'BYE, GEORGE

To Rex,

Enjoy some history written a bit differently.

John Ehrenreiter

11-26-16

'BYE, GEORGE

BLAZING A NEW NATION:
US WAR OF INDEPENDENCE

John Ebenreiter

'BYE, GEORGE
Blazing a New Nation: US War of Independence

iUniverse books may be ordered through booksellers or by contacting:

iUniverse
1663 Liberty Drive
Bloomington, IN 47403
www.iuniverse.com
1-800-Authors (1-800-288-4677)

Because of the dynamic nature of the Internet, any web addresses or links contained in this book may have changed since publication and may no longer be valid. The views expressed in this work are solely those of the author and do not necessarily reflect the views of the publisher, and the publisher hereby disclaims any responsibility for them.

Any people depicted in stock imagery provided by Thinkstock are models, and such images are being used for illustrative purposes only.
Certain stock imagery © Thinkstock.

ISBN: 978-1-4917-9130-1 (sc)
ISBN: 978-1-4917-9131-8 (e)

Library of Congress Control Number: 2016903796

Print information available on the last page.

iUniverse rev. date: 03/29/2016

To my wife, Sharon, who put up with my being hidden away for hours while writing, who put up with my absences while on research trips, and who spent countless hours proofreading my manuscript. To my stepdaughter, Heather, for suggesting the epistolary novel approach in writing *Bye, George.* To my mother, Paula Swart, whose ancestors' efforts helped establish the country we all love.

Table of Contents

Prologue

"Why are we discussing a battle in 1778 when independence was declared in 1776?" This was a question asked of the professor in a colonial history course I was auditing at a local university. In that instant, I decided to alter the thrust of the book I was beginning to write from being directed to youthful readers to those of all ages.

While I've been interested in history for as long as I can remember, as a youngster I found the War of Independence confusing. I didn't realize the war spanned eight years. It was hard to follow because it didn't flow easily from battle to battle. Confusion existed among the personalities in the war—were they all made up of the Founding Fathers, or were there other famous folks who really weren't considered among the founders of our country? And, of course, I thought every American was for independence and, therefore, against the British and King George III.

Two years before I audited the colonial history course, I became a tour guide at Brandywine Battlefield in Chadds Ford, Pennsylvania. As I became familiar with Brandywine, it whetted my appetite to learn more about the War of Independence. I voraciously read many books on the subject, and, to become more familiar, I visited many sites relating to the War of Independence.

As a result, this book is meant to convey that very learning that I so sadly missed. To express that message in this book, I decided to have seven Americans, who lived during the war, write a series of letters to one another to tell of their own experiences and to describe some of the major combatants whom they met or with whom they were associated.

Each chapter sets the stage for the events of which the letter writers will go on to describe their experiences or to share information received from others. Following is an introduction to those writers of the letters:

Ebenezer Chaplin: Mr. Chaplin (Uncle Eb) is the uncle of three of the letter writers. He is the father of one, is a distant cousin of another, and writes to his son's friend. Mr. Chaplin owns the Blaze Horse Tavern in Philadelphia. Philadelphia, being the capital and largest city of the American colonies, is the hub of political activity in the colonies. Many people frequented Mr. Chaplin's tavern—those for independence, those who wanted to stay loyal to the Crown, and those who didn't care one way or another.

Moses Chaplin: Moses, a student, is the son of Ebenezer Chaplin. When the Continental Army was being raised under George Washington, he immediately joined in 1775 and was not discharged until the war was over in 1783.

Ebenezer (Ben) Thompson: Ben is a nephew of Ebenezer Chaplin. He is a cordwainer, a person who makes shoes, and he lives in Salem, Massachusetts. He takes up the revolutionary cause almost immediately. He is soon engaged in the war and remains active until nearly the very end.

Zaccheus (Zack) Witt: Zack is a nephew of Ebenezer Chaplin. He is a ropewalker, is involved in making ropes used on ships, and lives in Boston, not far from his cousin Ben. He decides to stay loyal to the Crown. He fights with the British in many battles. At the end of the war, he decides he will not be able to continue living in the new United States of America.

Teunis Swart: Teunis is a nephew of Ebenezer Chaplin. He farms near Hoosick, New York. He hastens his involvement in the war to keep the British out of his home area. Later in the war he is involved in skirmishes with Native Americans (Indians) who, on behalf of the British, were attacking areas near his home.

Roelof Staley: Roelof's mother, a cousin of Ebenezer Chaplin, is married to the owner of a plantation (Boyne Manor) in King William, Virginia. Roelof gets involved in fighting even before we Americans have a fight with the British. Later he is involved in a secret offensive to the west.

Felix Porter: Felix is a friend and neighbor of Moses. As a farrier, a person who shoes horses, he moves from Philadelphia to Moncks Corner, South Carolina, near Charleston, where he could better use his talents in "horse country." He gets involved in some of the most vicious fighting of the war: Patriots versus Loyalists.

To assist in the reader's understanding, the following items are part of the appendixes.

- Maps: A series of maps is included to familiarize the reader with the geographic locations of the battles.
- Guide to Participants: The reader may find it confusing at times to discern on which side a participant mentioned might be. This guide provides the role of the participant during the war and then his/her role after the war is over. (Note: Many officers moved up in rank during the war. The guide usually lists the highest level the participant attained.)
- Pronunciation Guide: Many participants were French or German. This guide provides the proper pronunciation of their names. Also certain military terms need pronunciation guidance, and, in some cases, English and American participants require guidance on pronunciation.
- Battle Timeline: This list notes the date of the letter where the battle is covered.
- Noteworthy Events: The list of noteworthy events includes the date of the letter where the event is mentioned.
- What Happened to the Signers?: This is a listing of all signers of the Declaration of Independence, the colony that they represented, their age at signing, and their lives afterward.

The letter writers use the term "Indian" for Native American, and the term "Negro" for black American. The latter terms were not used in the time period in which these letters were written. "Loyalists," or "Tories," denote the term used to describe those Americans who wanted to stay loyal to the British Empire. "Rebels" denotes the term used by the British and Loyalists to describe the Patriots who were fighting for independence. The term "Signer" identifies one who signed the Declaration of Independence.

Chapter One

Give me Liberty, or give me Death.
—Patrick Henry

From 1754 to 1763, the French and Indian War was fought between Great Britain and France (with whom the Indians allied) for control of North America. British America consisted of the Atlantic Seaboard area north of Florida to Newfoundland. New France covered the territory from Quebec down through the area west of the Appalachian Mountains all the way to New Orleans. Britain and her American colonists defeated the French and Indians, taking what was New France.

In fighting this war, Britain supplied soldiers and munitions to their American citizens. As a result, Britain incurred enormous debt to finance the war. Britain felt that a portion of the debt payment should be borne by the people whom they defended. Over a course of several years, Parliament passed a succession of revenue-raising acts. Because American colonists were not represented in Parliament, these acts met with resistance, especially in Boston, resulting in the Boston Massacre and the Boston Tea Party. This set the stage for the War of Independence.

In 1774, a Continental Congress was called to deal with the deteriorating situation between the colonies and Britain. In February 1775, the first American bloodshed occurred at Salem, Massachusetts. Two months later, the first shots in the War of Independence were fired at Lexington and Concord, Massachusetts.

The Continental Congress established the Continental Army. George Washington became its commander in chief. A two-pronged invasion of Quebec was launched.

August 1, 1774

Dear Ben, Roelof, Teunis, Zack, and Felix,

Ever since Paul Revere rode from Boston to Philadelphia back in May, telling us of the Port Act, which basically isolates Boston economically, there's been a lot of conversation on how to deal with the deteriorating situation with our mother country over the past few years. Now the hot talk is about what might be coming out of the call in May for a Continental Congress when it convenes in September to address the issues.

Moses and I have been discussing what has led us to this situation. Of course, the constant effort by Britain to tax us to pay for the French and Indian War is a big reason. The Sugar Act, Stamp Act, Townshend Act, and Tea Act were all taxes imposed on the colonies without our having representation in Parliament to redeem the debts from that war. Many feel this is simply "taxation without representation."

Even though we've been subjects of Britain in most colonies for over one hundred years, even with having Crown governors, we've pretty much governed ourselves with elected local officials. The recently enacted Massachusetts Bay Regulating Act, one of the Coercive Acts, replaces elected officials with a mandamus council appointed by the governor. So far this practice relates to only Massachusetts. What colony might be next?

It is obvious that Parliament passed the Coercive Acts in response to the Boston Tea Party of last December 16. Just eight days later on Christmas Eve, the tea ship *Polly* came to Philadelphia. It was not allowed to unload the tea and was sent back to England still fully laden with its cargo of tea. We did not dump the tea, as had been done in Boston, but we too did not allow its unloading. Will Pennsylvania be next with its own Regulating or Port Act?

Many people here in Philadelphia were shocked when we heard the news that Ben Franklin, in London, had been brought before the privy council's cockpit in late January for exposing former Massachusetts governor Hutchinson. He was shamefully ridiculed. For years he has been a cool hand in London when things got hot between the colonies and Parliament. His attitude may now change.

In Philadelphia there is a lot of emotion between those who feel Britain, over the years, has become more and more oppressive in its treatment of the American colonists versus those who hold, and will continue to hold, a strong loyalty to His Majesty King George III and the Crown. Moses and I would appreciate hearing from you as to your own views and the sentiments in your area, as they might relate to the calling of a Continental Congress.

Sincerely, Eb Chaplin

August 15, 1774
Dear Uncle Eb,

So good to hear from you. I recently completed my apprenticeship as a cordwainer and have opened my own shop. I can only hope that all the unrest won't lead to military action now that I've started on my occupational career. I am part of the newly formed Minutemen in our militia. Being a Minuteman requires us to turn out on "a minute's notice." We each need to have our own firearm and supply of ammunition. We train four times a year. Because William Browne, a strong Tory, was sloppy in leading our militia, he was recently replaced by Timothy Pickering.

Several weeks ago our delegates were chosen here in Salem. When Thomas Cushing, John Adams, Sam Adams, and Robert Treat Paine left for Philadelphia, they made a point of parading their carriage right past the British troops in Boston. Having those troops in Boston makes the situation very tense. After all, when troops were sent in response to the Townshend Acts, they massacred five civilians four years ago.

We call the new British Coercive Acts the Intolerable Acts. The Port Act will have an enormous economic impact on Boston, with no shipments allowed in or out. The Quartering

Act is very repressive. If the military wants to use your home as an abode for their soldiers, you have no choice in the matter. The Port Act also moved the seat of government for Massachusetts from Boston to here in Salem.

The Quebec Act affects several colonies—Massachusetts, Connecticut, New York, Pennsylvania, and Virginia—that have land claims west of the mountains. The act now makes that territory off-limits to future development. Since the Quebec Act also gave recognition to the Roman Catholic Church in Quebec, will the next action of the British be the banning of our annual mockery of Catholics on Pope Day each November 5?

Uncle Eb, I cannot overempathize how tense the situation is up here. We have several cannons stored in town. Many other towns have gunpowder in storage so it can be accessed by the militia if the need arises. I hope the Continental Congress can work something out to defuse the tense situation. But with Sam Adams being a delegate, so passionate against the Crown, I wouldn't count on it.

Sincerely, Ben

∽

August 16, 1774
Dear Uncle Eb,

I am happy to give you my views regarding the present situation. It gives me a chance to sound off about the despicable Rebels here in Boston. The rebellious activities for the past ten years stem from the fact that Britain is trying to raise funds to reduce the debt incurred by our mother country in its armed support to save America from the French and Indians. My father fought in the French and Indian War and was most thankful there were British soldiers on our soil to assist us.

When the Stamp Act was imposed, the Rebels formed a group: the Sons of Liberty. They should be called the sons of anarchy for all the chaos they've stirred up over the years here in Boston. Do we forget the lawlessness shown against Lieutenant

Governor Thomas Hutchinson when they threatened his life, ransacked his house, and destroyed his property in 1765 when protesting the Stamp Act? How about the tar and feathering done to men who don't agree with resisting the British?

Due to all the protesting against the Townshend Acts, the British in 1767 sent enforcement troops. The friction that caused resulted in the so-called Boston Massacre on March 5, 1770. At least our justice system worked when John Adams worked on behalf of the accused troops, obtaining their acquittal. Did the Sons of Liberty feel any remorse for the bloodshed for those killed in that mob action?

To protest the Tea Act passed in May 1773, these so-called purveyors of freedom, not wanting to be identified, on December 16, 1773, dressed up as Indians to dump tea from the ships into the harbor. A tea party! What does that bring? It brought the Port Act, which forbids shipment of goods, including food, into Boston. Luckily, just yesterday, Israel Putnam drove 130 sheep from Connecticut into town to help feed the poor. In May, Thomas Gage was sent as our new governor, replacing Governor Hutchinson, who was recalled to Britain. Ironically, Gage was greeted by the Independent Company of Cadets commanded by John Hancock, who everyone suspects was heavily engaged in the Tea Party.

Because most of my fellow workers are ardent Rebels, being a ropewalker is not the best occupation for someone who feels loyalty to the Crown. They call me a brainless Tory. But tell me which is better—to be ruled by one tyrant three thousand miles away or to be ruled by three thousand tyrants not one mile away.

God Save the King, Zack

August 20, 1774
Dear Mr. Chaplin,

It was good to get your letter. After leaving Philadelphia, I have been quite happy pursuing my occupation as a farrier near

Moncks Corner, South Carolina. Horse racing is so popular here. There is hardly a Sunday when there isn't a horse race. The rice and indigo plantation owners are quite wealthy. Horse racing and, of course, the betting that goes with it are their main hobbies.

I couldn't help but snicker when you mentioned the Boston Tea Party of December 16, 1773. You may not have heard, but we had our own tea party two weeks earlier. On December 3, 1773, the *London,* loaded with tea, entered the harbor at Charleston. The ship was unloaded, but the tea was not allowed to be sold. The tea was stored in the Exchange Building. The last I heard it's all spoiled.

You asked about sentiment down here. The plantation owners I am familiar with lean toward resentment toward Britain. I've also heard that is the feeling of the tobacco planters in the Wilmington area of North Carolina. The most anti-British folks are the overmountain men in Western North Carolina. You may recall in May 1772 they established the Republic of Watauga and declared themselves independent of British rule.

On the other hand, the more recently arrived Scots Highlanders in both Carolinas have a strong loyalty to the Crown. Except for St. John's Parish, settled by Yankees from Connecticut, Georgia is basically Loyalist.

South Carolina has named the five delegates it is sending to the Congress: Christopher Gadsden, Thomas Lynch, Henry Middleton, Edward Rutledge, and John Rutledge. Ed Rutledge, better known as Ned, is about my age. I talk often to him at racing events. The news I have from North Carolina is that they are sending three delegates: Richard Caswell, Joseph Hewes, and William Hooper.

This is a nervous time. I am hoping fervently that Congress can come to some solution with Britain. If not, I have the feeling that down here, because of the deep feelings on both sides, we could have a really tough time of it.

Sincerely, Felix

⌇

August 21, 1774
Dear Uncle Eb,

While I appreciate hearing from you, the reason for your letter is frightening. As you know, I have a farm near Hoosick. Just last year I married a sweet young lady, Sarah van Vorst. Sarah also grew up on a farm, so she is familiar with all the hard work a farm requires. If things get so bad that we go to war, what would I do? I can't imagine going off to war and leaving Sarah with all the farm work.

The sentiment here is mixed. There are many folks very loyal to the Crown. Most of them are foreign-born. Their families have not been in America for generations like ours have been. They are not aware of the sacrifice we have had to make in fighting the French and then to be double-crossed by the Quebec Act.

For instance, there are the German Palatines. They are loyal to the Crown because the British let them settle here to escape starvation in their homeland. The Scots and Irish Catholics are loyal because they faced difficulty in practicing their faith before they came but are now free to practice their Catholicism. They are so disrespectful of their new environment. They still speak Gaelic!

When I heard of the Quebec Act, I was incensed. When I was just a baby, the French and Indians attacked our area. We were lucky to escape with our lives. And before that, at the turn of the century in King William's War[1] and Queen Anne's War[2], my ancestors had to fight the French. And now, with the British recognizing French civil law and extending the borders of Quebec south to the Ohio River and west to the Mississippi River—nice thanks for all of our efforts to defend ourselves and British territory from the French.

You mentioned the Boston Tea Party. On April 24, 1774, the *Nancy*, fully laden with tea, tried to dock in New York. She was

---

[1]   War between France and Britain in North America: 1688–97.
[2]   War between France and Britain in North America: 1702–13.

turned back to Britain still fully laden with her tea. New York is sending nine delegates to the Continental Congress. I am only familiar with three of them: James Duane, Philip Livingston, and John Jay. I pray they find some way to work things out with Britain so we don't go to war. At any rate, I hope they get the British to rescind the Quebec Act.

Sincerely, Teunis

❧

October 27, 1774
Dear Ben, Zack, Felix, Teunis, and Roelof,

Yesterday the First Continental Congress adjourned. I wanted to let each of you know what transpired. The Congress convened September 5 with fifty-six delegates from twelve colonies at Carpenter's Hall. It was opened by an Anglican minister with the very poignant Psalm 35. Georgia had a lot of fighting going on with the Creek Indians, which required support of British troops. As a result, their governor, James Wright, forbade any delegates to attend.

Some of the more prominent delegates included John and Sam Adams, Massachusetts; John Jay, New York; John Sullivan, New Hampshire; Caesar Rodney, Delaware; Roger Sherman, Connecticut; John and Edward Rutledge, South Carolina; and Patrick Henry (who early on declared, "I am not a Virginian but an American"), Benjamin Harrison, Richard Henry Lee, and George Washington, Virginia. Our most prominent delegates from Pennsylvania were Joseph Galloway and John Dickinson. Peyton Randolph of Virginia was elected president of the Congress.

Early in the meetings Galloway offered a *Plan of Union of Great Britain and the Colonies*. This plan urged compromise instead of any belligerent action. Before it could be voted on, Paul Revere arrived from Boston with the *Suffolk Resolves* primarily drafted by Dr. Joseph Warren. This document included the boycott of British products and urged colonies to raise militias of their own people. After much discussion, the *Suffolk Resolves* were endorsed and the *Plan of Union* was not adopted.

On October 20, Congress created the Continental Association to go into effect December 1. This is a plan of agreement among the colonies to ban import or consumption of any goods from Britain, Ireland, or the British West Indies. The goal is to bring pressure for repeal of the Intolerable Acts. On October 21, Congress resolved to send letters of invitation to Quebec (in French and English), Saint John's Island[3], Nova Scotia, Georgia, East Florida, and West Florida to the Second Continental Congress scheduled to meet on May 10, 1775. They then adjourned with a toast to King George III.

During the sessions, while at the Blaze Horse, the Virginia delegates told me their governor, Lord Dunmore, was sending a contingent of militia west to claim more western territory for Virginia from the Shawnee Indians. I just learned there was a pitched battle at Point Pleasant, where the Kanawha River flows into the Ohio, between Colonel Andrew Lewis's militia and Chief Cornstalk's men. While Lewis prevailed, he lost seventy-five men versus forty warriors.

Sincerely, Eb Chaplin

⁓

February 27, 1775
Dear Uncle Eb,

Yesterday afternoon while attending church service, Major John Pedrick, after galloping from Marblehead, threw open the doors and shouted, "The regulars are coming after the guns and are now near Malloon's Mills." Being a Minuteman, Colonel Timothy Pickering ordered us to hide the cannons. At the same time, Benjamin Daland raced off to Danvers to tell them of the march of the Regulars.

Many townspeople raced toward the bridge between Marblehead and Salem to rip up the planks. However, the

---

[3] Saint John's Island is now known as Prince Edward Island.

Regulars, led by Colonel Alexander Leslie, replaced enough of the planks to cross the river. Then as Leslie approached Spike Drawbridge over the North River, it was raised, preventing the Regulars from crossing. The townspeople shouted at the Regulars, "Soldiers! Red Jackets! Lobster coats! Cowards! Damnation to your government!"

After some time, Leslie was made aware of some scows in the river and sent his soldiers to commandeer them to cross the river into Salem. With this, several of the owners and their workmen got to the boats first and smashed the bottoms, making them useless. At this point things became quite scary when one of the workmen, Joseph Whicher, had a bayonet shoved at his chest, with blood spurting everywhere.

With sunset soon to arrive and getting colder, Leslie became desperate to locate and remove the cannons. About this time, Pastor Thomas Barnard of North Meetinghouse, a known strong Loyalist, shouted to Leslie, asking for a discussion. Barnard suggested to Leslie that if the drawbridge was lowered, Leslie could march into Salem no farther than thirty rods and, if he saw no cannons, march back out of town. Since by this time the Marblehead Regiment had formed at Leslie's rear and the Salem and Danvers militia in front, he took the offer and the incident was over, saving our nineteen cannons.

As I said in my last letter it is tense and getting hotter up here. Was Whicher's blood the first shed in a revolution?

Sincerely, Ben

⟨✥⟩

March 30, 1775
Dear Mr. Chaplin,

I apologize for not responding earlier to your request regarding the atmosphere in Virginia. When I got your letter I was well on my way to the Ohio country in response to a request in May 1774 by Governor Lord Dunmore to do battle with the Indians who were harassing citizens settling the region south of the Ohio River.

I was with Colonel Andrew Lewis while other troops were with Dunmore on his route to Fort Pitt.[4] Early on October 10, 1774, our camp was attacked by Shawnee Indians led by Chief Cornstalk. The battle raged all day, with heavy hand-to-hand fighting. Tomahawks were being used on both sides. Having more men, we eventually won, but at a cost of 75 killed and 140 wounded. The battle forced Cornstalk to cede all the territory south of the Ohio.

When we got back, we were told that Dunmore's effort dishonored the Crown because of encroachment on tribal lands. However, from a personal standpoint, I was glad I went on the raid because Dunmore granted me a patent for one thousand acres of land in what is called the Vandalia Colony.[5] The trouble is that it is in an area of dispute between Virginia and Pennsylvania.

Right now Dunmore is not happy about several actions taken in Virginia. On November 7, 1774, a ship arrived in Yorktown, and it included tea in its cargo. Because of the boycott enacted, the tea was dumped into the harbor and the ship was not allowed to load a shipment of tobacco destined for England. Then on January 20, the Fincastle Resolutions were published by prominent Fincastle citizens in western Virginia. One of the signers is William Campbell, a brother-in-law of Patrick Henry.

As you know, Patrick Henry was a delegate to the First Continental Congress. Back in 1773, he, Thomas Jefferson, and Richard Henry Lee organized the Virginia Committee of Correspondence. Patrick is quite a firebrand. I know him well, being a former neighbor in the next county. On March 23, he made a most forceful and eloquent speech at a meeting of the House of Burgesses, which included this exclamation: "Is life so dear, or peace so sweet, as to be purchased at the price of chains and slavery? Forbid it, Almighty God! I know not what course others may take; but as for me, Give me Liberty, or give me Death!"

Sincerely, Roelof

---

4 Fort Pitt is present-day Pittsburgh, Pennsylvania.
5 A proposed, but never approved, colony that would have included parts of present-day Pennsylvania, West Virginia, and Kentucky.

❧

April 20, 1775
Dear Uncle Eb,

Joe Whicher may have spilled the first blood at Salem in February, but yesterday the King's Men killed almost fifty Americans and wounded at least as many, or more. We got the alarm in Salem midmorning yesterday. Colonel Timothy Pickering quickly gathered the militia, and we made our way toward Charlestown. We encountered the Regulars just before they got to Charlestown but did not attack. Pickering didn't attack because he was adhering to the rules of engagement for the militia units set out by Provincial president Joseph Warren. To engage, the Regulars had to be a force in excess of five hundred troops; the force must include baggage and artillery; and five members of the committee of safety must vote in favor of arms. Only the first condition existed. If we had known what we learned overnight, I'm sure we would have engaged.

On the night of the eighteenth, Joseph Warren learned of General Thomas Gage's intent of marching British Regulars to Concord to capture powder stored there. Warren wasn't sure if the Regulars would go to Concord by land (leaving Boston at the Neck) or by water (crossing Back Bay to Cambridge). A signal was to be hung in Old North Church's steeple—one lantern if by land, two lanterns if by sea—for the benefit of Charlestown to know which way the Red Coats were coming. When word was known, William Dawes, after talking his way past two sentries on Boston Neck, was on his way to Lexington and Concord via Roxbury and Cambridge. Paul Revere rowed with muffled oars over to Charlestown to race toward Lexington to warn Sam Adams and John Hancock that the Regulars were coming. Sometime after midnight, as Dawes and Revere were on their way to Concord, they were overtaken by Dr. Samuel Prescott, who was returning to Concord after spending the night with his sweetheart. Soon all three ran into a British patrol. Prescott jumped his horse over a stone wall and continued on to alarm Concord. Dawes was able to speed back toward Lexington.

Revere was captured, but he was eventually released, making his way back to Lexington on foot.

The Regulars, seven hundred strong, were led by Lieutenant Colonel Francis Smith, with his second in command Marine Major John Pitcairn. The alarm traveled fast. By 1:00 a.m., 130 militiamen were gathered at Lexington's Green and the citizens of Concord were frantically hiding food, gunpowder, cannons, and other military stores.

At dawn when the Regulars got to Lexington, they encountered the militia under Captain John Parker. Parker's men were under orders not to fire unless first fired upon. Pitcairn advanced toward Parker's men and ordered them to disperse. As Parker gave orders to disperse, a shot rang out from the Regulars. Before it was over, eight men were killed and ten were wounded. One of the deceased was Jonathan Harrington, who was hit in the chest. He crawled to the doorstep of his home, where he died before the horrified eyes of his wife and son.

Many British officers tried to convince Smith not to continue on to Concord. He argued he would obey his orders, and he got to Concord at around 8:00 a.m. The Brits searched for war material, but it was well hidden. Meanwhile, because of the alarm, militia units were pouring in from all directions from many localities. Fighting eventually broke out in Concord at the North Bridge, and Smith decided to return to Boston. The trip back was disastrous for him and the troops.

Militia members were firing from behind every stone, fence, tree, and house, which caused much panic in the British line. The Brits killed several people who fired at them from inside their home. There is word that some prisoners they took were executed. On the way back through Lexington, Smith was wounded. At about 3:00 p.m. General Hugh Percy, with 1,350 reinforcements, arrived. But even with these extra men, the Brits were trying to get back to Boston with many thousands of militia pursuing them.

If only we had known all this, we might have finished the job by blocking their way into Charlestown and, perhaps, making prisoners of the whole lot. It is estimated the Brits suffered 73 killed and 174 wounded. I think they are fortunate to have lost only that amount.

The Bedford Minutemen, the first outsiders to arrive at Concord, carried an interesting flag. It was a crimson flag depicting an armored arm, reaching out of the clouds, with a sword clenched in its fist; around the appendage were the words *Vince Aut Morire* (Conquer or Die), a very fitting war cry. Many are wondering how Warren learned of the timing and destination of the attack. Some are speculating he got the intelligence from Margaret Gage, the British general's American-born wife.

I'll keep you informed on any future actions. This surely has ignited a revolution.

Sincerely, Ben

May 14, 1775
Dear Uncle Eb,

We got the news up here in New York about Lexington and Concord in late April. We were shocked and outraged. A few days later I heard that Ethan Allen's Green Mountain Boys over in the Hampshire Grants[6] were talking of attacking the British forces at Fort Ticonderoga. The idea had been broached by John Brown, a confidante of Sam Adams, who had been doing some spying in Canada to determine if there was sympathy for our cause there. He found there were few Canadians interested in defying Britain.

Even though I knew Allen was no friend of us Yorkers, I decided to go to Bennington and join up with his forces. While in Bennington on May 2, some men arrived from Massachusetts and Connecticut. The plan was made to make a dawn raid on May 10. We then went to Castleton to position ourselves for the raid. On May 8, Benedict Arnold, who had been commissioned a colonel by the Massachusetts Committee of Safety, arrived in

---

[6] Hampshire Grants is now Vermont. At the time, the territory was disputed by New Hampshire and New York colonies.

Castleton. He was aware that there was a great store of ordnance at Fort Ticonderoga that might be helpful to the American cause. Arnold insisted on being in command of all the forces assembled. Allen, of course, didn't think much of this idea. Allen finally decided to share command, because Arnold was officially commissioned. Allen's Green Mountain Boys were acting without official sanction. Therefore, if anything went wrong they could face severe disciplinary action.

During the night of May 9, troops were being ferried across Lake Champlain to the New York side. At the first light of dawn on the tenth, we attacked the fort. A British sentry spotted us and fired. Luckily, he had a misfire and ran into the fort. We continued into the fort, where Allen demanded to be shown to the commander's quarters. A lieutenant tried to stall Allen and Arnold, but finally Captain William Delaplace appeared. Delaplace asked under what authority the leaders were acting. Allen shouted, "In the name of the Great Jehovah and the Continental Congress." Delaplace had no choice but to surrender. We took this most important citadel without a drop of bloodshed.

Today Arnold is sailing with some troops to the other end of the lake to determine if he can take Fort St. Johns.[7] I have decided to go back home. In April I was able to sow my wheat crop. It is now the time to plant corn. It would be unfair to expect my wife, Sarah, to take care of that chore. Hopefully our taking of Fort Ticonderoga will convince the British to stop their terrorist actions.

Sincerely, Teunis

June 18, 1775
Dear Uncle Eb,

Today was the day that the Brits were going to attack the besiegers of Boston. British general William Howe was to attack

---

[7] Also known as Fort Saint-Jean.

Dorchester Heights, and British general Henry Clinton was to attack Cambridge and then take the Charlestown Heights. Our general, Joseph Warren, got word about the plans, and the decision was made to fortify Bunker Hill on the Charlestown Heights.

During the night, Colonel William Prescott's men were sent to Bunker Hill to build fortifications. But instead of fortifying Bunker Hill, his men dug in on Breed's Hill closer to Boston. They had a tough time of it, being very hot and having little water. When the British awoke in the morning, upon seeing the fortifications, British Admiral Samuel Graves opened a cannonade from his fleet in Boston Harbor. He also fired hot shot and carcasses[8] at Charlestown, setting it on fire, which sent smoke directly into the British soldiers' eyes. Howe could not attack until the tide was in his favor in the afternoon.

Being with Colonel John Stark early in the afternoon, we were marching on Charlestown Neck at a very deliberate pace under tremendous fire. I heard Captain Henry Dearborn ask Stark if the pace shouldn't be quickened. Stark's answer was "One fresh man in action is worth ten fatigued ones." We went toward the Mystic River to take on Howe's attack. We managed to throw up a breastwork of stones and heavy grasses to defend against Howe's attack. Stark ordered, "Hold your fire until you see the enemy's half-gaiters." He also had us fight with continuous fire from three ranks to repel the Brits coming up Mystic River—first rank kneeling, second rank stooping, third rank standing, and then reloading to be ready for the next volley.

Because of our success, Howe's flanking move didn't work. Then he attacked Prescott's redoubt.[9] Because of the officer's gorgets[10] gleaming in the sun and their scarlet uniforms, as opposed to the red uniforms of the Regulars, they were easily picked off. Prescott's men held off two charges but had to retreat due to a lack of gunpowder. As they were retreating, General Warren was killed by Lord Francis Rawdon. Near the end, as

---

[8] Carcasses were hollow balls filled with burning pitch or with gunpowder, saltpeter, and tallow.

[9] A small enclosed defensive work.

[10] A piece of plate armor hanging from the neck.

British Major John Pitcairn shouted, "The day is ours," he was shot by Salem Poor, a free Negro.

Because of running out of powder we had to retreat. However, our losses were much less than those suffered by the Brits, especially by the officers. In retrospect, if General Warren had not sent two hundred pounds of powder with Arnold on his foray to Fort Ticonderoga, we very likely could have been the victors.

Sincerely, Ben

June 20, 1775
Dear Uncle Eb,

Things have gotten quite bad here in Boston. As you are by now aware, the Rebels attacked the British troops when they tried to seize the illegally stored powder at Concord on April 19. When those Rebels fired on His Majesty's troops at Lexington, it started a revolution. Do they really want that? Not only were the Crown troops fired upon, but shameful tactics were used by the Rebels as they tried to return to Boston. It was fortunate that General Hugh Percy came to the rescue of Colonel Frances Smith and Marine Major John Pitcairn, or who knows how many more the Rebels would have slaughtered.

Ever since, we've been under siege. General Thomas Gage offered the people to leave Boston with all the baggage they could take with them, but they would have to give up their weapons. The Loyalist leadership protested, saying they needed hostages; nine thousand had already left. Gage had asked Britain for twenty thousand troops before the Concord event. Instead, on May 25, he received three generals: William Howe, John Burgoyne, and Henry Clinton! Clinton is living in John Hancock's house. Food and animal forage is running low. This became worse on May 27 when General Israel Putnam attacked Noddle's Island, where many of our supplies were provided.

Just three days ago we had a major battle over at Bunker Hill. I was able to watch much of it from Copp's Hill. The noise was deafening from Graves's cannonade of the Rebel positions. Howe's troops left from North Battery and Long Wharf. The navy would not go up the Mystic River to support Howe, which resulted in disaster. But eventually he would win the day. His words "I shall not desire one of you to go a step further than where I go myself at your head" surely gave inspiration. The Rebels shot low and held their fire until the Crown's troops were within fifteen to thirty yards, which had a crippling effect, causing many amputations, especially among the Welsh Fusiliers. The Regulars heard Prescott commanding, "Don't fire until you see the whites of their eyes." To protect themselves, the Regulars piled their dead compatriots as breastworks. While we "won" the battle, it was purely pyrrhic. Of our 2,200 soldiers, we lost 1,054 to death or wounds. The Rebels had a little over 400 casualties.

Boston is filled with wounded bleeding soldiers—some in coaches, horse chaises, even handbarrows. Many residents and soldiers are dying due to lack of veggies and meat. Dismal now, but we Loyalists must prevail for the Crown.

God Save the King, Zack

June 25, 1775
Dear Ben, Teunis, and Zack,

There's been a lot of activity the past two months taken by the Second Continental Congress I need to tell you about. Proactive actions taken by the Congress will undoubtedly have an effect on all three of you.

The Second Congress convened on May 10. They reelected Peyton Randolph of Virginia to serve as president. However, he shortly was summoned back to Virginia to preside over their House of Burgesses. As a result, John Hancock, of Massachusetts, was elected the new president on May 24. He is a new delegate along with another new delegate, Benjamin

Franklin, of Pennsylvania, who recently arrived from London. When Randolph had to leave, Virginia replaced him with a young red-haired fellow, Thomas Jefferson.

As you know, Georgia did not send a delegate to the First Congress. This time Lyman Hall of St. John's Parish in Georgia arrived on his own volition. Several weeks later Georgia sent an official delegation.

When the Congress heard about Arnold and Allen taking Ticonderoga, they were not happy with their bellicose action. However, on June 14, Congress created a Continental Army. The next step was to choose a commander in chief. The scuttlebutt heard in the Blaze Horse was that John Hancock expected the role. However, John and Sam Adams felt it would be better not to choose a Boston firebrand who might not be endorsed by the rest of the colonies. John Adams nominated George Washington, a delegate from Virginia. Sam Adams, who by the way is one of Hancock's best friends, seconded the motion. Earlier, Artemas Ward (considered too timid), Israel Putnam (considered too old), and Charles Lee (considered too British) were rejected. By the way, Washington wears his Virginia militia uniform to every session.

The Congress also made New York delegate Philip Schuyler commander of the Northern Department. Congress authorized a foray into Quebec by Schuyler. There is a large cache of military supplies in Quebec City. Schuyler was also instructed to take possession of St. Johns, Montreal, and any others "to promote peace and security to these colonies."

Moses left with the Continental Army headed toward Boston.

Sincerely, Uncle Eb

July 15, 1775
Dear Father,

The trip from Philadelphia to Boston was tougher than I ever expected—a lot of walking! Along the journey many units of troops joined us. They included German speaking units from Pennsylvania and Maryland. As we went through New Jersey many more joined us. Very few joined us as we traveled though Connecticut and Rhode Island, for they already had many militia units in the Boston area.

When we got to New York City on June 26, we had an interesting situation. A parade was planned for General Washington and his troops. However, Royal governor William Tryon, who had no idea the revolution had begun, was returning from his trip to England. So as not to interfere, we paraded at 10:00 a.m. After we were out of town, Tryon was welcomed at 3:00 p.m.

When we arrived on July 2, Washington made his headquarters at Cambridge, Massachusetts. He was disturbed by the encampments—unsanitary conditions and undisciplined soldiers. All the troops here were militia loyal to their respective colonies. Washington made it clear that henceforth the militia units "are troops of the United Provinces of North America." Major General Artemas Ward had been commander in chief of New England militias but became second in command when Washington arrived. However, due to Ward's ill health, Charles Lee assumed most of his duties. Lee had expected to be named commander in chief, and it is obvious he does not respect Washington. He is known to have said, "Washington is not fit enough to command a Sergeant's Guard." They've known each other since serving together in General Braddock's campaign during the French and Indian War. Incidentally, British general Gage also served with them.

Washington had been assured that there would be an ample supply of powder. But when we got here there were only 36 barrels. Washington quietly had word "leaked" inside Boston that we had 1,800 barrels. However, these barrels were filled with sand to impress any British spies who might enter the encampment. I sure hope we can get a supply of powder before anything major might start.

Your son, Moses

July 31, 1775
My dear son Moses,

John Adams shared news he received from his wife, Abigail, regarding the Battle of Bunker Hill. From their house he said his wife, along with their son John Quincy, could hear the bombarding and could see the smoke as Charlestown burned. They were grief stricken to hear of Dr. Joseph Warren's death. He had filled the leadership vacuum of the Sons of Liberty when Sam Adams came down to Philadelphia to serve in Congress. Additionally, he was their family physician.

There have been some interesting discussions in the Blaze Horse regarding sentiments as to whether or not rebellion should be pursued. Congress is wrestling with the subject. Many hope reconciliation can yet be achieved. On June 26, when Benjamin Franklin heard the detailed recitation of the carnage at Bunker Hill, he felt the idea of reconciliation was out of the question. John Adams also feels war is inevitable. Yet, a few days later, Congress formed a committee to draft a reconciliatory proclamation.

Thomas Jefferson penned the first draft of the Olive Branch Petition. However, John Dickinson, who is strongly in favor of working out a plan of reconciliation, found Jefferson's language too offensive. Dickinson rewrote the document, which claimed that the colonies did not want independence but that they merely wanted to negotiate trade and tax regulations with Great Britain. His draft was approved by Congress on July 8. Richard Penn was dispatched to London to deliver the Olive Branch to King George. But even after this, Franklin proposed declaring independence. Jefferson was enthusiastic about the idea but felt many of the delegates would be "revolted at it."

Your letter on the fifteenth hinted at possible sectional differences. I have a good example to report. John Adams made his displeasure well-known on Washington's selection of Thomas Mifflin as the new quartermaster general. Adams felt a New Englander should have been chosen. Mifflin, who had been a member of Congress, is an extremely successful Philadelphia businessman. With his background, I feel he will fill this position very ably.

May God bless you, Father

⸙

October 4, 1775
Dear Father,

After we were here for a while, Captain Daniel Morgan arrived with one thousand rambunctious soldiers from the backcountry of Virginia and Pennsylvania. His arrival gave further evidence that the rest of the country is supporting New England. His soldiers came with their long-barreled rifles. The rifles are astonishingly accurate, but they do take more time to reload than a musket. He too served in the Braddock campaign as a wagon master. When he got into a fight with a British officer, he was sentenced to 500 lashes. He showed me the scars but insisted that by his count they only laid on 499.

On September 11, General Benedict Arnold left for an invasion of Canada. Cousin Ben went with him. Before he left, I had Ben make two pairs of shoes for me costing thirteen shillings. Daniel Morgan and his riflemen went with Arnold.

Ben told me that word was received back from London that John Derby of Salem got the news of Lexington and Concord to London on his speedy ship *Quero* two weeks before Gage's report arrived. Gage had sent his report on the *Sukey*, which left four days before *Quero*. John Derby reported the news to Massachusetts agents who took it to the pro-American lord mayor of London. Maybe this will have some impact on the British Parliament.

Today we learned that one of the Sons of Liberty in Boston, Benjamin Church, our surgeon general of the Continental Army, was a spy for Gage. Being with the Sons of Liberty, he was a trusted confidante of Sam Adams and Joseph Warren. We learned he had passed on the Massachusetts Provincial rules of engagement to Gage, and that is why Gage did not send baggage or artillery on the Concord mission. By the way, Gage was recalled back to Britain on September 26.

We just got the news that King George on August 13 issued "A Proclamation for Suppressing Rebellion and Sedition." In it, he declared that all colonies were in a state of "open and avowed rebellion." I guess that's his answer to the Olive Branch petition! What does he expect when he sends his troops to attack his own subjects? I think it is time to say, "Bye, George!"

Your son, Moses

❧

January 2, 1776
Dear Uncle Eb,

Since things were pretty quiet up here after Bunker Hill, I decided to join General Benedict Arnold's expedition to Quebec. Besides the £2-per-month pay, I joined him because of Arnold's reputation for taking Fort Ticonderoga last May, along with Ethan Allen, and also because Henry Dearborn joined the expedition.

To our fortune, the 1770 journal of British engineer John Montresor's trip from Quebec down the Kennebec River to Maine fell into Arnold's hands. And then in August, Reuben Colburn arrived in Cambridge from Maine with several chiefs of the St. Francis Abenaki[11] tribe willing to join our cause. General Washington welcomed them with open arms and enlisted them on the spot. Colburn, being a shipbuilder, offered to build two hundred batteaux[12] for the expedition.

Arnold formed two battalions—one under Lieutenant Colonel Christopher Greene, of Rhode Island, and the other under Lieutenant Colonel Roger Enos, of Connecticut. General Washington added 250 Virginia and Pennsylvania riflemen under the command of Captain Daniel Morgan. Aaron Burr,

[11] Referring to the mission village of Saint Francois-de-Sales.
[12] Flat-bottomed boats used to haul cargo, men, or artillery.

who had been unsuccessful in obtaining a commission from Washington, also joined us.

We left Massachusetts with about 1,050 men on September 11, sailing to the Maine district of Massachusetts.[13] When we arrived in Pittston, Maine, Colburn had the batteaux ready. He had built them in fifteen days! The batteaux were twenty-two feet long. Arnold had wanted them longer. However, Colburn told him that if they were longer they would be difficult to lift when portaging. They were not meant to carry men but to haul casks of supplies.

We left and worked our way through Maine up the Kennebec River toward Quebec. The trip was horrible. The boats, made from green wood, often leaked, spoiling our food and gunpowder. Our first portage was from the Kennebec River to the Dead River. We also had to portage along the unnavigable areas of the Dead River. Then we had to portage to the Chaudière River, which was brutal because of swampy bogs.

Early in the trip we were able to shoot moose, grouse, and ducks to survive. After a while things were getting desperate, and some resorted to eating dogs some men had brought along. I also heard some men resorted to cooking their leather shoes to survive. All the while, the howling of wolves at night was frightening. I believe the information for the expedition from Montresor's journal was not accurate, because the trip took much longer than anticipated.

Captain Daniel Morgan was in the vanguard the entire trip. On October 30, we got into Quebec. While the local Canadians provided food, we found out some of the letters regarding battle plans sent to General Richard Montgomery from General Arnold had been intercepted by the British. As a result, all the boats on the south shore of the St. Lawrence River were destroyed.

On November 13, we crossed the St. Lawrence and got to the Plains of Abraham the next day, whereupon General Arnold demanded the surrender of Quebec City, which was refused. At this point, we had only about six hundred men due to casualties on the trip, desertions, and the fact that Enos's men had turned back. On November 19, we withdrew to await Montgomery,

---

[13] Maine was part of Massachusetts until 1820.

who was coming from New York. Arnold sent Aaron Burr to Montgomery to guide him from Montreal to Quebec. The siege began on December 3.

In a raging snowstorm early in the morning of December 31, the assault on Quebec City began. Captain Morgan, coming from the north, used a scaling ladder to get inside the fortress. Montgomery was to come in on the other side. After we got in, there was no sight of his men. We found out later that Montgomery had been killed. After General Arnold was wounded in his left leg, Morgan took leadership. Soon he was surrounded by troops, but he refused to surrender his sword to the British. However, when a French Canadian priest appeared, he surrendered his sword to him and was taken prisoner.

Yesterday, as we were regrouping, I had the happy experience to run into Teunis. I also learned the unfortunate news that Henry Dearborn and Christopher Greene were also captured.

Sincerely, Ben

January 3, 1776
Dear Uncle Eb,

Your letter to us in July suggesting we could be affected was true enough. After General Schuyler got back from Philadelphia, he organized forces for an invasion of Canada. We gathered at Fort Ticonderoga in August. There, I found out that Colonel John Brown, who'd been with us in the May capture of Fort Ticonderoga with Allen and Arnold, was on this expedition too.

On September 16, due to Schuyler's illness, General Richard Montgomery took command. We went down Lake Champlain to attack Fort Saint-Jean and started a siege of the fort a day later. We were not doing well, and morale was bad. On October 16, some of our men slipped past the fort to attack Fort Chambly. After two days of bombardment, Fort Chambly surrendered. Finally, after forty-five days, on November 2, Fort Saint-Jean surrendered. On November 3, the British marched out. The prisoners, including an engaging young officer, John André, were sent to Lancaster, Pennsylvania.

During the siege of Fort Saint-Jean, Montgomery sent John Brown and Ethan Allen down the St. Lawrence to prevent the British from relieving our siege. We later learned that Allen was captured by the British on September 25 at Montreal.

Now we were on our way to Montreal. On November 13, Montreal surrendered. Because our uniforms were in tatters, we began taking uniforms from the British prisoners. Montgomery stopped it. British general Guy Carleton fled from Montreal on a flotilla down the St. Lawrence River to Quebec City.

As we were heading to Quebec City, we were met by Aaron Burr, from Arnold's expedition, who guided us to Arnold's forces. Burr became a member of Montgomery's staff, and Arnold placed himself under Montgomery's command.

It was decided to attack Quebec City if a snowstorm hit. On December 30, it started to snow. At 2:00 a.m. on the thirty-first we attacked. The plan was for us to attack the lower town while Arnold's forces would lead an assault from the other side.

As we attacked, we came across a log house that was occupied by British soldiers and sailors. We took a heavy barrage from their guns, as well as grapeshot fired from cannons. General Montgomery was struck in the heart. Several of us tried to drag him off, but because of the heavy snow and continuous firing from the Brits we had to abandon him. After meeting up with Ben, he told me Arnold's group fared no better.

Sincerely, Teunis

January 5, 1776
Dear Mr. Chaplin,

Norfolk is gone! On New Year's Day, Lord Dunmore bombarded the city, causing it to catch fire, eventually destroying it. After the Battle of Great Bridge, which I write about below, General Robert Howe arrived from North Carolina. He, along with

Colonel William Woodford and his Virginia militia, had been attacking the Tory stronghold of Norfolk.

Because of the rebellious mood of the House of Burgesses, especially after Patrick Henry's speech, Governor Dunmore has taken actions to thwart rebellion. On April 21, he ordered twenty marines from HMS *Magdalen* to confiscate fifteen and a half barrels of powder from Williamsburg. Then on June 8, he fled Williamsburg to make his headquarters on HMS *Fowey,* from where he ordered raids on plantations, plundered homes, carried off slaves, and threatened to use Indians to assist him.

During October and November he gained control of Norfolk and portions of Virginia's eastern shore of the Chesapeake. He formed two new units to augment his troops—the Ethiopian Regiment, consisting of three hundred runaway slaves, and the Queen's Own Loyal Virginia Regiment, consisting of local Tories. In mid-November it was learned that Dunmore had a large store of gunpowder at Kemp's Landing.[14] On the fifteenth, a small militia force laid an ambush for Dunmore's troops but was easily driven off.

On December 9, Dunmore decided to attack the Patriots at Great Bridge[15] in his defense of Norfolk. I joined Colonel Woodfords's forces to repulse and drive the British away from Great Bridge. Part of the success was due to Woodford's Culpeper Minutemen, who were armed with rifles. We had one man slightly wounded, while they lost fifty to a hundred. I met and got on quite well with John Marshall, one of the Minutemen. Later that same day Dunmore declared Virginia in a state of rebellion, under martial law, and that any Rebel's slave serving in the British Army would be a free man.

This news is very disturbing to my father. Our plantation, Boyne Manor, depends on its slaves. One recaptured runaway slave from a neighboring plantation was punished with eighty lashes. Having that news get around should discourage more slaves from taking up Dunmore's Emancipation Proclamation.

We now await Dunmore's next action. I will keep you informed.

Sincerely, Roelof

---

14 Present-day Virginia Beach, Virginia.
15 Present-day Chesapeake, Virginia.

Chapter Two

THESE are the times that try men's souls.
—Thomas Paine

On July 4, 1776, the Continental Congress took the bold step of adopting the Declaration of Independence. This action establishes the fact that the American colonies no longer considered themselves to be a part of the British Empire. King George III considered the colonies in a state of revolution.

Militarily, 1776 was a year of ups and downs. The year started out with the disappointing news that the Quebec invasion failed. On the other hand, in March, the British evacuated Boston.

The British didn't stay away for long. In July and August, large expeditionary forces landed on Staten Island. Near the end of August, the British attacked on Long Island. Their victory was decisive, but the Americans escaped annihilation.

The Patriot forces were eventually pushed out of New York. On Christmas night, in a move that rescued the revolution, General Washington made an attack on Trenton, New Jersey, resulting in a resounding victory. While all this was going on in the Northern theater, Patriots were victorious in North Carolina, South Carolina, and Virginia.

⟨∽⟩

March 5, 1776
Dear Mr. Chaplin,

Even though we have no British soldiers in South Carolina at this point, because of the strong feelings, Tory versus Rebel, the bloodshed has begun. In this part of South Carolina the Rice Kings are strongly for independence. The folks in the up-country of both Carolinas are split in their feelings. Georgia is mostly made up of "King's Men." This episode will give you a picture of what things have become. Last August 2, a crowd of Sons of Liberty confronted Thomas Brown at his house in Georgia. When he said he would not take up arms against his country, he was taken prisoner with a fractured skull and tied to a tree where his feet were roasted by fire, and he was scalped, tarred, and feathered. He survived and is now a formidable Tory leader referred to as "Burnfoot" Brown.

On November 19, 1775, 1,900 Tories attacked a small fortification in the town of Ninety Six in the South Carolina up-country. The Rebel force of six hundred held out for three days. On the twenty-second, a cease-fire and treaty, in which the Tories agreed to disband, ended the affair. However, in December it was learned that two hundred Tories were encamped in the "Great Cane Brake." Colonel William "Danger" Thomson, with 1,300 cavalry and infantry, went after them, surrounding their camp on December 22. Most Tories escaped, and Thomson controlled his men to avoid a slaughter. The campaign ended because of heavy snow. Not prepared for that kind of weather, Thomson and his men moved back down toward the coast.

Word was just received of another Patriot victory in North Carolina on February 27. Loyalist Scottish Highlanders led by General Donald MacDonald, with 1,600 men, went on the march toward Cape Fear to join the British with the expectant arrival of troops under General Henry Clinton. Patriot forces coming from Wilmington and New Bern, commanded by Colonels James Moore and Richard Caswell, respectively, set up their defense at a bridge on Moore's Creek with one thousand militiamen. The bridge's planks were removed and the two stringers greased with soap and tallow. When the Loyalists got there, General MacDonald urged caution and then became ill. Taking over, Lieutenant Colonel Donald McLeod stormed his men across the bridge, with bagpipes screeching. The Patriots opened with cannons. The battle quickly ended. One Patriot died. Many Loyalists were taken prisoner, including MacDonald.

Last summer our little South Carolina Navy managed to capture some British ships that yielded twenty-five thousand pounds of powder. If the British come to Charleston, their ship captains are going to have quite a challenge. Last summer, vessels were sunk in the channels, beacons were removed from lighthouses, and landmark trees used by pilots for crossing sandbars were chopped down. To be able to build forts, two thousand palmetto logs were floated to Fort Johnson and thousands more to Fort Sullivan.

Sincerely, Felix

March 17, 1776
Dear Father,

On November 15, I left with several other soldiers with Colonel Henry Knox for Fort Ticonderoga to bring cannons back to Cambridge. We covered the three hundred miles in twenty days, arriving on December 5. We lost no time in gathering up fifty-nine weapons for the return trip. To haul the cannons, we used boats, horses, and ox-drawn sledges. Sometimes we did not have ice strong enough to bear the cannons. We would cut holes in the ice and let the water bubble up, and when the water froze it strengthened the ice. We used Lake George and the Hudson River at the beginning, but when we got to Kinderhook, New York, we had to come overland. We dropped a few cannons into lakes but were able to recover them. We delivered the cannons to General Washington on January 25.

On February 16, Washington proposed an attack on Boston from various points over the ice. However, General Artemas Ward suggested that we fortify Dorchester Heights and attack from there. He had been gathering a supply of fascines and gabions for just such an event. It was also suggested by Quartermaster Thomas Mifflin that the date of the attack should be set for March 5, the sixth anniversary of the Boston Massacre.

At dark on the fourth, we assembled to build the fortifications on Dorchester Heights. Mifflin had 350 oxcarts with supplies, including chandeliers suggested by Rufus Putnam. The chandeliers were wooden scaffolds set next to one another filled with bundles of tree branches and covered with dirt. Before we started the work, the path was lined with hay bales to muffle the troop movements. While there was a full moon, the sky was very hazy. We also chained together rock-filled barrels to roll down the hill if the Red Coats attacked.

While we were building the fortifications and hauling the cannons in place, Generals Israel Putnam, John Sullivan, and Nathanael Greene were assembling on the Charles River for their attack on Boston. They were doing some cannonading to help camouflage our actions. As Washington circulated among his forces, he would remind us, "Remember this is the Fifth of March."

When Howe awoke and saw what we accomplished, he sent a message to Washington requesting that we not bombard Boston, and if we did not, he would not burn Boston when he evacuated. We were happy that Howe was impressed by our work, because unbeknownst to him we had precious little powder to effect a bombardment. Today the British are evacuating. Henceforth, March 17 will no longer be St. Patrick's Day but instead Evacuation Day in Boston. I must say I worry about Zack.

Your son, Moses

April 1, 1776
Dear Moses, Ben, Teunis, Roelof, Felix, and Zack,

With this letter I am sending each of you a copy of *Common Sense*, a powerful pamphlet written by Thomas Paine. Paine emigrated from England with the help of Benjamin Franklin two years ago. Moses, you may already be familiar with *Common Sense*, because I've heard that many copies were distributed to the Continental Army. The pamphlet was published in mid-January anonymously because of its "treasonable" content. Due to all the interest in the pamphlet and its phenomenal sales (over one hundred thousand copies so far), Paine's name was just recently attached to it.

His pamphlet openly asks for American independence from Great Britain. He points out why people should not be ruled by a monarch with its tyranny of hereditary succession. He discusses the relationship between government and society. He argues that Britain should not be the "mother country" because America is composed of influences and peoples from all over Europe. He also outlined a proposal as to how America should be governed when independent.

We heard earlier in the year that King George III announced to Parliament that mercenaries would be procured to help suppress the "rebellious war." King George turned first to Czarina Catherine II (the Great) of Russia asking for twenty thousand soldiers. As they say in London, "Sister Kitty" refused. Then Holland refused his next request for the Scottish Brigade serving there. Word is that King Frederick II (the Great) of Prussia counseled Catherine not to send troops because it would be improper to send troops to another hemisphere to save a foreign government.

Now we have the details around his procurement of mercenaries from six German principalities. Landgrave Frederick II of Hesse-Kassel supplied 17,000 for £7 each and an annual payment of £108,000, plus £7 for any killed or for every 3 wounded. Duke Charles I of Brunswick supplied 5,700; Count William of Hesse-Hanau supplied 2,400; Prince Frederick of Waldeck supplied 1,200; Prince Frederick Augustus of Anhalt-Zerbst supplied 1,200; and Margrave Charles Alexander of Ansbach-Bayreuth supplied 2,400. Each of them was also paid £7 per soldier. Except for Ansbach-Bayreuth, they also received the same amount of "blood money" for dead and wounded soldiers. That means there will be 29,900 German soldiers that will be fighting against us. We've heard that Voltaire told Franklin that King Frederick of Prussia deplored this action by the Germans of selling their subjects to the English as "one sells cattle to be dragged to slaughter."

Sincerely, Eb Chaplin

May 2, 1776
Dear Uncle Eb,

Both Teunis and I survived the winter. After our attempt to take Quebec City, General Arnold continued to besiege it through the winter but to no avail, even after General David Wooster arrived from Montreal in April. Besides the cold, we survived a terrible smallpox epidemic. I feel so fortunate that I had been inoculated for smallpox a few years ago. We lost many men, and those who survived were too weak to do battle. Yesterday General John Thomas took command. The best thing we could do was to get back down to Fort Ticonderoga. During the siege at Quebec City we noticed British soldiers sliding flat rocks on the ice as some type of game. When we asked a deserter about it, he explained the "players" were from the Royal Highland Emigrants Regiment. They were emigrants from Scotland who brought the game, called curling, to Canada.

Teunis and I have had some discussions regarding General Arnold. As I told you previously, I joined his expedition because I was impressed with his capture of Fort Ticonderoga last May. I was also impressed with his leadership as we went through Maine on our way to Quebec City. Likewise, as a fervent Patriot, just five days after Concord, Arnold led the Governor's Foot Guards of New Haven to Cambridge, Massachusetts, in support of the Patriots there.

Teunis has some different feelings. As you know, he was on the raid to Fort Ticonderoga last May, initiated by Ethan Allen. He told me that Arnold insisted on being in command. Eventually he and Allen agreed to share it. One of the men with Allen was Colonel John Brown, who's become a friend of Teunis. I too have met him and have great respect for him. He went to Yale with Arnold's brother and knows Arnold well. His feeling about Arnold is that "money is this man's God, and to get enough of it he would sacrifice his country."

Brown also reminded us that shortly after Arnold joined the British Army in the French and Indian War, he deserted. Brown then told us about Arnold's actions at Fort Ticonderoga after Connecticut governor John Trumbull sent one thousand troops under Colonel Benjamin Hinman to take command at Fort Ticonderoga. When Hinman got there, Arnold refused entrance of the Connecticut troops to the fort. While Ethan Allen and Seth Warner yielded to Hinman's command, Arnold refused. He resigned in a rage. And worse yet, he threatened to sail ships, captured from the British, to Fort Saint-Jean and surrender them.

At this point, my regard for Arnold is high, but Teunis's points could give pause.

Sincerely, Ben

⧼∽⧽

June 8, 1776
Dear Uncle Eb,

This past year has been quite a challenge. After the Rebels started the rebellion at Lexington, the Boston citizenry has been besieged continuously. At times we've been surrounded by many thousands of troops. Of course, many of those rebellious to the Crown did leave the city, perhaps 50 percent or more. But nevertheless food and fuel supplies got very scarce.

We depended on the many islands throughout Boston Harbor for our own food, plus foraging food for our horses, cows, and sheep. We also depended on wood for fuel from them. The greatest loss took place when the British soldiers on Noddle's Island were chased off by General Putnam. The word is that his action led to the illegal Continental Congress's granting his commission as a general. Many Rebel whaleboats are in action taking food and fuel from many islands in the harbor. The whale boaters have even destroyed lighthouses. This makes it difficult to get shipments of food and fuel into Boston, but we did get a shipment of rice seized in Savannah. Furthermore, the ships can no longer obtain pilots to navigate them into Boston, because pilots who aid the British are threatened with death.

We have been able to survive by getting supplies from England and Ireland and the remaining loyal colonies—Quebec, Nova Scotia, and East Florida. Also, as Rebels left the city we utilized any food or fuel abandoned. Boats returning from fishing often have had their catch seized by the Rebels. Occasionally a dead whale appears on shore, which immediately becomes a food source.

I decided I could not remain in Boston. I managed to get on a boat when Howe evacuated on St. Patrick's Day. I was fortunate to be on the one with General Clinton. Since he was using John Hancock's house, he appropriated his total supply of Madeira wine, which was much enjoyed!

From Boston we sailed for Halifax, Nova Scotia, arriving on April 2. On King George's birthday, June 4, we celebrated with a *feu de joie*.[16] I have decided to fight for the Crown by joining a Loyalist provincial unit, the Queen's Rangers. We've been ordered to board ships tomorrow—destination unknown.

God Save the King, Zack

June 20, 1776
Dear Uncle Eb,

Well, we are now not far from Fort Ticonderoga, but it is not how we expected to get here. Just after Ben wrote his letter, General Carleton attacked and chased us from outside Quebec City. As we were traveling up the St. Lawrence River, General Thomas

---

[16] *Feu de joie* is a salute of musketry fired successively by each man in turn along a line and back.

contracted smallpox and died on June 2. Meanwhile General William Thompson was arriving with two thousand troops to try to evict the British from Canada. At the same time, Carleton was getting additional British troops with the arrival of General John Burgoyne and troops from Brunswick and Hesse-Hanau under Friedrich Riedesel.

As Thompson was coming north, General Simon Fraser was driving toward Trois-Rivières. In early June, General John Sullivan was put in command of the American forces in Canada. When Sullivan got there, he ordered Thompson to attack Trois-Rivières. During the night of June 7, Thompson and Colonel Arthur St. Clair crossed the St. Lawrence. However, they were spotted by local Quebec militia, who reported our arrival to General Simon Fraser. Thompson convinced a local farmer, Antoine Gauthier, to lead us to the British. The treacherous soul led us into a swamp. Some of us got extricated, but there was a heavy battle the rest of the night and the next morning. Many of our troops caught grapeshot from a ship in the St. Lawrence River.

Eventually, as we were finding our way out of the swamp, we met up with Colonel Anthony Wayne. He formed a rear guard action, which allowed us to retreat. However, many of Thompson's men, including the general himself, were captured. The total captured were 236. We lost between thirty and fifty. The Brits lost about twenty.

We got on our way to Montreal and Fort Saint-Jean. We set both places ablaze, most importantly the sawmill at Saint-Jean to prevent British shipbuilding. At Fort Saint-Jean we took boats that could be used to navigate Lake Champlain. General Arnold directed this task and was the last to push away from the burning remnants.

Now that we are out of Canada, I am looking forward to getting back to the farm and once again seeing Sarah. Because I left for Quebec before the crops were harvested, she did this by herself. She has also planted this year's crops. In addition to all the farm work that has to be done, I need to cut a supply of firewood to get us through the next winter.

Sincerely, Teunis

June 29, 1776
Dear Mr. Chaplin,

Yesterday we managed to hold off a British attack on Charleston.[17]
On March 12, General Henry Clinton arrived at Cape Fear,
North Carolina. He had been initially sent by General Howe
from Boston to rendezvous with Commodore Peter Parker's
fleet coming from Cork, Ireland, with General Charles
Cornwallis. They went to North Carolina at the behest of their
royal governor Josiah Martin. But when hearing the news of the
Moore's Creek Bridge Battle, the British commanders decided
to attack Charleston.

Clinton put ashore 2,200 troops on Long Island[18] between the
sixth and the fifteenth of June. Early in June, after being named
Southern Department commander, General Charles Lee arrived.
Lee went to Sullivan's Island to inspect the fort that Colonel
William Moultrie was building. Lee called it a slaughter pen and
wanted to evacuate it, but Governor John Rutledge sent a note to
Moultrie that he could not abandon without a direct order from
him. Moultrie built the fort with four double walls of palmetto
logs placed sixteen feet apart, with the space between the walls
filled with sand and marsh clay. Palmetto is soft and spongy. As
a result, cannonballs hitting it would not produce lethal flying
splinters. Apple trees were perfect for constructing abatis.

At 10:00 a.m. on the twenty-eighth, Parker's squadron
of several ships opened fire from the harbor. Because of the
dangerous shoals, Parker could not get very close to the fort.
Many shells fell short, and others were absorbed into the
palmetto and sand. Clinton then tried to cross from Long
Island using the Breach to Sullivan's Island. He thought the
Breach would be easy to ford, but it was seven feet deep and the
Brits couldn't get across. Lieutenant Colonel William "Danger"
Thomson was facing Clinton with 780 men. In the fort, we
had 420 men. Assisting Moultrie were Peter Muhlenberg and

[17] At the time known as Charles Town.
[18] Currently known as Isle of Palms.

Francis Marion. By the way, Moultrie's bother John, a fervent Tory, is lieutenant governor of East Florida.

We had to be very selective with our shots, because Lee had taken ten thousand pounds of powder from the fort to use in Charleston if he was attacked there. Our fire was extremely accurate, killing many on board the ships, including former South Carolina Royal governor William Campbell. At dusk many British ships were in very bad shape. Those that were able withdrew. During the battle our flag was knocked down. To make sure the British didn't think we were surrendering, it was quickly hoisted back up. Our flag, designed by Moultrie, is blue, bearing a white crescent with the word "Liberty" on it.

Sincerely, Felix

June 30, 1776
Dear Moses, Ben, Teunis, Roelof, Felix, and Zack,

I really appreciate the letters from each of you. Because of the timeliness of your letters, Felix and Roelof, the Blaze Horse had the first news in Philadelphia of those two events (victory at Moore's Creek and burning of Norfolk). Ben and Teunis, your letters regarding the siege of Quebec were gut-wrenching. What an awful winter you two have endured. When the British evacuated Boston, Moses was concerned about Zack. Zack wrote to say he went to Halifax with the British. His last letter mentioned he was leaving Halifax on June 9, destination unknown.

Ben and Teunis, I don't know if you saw the commissioners to Canada arriving in April. Congress decided to send Benjamin Franklin, Pennsylvania delegate; Charles Carroll and Samuel Chase, Maryland delegates; John Carroll, a Jesuit priest educated in France and cousin of Charles; and General Baron Frederick William de Woedtke, a twenty-six-year-old Prussian. They left on March 26 to attempt to form a union with the people of Canada.

Franklin and Father Carroll arrived back in Philadelphia on June 11. Franklin stopped by the Blaze Horse to tell about the trip. When they got to General Schuyler's estate at Saratoga, they were entertained for a few days and then—except for the baron, who joined Schuyler's staff—left for Montreal on April 16. When they arrived in Montreal on April 29, they were received in grand military style by General Benedict Arnold. They may have had a good reception by Arnold, but the Canadians were not impressed. Father Carroll was snubbed by the bishop of Quebec and then excommunicated. Franklin decided he'd had enough. He and Father Carroll left. Charles Carroll and Samuel Chase decided to stay but upon returning reported that Canada is staying loyal to the Crown.

Now the BIG NEWS. On June 7, Delegate Richard Henry Lee introduced the following resolution to Congress: "Resolved, That these United Colonies are, and of right ought to be, free and independent States, that they are absolved from all allegiance to the British Crown, and that all political connection between them and the State of Great Britain is, and ought to be, totally dissolved." After hours of debate, Congress on June 11 agreed to table the issue for three weeks. Nevertheless, it appointed a committee to prepare a statement of independence during the interim. The members of the committee are Thomas Jefferson, Benjamin Franklin, John Adams, Roger Sherman, and Robert Livingston. Two days ago the draft was presented, but due to Maryland and New York not having yet received instructions on how to vote, the vote was delayed until July 1. Since Rhode Island declared independence on May 4, there is for sure one yes vote. I will keep you informed on what happens.

Sincerely, Eb Chaplin

July 8, 1776
Dear Moses, Ben, Teunis, Roelof, Felix, and Zack,

On July 4, the Declaration of Independence was adopted by the Continental Congress. As I mentioned in the last letter, the vote on Richard Henry Lee's resolution was delayed to July 1. Felix, your friend Ned Rutledge played an important role in Congress that day even though John Adams said, "Young Ned Rutledge is a perfect Bob o' Lincoln, a swallow, a sparrow, a peacock, excessively vain, excessively weak, and excessively variable and unsteady – jejune, inane, and puerile." Yet twice Ned saved the day for Adams, who is very vocal for independence.

On July 1, the debate was begun by John Adams. After an hour of speaking, the New Jersey delegation entered the room. When they asked Adams to repeat the speech that they missed, Adams objected. However, Ned urged Adams to do so because only he, Adams, had the facts at his command. That was his first occasion of helping Adams, because the repeated speech convinced the New Jersey delegation to vote for independence.

Parliamentary procedure required two ballots: a vote by the committee of the whole followed by Congress's formal vote for independence. On the first ballot, nine colonies voted for independence, Pennsylvania and South Carolina voted against, New York abstained, and Delaware's delegation was split and, therefore, could not vote. Now the second occasion of helping Adams occurred. Ned rescued the moment by moving that the second vote be postponed to the next day. He hinted that South Carolina might change its vote for the sake of unanimity.

On July 2, things looked different in the room. After an all-night ride, Caesar Rodney was there to break the Delaware split. Missing from the Pennsylvania delegation were John Dickinson and Robert Morris, two nay votes on the day before. Voting yea for Pennsylvania were Benjamin Franklin, James Wilson, and John Morton. Voting nay for Pennsylvania were Thomas Willing and Charles Humphreys. Now, the two colonies voting against the day before, South Carolina and Pennsylvania, voted in favor of independence. This time the vote was twelve for independence and an abstention by New York. Even though the New York delegates were for independence, they did not have instructions to cast a yea vote. On July 3 and 4, the delegates worked on the draft that Thomas Jefferson and his committee submitted. After changes, the wording was approved on the fourth and sent to be printed. John Adams is telling everyone that this date should be celebrated with illuminations from this time forward forever more.

The Declaration begins with an introduction: "When in the Course of human events, it becomes necessary for one people to dissolve the political bands which have connected them with another, and to assume among the powers of the earth, the separate and equal station to which the Laws of Nature and of Nature's God entitle them, a decent respect to the opinions of mankind requires that they should declare the causes which impel them to the separation."

This is followed by a preamble:

> We hold these truths to be self-evident, that all men are created equal, that they are endowed by their Creator with certain unalienable Rights, that among these are Life, Liberty and the pursuit of Happiness.
>
> That to secure these rights, Governments are instituted among Men, deriving their just powers from the consent of the governed, That whenever any Form of Government becomes destructive of these ends, it is the Right of the People to alter or to abolish it, and to institute new Government, laying its foundation on such principles and organizing its powers in such form, as to them shall seem most likely to effect their Safety and Happiness. Prudence, indeed, will dictate that Governments long established should not be changed for light and transient causes; and accordingly all experience hath shewn, that mankind are more disposed to suffer, while evils are sufferable, than to right themselves by abolishing the forms to which they are accustomed. But when a long train of abuses and usurpations, pursuing invariably the same Object evinces a design to reduce them under absolute Despotism, it is their right, it is their duty, to throw off such Government, and to provide new Guards for their future security.

Then follows the indictment: A bill of particulars documenting the king's "repeated injuries and usurpations" of the Americans' rights and liberties. Following this is a denunciation and conclusion.

On July 5, our German newspaper, *Der Wochentliche Philadelphische Staatsbote*, was the first to publish a notice that a Declaration of Independence was adopted. Moses, since I know you are among many German-speaking soldiers, I am sending along a copy. On the sixth, the *Philadelphia Evening Post* published the full text of the Declaration of Independence. I am sending a copy to each of you. Today the Declaration of Independence was read aloud at the State House yard followed by the ringing of the bell in the Pennsylvania State House. We now refer to the State House bell as the Liberty Bell.

Sincerely, Eb Chaplin

July 13, 1776
Dear Father,

It's been some time since I wrote to you. I appreciate your sending a copy of *Common Sense*. I have shared it with many other soldiers. I have also read it to many soldiers who cannot read. It has been very helpful for us all to remember why we are involved in this rebellion.

Your letter about the commission to Canada was interesting. It was the tradition for years in the Boston area to celebrate Pope's Day on November 5. When it started it was reminiscent of Guy Fawkes Day[19] in Britain but soon became an anti-Catholic celebration. In an attempt to assist in winning over Quebec, General Washington, last September 14, issued a general order that banned Pope's Day.

At the end of January, General Washington sent General Charles Lee to New York to supervise building defense fortifications. He stayed there until March, when he was sent to Charleston. We left Boston on April 4 and arrived here in New York ten days later. While in Boston we were grateful when we received 15,000 pounds of powder sent from Georgia and 111 barrels of powder sent from

---

[19] A celebration of the foiled attempt to assassinate King James I in 1605 by Catholic conspirators.

South Carolina, which had been captured from the British. Until we left for New York, we passed our time by playing cards (All Fours and Whist) and playing dice (Going to Boston and hazard). Hazard[20] is a complicated game, but I really like it. Now that it is warmer, when we are not working on fortifications, we play tip-cat. We use a stick and a block of wood (the cat). We tip the cat with the stick and then hit it for distance to determine a winner.

On June 28, we had quite a shock. One of Washington's Life Guards, Thomas Hickey, was hanged as a traitor before twenty thousand spectators. He was part of a large conspiracy against Washington. During his court-martial he was accused of being part of the conspiracy to assassinate Washington or kidnap him to turn over to the British when they arrived.

My German American friends really appreciated your sending *Der Wochentliche Philadelphische Staatsbote*. I constantly receive *"viel danke"*[21] from them. We had the Declaration of Independence read to us on July 9. After the reading, the Sons of Liberty tore down the statue of King George III in New York. It is being sent to Connecticut to be melted down for lead bullets. It is estimated it can produce 42,000 bullets.

On June 29, forty-eight British ships from Halifax under General William Howe appeared on the horizon. On July 2, they landed on Staten Island. Then yesterday, another eighty-two ships under the command of Admiral Richard Howe arrived. When I look out at the harbor, the masts appear as a huge forest. With so many British troops here, I fear an enormous battle.

Your son, Moses

August 2, 1776
Dear Moses,

Last year Ben wrote about the lack of gunpowder at Bunker Hill and at Dorchester Heights. You mentioned that General

---

[20] The present-day dice game of craps was developed from hazard.
[21] German for "many thanks," pronounced *feel dung-kah*.

Washington leaked word that he had 1,800 barrels of gunpowder to intimidate the British. The lack of gunpowder has been a big problem.

I'm not sure if I told you about the gunpowder we got from Bermuda a year ago. Because all trade was banned by the Continental Congress with any colony staying loyal to the Crown, Bermuda was desperate for food. We managed to obtain one hundred barrels of gunpowder from storage in St. George's by providing much-needed food. Half of the powder was sent to Charleston and the other half here to Philadelphia. Just a few days ago, we got word that ninety-eight kegs of powder got to Fort Pitt from New Orleans. It was supplied by Oliver Pollock, originally from Carlisle, Pennsylvania, now living in New Orleans. His billings were denoted with "$," signifying dollars, instead of merely using the word.

On April 8, Commodore Esek Hopkins arrived in New London, Connecticut, with twenty-four barrels of powder. But there is more to the story. In January, Hopkins, as commander in chief of the Continental Navy, took over a fleet here in Philadelphia. When he raised the Navy Jack, Lieutenant John Paul Jones took displeasure with it because it contained a serpent with the words "Don't Tread on Me." Finally on February 17, when he could get through the ice, he sailed down the Delaware River. His orders were to go after Lord Dunmore's navy roving in the Chesapeake Bay area.

Instead, he sailed to the Bahamas, where it was learned that Lord Dunmore had sent a cache of powder from Virginia, getting to Abaco Island on March 1. On the third, he initiated our first amphibious landing under Marine Captain Samuel Nicholas[22] at Nassau on New Providence Island, capturing seventy-one cannons, fifteen brass mortars, and twenty-four barrels of powder. Before Governor Montfort Browne was taken prisoner, he managed to get 150 barrels out, sending them to St.

---

[22] Nicholas was the first officer commissioned in the United States Continental Marines by Congress on November 5, 1775, and by tradition is considered to be the first commandant of the Marine Corps. On November 10, 1775, Tun Tavern in Philadelphia was established as recruiting headquarters for the Marines.

Augustine, East Florida. On his way to New London, Hopkins's fleet was badly damaged by the British HMS *Glasgow*.

The talk in the Blaze Horse is that Hopkins is in big trouble with Congress for not going after Dunmore and then for letting so much powder get away. Today was a very busy day at Blaze Horse. Delegates were in town to sign the Declaration of Independence.

May God bless you, Dad

August 10, 1776
Dear Mr. Chaplin,

It was great to get your letter telling us of the Declaration of Independence. Being a Virginian, I was really glad to see the roles Virginians played. I was proud to see that Richard Henry Lee formally proposed the motion for independence to Congress. Thomas Jefferson's words were so eloquent. I was particularly happy to learn that George Washington was named commander in chief. I couldn't help but to laugh aloud when I learned of Benjamin Harrison's remark to Elbridge Gerry: "When the hanging scene comes to be exhibited I shall have the advantage over you on account of my size. All will be over with me in a moment, but you will be kicking in the air half an hour after I am gone." Harrison's plantation, Berkeley, is about forty miles south of ours.

When George Washington heard of Dunmore's November 1775 Emancipation Proclamation, he exclaimed that Dunmore must be crushed. Washington should be pleased—Lord Dunmore is out of Virginia! After he burned Norfolk, Dunmore went to Tucker's Point, not far from Portsmouth. By February, forces were closing in on Dunmore. Luckily for him, Captain Andrew Snape Hamond on HMS *Roebuck* was in the Virginia Capes waiting to join Cornwallis's foray to Cape Fear. Hamond managed to extricate Dunmore and his troops to Gwynn's Island in the Chesapeake. From there he continued to harass the Virginia settlements.

General Andrew Lewis was ordered to evict Dunmore from Gwynn's Island. On July 8, we started a cannonade. When we got on the island, we found that Dunmore had escaped by ship. The scene at which we arrived was unbelievable. While many of the British and Tory troops were inoculated against smallpox, most of his Negro troops had not been inoculated. We found over five hundred dead Negroes who were not even buried. These slaves had been induced to join the British forces in exchange for their freedom, and this is how they were treated! Totally shameful.

Now that we've declared independence, I hope we can achieve it. I understand that Washington left Boston and went to New York. Please keep me in the loop as news happens.

Sincerely, Roelof

~

August 21, 1776
Dear Uncle Eb,

On June 29, we got to New York Harbor after having left Halifax, Nova Scotia, on the ninth. We disembarked onto Staten Island on July 2. A few days later we got the news that the colonies declared their independence. Then I got your letter and couldn't believe some of the things I read! One of the lines you quoted was "that all men are created equal." You also indicated Thomas Jefferson penned most of the document. If all men are created equal, where did it say the slaves were now free? How many of these "men created equal" does he still own?

On July 12, General William Howe sent two ships up the Hudson River to test things out. Even though receiving shelling, the ships not only easily made it past Rebel fortifications but continued all the way up to Tappan Zee. Also, on the twelfth, Admiral Lord Richard Howe arrived with troops from England. In addition, he carried peace overtures from Parliament. When Ben Franklin served in London, Lord Howe and he were acquaintances.

On the fourteenth, Lord Howe sent an officer under a flag of truce to New York with a letter addressed to "George

Washington, Esq." The answer he got was "Sir, we have no person in our army with that address." When asked what title Mr. Washington chose, the reply was "You are sensible, sir, of the rank of General Washington in our army." More letters were sent addressed to "George Washington, Esq., etc., etc." and were again sent back unopened. On the twentieth, Washington agreed to meet with Colonel James Paterson, adjutant to General Howe. When Paterson once again placed the same letter on the table between them, Washington let it lie, not touching it. Paterson then told Washington that Lord Howe had come from London with authority to grant pardons. Washington replied, "Those who have committed no fault want no pardon. We are only defending what we deem our indisputable rights." Based on that stubborn act and the so-named Declaration of Independence, it looks as if a major fight may soon ensue.

On August 1, Generals Henry Clinton and Charles Cornwallis arrived back from Charleston with three thousand troops. And then on August 12, one hundred ships arrived, which included eight thousand Hessian troops. We have over 32,000 troops now on Staten Island. The British soldiers are having some fun with the Hessians. They tell the Hessians that the Rebels are cannibals and will cook them with sauerkraut if they are captured!

God Save The King, Zack

August 31, 1776
Dear Father,

Today I and the entire American Army are lucky not to have fallen entirely into the hands of the British. Because we were able to escape from Long Island, with what I believe was providential interference, we live to fight another day. Let me tell you what has transpired since I last wrote about all the masts in the harbor.

While there were an estimated 32,000 British troops on Staten Island, General Washington didn't know how or when they would attack. He had troops under General William Heath at King's Bridge on the north of York Island[23] at the Harlem River. He had troops at Brooklyn on Long Island under General Nathanael Greene. Washington was headquartered on York Island with more troops. On August 19, in an effort to block the British from coming up the East River between New York City and Brooklyn, several old ships were sunk at the mouth of the East River.

On the twentieth, General Greene became so ill that Washington named General John Sullivan to replace him. As it turned out, this was disastrous for us, because whereas Greene was intimately familiar with the terrain on Long Island, Sullivan was not. On the twenty-first, a most terrifying lightning storm struck. Many houses were set on fire, and several soldiers were killed by lightning bolts.

On the twenty-second, the British started to transport troops from Staten Island to Long Island. Washington was not sure if this was to be the real attack or if it was a feint to cover a possible attack up the Hudson River. On the twenty-fourth, Washington decided to name General Israel Putnam to replace General Sullivan. Finally the British attacked. Putnam, at 3:00 a.m. on the twenty-seventh, signaled that fact from Brooklyn to Washington in New York.

The sun rose the morning of the twenty-seventh with a red angry glare. In front of the Brooklyn Heights, fortifications were under the command of General Putnam. Generals Lord Stirling and John Sullivan were positioned on the Guan Heights. Stirling had one thousand troops on the right in front of the Gowanus Swamp. Most of his men were from Colonel John Haslet's Delaware Blues and Major Mordecai Gist's Maryland Battalion. Sullivan had 1,500 troops on the right. Still further to the right were four hundred of Colonel Samuel Miles's Pennsylvania State Rifle Regiment.

Stirling faced a much superior force to his under the command of General James Grant. Initially his men fought gallantly. The Delaware Blues almost took some British prisoners, because the British mistook them to be Hessians. The

---

[23] Present-day Manhattan.

Blues wore tall leather helmets, which resembled the Hessian tall mitered helmets. Stirling's troops were overwhelmed, and the Maryland forces lost most of their men. Watching from Brooklyn, Washington cried out, "Good God, what brave fellows I must this day lose." Many, in trying to escape, drowned in the Gowanus Swamp.

Sullivan was attacked by General Leopold Philip von Heister frontally and was hit from his left flank by General Henry Clinton. His left flank had been left undefended. Sullivan's forces were soon surrounded, and he was taken prisoner. Stirling too was taken prisoner when he surrendered his sword to von Heister.

Howe decided to stop the attack in front of Brooklyn Heights late on the twenty-seventh. On the twenty-eighth, Washington sent more men over to Brooklyn. All day on the twenty-ninth, we were drenched by heavy rains. The same day Washington sent an order to General Heath to gather boats and send them down York Island across from Brooklyn. Also on the twenty-ninth, General Thomas Mifflin suggested that Washington retreat with his Pennsylvanians serving as a rear guard.

Colonel John Glover's Marblehead, Massachusetts, men were called on to ferry us across the East River. Orders were given for complete silence and to keep campfires burning. However, due to a northeast wind, it looked as if this couldn't be accomplished. Then at 11:00 p.m., the wind shifted to the southeast. The disembarkation across the East River began. Then as dawn approached, without all the men across, a heavy fog settled in. This allowed the completion of the escape of nine thousand troops. Some boats had to complete eleven crossings during the night.

Our losses were approximately three hundred killed, seven hundred wounded, and one thousand prisoners. In addition to Stirling and Sullivan, Colonel Miles and his men were captured. Later we learned that Miles had warned Sullivan that the British might make a flanking move and that troops should be placed in the Jamaica Pass, through which they came. After the battle and with hindsight based on this almost disaster, General Greene suggested to Washington that in the future, American forces "take post where the enemy is obliged to fight us, and not us them."

Your son, Moses

⟨∿⟩

September 1, 1776
Dear Uncle Eb,

I am pleased to report we had a resounding victory on Long Island. After a horrendous lightning storm the night before, a huge amphibious landing was launched before dawn on a clear, cloudless August 22. By noon, over fifteen thousand men and forty pieces of artillery had landed at Gravesend on Long Island. We were met by many happy Loyalists. General Charles Cornwallis led the vanguard inland six miles to establish at Flatbush. Meanwhile General Henry Clinton, along with Lord Rawdon, went off to reconnoiter the Rebel defenses. They discovered the undefended Jamaica Pass. After much discussion between Generals Clinton and William Howe, Clinton convinced Howe to make a flanking move to the Pass.

On the twenty-sixth, we could see General Washington on the Guan Heights looking at our encampment through his spyglass. That night at 9:00 p.m., General Clinton, led by Loyalist scouts, commenced the right flanking move on Jamaica Pass. Clinton was followed by Generals Cornwallis, Howe, and Hugh Percy. General James Grant attacked on the left toward the Gowanus Swamp, and General Leopold Philip von Heister attacked straight on toward the Guan Heights.

While Grant met fierce resistance from a small force, he managed to roll them back into the Gowanus Swamp. Our forces swept through the Jamaica Pass, and soon we and von Heister had General John Sullivan's troops surrounded. He surrendered, as did General Lord Stirling. We were about to attack the fortifications on Brooklyn Heights when General Howe halted the attack. On the twenty-eighth and the twenty-ninth, we busily dug entrenchments in anticipation of an attack on the Heights. When we awoke on the thirtieth, the Americans were gone.

Much discussion has ensued as to why Howe stopped the attack rather than finishing it off. After seeing what happened at Bunker Hill, I feel that he did not want to risk another such slaughter. Our losses were minimal: 65 killed and 293 wounded. If Howe loses men, he can't just go into the countryside and round up more troops. He has to send for them thousands of miles across the sea.

You will probably hear of some horrible atrocities committed by the Hessians. Instead of taking prisoners, they pinned Rebel soldiers to trees with their bayonets. While I am disappointed at not having a total victory, General James Grant informed London, "If a good Bleeding can bring those Bible faced Yankees to their senses, the Fever of Independency should soon abate." Perhaps his view is true, and soon this ridiculous rebellion will come to an end. I so much would like to get back home to Boston.

God Save The King, Zack

September 14, 1776
Dear Moses, Ben, Teunis, Roelof, Felix, and Zack,

Before I tell you about the very interesting evening last night at the Blaze Horse, I was so thankful to hear from Moses and Zack that they both survived that large battle on Long Island.

Last night John Adams and Ned Rutledge were here telling us about the Peace Conference they attended on the eleventh at Billopp House on Staten Island with Admiral Lord Howe. After General John Sullivan was captured, Howe suggested that Sullivan go to Philadelphia and deliver a peace conference proposal to Congress. Sullivan was willing but felt Washington should know about it. On August 30, under a white flag of truce, Sullivan spoke to Washington. While Washington was not pleased, he did not object.

On September 2, Sullivan delivered the proposal to Congress. John Adams nearly exploded, totally incensed at Sullivan for even thinking that Congress might renounce independence. Pennsylvania delegates George Ross and Benjamin Rush, along with New Jersey's John Witherspoon, joined in the outrage. However, on the fifth, Congress agreed to send a committee of Benjamin Franklin, John Adams, Richard Henry Lee, and Ned Rutledge. Lee refused to go. Adams finally agreed.

On the ninth, the first night out, Franklin and Adams, sleeping in the same room, got into a discussion about whether or not the window should be open or closed. Franklin lectured Adams on the virtue of fresh air, and the window was left open. We had quite a laugh about that. On the eleventh, the group got to Perth Amboy, New Jersey, and was escorted across the Arthur Kill by spotlessly attired Hessian soldiers. They told us the Hessians wore cone-shaped helmets with a pointed, highly polished tin plate embossed with the lion of Hesse-Kassel. The Hessian soldiers wore thick mustaches, blackened with wax, twirled into sharp points, making them look even more ferocious—a little different from the clean-shaven rules for our soldiers.

They met in the Billopp House, owned by a Loyalist, which was used to house the Hessian military guards. When they arrived they were escorted to a room that had a carpet of moss and green sprigs from bushes and shrubs. Another laugh—they mentioned even though a nice try, it did not hide the stench of housing so many soldiers! Before the conference commenced, they were served a dinner of cold ham, tongue, and mutton with a good claret wine.

After dinner Howe opened by noting that he, as a member of Parliament, had often opposed the taxes aimed at the colonies and felt that the differences between the colonies and Britain might be accommodated to the satisfaction of both. He mentioned his gratitude to the people of Massachusetts who had erected a monument in Westminster Abbey in memory of his brother, George Augustus, who was killed in the French and Indian War near Fort Ticonderoga.

Howe told the committee he did not have the power to deal with the colonies as anything but colonies and could not acknowledge the legitimacy of the authority of Congress. Howe and Franklin had some interchange as to how to consider each other as they proceeded. Adams at that point said he could be considered as Howe wished, except that of being a British subject. When discussion turned to the Declaration of Independence, Rutledge, speaking on behalf of South Carolina, flatly told the admiral that if Congress revoked independence, South Carolina would never do so. Howe stated that if the colonies would not give up independency, it was impossible for him to enter into any negotiations—helping us to say, "Bye, George"?

The conference ended with the committee returning to Philadelphia yesterday. Succinctly Caesar Rodney of Delaware declared, "This business is put an end to by their return." On the twelfth, General Sullivan and General Lord Stirling, who had been taken prisoner at Long Island, were exchanged for General Richard Prescott, captured near Montreal by Armstrong's expedition to Quebec in 1775; General Donald MacDonald, captured at Moore's Creek, North Carolina, in February, 1776; and Governor Montfort Browne, captured at New Providence, Bahamas, in March, 1776.

Being tired from his trip back from Billopp House, Ben Franklin did not make it last night to the Blaze Horse. Speaking of Franklin, I may have neglected to tell you that his son, William Franklin, who has been New Jersey's colonial governor since 1763, was placed under house arrest in January by colonial militia because of his Loyalist stance. After the Declaration of Independence, the Provincial Congress of New Jersey, which he refused to recognize, took him into custody. The word is that he is being sent to Simsbury Copper Mine at Newgate Prison in Connecticut for incarceration. We all feel so sorry for Dr. Franklin to have to bear this heavy personal burden.

Sincerely, Eb Chaplin

September 23, 1776
Dear Uncle Eb,

The Rebels are still in full force on York Island. Since they escaped Long Island on August 30 until September 15, General

Howe made no moves against them. Howe and General Clinton always seem to have differing views on how to move forward. Clinton's idea on the flanking move through Jamaica Pass won the day for us on Long Island. This time Clinton's view was that we should attack the Rebels up at King's Bridge and the Harlem River. He felt that if York Island was a bottle, then Harlem was the neck. However, Howe, based on input from the Royal Navy, overruled him because to get there we'd have to get ships through Hell's Gate, with its treacherous currents at the confluence of the East and Harlem Rivers.

The decision was to attack at Kips Bay. On the fifteenth, with four thousand troops, we crossed the East River. During the crossing we Loyalists and Brits shouted profanities at the Rebels. The Hessians sang hymns, which is traditional. Upon landing, we easily routed the Rebel forces. Even General Washington couldn't rally them. Our advance on the island was virtually stopped when a Quaker lady, Mary Murray, invited General Howe to afternoon tea. We tarried there for at least two hours while Howe and his generals enjoyed cake and wine! The next day we attacked the Rebels at Harlem Heights but were thrown back.

During the night of the twenty-first, a huge conflagration consumed a large portion of New York City. We are totally convinced that Washington had the dirty deed done. Citizens and soldiers were so incensed that persons suspected of starting the fire were unceremoniously hanged. The Brits hung a man by his heels until he died, later learning he was a Loyalist! General Howe stopped soldiers from fighting the fire, suspecting it was a trap set by the Rebels to attack while they were firefighting.

Yesterday a Rebel spy, Nathan Hale, was hanged. He was a very young man who volunteered for the task with no training. Hale was spotted on a road conspicuously asking questions and making notes by none other than Robert Rogers, who, as you may recall, so admirably led Rogers' Rangers during the French and Indian War. He is now commander of the Loyalist Queen's American Rangers. In conversation Hale admitted to Rogers that he was a spy and was captured.

God Save The King, Zack

⋅October 22, 1776
Dear Uncle Eb,

What a summer and fall this was. My soldiering abilities were switched to the navy! After burning Fort Saint-Jean, we arrived at Fort Ticonderoga. There we learned General Horatio Gates, appointed by Congress to replace General John Sullivan, was in command of the fort and the defense of Lake Champlain. To defend Lake Champlain, we had to expand the fleet, which meant building ships. Since General Arnold had been a former merchant captain, Gates put Arnold in charge of building ships to expand the fleet. We built the ships at Skenesborough,[24] New York, located at the southern end of the lake. We managed to build three ten-gun galleys and eight three-gun gundalows to add to the existing fleet. Word came from Fort Saint-Jean the British were also busy building ships.

After these ships were completed in August, we sailed north to meet the British. After getting there, Arnold decided on September 30 to go back up the lake. His decision to hide the fleet behind Valcour Island met resistance with several of the captains who wanted an open-water fight, which would allow an escape if things went badly. Arnold explained our primary purpose was not survival but to avoid Carleton from taking Fort Ticonderoga this year.

Early on the morning of October 11, thirty British vessels started past Valcour Island, followed by many Indians in canoes, unaware we had fifteen vessels behind the island. At about 11:00 a.m., the Battle of Valcour Island started in earnest. The battle raged on all day. Due to the British having more and much larger ships, we were beat up badly. We managed to get some vessels back behind Valcour as night fell. We could not escape by land, because hordes of Indians were there.

During the night, we muffled the oars. Luckily it was a foggy night too. With our muffled oars, the fog, and the darkness of night we managed to slip past the British ships. We also

---

[24] Present-day Whitehall, New York.

managed not to be detected by the Indians on shore, whose campfires were a frightful reminder of what our fate may have been if they had sighted us. We were able to outrace the British ships and made it to the Vermont shore above Fort Ticonderoga.

On October 20, snow fell and Carleton withdrew back to Canada. He was also intimidated by the strong defenses built on Mount Independence during the summer. Arnold's purpose was met. *Royal Savage* was one of our ships sunk. It carried all of Arnold's personal papers. I hope that doesn't cause him trouble when he files for expenses from the Quebec Expedition. I'll be spending the winter at Fort Ticonderoga.

Sincerely, Ben

November 14, 1776
Dear Father,

After the debacle on Long Island it was said that the roads in Connecticut and New Jersey were filled with soldiers streaming home. We had twenty thousand troops on York Island stretching from the Battery in the south to King's Bridge in the north. We were encamped at Harlem Heights.

After Long Island, there was talk about burning New York City. General Washington was contemplating it. General Greene and John Jay were arguing for it to be done. That question was settled on September 7 when Washington received a letter from John Hancock stating that Congress wanted no damage done to the city.

On September 15, a force of four thousand Brits and Hessians landed at Kips Bay. It was too large a force for the Connecticut men, who soon retreated. Washington, hearing the cannons roar and seeing smoke rising in the distance, galloped down from Harlem Heights to personally rally the troops, but to no avail. As our men tried to surrender, the Hessians shot or bayoneted them. One was seen to be beheaded.

When General Putnam started his retreat, he was directed by Lieutenant Aaron Burr to take a route along the Hudson River. If Putnam had not done so, he would have run into the British forces, facing capture. Interestingly, Burr had been on Washington's staff but was removed because Washington felt he had "certain character flaws," not trusting him.

On September 16, a reconnoitering party found five thousand British advancing toward Harlem Heights. As they got closer they were sounding their bugles, as if they were on a fox hunt. Washington ordered a counterattack. After some heavy fighting, we managed to drive them back quite quickly. We chased them for three miles. Washington called off the attack, fearing we might be running into a trap. Their casualties were ninety killed and three hundred wounded, while ours were thirty killed and one hundred wounded.

On the evening of September 21, we were aghast to see that New York City was aflame. No one knows how it started. Unfortunately for the residents, they could not ring any warning bells, because Washington ordered that all bells in the city be removed so they could be recast for cannons. The fire finally stopped when the wind changed. Approximately 25 percent of the city was destroyed.

On September 22, we received distressing news. Under a white flag of truce, British Captain John Montresor came to our lines to inform Captain William Hull that his friend Nathan Hale had been hanged for espionage. He also mentioned that Hale's last words were "I only regret that I have but one life to lose for my country."

On October 14, General Charles Lee rejoined our forces upon returning from Charleston. On the seventeenth, we made our exodus from Harlem Heights heading to White Plains, New York. On the eighteenth, as we were still moving out, four thousand British troops landed at Pell's Point. Colonel John Glover, with 750 men, managed to slow them down before they had to make a retreat.

On October 28, the British, with a force of thirteen thousand, attacked us at White Plains. We were hit on the right by General von Heister and on the left by General Clinton.

The Hessians attacked Chatterton Hill, defended by Haslet's Delaware Blues and Smallwood's Marylanders. As at Gowanus Swamp, they put up a gallant fight before retreating. We pulled back to higher ground, and then General Howe halted further action. On November 5, the British left. Each side had about fifty men killed.

We left White Plains on the twelfth, heading for New Jersey. Washington left seven thousand with General Lee to check any British moves to New England. He left three thousand with General Heath to guard the Hudson Highlands. He left General Greene in command of the troops at Fort Washington and Fort Lee. General Lee advised that Fort Washington should be abandoned, but General Greene, based on the feelings of Colonel Robert Magaw, the fort's commander, felt it could be held.

Before signing off, I must tell you about an incident that happened back on September 7. David Bushnell of Connecticut invented a submersible vessel that he called the *Turtle*. It resembled a large barrel that could maneuver underwater with a device that could attach explosives to the bottom of a ship's hull. On that night Bushnell became ill. Ezra Lee volunteered for the mission, maneuvering the *Turtle* under Admiral Lord Howe's HMS *Eagle*. However, he could not attach the torpedo, because the drill could not penetrate the hull. The *Turtle* had to escape. During its escape the *Turtle* was spotted by British sailors, so Lee released the torpedo and submerged. An hour later, with Lee safely back on shore, the torpedo went off with a tremendous explosion.

Your son, Moses

☙◗

November 18, 1776
Dear Uncle Eb,

After chasing the Rebels around for over a month, we had a decisive victory yesterday. Our forces completely over ran and captured Fort Washington. Today it was renamed Fort Knyphausen. I think our next target will be Fort Lee located on ·the New Jersey side of the Hudson River.

On October 12, General Clinton, commanding a force of four thousand, went through Hell's Gate and landed on Throgs Neck. To our dismay, instead of being a peninsula, it was virtually an island. Colonel Edward Hand, with a minute force, managed to bottle us up for six days. On the eighteenth, General von Knyphausen brought up seven thousand more troops and moved off to Pell's Point. After subduing a small party of Rebels, we were on our way, chasing Washington to White Plains.

When we got to White Plains on October 28, the main force of Rebels was in a well-fortified position. However, some Rebel forces were on Chatterton Hill. Howe sent General von Heister to dislodge them. Colonel Johann Rall went to the left, with Colonel Karl von Donop taking the right. After a spirited battle, the Rebels were chased off the hill. Howe decided not to take major action. After Washington moved to higher ground on November 1, Howe pulled out on the fifth.

On the second, a deserter from Fort Washington gave the British plans of the fort, including cannon placements. On the fifteenth, General Howe sent Colonel James Paterson under a white flag of truce with a message to the fort's commander, Colonel Robert Magaw, to surrender or face annihilation. Magaw refused the demand. On the sixteenth, a three-pronged attack commenced—from the north, General von Knyphausen with four thousand Hessians; from the east, General Cornwallis with one thousand; and from the south, General Percy with three thousand. The Hessians, fighting under Colonel Rall, took a terrific pounding. When they got to the fort, they wanted to enter it. Von Knyphausen refused to let Rall's men enter, which avoided a horrible slaughter.

With almost five hundred casualties, our losses were almost three times greater than theirs. However, we captured over 2,800 prisoners. One of the prisoners is Molly Corbin, who took over her husband's cannons when he was killed. She is going to be released. The rest of the prisoners are being marched to the prison ships in Wallabout Bay. The angry Hessians hitched many of the prisoners as "horses" to cannons to drag them off.

God Save The King, Zack

⟨❧⟩

December 15, 1776
Dear Uncle Eb,

After the capture of Fort Washington on November 16, I joined General Charles Cornwallis with over five thousand troops to capture Fort Lee. Fort Lee is situated atop the New Jersey Palisades, very high cliffs on the Hudson River. We sailed six miles upriver beyond Fort Lee. We then had an arduous climb on a steep, twisting, almost perpendicular path over the 300-foot cliffs. Sailors dragged up the artillery.

Our plan was to trap Washington's forces between the Hudson and Hackensack Rivers. Unfortunately, Washington received warning and directed General Nathanael Greene to evacuate Fort Lee. Greene's men left in such a hurry that they left fifty cannons, one thousand barrels of flour, and stores of ammunition. In the fort we captured 12 drunken soldiers and another 150 prisoners in the vicinity. We then began our chase of the Rebels across New Jersey. Our going was slow because of muddy roads. In addition, the Hessians were pillaging the locals as we went. Unfortunately many of those pillaged were Loyalists, because the Hessians didn't know the difference. On the thirteenth, General Howe halted the pursuit to winter in New York. General Cornwallis, believing with all the success we've had since July that the war was virtually over, requested a leave to return to England. Howe granted his request.

On the thirteenth, we got some other great news. On the twelfth, Colonel William Harcourt and his Light Dragoons got word from Loyalist informers that Rebel general Charles Lee was in the area of Basking Ridge, New Jersey. On the morning of the thirteenth, Cornet Banastre Tarleton made a raid on White's Tavern, capturing Lee. Tarleton received a promotion to brigade major of cavalry for his action. The British high command is elated with the capture of Lee. They feel he is the most competent of the Rebel generals. Word is that Lee is offering thoughts to Howe on how the British can defeat the Americans. Lee more than likely is fighting for his life, because the British consider him a deserter due to his not resigning his British commission before declaring for the Rebels. However, if they hang him, I'm sure the Americans will certainly retaliate by hanging their British prisoners.

Hopefully, with the capture of General Lee, Fort Lee, and all the defeats handed the Rebels since July, this rebellion to the Crown can cease.

God Save the King, Zack

December 27, 1776
Dear Father,

After what we've been going through since July, I cannot tell you how ecstatic I am today. Yesterday morning we laid a total defeat on the Hessian garrison at Trenton, New Jersey. Since we started across New Jersey in late November, the trek has been extremely difficult, but we were able to evade the British chasing us.

We were desperately trying to get to the Pennsylvania side of the Delaware River to be able to defend Philadelphia from the British. General Israel Putnam had been sent ahead to prepare for the defense of Philadelphia. We crossed to Pennsylvania on the seventh. General Washington then instructed Captain Daniel Bray of the Hunterdon County New Jersey militia to remove all boats from the east side of the Delaware. If the boats couldn't be moved to the west side, they were to be destroyed. Astonishingly, Bray's men did the task for a sixty-mile stretch.

On December 1, we lost over two thousand men, because their enlistments were up. We kept waiting for four thousand troops under General Charles Lee's command to arrive. Finally on the twentieth, they showed up under General John Sullivan, but there were only two thousand and many had no shoes. That is when we learned that General Lee had been captured by the British. The same day General Horatio Gates showed up with six hundred men from Fort Ticonderoga.

During the retreat across New Jersey, Thomas Paine, accompanying the troops, witnessing the pain and suffering, wrote a pamphlet he called *The American Crisis*. On the twenty-third, he read aloud to the troops what he had written. These opening words were a great inspiration to all: "THESE are the times that try men's souls. The summer soldier and the sunshine patriot will, in this crisis, shrink from the service of their country; but he that stands by it now, deserves the love and thanks of man and woman."

We learned on Christmas Eve that we were going to attack Trenton in a three-pronged attack. We, with Washington, would cross the Delaware at McKonkey's Ferry with 2,400 troops. General James Ewing, with 700, would cross directly across from Trenton and hold the bridge at Assunpink Creek. General John Cadwalader, with 1,500, would cross downriver at Bristol, Pennsylvania, and advance to Burlington, New Jersey.

Late afternoon Christmas Day we started to cross the river. The password was "Victory or Death." The crossing operation was directed by General Henry Knox. Colonel John Glover's men from Marblehead, Massachusetts, operated the boats. We, along with horses, were shipped across in Durham[25] boats holding forty to fifty men each propelled by eighteen oars. Ferryboats used by McKonkey's Ferry and Johnson's Ferry on the New Jersey side were used to carry artillery pieces and also horses. The crossing was brutal because of the ice chunks in the river.

The landing was completed around 4:00 a.m., several hours later than planned, which caused concern that the Hessians would not be surprised. Even so, the decision to attack was made. We had a nine-mile march to Trenton with very icy conditions and a horrible snowstorm. Washington sent General Nathanael Greene to the left and General John Sullivan to the

---

[25] Large flat-bottomed boats that hauled cargo such as ore, pig iron, timber, and produce from up-country mines, forests, and farms down the Delaware River to Philadelphia's markets and port.

right. When we got to Trenton at 8:00 a.m., we totally surprised the Hessians. Knox opened up his cannons with deadly effect. Along with Captain William Washington and Lieutenant James Monroe, several of us rushed a Hessian field gun and managed to turn it on them.

The Hessians—after realizing their commander, Colonel Johann Rall, was wounded—soon surrendered. The Hessians' casualties were twenty-one killed, ninety wounded, and about nine hundred prisoners. Rall died of his wounds. Remarkably, after his death a note was found in his pocket warning him of the attack, which undoubtedly he had never read. Unbelievably, we had no battle fatalities, although two men froze to death on the march to Trenton. We had four wounded, including William Washington and James Monroe.

After we got back, we learned that Ewing called off his portion of the attack because of the ice in the river. Cadwalader had landed some forces but then because he could not move his cannons across the river called off his attack. We also learned that a local farmer, John Honeyman, who was brought to Washington suspected as a British spy, was instead a spy for him, posing as a Loyalist. Honeyman was sent back to Rall to inform him that our army was suffering from very low morale.

I am so thankful to inform you of "Victory," not "Death."

Your son, Moses

January 5, 1777
Dear Father,

After Trenton, we had more success. Washington got word that General Cornwallis and General Grant had eight thousand troops at Princeton, New Jersey. Washington decided to attack, and on the twenty-ninth and thirtieth, we crossed back over to Trenton. Washington knew that most enlistments would be up on January 1. On the thirty-first, he made an eloquent plea for the soldiers to continue their service for six more weeks.

There were no takers. He appealed once again, offering $10 as a bounty for staying. Finally, one soldier stepped forward. Others followed, and we had our army back to fight the British once again.

We positioned ourselves along the Assunpink Creek on the south side of Trenton. We received reinforcements from Crosswicks and Bordentown, under the commands of General John Cadwalader and Thomas Mifflin, respectively. On the second, Washington sent General Matthias de Fermoy to harass Cornwallis's troops as they moved from Princeton. Unbelievably, de Fermoy rode back to Trenton drunk. Colonel Edward Hand took command but had to retreat to our position. Cornwallis, arriving near twilight, made three assaults, but we held firm.

During the night, we lit fires and had men digging with picks and shovels to induce the British to think we were still there. We made a circuitous route—first east and then north toward Princeton. It was easy traveling, because the muddy roads were frozen. Outside of Princeton, General Hugh Mercer's forces were attacked by British Lieutenant Colonel Charles Mawhood. Mercer was thrown from his horse and was brutally stabbed by bayonets several times. Trying to rally Mercer's men, Colonel John Haslet, 1st Delaware, was shot in the head. Next, General Cadwalader's forces were engaged but hastily retreated. Then General Washington appeared, bravely leading troops right to the British lines and at thirty yards ordered them to fire. The British lines faltered, and Washington shouted, "It's a fine fox chase my boys."

Washington decided not to pursue the British further, deciding to make our way to Somerset Courthouse. When we leave here we will go into winter quarters in Morristown, New Jersey. A prisoner told us that when other British officers tried to convince Cornwallis to attack at night at Assunpink Creek, he commented, "We've got the old fox safe now. We'll go over and bag him in the morning."

I guess we now know who the better fox hunter is! Because of their distinguished service in these two battles, Washington appointed the Dover Light Infantry from Delaware "to be his own guard" for a period of time. It is thought that General

Mercer's wounds are mortal. He and Washington are the dearest of friends from their days in the French and Indian War.

Your son, Moses

❧

January 18, 1777
My dear son Moses,

Perhaps the victory at Trenton has "rescued the revolution." I am so glad you were part of it. The mood here in Philadelphia is once again optimistic. It surely has changed from a city of jitters, which it had been when Washington sent a warning that after the capture of Fort Lee "Philadelphia would be next." Many members of Congress were absent. Thomas Jefferson and John Adams returned to their homes. Ben Franklin had departed on his mission to act as the American commissioner to France. Another signer, William Hooper of North Carolina, described Congress as being in a "torpor." In mid-December President John Hancock moved the Congress to Baltimore.

Since you wrote, we've learned that General Mercer's wounds were indeed mortal, as you suspected. One rumor is the reason that he was bayoneted so many times is that the British mistook him for Washington. Mercer had escaped with the Jacobites after the Battle of Culloden in Scotland, escaped when General Braddock was cut down in the French and Indian War, and was later badly wounded in that same war. We not only lost a fine soldier, but we also lost a noted physician.

Zack wrote to me about General Lee's capture. I am not so sure Washington is all that displeased. According to word I've received, Lee was dallying in getting his troops from Fort Lee to joining Washington's contingent. Zack indicated that the British are overjoyed in getting Lee out of command because they feel he is the superior general in the American Army. Sam Adams has the same feeling.

Zack also wrote that General Cornwallis had been granted a leave to go back to London. Cornwallis felt the war was basically over. His leave must have been canceled, because you wrote about his leading British troops at Assunpink Creek.

When the Declaration of Independence was voted upon on July 4 last year, it contained only the signatures of President John Hancock and Secretary Charles Thomson. On August 2, the other delegates signed. Their signatures were never printed to protect them. Because of Trenton and Princeton, Congress today approved the printing of the Declaration of Independence with all the signatures.

May God bless you, Dad

Chapter Three

We had something more at stake than fighting for six pence per day.
—Henry Dearborn

In 1777, the British made an all-out effort to crush the revolution. One large force attacked from Canada with the intention of driving to Albany, New York, to split the New England colonies from the other colonies. The other force attacked Philadelphia, the capital and largest city of the colonies.

Philadelphia fell to the British. General Washington encamped for the winter at Valley Forge. During this time an attempt was made to remove Washington as commander in chief.

The British expedition from Canada faced extreme difficulty. After two major battles near Saratoga, New York, the British surrendered. When the word of this decisive American victory reached France, the French decided to assist the United States.

༄

March 15, 1777
Dear Uncle Eb,

Because of the lack of housing in New York City, due to the immense fire, I am spending the winter at a Rebel farmhouse on Long Island. Because this is quite a prosperous farmer, we have plenty of cattle and pigs to slaughter to provide good amounts of beef and pork. There are plenty of chickens to provide enough eggs. We were also able to harvest his good crop of carrots, turnips, and cabbage. Having very little money, I consider myself lucky, but I do miss having chocolate for breakfast, which I was used to having in Boston.

On the other hand, the Hessians camped nearby have no trouble purchasing food or warm clothing because they are well paid. I've become friendly with Johann Ewald, a captain of the Hesse-Kassel Jägers. To pass the time, a lot of soldiers are playing faro[26], but in all cases the Hessians keep the faro bank!

The area north of the city has become a vicious no-man's land between Rebels and Loyalists. The Loyalists are known as "cowboys." They got their name by ringing cowbells to lure Rebels who were looking for their stray cows. The Rebels are known as "skinners," because they skin their victims of their purses and valuables. Here on Long Island we've not escaped the predations of the "skinners." Many come across Long Island Sound from Connecticut to join with the local Rebels here to engage in their treacherous tactics.

Christmas was truly a new experience for me this year. The Hessians would cut down a fir tree and then stand it up in a base to decorate it. After decorating it with ribbons and small pieces of fruit, they attached candles to the tree. On Christmas Eve they lit the candles and stood around the tree and sang Christmas songs. During all this celebrating quite a lot of alcohol was consumed. This, I am sure, would be considered a pagan observance in Boston. I am also quite sure, because

---

[26] A gambling card game originating in France.

of the Quakers, this would not be a tolerated observance in Philadelphia.

It was fortunate for the British that General Washington took his army to winter quarters after the Battle of Princeton instead of pursuing the British back to New York. If he had, he more than likely would have captured General Cornwallis's baggage train, which included a wagon containing £70,000 of hard currency.

God Save the King, Zack

෮

April 30, 1777
Dear Uncle Eb,

I just returned from a raiding mission into Connecticut. General Howe learned that the Continental Army had built a large supply depot in Danbury, Connecticut. Howe commissioned New York Royal governor William Tryon a major general with the mission of destroying the depot in Danbury. On April 22, we left New York City, navigating our way along Long Island Sound, landing at Compo Point[27] on the twenty-fifth.

We got to Danbury on the twenty-sixth. The little resistance the Rebels had was easily overcome. We secured the depot and proceeded to burn 4,500 barrels of pork, beef, and flour; 5,000 pairs of shoes; 2,000 bushels of grain; and 1,600 tents, along with other supplies. While going about the task, we located and then consumed a large supply of rum. At 1:00 a.m. on the twenty-seventh, we learned American troops were nearby. As we left town, we set about torching Rebel homes. Loyalists had marks on their chimneys, enabling us to spare their homes.

General David Wooster pursued us. We had two engagements with him. During the second one, he was severely wounded. As we got to Ridgefield, Connecticut, General Benedict Arnold was waiting for us. We eventually overwhelmed his forces. Arnold's horse was shot, and he got tangled up in its trappings. A British

---

[27] In present-day Westport, Connecticut.

soldier tried to capture him, but Arnold shot him. We encamped near Ridgefield that night. We were heavily pursued the next day as we made our way back to Compo Point. We were warned by a Loyalist that Arnold was setting up to intercept us. With that knowledge we managed to get around him and get back to our fleet.

I learned from a prisoner that some of the troops pursuing us out of Ridgefield were New York militia from Dutchess County under the command of Colonel Henry Ludington. Ludington had learned of our raid. He needed to round up the militia. He sent his sixteen-year-old daughter, Sybil Ludington, on the task. She left at 9:00 p.m. and rode over forty miles, arriving back near dawn as soldiers were arriving to join the attack on us. Amazingly she rode through territory controlled by the bands of "cowboys" and "skinners" and survived.

While this was a fruitful mission, I am not so sure it is smart to make raids so far inland.

God Save the King, Zack

⟨∾⟩

June 15, 1777
Dear Mr. Chaplin,

I have some distressing news and some interesting news to report. Earlier this year the Georgia Council of Safety authorized Signer Button Gwinnett, serving as Georgia's president, to organize a force of militia to proceed with an attack on St. Augustine, East Florida. Having difficulty gathering enough troops, he asked General Robert Howe, the new Southern commander, for assistance from the Continental Army. Howe appointed General Lachlan McIntosh to join Gwinnett. McIntosh and Gwinnett did not get along and could not agree on strategy.

With the void in leadership, Colonel Sam Elbert took charge. He took three hundred troops on a flotilla to Sawpit Bluff in East Florida to rendezvous with Colonel John Baker who went overland with two hundred cavalry. When Baker got there, Elbert had not arrived. On the night of May 14, while encamping there, Colonel "Burnfoot" Brown sent fifteen Indians to steal Baker's horses. While Baker recovered most of the horses, he decided to move west. On the seventeenth, he ran into an ambush set up by "Burnfoot" Brown's Loyalist East Florida Rangers and Creek Indians at Thomas Creek.[28] In trying to escape, his forces ran smack into Major Mark Prevost's British Regulars who had been following behind. Baker had few men killed, but over thirty were captured and subsequently over half of them were tortured to death by the Indians.

On May 1, Lachlan McIntosh addressed the Georgia assembly, calling Button Gwinnett a "scoundrel and lying rascal." When McIntosh refused to apologize, Gwinnett challenged him to a duel. The duel took place on May 16. Both were wounded in the leg, with Gwinnett dying three days later.

Yesterday I met quite an interesting young Frenchman. His name is Marie-Joseph Paul Yves Roch Gilbert du Motier, marquis de Lafayette. He arrived in South Carolina on June 13 and was staying with Major Benjamin Huger before embarking to Philadelphia. He is enthusiastic about our cause but was denied joining us by King Louis XVI. He managed to get to Spain and, being very rich, purchased *La Victoire*, hired a captain, and came over with several friends who also wanted to join our cause. Some of the friends who came with Lafayette are Baron Johann de Kalb, a Bavarian in the French military, Jean-Joseph de Gimat, Chevalier Du Buysson des Aix, and Chevalier de la Colombe. I anticipate you will meet Lafayette when he gets to Philadelphia.

Sincerely, Felix

⟨∽⟩

July 9, 1777
Dear Uncle Eb,

---

[28] Near present-day Jacksonville, Florida.

Things surely got hot up here after a cold and hungry winter at Fort Ticonderoga under General Anthony Wayne. We had to cut a lot of wood to keep warm, and we built a bridge from the fort across Lake Champlain to Mount Independence, also known as Rattlesnake Hill. We started the bridge on March 1. We built caissons and then dragged them across the ice to be sunk in holes cut through the ice. In June, a Polish engineer, Tadeusz Kościuszko, arrived to direct fortification activities. Also, General Arthur St. Claire arrived to replace General Wayne. Then to our fright, we learned a large British force under General John Burgoyne was headed our way from Canada.

On July 5, we noticed British general William Phillips's troops had managed to get cannons up onto Mount Defiance. Our officers didn't think a goat could get up that mountain, much less men and cannons. St. Claire decided to retreat during the same night. We were ordered to retreat under total silence with no fires, not even lit candles. To our dismay, the French general Matthias de Fermoy decided to burn his house, which alerted the British to our retreat intent.

We headed to what is now called the Republic of Vermont, also known as the Green Mountain Republic, under Colonel Seth Warner. Previously it was known as the Hampshire Grants and more recently as the Republic of New Connecticut. Another force under Colonel Pierse Long left Ticonderoga up the lake with many sick men and supplies. On July 6, we encamped at Hubbardton. Early on the seventh, as we were awakening, the British under General Simon Fraser attacked. We nearly turned his flank, but the Brunswick general Friedrich von Riedesel sent in reinforcements and we had to run for it. Before we fled we inflicted heavy casualties on the British: 49 killed and 141 wounded. We lost 41 killed and 96 wounded. But worst of all, 230 of our men were taken prisoner.

Yesterday we heard Long's men tried to make a stand at Fort Anne in New York but had to eventually flee from Burgoyne's men. At this point I am not sure what is next. I would like to get back home, but I am not sure what is planned.
Sincerely, Ben

⟨～⟩

August 5, 1777
Dear Father,

We are marching south. We had been watching Howe in New York City and wondering what he was planning. In mid-July he started loading ships. We weren't sure if he was going up the Hudson River to join Burgoyne or if he was planning a sea voyage. Then our spies noticed the horse stalls built on the ships were being lined with sheepskin, with the wool side being turned to the inside of the stalls. This told us the British were going on a long sea voyage, not up the Hudson. But we didn't know if they are headed to Boston, Philadelphia, or Charleston.

On July 23, General Howe left New York with a fleet of 266 ships under the command of his brother, Admiral Richard Howe. A few days ago the fleet was spotted off New Jersey. Now we know they are headed south.

Since we left winter quarters in Morristown, we had only one major action. During June, Howe was attempting to draw Washington's army into battle. On the night before June 26, our group was encamped at Metuchen Meetinghouse in New Jersey under the command of General William Alexander, also known as Lord Stirling. On the twenty-sixth, Howe marched out of Amboy to attack us with the intent of then engaging Washington's main force. The British forces proved too strong, and we needed to move out. The British losses were minimal—five killed—while we lost about thirty. Even though most of the fighting occurred at Scotch Plains and Edison, for some reason it is being called the Battle of Short Hills.

We just got word that when we get to Philadelphia, General Washington is planning a huge parade of the troops. I will be so glad to be in Philadelphia so I can see you for the first time in two years. Hopefully you will invite many of our friends to see the parade. And, oh, I hope you have some of your famous porter on tap at the Blaze Horse. I've told a lot of my soldier friends you make the best beer in Philadelphia.

Your son, Moses

❧

August 16, 1777
Dear Uncle Eb,

While I had wanted to go home after Hubbardton, an incident happened in nearby New York that really got the locals indeed riled up. Word came through that a beautiful red-haired young lady, Jane McCrea, was killed and scalped by Wyandot Indians working for Burgoyne. Ironically she was the fiancée of a New York Loyalist fighting with Burgoyne. Also, the British were issuing proclamations for New Englanders to join Burgoyne's forces. Many signed up to appease the British but were intending to fight them.

Seth Warner learned that the British wanted to raid Bennington, Vermont, to secure horses for their German troops. Burgoyne had neglected to bring enough horses from Canada. Then we learned General John Stark was coming west from New Hampshire. We joined Stark's forces, which culminated in quite a battle today with the British in New York, just west of Bennington. As I learned at Bunker Hill, Stark is a superb soldier and leader of men. Before the battle, General Stark yelled an inspiration to us: "There are your enemies, the Red Coats and the Tories. They are ours, or this night Molly Stark sleeps a widow."

We faced a force of mostly German soldiers from Brunswick, along with some Canadians, Indians, and Loyalists under Lieutenant Colonel Friedrich Baum. We found out the Loyalists were to have white paper on their hats so the Germans wouldn't fire on them. When we learned this, we also put white paper on our hats. And many of those who "signed up as Loyalists" fought with us.

It was a resounding victory. The British lost 207 men, and we captured around 700. Our losses were thirty dead and forty wounded. Finally I can go home. I will be in the group to march the prisoners to Boston.

I am sure you'd be interested in this bit of information. After the battle, General Stark told us a nobleman, Count Casimir

Puławski, from Poland arrived at Marblehead in hopes of joining our cause. He carried a letter of introduction from Benjamin Franklin. His specialty is the cavalry.

Sincerely, Ben

❧

August 25, 1777
My dear son Moses,

It was so good to see you over the past few days. I must say I was disappointed to see you are not as nourished as I would expect. And then I was appalled when you told me there are days when no food is available. Since many members of Congress come to the Blaze Horse, I am going to make sure they know the plight of the army.

I enjoyed meeting your friends. I was especially impressed by your friend from Virginia, James Monroe, who is so dedicated to the fight for freedom. It's really nice to find he too speaks French. It seems all your friends enjoyed the porter. They ran me out, but I'm busy brewing a fresh batch.

The parade was outstanding. Having so many of our freedom fighters marching by for hours on end was touching. It was interesting to see the young Frenchman, the marquis de Lafayette, riding next to Washington. It is hard to believe he is only nineteen years old, just a year older than you. To come to America on a ship he purchased with his own funds proves he really believes in the cause. John Adams was here today. He couldn't stop talking about how impressed he was with not only the parade, but with the attitude shown by the soldiers. Coming from Adams, who has not been too flattering about Washington or the army, was quite something.

Also, we heard today Howe's fleet has landed at Head of Elk near the top of Chesapeake Bay in Maryland. More than likely this means Howe has his sights set on Philadelphia. Folks are wondering where Washington will make his defense of our city.

Son, my prayers are with you, as you are surely going to be in another strong engagement with the enemy. If Washington is not victorious, our town will be under British occupation. No one knows how it will affect us Patriots. It is interesting to see how some citizens are trying to play both ends between the Patriots and Loyalists.

May God bless you, Dad

⁌〜⁌

August 30, 1777
Dear Uncle Eb,

I am happy to be able to tell you I survived a furiously bloody battle on August 6. While we were aware that the British, under General Burgoyne, gained Fort Ticonderoga on July 6, we got a surprise in mid-July. We learned the British were sending a flanking force from Canada to Lake Ontario and then across western New York to take Fort Stanwix under Lieutenant Colonel Barry St. Leger.[29]

I joined a force of eight hundred militiamen, including fifty to sixty Oneida Indians, under General Nicholas Herkimer to assist Colonel Peter Gansevoort at Fort Stanwix. The Oneida[30] were led by War Chief Han Yerry Tewahangarahken ("He Who Takes Up the Snow Shoe"). On the sixth, just a few miles short of Fort Stanwix we were attacked by a combined force of the Loyalist King's Royal Regiment, Hanau Jägers, and many Mohawk and Seneca Indians led by Joseph Brant. The attack occurred along a small stream near the Oneida village of Oriska, meaning "Field of Nettles."

Early in the fight, General Herkimer was wounded. He ordered that he be propped against a tree. While smoking his pipe, he commanded his troops. One of his orders was for us to double-team, meaning two soldiers team up—while one fires,

---

[29] Prior to the campaign, General Burgoyne brevetted St. Leger a general to ensure he was superior to any American Loyalist or Canadian militia commanders.
[30] "Oneida" (Onyata'a:ka) means "People of the Standing Stone."

the other reloads. This tactic allowed us to have fewer losses than we did. After killing nine attackers, Han Yerry was wounded, but his wife, Tyonajanegen (Two Kettles Together), loaded his musket so he could keep fighting.

Because of the Indians' tomahawking, the battle was terribly bloody. With Indians on both sides we had to identify them by their headdress—Oneida, two feathers up, one down; Mohawk, three feathers up; Seneca, one feather up. The Oneidas named the battle Blood Shed a Stream Running Down.[31] Our losses were staggering: 160 killed, 50 wounded, and 200 captured. I can't imagine the horrors committed by the Indians on those captured. After the battle the Oneidas were sent a bloody hatchet by the Iroquois Nation, signifying they were now enemies.

While the battle was raging, Gansevoort sent Lieutenant Colonel Marinus Willett to destroy the Tory camp of Sir John Johnson. Then on August 13, General Philip Schuyler sent General Benedict Arnold to relieve Fort Stanwix. He got messages to the British lines, overemphasizing the size of his force. With this news, along with Willett's action, St. Leger lifted the siege on Fort Stanwix on the twenty-second. I, along with a portion of Arnold's forces, pursued St. Leger, only to catch up to him as he escaped on Oneida Lake. When we returned, I learned that General Herkimer had died from his wounds.

Sincerely, Teunis

September 9, 1777
Dear Uncle Eb,

On July 23, General William Howe, with 266 ships under the command of his brother, Admiral Richard Howe, left New York City. Our outfit, the Queen's Rangers, sailed on the *Augusta*. Included on our ship were the troops of Captain Patrick Ferguson who were armed with Ferguson's breech-loading rifles. We had

---

[31] Later it became known as the Battle of Oriskany, by adding "ny" for "New York" to the village name of Oriska.

bad storms. One of the ships carrying Hessians was struck by lightning. Fortunately for them, they were able to put the fire out. When we got to Cape Henlopen, Captain Andrew Snape Hamond sailed out to our fleet. He suggested to Admiral Howe to go up the Delaware River to Philadelphia. Howe said his intelligence told him the river was heavily defended.

We finally arrived at Head of Elk, Maryland, at the top of Chesapeake Bay on August 25. As we were trying to disembark, many slaves swam out to our ships and attempted to get on board. Of course, we couldn't let them on. When we disembarked, during a lightning storm, the countryside was virtually uninhabited. The Rebels got out of town! We were very hungry, because we ran out of food on the long trip. However, wild game was quite plentiful, and we feasted on turkeys, ducks, and passenger pigeons. And because so many horses died on the voyage, we were busy trying to round up new mounts. It was difficult because the locals had taken their horses and cattle with them.

On September 2, we headed out for Philadelphia. We encamped at Aitken's Tavern in Delaware. The next morning Captain Johann Ewald's Hessian jägers led the way. Suddenly they were ambushed by General William Maxwell's light infantry, and Ewald lost several men. General Charles Cornwallis immediately sent three companies of field jägers—two of Hessians and one of Ansbachers—under Lieutenant Colonel Ludwig von Wurmb to drive out Maxwell's men. There was quite a skirmish at Cooch's Bridge. Finally, General Howe sent in his grenadiers. With that action, the Rebels ran off. We had three killed, but several wagonloads of wounded were sent back to the ships. The number of Americans killed ranged from twenty to forty.

After the battle we went through the deserted town of Newark on our way toward White Clay Creek, where Washington was encamped. Howe decided not to fight there and did a "George Washington" trick by slipping out of the area during the night. As we slipped away, we were treated to a grand display of the aurora borealis. We are presently encamped at New Garden, Pennsylvania.

God Save the King, Zack

〜

·September 12, 1777
Dear Father,

Yesterday we had a huge and vicious battle along the Brandywine Creek. We came to the area on the ninth with almost fifteen thousand troops. General Washington set up headquarters at Benjamin Ring's farmhouse about a mile east of the creek, where he decided to make his defense of Philadelphia. On the evening of the tenth, a sermon was offered to the gathered troops as our new stars-and-stripes flag waved. It is said the flag was made in Philadelphia by a seamstress, Betsy Ross. Washington had these nearby fords[32] protected—Pyle's by General John Armstrong; Chads by Generals Anthony Wayne and Nathanael Greene; Brinton's by General John Sullivan; Jones's by Colonel David Hall's Delaware Regiment; and Wister's and Buffington by Colonel Moses Hazen's Canadian Regiment. Later in the day we found, to our surprise, there were two more fords farther upstream—Trimble's and Jefferis's.

As the morning progressed, we heard gunfire from skirmishing troops as the Brits came from Kennett Square. There were artillery exchanges between the British troops commanded by General Wilhelm von Knyphausen and General Henry Knox's artillery along both sides of the Brandywine. Thinking the entire British force was ahead of him, Washington ordered Greene, Wayne, and Sullivan to cross the creek. He did this even though a local farmer, Thomas Cheyney, had told him he saw British troops to the north. Cheyney insisted he could be vouched for by some of Washington's officers. The general was convinced Cheyney was a Loyalist giving false information.

Being with Lord Stirling, we were being held in reserve near Mr. Ring's house. Later in the day, soldiers from an upper ford sent word the British were flanking us. With this news, Washington pulled back Sullivan and Greene, sending them north. He also sent us and General Adam Stephen, both of

---

[32] A shallow place in a body of water, such as a river, where one can cross by walking or riding on an animal or in a vehicle (wagon).

whom he had been holding in reserve, north. We had some rough terrain to traverse but made three to four miles in forty-five minutes. When we got up to the heavy fighting area of Birmingham Hill and Sandy Hollow, the British cannonade from Osborne's Hill was terrifying, showering tree leaves all about us. Then to add more fright was the sound of bagpipes, fifes, and drums as the British and Hessian troops started their advance.

All the while, Knox was trying to move artillery from the creek to his northern front. And Sullivan, who was way out of position on the left, was trying to maneuver closer to the center of action. The fighting became very close, intense, and hand-to-hand (having your victim's blood spurt on you isn't pleasant, but better his than mine). In the thick fighting, General Peter Muhlenberg, born in Germany, was recognized by some Ansbachers who yelled out, "Hier kommt Teufel Piet" ("Here comes devil Peter").

We were getting beat pretty badly, but then General Marquis de Lafayette rallied some troops who were trying to escape the onslaught. Soon we heard Lafayette was wounded. My friend James Monroe, who speaks French, went along with a surgeon to attend to him. Fortunately the wound was not life threatening.

Just as we thought all was lost, Count Casimir Pułaski went to Washington and requested the use of thirty of his mounted Life Guards. With these men, Pułaski made a mini-cavalry charge into the British lines, completely surprising them and momentarily halting them. Meanwhile, General Greene was doing a superb job of holding off the Brits to allow an orderly retreat by us. During this time, General Wayne had been forced back east by von Knyphausen's onslaught once the battle started in the north. He also organized an orderly retreat.

The fighting subsided at dusk. The British did not pursue our retreat. More than likely, because their effort started at 4:00 a.m. on a very hot day and after an excruciating battle, they were just plain tired. We retreated to Chester, getting there at about midnight. When I got there I learned of the bravery of Ned Hector, a free Negro, serving as a teamster and a bombardier. When he was ordered to retreat and abandon everything, he refused and replied, "The enemy shall not have my team; I will save my horses and myself!" While at Chester, I also learned Peter Francisco had been wounded. His is an interesting story I want to tell you when I see you next.

While we lost the battle, we stood up very well against a superior force. While Washington was outwitted by Howe's flanking move, we had an opportunity to retreat from the enemy to be able to fight another day. I am not sure what our next move will be, but we need to keep the British from taking Philadelphia.

I learned today General Howe told Washington that he did not have enough surgeons or physicians to treat the wounded from both sides. If Washington wanted his troops cared for, he would need to send his own surgeons and physicians. In response, Washington sent surgeons and physicians to Birmingham Meetinghouse, being utilized as a hospital, under a white flag of truce. One of them was Signer Dr. Benjamin Rush. Being behind enemy lines as a traitor to the Crown, we can only hope Howe will respect the fact that Rush is merely performing the duty of his profession.

Hopefully we will be able to keep the British out of Philadelphia so I can see you again.

Your son, Moses

September 17, 1777
Dear Uncle Eb,

We encamped the night of September 10 in Kennett Square, Pennsylvania. At 4:00 a.m. on the eleventh, Howe broke camp. He and Cornwallis went north to flank Washington's troops. Howe used the same flank strategy as he did at Long Island. He was led by Loyalist guides, one being Sandy Flash, who knew two fords on the Brandywine were undefended. And then Captain Johann Ewald had his jägers lead the troops up an undefended road. Our outfit left camp under the command of

General Wilhelm von Knyphausen, marching toward Chads Ford on the Brandywine Creek to take on General Washington's army. Included in this force was an ex-slave of Washington. We met up with General William (Scotch Willie) Maxwell's men, who grounded their rifles as a sign of surrender. When we went to take the surrender, they grabbed their muskets and killed many of the Queen's Rangers. I feel because of our green uniforms they knew we were Loyalists and were singled out. We eventually crossed the Brandywine and forced General Anthony Wayne to retreat. At about 4:00 p.m., Howe and Cornwallis engaged the Americans and drove them off at dusk in a retreat to Chester. We learned the next day Patrick Ferguson, inventor of a superior breech-loading rifle, had General Washington in his sights at the Brandywine but refused to shoot an unoffending officer in the back.

We joined with General Cornwallis and went to Village Green. Cornwallis stayed in the Seven Stars Hotel. We encamped on Mount Hope. On September 15, a very disturbing incident occurred. Two young ladies, Miss Martin and Miss Coxe, came to camp, saying their homes were marauded the previous night by three British soldiers. Because General Howe had put out an order that marauding was a capital offense, General Cornwallis told the young ladies if they could identify the soldiers they would be punished. Three times they picked these men out of the thousands of troops. Cornwallis told the men to roll dice to determine lots. The soldier rolling the highest number had to hang the other two. These men were hanging in apple trees as we broke camp later in the day.

The next day, September 16, as we marched up the Chester Road toward Great Valley, rain started to fall. As we encountered the Americans, we expected a very large battle. However, it rained torrents, most likely the remnants of a hurricane. Because of the rain, which made our gunpowder useless, the Battle at Goshen[33] quickly came to a conclusion.

God Save the King, Zack

---

[33] Later this became known as the Battle of the Clouds.

༺⁓༻

·September 20, 1777
Dear Uncle Eb,

After the relief of Fort Stanwix, I came with General Benedict Arnold to join General Horatio Gates's forces along the Hudson River at Stillwater, New York, on the ninth. Gates had been named Northern commander, replacing General Philip Schuyler in August after the fall of Fort Ticonderoga. Gates planned to make his defense against the British forces under General John Burgoyne at Stillwater. However, local residents informed Gates that a better position would be a few miles north at Bemis Heights. After seeing Bemis Heights, Gates agreed it provided greater advantage. He immediately put Colonel Tadeusz Kościuszko to work building fortifications. The fortification work was completed on the fifteenth.

On the thirteenth, General Benjamin Lincoln, who General Washington had sent to aid Gates, sent Colonel John Brown around British lines on a raid to Fort Ticonderoga. Having accompanied Brown on the taking of Fort Ticonderoga with Benedict Arnold and Ethan Allen and being with him in Canada coming back from Quebec, I am confident he can get the job done.

Also, on the thirteenth, I joined General Arnold with a small detachment to "take a view of the enemy's encampment." While we were not successful in learning much about the enemy, we took eight prisoners. They told us of the horrible conditions they faced coming from Fort Ticonderoga to this area. The terrain was very difficult for more than a 500-wagon train of baggage followed by 300 women and children. Several wagons were carrying large amounts of gin, rum, and wine for the officers. As General Arthur St. Clair retreated from Fort Ticonderoga, his forces took great efforts to impede the British march by felling trees across the roads and burning bridges. The prisoners also told us about their great fear of copperheads and rattlesnakes. We learned that Charles Langlade brought over five hundred

Sauk and Fox Indians from as far away as La Baye.[34] Burgoyne was disappointed because he expected several thousand. On their route, a great many Indians deserted the British when their officers complained of their "horrid enormities."[35]

Yesterday morning dawned extremely foggy. We figured something must be up because we could hear the enemy's drums. Then at 10:00 a.m., our scouting parties reported that the British were on the move. What we didn't know until later is that Burgoyne was lining up his forces to make a three-pronged approach simultaneously. He was sending General Friedrich von Riedesel's Brunswickers, General William Phillips's British artillery, and Captain Georg Päusch's Hesse-Hanau heavy artillery toward our right on Bemis Heights. Burgoyne and General James Hamilton were coming to the left of our position on Bemis Heights. Meanwhile, General Simon Fraser was making a flanking move far to our left to cut off any possible escape.

While all this was happening, General Gates made no moves. General Arnold, who is intensely disliked by Gates, finally convinced Gates that we should meet the enemy instead of waiting to be attacked. Arnold sent Colonel Daniel Morgan's riflemen and Major Henry Dearborn's light infantry to keep a sharp eye on the enemy's flank and to harass enemy troops. Some of their men got to a farm formerly owned by John Freeman, a Loyalist who had gone to join Burgoyne. There they routed the Red Coats and while chasing them were surprised by Hamilton's forces. Morgan collected his men with his high-pitched "gobble-gobble-gobble" imitation turkey call. Morgan's men singled out men to shoot at who were wearing silver gorgets at their throats, knowing they were officers.

The battle was high-pitched and deadly for hours. Arnold was dashing to and fro, rallying the troops. We were desperately trying to capture their artillery pieces. But even if we had captured them, there was no way to get them for our use, because all the horses were dead. Just as we were gaining an advantage, Riedesel and Päusch charged in from our right flank and turned the tide. Mercifully darkness came to end the battle.

---

[34] Present-day Green Bay, Wisconsin.
[35] Words used to describe Indian pillage and torture tactics.

While we didn't actually "win," we inflicted higher losses than we took. The British had 160 killed, 364 wounded, and 42 missing. We had 65 killed, 218 wounded, and 36 missing. As Henry Dearborn so aptly stated, "we had something more at stake than fighting for six pence per day." Last night was agonizing. As many wounded were left on the field, we could hear the wolves howling and we could hear dying men scream as the wolves tore at their flesh. Today we fully expected an attack, but nothing happened. I'm sure there will be more bloodshed, because we cannot allow the British to get to their destination of Albany.

Sincerely, Teunis

September 21, 1777
Dear Uncle Eb,

While I mentioned there was little action at the Battle of Goshen, there was one heroic incident by Colonel Karl Emil Ulrich von Donop's Hessians. During the morning of the sixteenth, his forces became entirely surrounded by General James Potter's men. They eventually freed themselves from the encirclement with a bayonet charge. Bayonets usually do the trick against the Rebels. Von Donop is something of a character. He's been telling his men that when they are finished with the Americans, they'll be off to Mexico and Peru!

On the eighteenth, while encamped at Tredyffrin, we heard there was a large cache of supplies at Valley Forge. Howe sent Colonel William Harcourt's dragoons to capture the supplies. They were able to run off the Rebel troops trying to move the supplies out. Harcourt managed to collect 3,800 barrels of flour and thousands of tomahawks.

While encamped we were constantly being harassed by General Anthony Wayne's troops. He was encamped in the area of the Admiral Warren Tavern and White Horse Tavern. On the twentieth, General Charles Grey, along with his aide, Captain

John André, decided to make an attack on Wayne's camp. André despises the Rebels because of the treatment he got from them while being held prisoner.

At about 11:00 p.m., we gathered together for the attack. We were ordered to remove the flints from our muskets. Grey did not want any accidental discharges to warn the Rebels. This was a bayonet and saber-only charge. At the Warren Tavern, a blacksmith was forced to guide us to Wayne. The idea was to get behind Wayne and drive him east toward Colonel Thomas Musgrave. Our guide was either stupid or duplicitous. He guided us into Wayne's camp from the east.

It was pouring rain. Most Rebels were in tents, but being perfectly silhouetted by their campfires made for perfect targets. Rebel getaway was difficult because the heavy rain made the roads difficult and wagon jam-ups blocked escape. The Action Near White Horse Tavern[36] by General Grey was a great success. Rebel deaths were around 150, while ours were very minimal.

God Save the King, Zack

September 22, 1777
Dear Father,

Since I last wrote following the Battle at Brandywine Creek, there has not been much good news. A few days after that battle, I accompanied Lieutenant Colonel Alexander Hamilton and Lieutenant Colonel Anthony Walton White into Philadelphia on a specific mission. Hamilton's orders were to collect blankets and White's to commandeer horses for the army. I so badly wanted to stop by the Blaze Horse to see you, but our task did not permit that.

On the sixteenth, we thought we were going to have a major battle near Goshen. Howe and von Knyphausen converged toward us from Turks Head,[37] while Cornwallis came up

---

[36] Later this battle became known as the Paoli Massacre.
[37] Turks Head is now known as West Chester, Pennsylvania.

from Aston. Generals Wayne and Potter drove toward them, encircling von Donop's Hessians, who managed to escape. Then a torrential downpour hit us, making a battle useless because of wet powder.

On the eighteenth, while Hamilton, General Maxwell, and Captain Henry "Light-Horse Harry" Lee were trying to move supplies out of Valley Forge, a British dragoon force attacked. They managed to capture 3,800 barrels of flour, 25 barrels of horseshoes, many tomahawks, soap, candles, and kettles. As Hamilton was crossing the Schuylkill River, his horse was shot. However, he managed to get across and was able to send a warning message to President Hancock that the British were on their way to Philadelphia.

During the night of the twentieth/twenty-first, General Anthony Wayne's troops suffered a terrible massacre. General Charles Grey attacked with bayonets and sabers only. There was much confusion. Teamsters couldn't get their wagons out due to muddy roads. This blocked escape routes for Wayne's troops. While Wayne had pickets[38] around his encampment, the British managed to get past them, leaving Wayne with no warning. Wayne knew Generals William Smallwood and Mordecai Gist were coming in from Maryland, but unfortunately they were too far away to assist. After the battle, many mangled bodies were found. We think we lost about 150 but have no idea how many were wounded. The Brits took seventy-one prisoners. Their losses were very few. Rumor is that Wayne may be up for court-martial.

Your son, Moses

September 26, 1777
My dear son Moses,

Due to Alexander Hamilton's warning to John Hancock, the Continental Congress fled Philadelphia in the early morning

---

[38] A soldier or detachment of soldiers placed on a line forward of a position to warn against an enemy advance.

hours of the nineteenth. There was much confusion as to where they should head. The last word was that they were heading north to Bristol. In addition, many citizens have left the city, fearing what is to come. The Liberty Bell has been sent north to Allentown.

I have some news since Brandywine. The day after the battle, on the twelfth, many prominent Quakers were arrested and sent as prisoners to Virginia. Of course, Justice Benjamin Chew and John Penn were sent to detention in New Jersey earlier. You wrote about Count Pułaski's action at Brandywine. On the fifteenth, Congress made him a brigadier general and commander of the Corps of Continental Light Dragoons. The marquis de Lafayette was sent to Bethlehem for treatment of his wounds suffered at Brandywine.

Today the British formally occupied Philadelphia. If it weren't such a sad situation, one could say the procession was beautifully arranged. The British and Hessian troops were all "spit and polish" and colorfully adorned. The escorts for the commanders were the light horsemen led by Colonel William Harcourt and leading Loyalist Joseph Galloway. General Howe gave the honor of leading the march-in to Lord Cornwallis. They came in stepping to a slow-march rate of sixty-four steps per minute. Fifers trilled "God Save the King" above the solemn rumble of drums. It is kind of ironic that on this past July 4, a band of Hessian prisoners were playing patriotic songs outside the Blaze Horse as we celebrated the first anniversary of independence.

Cornwallis and his staff wore fine scarlet coats laced with black velvet and gleaming gold embroidery. Count von Donop was splendid in a lace-encrusted blue coat with a silver sash and black cocked hat. A German woman, upon seeing the Hessians, shouted in German, asking why they were here to kill her and her family. As the Queen's Rangers marched by, I waved to Zack.

We have now witnessed our fate. I wonder what is happening at Saratoga.

May God bless you, Father

⌁

October 4, 1777
Dear Father,

Last night glorious plans were laid out for General Washington's first attack on an entire British army. Tonight we are back at Pennypacker Mill[39] after a retreat of about twenty-five miles from Germantown. Washington had eleven thousand men under command, with intelligence telling him there were eight thousand men under General Howe at Germantown. The plan was to push the British into the Schuylkill River. Generals Armstrong and Potter were on the far right along the Schuylkill. Generals Sullivan, Conway, and Wayne were to hit hard on the right, while Generals Greene and Stephen were to hit hard on the left. General Smallwood's Maryland militia and General David Forman's New Jersey Red Coats were on the far left. Many of us put buckshot in our cartridges, hoping it would improve our effectiveness. We left at dusk last night, and having a new moon, it was very dark.

We started our attack around 5:00 a.m. It was very foggy. Wayne's men were charging hard to avenge Paoli and taking no prisoners. His men and Thomas Conway's men came upon Cliveden, Justice Benjamin Chew's house. The house was heavily defended by Lieutenant Colonel Musgrave and one hundred men. As General Washington came upon this action, he conferred with his staff. Both Pickering and Hamilton suggested the forces pass by the house, but Knox insisted that the British be driven out so that no British forces would be behind the Americans. Musgrave's men could not be driven out. Meanwhile, Generals Stephen and Greene had taken the wrong route and came up behind Wayne's men. In the confusion of the fog and the heavy smoke from gunfire, Stephen ordered his men to fire on Wayne. Wayne, not understanding how the British could have gotten behind him, returned fire.

At about this time, Howe had rallied his forces. Generals Grey and Grant drove us out. I learned later that the same

---

[39] Today located in Schwenksville, Pennsylvania.

cannonball shot killed both Major James Witherspoon, son of Signer John Witherspoon, and General Francis Nash. About 150 men were killed, over 500 were wounded, and about 400 men were captured.

The battle was basically over by 10:00 a.m. I believe this battle could have been won if Greene didn't get lost, if Cliveden had been passed, and if Stephen were sober. Rumor is that General Stephen is to be court-martialed for having been drunk.

Your son, Moses

❦

October 5, 1777
Dear Uncle Eb,

Yesterday General Washington received another comeuppance. However, I must admit we were totally surprised by the attack. On the third, a preacher told Captain Ewald to expect an attack. When Howe was told, he answered, "That cannot be." Early yesterday morning a picket intercepted an American soldier who had become lost. Upon questioning, it was learned that Washington was on the move. The intelligence was relayed to General James Grant, who took decisive action.

Lieutenant Colonel Thomas Musgrave was near Cliveden, a huge mansion. When he learned Wayne's men were attacking, fearing retribution from Grey's action near White Horse Tavern, he and one hundred men occupied the house. The Americans brought up artillery to bombard the house. When that failed, they tried to light fire to Cliveden. The Americans could not make any headway. Eventually they were driven off by General Grey, rescuing Musgrave's forces.

We had about eight thousand troops in the area. Howe sent word to Cornwallis in Philadelphia to send reinforcements. He and the British grenadiers arrived just before the heavy fighting quieted down. It was very foggy. That caused the gunpowder to hang in the air close to the ground, adding to the difficulty of distinguishing friend or foe.

We encountered troops firing at us. As we got closer, we found that they wore red coats. We thought we were caught in "friendly fire." It turned out they were a New Jersey militia unit known as Forman's Red Coats. One of the prisoners we took claimed to be a member of the New Jersey militia. It turned out he was a British deserter and was subsequently hanged. Many prisoners we took smelled heavily of liquor. It may have provided fortification, but it surely can't help when one has to make decisions in a foggy, smoke-laden atmosphere.

I learned that General James Agnew was shot and killed by a civilian sharpshooter. Our losses were listed at 71 killed, 428 wounded, and 14 missing. We took over 400 prisoners.

God Save the King, Zack

October 6, 1777
Dear Uncle Eb,

Militarily, except for the occasional skirmish, things have been very quiet since the battle at Freeman's Farm on September 19. Politically there has been a lot of drama. When Gates sent his account of the battle to Congress, there was no mention of Arnold. On the twenty-second, Gates ordered that Morgan's corps would no longer be under Arnold's command. Arnold was enraged and confronted Gates, suggesting that since he was unable to serve his country here he requested permission to return to Washington's army. Gates then sent a letter to John Hancock, indicating that he granted permission for Arnold to leave. As the fight went on, every general officer, except Gates and Lincoln, signed a petition asking Arnold to remain, which he did.

One afternoon a party of Stockbridge Indians brought a Loyalist to Arnold. He allowed the Indians to have some fun. The Indians buried the Loyalist up to his neck, building a fire while they held a powwow in a circle around him. Pulling him out of the ground, they alternately held his feet and head to the flames. Finally, Arnold stopped them and sent the Loyalist off to jail in Albany.

I had an interesting discussion with a new friend, Benjamin Pierce[40] of Massachusetts, who came in with Lincoln's forces. The discussion was around Arnold's leadership and the difference between the British generals and General Gates. While Burgoyne, Phillips, Hamilton, Fraser, and Riedesel were all visible in the action, our general remained in his headquarters.

A deserter recently gave us a clue about the inactivity. Burgoyne is hoping that General Henry Clinton will come up the Hudson Valley to relieve him. He also told us that before the battle, the British forces numbered 7,200, but with their losses they are down to about 6,600. Before the battle we had 9,000, and with all the militia units pouring in we are now close to 12,000.

We just got word that John Brown is now in Fort Anne. Even though he was not able to recapture Fort Ticonderoga, his mission was very successful. He released 118 Americans from prison and captured 165 British soldiers and 119 Canadian militiamen. He also captured 150 batteaux on Lake Champlain and another 50 vessels on Lake George.

Sincerely, Teunis

❧

October 9, 1777
Dear Uncle Eb,

On the seventh, a British deserter alerted us to an impending move by Burgoyne. Again, Burgoyne staged a three-pronged assault. Fraser commanded their right, Riedesel commanded the center, and Major John Dyke Acland was on their left. At around 1:00 p.m., a picket who'd been hidden in the woods warned Gates the British were attacking. Gates sent Colonel James Wilkinson to investigate. When Wilkinson verified the report, Gates ordered Morgan "to begin the game." Arnold

---

[40] He would father the fourteenth US president, Franklin Pierce.

requested permission to investigate. Reluctantly Gates allowed it but sent General Lincoln to accompany him. When Arnold reported back, he told Gates he needed a much larger force than was sent. Gates retorted, "I have nothing for you to do. You have no business here." However, Lincoln prevailed on Gates to send more men.

Early in the fight, Major Acland was wounded in both legs. Wilkinson, after saving Acland from being finished off by a boy soldier, took him to Gates's headquarters. With all the activity, Arnold, ignoring orders, bolted toward the action. Gates sent a major to order him back, but he was outrun by Arnold. Generals Fraser and Burgoyne were quite conspicuous on the battlefield. Morgan ordered rifleman Tim Murphy, sitting up in a tree, to try to pick off Fraser. The first shot cut the crupper[41] of Fraser's horse. The second went through the horse's mane. The third hit Fraser in the stomach.

Before this the Brunswickers were determinedly holding us off. The loss of Fraser had an effect on the British. Arnold led a gallant charge against a redoubt being stubbornly held by Major Alexander Lindsay, earl of Balcarres. Meanwhile, Morgan was making a frontal assault on a redoubt under command of Colonel Heinrich Breymann. Noticing this and the Balcarres assault working, Arnold charged off to the rear of Breymann's redoubt to their total surprise. Here Arnold's luck ran out. He was shot in the same leg wounded at Quebec. When his horse was killed, his leg was broken when he was pinned beneath the horse. The battle was essentially over. I believe Arnold's bravery, magnetism, and energy contributed highly to the victory. We learned today from a German prisoner that Breymann had been killed by his own men because he was sabering soldiers to convince them to keep fighting.

Our losses were 30 killed and 100 wounded. The British lost 300 to death and over 350 wounded. Militia units continue to stream in. There might be fifteen thousand Americans in the area now. Yesterday some cannonballs were lobbed at a gathering of British officers. We learned today that the gathering was the funeral for General Simon Fraser. The report is that the British

---

[41] A strap looped under a horse's tail to help anchor saddle.

have moved north to Saratoga.[42] Will they decide to surrender, or will they try to retreat back to Canada?

Sincerely, Teunis

❦

October 17, 1777
Dear Uncle Eb,

After conducting the Bennington prisoners to Boston, my time home was short-lived. In mid-September we received word a large battle was taking place near Saratoga, New York. Because the British were not totally defeated, we rushed to assist the Continental troops. By the time we got here, another major battle took place. No one knew if the British would surrender, retreat, or fight again. Today I can tell you I witnessed a sight I never thought I would see—the surrender of General John Burgoyne's British forces to General Horatio Gates's Americans.

On our way to Saratoga, we were met by a soldier who had escaped from the British capture of Fort Clinton and Fort Montgomery. These forts are along the west side of the Hudson River across from each other on Popolopen Creek—Fort Clinton to the south and Fort Montgomery to the north.

On October 6, General Henry Clinton, coming up from New York City, landed three thousand troops—British, Hessians, and Loyalists—on the western side of the Hudson at Stony Point. Knowing General Israel Putnam was on the eastern side of the Hudson, he also landed some troops as a feint move to confuse Putnam.

After landing and marching to Fort Clinton, Clinton split his forces. He sent Lieutenant Colonel Mungo Campbell on a flanking move toward Fort Montgomery. Clinton sent General John Vaughan to take Fort Clinton. Campbell was killed early in the action and was succeeded in command by Colonel Beverly Robinson of the Loyal American Regiment. All the while British ships were bombarding the forts from the river. Pleas were sent

---

[42] Present-day Schuylerville, New York.

to Putnam for assistance, but help never came. While the six hundred men under General James Clinton at Fort Clinton and his brother, General George Clinton, at Fort Montgomery made a valiant fight, they were routed by the British. The British lost 41 killed and 142 wounded. The American generals escaped, but 263 were taken prisoner and 75 were killed or wounded. After the battle the British were able to break the iron chain across the Hudson River, which now allows the British to traverse it. Fortunately Henry Clinton did not continue north to assist Burgoyne.

We later learned Clinton attempted to send a message to Burgoyne. The messenger, unfortunately for him, was captured. At his capture, he swallowed a silver bullet. An emetic brought up the bullet containing a message. He was hanged as a spy.

Sincerely, Ben

October 18, 1777
Dear Uncle Eb,

What a wonderful scene I witnessed yesterday when General Burgoyne surrendered to General Gates. At around noon, Burgoyne handed his sword in surrender to Gates, who held it for a few moments and, after exchanging words, returned it. Our entire force, standing in absolute silence, lined both sides of the road as the prisoners passed by without arms, for they had been stacked earlier under the supervision of their officers.

After the surrender ceremonies, Gates provided a dinner for his and Burgoyne's staff. Gates and Burgoyne knew each other, having served together in the French and Indian War. General von Riedesel had sent for his wife, Baroness Frederika Riedesel. When she arrived she realized it would be awkward if she and her children attend. At this point, General Philip Schuyler invited her and the children to have dinner with him. Burgoyne apologized for torching Schuyler's house in Saratoga. The fire burned to death a Brunswick soldier who was too wounded to leave.

Two interesting things happened on the twelfth. General Gates sent the account of the battle at Bemis Heights on the ninth to the president of Congress, John Hancock, but ignored sending an account to his commander in chief, General Washington. Also General John Stark appeared with one thousand New Hampshire militiamen to seal off Burgoyne's northern escape route. Back on September 18, Stark had gotten into a tiff with Gates, marching his six hundred men out of camp the day before our first big battle.

One of the prisoners I am guarding is the earl of Balcarres. I received some very interesting insight from him. He told me that on October 5, two days before the second big battle, General von Riedesel suggested to Burgoyne that if General Clinton wasn't going to come to the rescue, Burgoyne move his forces back to Fort Ticonderoga. That would allow Burgoyne's army to get back to Canada before winter set in. Burgoyne would have none of it. By this time morale was very low. In an effort to boost morale, Burgoyne, on October 6, distributed twelve barrels of rum to the troops. Then after the battle on the ninth, Riedesel again suggested a retreat to save what was left of the army. Again, Burgoyne refused and even considered another attack. That delay allowed Stark to seal off the escape route.

After a council of war on October 14, Burgoyne sent a messenger to Gates with a proposal to cease fighting while they discussed preliminary terms "to spare the lives of brave men upon honorable terms." Gates dismissed the proposal and demanded an unconditional surrender. The truce would last until sunset. Burgoyne countered that his troops were to march out of camp with honors of war, his troops were to march to Boston and embark to England, and Canadians would be given a free pass to return home. Astonishingly Gates accepted, provided Burgoyne's troops march from their encampments at 5:00 p.m.

At 10:30 p.m. on the fifteenth, Burgoyne sent word that Gates's terms would be accepted if one word was changed—that it be a treaty of *convention* instead of a treaty of *capitulation*. Again, Gates accepted. But later that night, a Loyalist from Albany reported that many Rebels were leaving camp and that General Henry Clinton was near Albany. The next day Burgoyne sent word that he wanted to determine his enemy's strength by a count by two of his officers.

Gates sent an ultimatum to Burgoyne that he had one hour to answer his terms agreed to on the fifteenth. Gates also ordered the army to be ready to attack early the morning of the seventeenth. Finally, the signed convention was delivered to Gates.

While Balcarres was not happy being a prisoner, he had some other interesting comments. The Europeans were totally awed at the sight of the colored foliage. They had never experienced those beautifully colored leaves. He told me how many of Burgoyne's officers were sickened by Burgoyne's early use of Indians due to their pillaging and cruel treatment of Rebel citizens. Burgoyne thought they'd be an advantage, but in fact their use provoked the Americans to continue sending troops. Burgoyne had little respect for Riedesel and the Brunswick troops. Yet, as Balcarres intimated, Riedesel had much more experience leading troops in warfare. The disrespect the English had for the Germans led to massive desertions by the Germans. He also told me he could not believe the respect the Americans paid to their captives as they marched out in surrender.

I can't forget to mention the great surprise yesterday. With all the troops here, I actually ran into cousin Ben. The last time we met we had a discussion regarding General Arnold. I told him about Arnold's inspiring conduct in the two battles here. He told me about taking the prisoners from Bennington to Massachusetts and then coming all the way back, arriving just before the surrender. He told me he is being assigned to General John Glover to take 5,800 prisoners back to Cambridge. I will be glad to get back to the farm. Once again, Sarah was stuck with the harvesting tasks.

Sincerely, Teunis

November 1, 1777
My dear son Moses,

Even though under occupation by the British, lots of information is trickling into the Blaze Horse. I just heard General Wayne was acquitted at his court-martial for the Paoli affair. From everything I've heard, it seems that Germantown was "a defeat snatched from the jaws of victory." I heard a cute story. After the battle a terrier was found. It had a name tag indicating General Howe as its owner. Washington had the terrier returned to Howe.

The British are desperate to break the blockade on the Delaware River due to the chevaux de frise.[43] Howe had to send troops to the Chesapeake to get supplies off the ships. Washington has taken steps to further hinder the British, sending Lieutenant Colonel Samuel Smith to Fort Mifflin on Mud Island; Colonel Christopher Greene, newly arrived from Rhode Island, to Fort Mercer at Red Bank, New Jersey; Captain Thomas-Antoine de Mauduit du Plessis, French engineer and artillerist, to Red Bank; and Commodore John Hazelwood's Pennsylvania Navy to patrol between Mifflin and Mercer. One of du Plessis's first acts was to pack the outside of Fort Mercer with abatis[44] made from apple and peach trees. This wood is small but tough with dense branches.

Colonel von Donop, sent over by Howe, arrived at Fort Mercer on October 22. Greene twice refused requests to surrender. The Hessians had two thousand men. Initially Greene had two hundred, but Colonel Israel Angell arrived from Fort Mifflin to raise the total American force to five hundred. When the Hessians attacked, their soldiers were burdened by carrying fascines[45] to facilitate their getting into the fort. A heavy bombardment came from the fort's artillery and from Hazelwood's navy. Many Hessian officers were hit, including von Donop. Hessian losses were nearly four hundred. At dusk they left the battle but had to leave von Donop behind. Later that evening he was taken into the fort by du Plessis. On the twenty-ninth, he died.

---

[43] Huge timbers tipped with iron spikes sunk in the riverbed to block shipping.

[44] A defensive obstacle formed by felled trees with sharpened branches facing the enemy.

[45] A rough bundle of brushwood or other material used for strengthening an earthen structure or making a path across uneven or wet terrain.

Zack's friend Johann Ewald stopped by the Blaze Horse. He told me he was sorrowful at the pounding the Hessians took. He told me von Donop's gorget carried the Hessian motto—*Nescit Pericula* ("No Fear of Danger")—quite appropriate, considering the facts.

Did you hear the explosion of HMS *Augusta*? On the twenty-third, it ran aground. The next day, after fire ships were launched, it caught fire and eventually exploded. The sound was deafening. Several Blaze Horse windows were shattered. A huge mushroom cloud hung in the air for hours.

May God bless you, Father

November 22, 1777
Dear Moses,

As if we have not had enough excitement with exploding and burning ships, today we had an earthquake! With the fall of Fort Mifflin and abandonment of Fort Mercer, British ships have arrived in Philadelphia, bringing much-needed supplies to the city. You name it—we were running short. The British succeeded in clearing the Delaware River, but at a high cost of resources, time, and lives.

When I last wrote, Fort Mifflin on Mud Island was intact. On the fifteenth, it was literally obliterated. Because Washington knew access to the fort would be difficult once the British were here, he sent a small force to create a garrison on September 23. Then on October 14, Washington sent French engineer Major Francois-Louis Teissedre de Fleury to assist in fortifying it. To impede an infantry attack, he had it surrounded with trous de loup.[46] While Fort Mifflin was being improved, British Captain John Montresor was constructing a large battery on Carpenter's Island. Ironically it was Montresor who designed Fort Mifflin in 1771, but due to lack of funds it was never completed.

---

[46] Shallow holes with sharpened stakes to impale the feet of attackers.

On November 3, General James Varnum arrived at Fort Mercer, sending additional troops across the river to Lieutenant Colonel Samuel Smith at Fort Mifflin. On the tenth, the Brits opened their batteries. The bombardment from Carpenter's Island and British ships never stopped. On the eleventh, Smith was wounded when a collapsing chimney fell on him. He was removed from the fort, turning command over to Major Simeon Thayer. At 2:00 a.m. on the sixteenth, Thayer set fire to the fort, left the flag flying, and rowed to safety with the last soldiers to Fort Mercer. On the fifteenth, Admiral Howe came up from Wilmington to view the bombardment along with Generals Howe, Cornwallis, and Grant. On the nineteenth, Fort Mercer was abandoned, opening up the Delaware River for the Brits.

On November 2, we finally received word about the Saratoga surrender. James Wilkinson, who delivered the news, took fifteen days to get here. Based on General Gates's recommendation, Wilkinson was brevetted a brigadier general by Congress. Sam Adams suggested that perhaps Wilkinson should have been given a pair of spurs instead of one brigadier general star.

Congress is now in York, Pennsylvania. On the fifteenth, after a year of debate, the Articles of Confederation were adopted. They were sent to each state for ratification. I also heard today that General Stephen was found guilty at his court-martial and has been cashiered from the army.

May God bless you, Father

✺

December 20, 1777
Dear Father,

Since the Battle of Germantown, for most of the time we were encamped at Whitemarsh. We did indeed hear the *Augusta* explosion way out here. Your hearing of Saratoga was interesting. General Washington got the news on October 25 in a note from General Israel Putnam. Several days later, Washington finally got notice from General Gates. The news of Wilkinson's promotion to general was greeted here with fury by many officers. Before telling you of recent actions, I must relay a beautiful scene displayed on an aurora borealis the night of November 27. The sky was blood red with white streaks shooting upward. At times the heavens appeared to be covered with crimson velvet.

On December 3, a lady passed a note with news that Howe was planning to attack us. During his attack on the fifth, our general James Irvine was captured near Chestnut Hill. On the sixth, Howe moved many forces out of Chestnut Hill toward Edge Hill. On the seventh, Howe ordered an advance on Edge Hill. Washington had Morgan's riflemen on the right, but they were eventually driven back. As the battle commenced, Pickering was riding unit to unit to remind everyone not to fire too high. On the eighth, Washington, after seeing British campfires all night, sent Major Allan McLane to gather intelligence. He reported that as the campfires burned, Howe was headed to Philadelphia. Howe will likely winter his soldiers utilizing the city's comforts.

In mid-November, Generals Greene and Lafayette were sent to New Jersey to assist Red Bank, if necessary, and to receive troops coming from Saratoga. Eventually we welcomed four thousand reinforcements from Saratoga. On November 19, General Cornwallis crossed over to Red Bank. On seeing the overwhelming force, Red Bank was abandoned without a fight. On the twenty-fifth, as Cornwallis was trying to cross back at Gloucester, Lafayette attacked his rear guard in a furious skirmish.

On December 11, as we were moving westward toward Valley Forge, we came across General Potter's troops at Matson's Ford on the Schuylkill River. They were in an intense engagement with a huge foraging party led by General Cornwallis. On the eighteenth, due to a resolution by Congress, we had a day of thanksgiving. We each got half a gill[47] of rice and a tablespoon of vinegar—a joke! Yesterday, the nineteenth, we got to Valley Forge. It will be our home for the winter. I am not looking forward to it.

Your son, Moses

---

[47] A gill equals one-quarter of a pint.

January 21, 1778
Dear Moses, Ben, Teunis, Roelof, and Felix,

I want to give all of you an update of events in Philadelphia since the occupation. The most distressing is the fact that so many Patriots from town and outlying locations are imprisoned. Many are imprisoned in Independence Hall. Also, many are billeted in taverns around town. Since I have a big clientele of British and Hessian officers, I hope my congeniality will not give them the idea to use the Blaze Horse as a prison. Even though Moses is close by in Valley Forge, but not being able to visit, I need to include him in this update.

Of course, many abodes in the city are now housing British and Hessian officers. Ben Franklin's house is home to Captain John André, an aide to General Charles Grey. We refer to him as General "No Flint" Grey because of his tactics at Paoli. André has been seen a lot with Peggy Shippen, the daughter of Judge Edward Shippen, a highly suspected Tory. Shippen is close with Joseph Galloway, who was placed as the head of civil government in Philadelphia by General Howe.

With Washington's defeats at Brandywine and Germantown, coupled with Gates's success at Saratoga, we've had four months of intrigue between the Continental Army and the Continental Congress. It all started when General Thomas Conway sent a letter to Congress, asking for a promotion and protesting the promotion of Johann de Kalb to general. Conway was upset because in France he had held a higher rank than de Kalb.

Meanwhile, Sam Adams, Thomas Mifflin, Richard Henry Lee, and Benjamin Rush became noted Washington detractors and came to favor Gates. John Adams agreed with Rush, because Adams was not a fan of Washington's Fabian tactics.[48] My view is without those tactics, this rebellion might well be finished. Washington wrote Lee, protesting Conway's

---

[48] The Fabian strategy is a military strategy where pitched battles and frontal assaults are avoided in favor of wearing down an opponent through a war of attrition and indirection.

promotion. Congress promoted Conway to inspector general under Washington but reporting directly to the Board of War. When the Board of War was created, General Horatio Gates was named president and General James Wilkinson secretary.

Conway had written a letter to Gates, thoroughly disparaging Washington. Gates shared the letter with Wilkinson, whose promotion to general after Saratoga was greeted with derision by many officers. Wilkinson revealed the contents to General Lord Stirling. Stirling told Washington about it. Washington informed Congress, while totally ignoring Conway's role as inspector general. Gates and Conway went to see Congress. By this time Congress had many letters of support for Washington from his officers, especially Alexander Hamilton and John Laurens. Congress, in light of this duplicity, asked Gates, Wilkinson, and Mifflin to resign from the Board of War. This affair became known as the Conway Cabal and is now over.

Zack comes to Blaze Horse on occasion with various friends. He told me that Hessian Jäger Captain Johann Ewald really likes our porter. Coming from a German, that's a real compliment! Lately he's been in here with Lord Rawdon, the British hero of Bunker Hill. Zack knew him during the British occupation of Boston. Rawdon was here recruiting for a Loyalist unit called the Volunteers of Ireland. Moses, I mentioned that you were friends with Lafayette. To my astonishment, Rawdon told me he had met Lafayette in London in March 1777. Zack is also involved in recruiting for another Loyalist unit, the Bucks County Dragoons.

On another occasion, Zack told me that Major John Graves Simcoe was named as the new commander of the Queen's Rangers, replacing Major James Wemyss. Both were wounded at Brandywine. Zack got to know Simcoe during the siege of Boston.

The Articles of Confederation were adopted last November 15 and sent to each state for ratification. Upon ratification the Continental Congress will cease to exist. The new body will be known as the Unites States in Congress Assembled. Some of the main points are: provision for common defense of all states; one vote per state; only USCA can conduct foreign relations and declare war; expenditures by USCA to be paid by funds raised by states based on real property values of each; if Canada accedes to this confederation, it will be admitted; and admission of any other new state requires the vote of nine states.

It will be interesting to see if it is ratified. Maryland is opposed to claims of western lands by Virginia, Connecticut, and Massachusetts. And what if states don't provide funds? The USCA has no power of taxation.

Sincerely, Eb Chaplin

❧

March 23, 1778
Dear Father,

I apologize for not having written sooner. I hope you haven't worried about me. When twelve thousand of us arrived, there was no housing or any supplies of food. As a result, it's been dawn-to-dusk labor to build housing and to forage for food. The encampment at Valley Forge is on farmland—therefore, very few trees. We've had to range out quite far to cut logs to build cabins.

We need to build the cabins based on specifications: twelve feet by sixteen feet; fireplace made of wood, lined with eighteen inches of clay; doors on the south side; and optional materials for roofing. After experimentation, oak shingles work best for the roof. Cabins will lodge twelve enlisted men. We've learned the best firewood is oak, chestnut, or hickory.

We've lost a lot of men, but to disease rather than cold weather. It's averaged 33 degrees thus far. The rain, making roads muddy, has hampered foraging efforts. Many horses have died of starvation for lack of hay. For many of the men, corn is considered animal food. Washington's cook, Polly Cooper, an Oneida Indian, has shown the men how to prepare corn for human consumption. A huge bakery is in operation under the command of Baker General Christopher Ludwig. Each person gets about a pound of bread a day.

When we did have leisure time, we had races. John Marshall, from Virginia, always seems to win. We also have been taught the game of lacrosse by the Oneidas. Leisure time is rare now. On February 23, Baron Friedrich von Steuben arrived; he had served Frederick the Great of Prussia. Since Conway hadn't been seen much, Washington named Steuben as acting inspector general. He is in charge of proper military training—how to aim muskets, how to correctly charge with bayonets, and how to maneuver together in compact rank. At first the soldiers were not happy doing this, but now there are friendly competitions between units to prove their superiority to each other.

Steuben doesn't know any English. At the start, when exasperated by poor performance, he would swear in German. Most didn't know what he was saying. They just laughed and mocked him. Some called on our German units to learn German swear words so they could swear back at him. I've gotten to know von Steuben quite well because of the translation project on which I am working. He asked me in French if I could teach him some English swear words. He surprised the soldiers when he swore back in English, but they got a good laugh out of it. Steuben is compiling a training manual titled "Regulations for the Order and Discipline of the Troops of the United States." We refer to it as "The Blue Book." Each evening von Steuben dictates in French to his secretary, Pierre Du Ponceau, who came to America with him. Du Ponceau then translates to English. He knew Lafayette in France. Lafayette asked if he needed any assistance and offered my services. Believe me, that is more fun than chopping wood or going out foraging.

Due to Mifflin's resignation, Nathanael Greene became quartermaster general. He did not want the position but has performed admirably. While it is hard work going out on foraging trips, at least at night if we couldn't return, we usually had a warm and dry place to sleep at some farm.

The British are also foraging in the area. We often find the farmers will not sell to us. They want to do business with the British, because they pay in hard currency instead of paper money. One farmer learned a lesson the hard way. He was tied to the tail of one of his horses and dragged for quite a way; we took his horse. In January, Henry "Light-Horse Harry" Lee had a close encounter with two hundred British Light-Horse under Major Banastre Tarleton, who was sent to capture him as he was harassing British forage parties. Because of his actions to escape Spread Eagle Tavern, where he was taking cover, a new cavalry unit—Lee's Legion—was formed.

General Wayne was sent to southern New Jersey to forage. The British are also foraging there. He brought back two distressing stories by troops under British Lieutenant Colonel Charles Mawhood's command. On the eighteenth, a New Jersey militia unit from Salem was ambushed at Quinton's Bridge by the Queen's Rangers and Skinner's Greens, a New Jersey Loyalist unit. Losses were thirty to forty, many of whom were drowned. Then on the twenty-first, the Queen's Rangers learned that New Jersey militia were occupying Loyalist Judge William Hancock's home at Hancock's Bridge. When they attacked, Simcoe gave no quarter.[49] Twenty militiamen were bayoneted. The judge and his son also became victims of the massacre. I wonder if Zack has blood on his hands from this affair.

Washington is making his headquarters in the house of Isaac Potts, who owned a gristmill until it was burned by the British when they were here last September. The massive bakery was built close to Potts's house. Mrs. Washington, Martha, arrived a few days ago. She had to take a very circuitous route from Mount Vernon to avoid the British.

By the way, when General Stephen was cashiered, Washington gave Stephen's command to Lafayette. He was very impressed with Lafayette's encounter with Cornwallis at Gloucester.

Your son, Moses

---

[49] A victor gives "no quarter" when the victor shows no clemency or mercy and refuses to spare the life in return for the surrender at the discretion (unconditional surrender) of a vanquished opponent.

Chapter Four

Sir, I have not yet begun to fight.
—John Paul Jones

The activities in the War of Independence during 1778 and 1779 were widespread, not only across America, but also across the Atlantic Ocean. The British were put into panic when John Paul Jones boldly attacked them on their own shores.

In 1778, a secret mission was sent from Virginia to Illinois to control the areas west and north of the Ohio River. General Washington ordered a "scorched earth" policy against the Indians in northern Pennsylvania and western New York.

The major action in the Northern theater occurred in Rhode Island in 1778. In the Southern theater, the British captured Savannah and Augusta, Georgia. They were repulsed for a second time, trying to take Charleston, South Carolina. The Americans, with assistance from the French, tried to retake Savannah. It was a bloody defeat for the Americans.

༺ঌৣৗ༻

June 18, 1778
Dear Moses,

They're gone! The British occupation of Philadelphia is over. This morning the entire British army, with 1,500 wagons, crossed the Delaware River into New Jersey on their way to New York City. They chose not to leave by ship because the rumors were rampant that a French naval fleet was nearing Delaware Bay to attack the British here. The ships brought up, initially for troop movement, were used to transport Loyalists who were eager to escape. Joseph Galloway left with them to New York.

The Treaty of Alliance with France was received by Congress on May 2 and ratified on May 4. Some states were not represented, but urgency overrode the necessity of having all thirteen states ratify the document. In addition to French military support to America, the treaty effectively guarantees control by the United States of any land it is able to gain possession of in North America (except the islands of Saint Pierre and Miquelon, which France had retained possession of after the Seven Years' War) and of the Islands of Bermuda. The treaty was signed in Paris on February 6 by Benjamin Franklin (wearing the same suit he wore when ridiculed in the privy council's cockpit), Silas Deane, and Arthur Lee for America and Conrad Alexandre Gérard de Rayneval of France. As a result of the treaty, Great Britain declared war on France. Now we have a second worldwide war. While Washington sparked the first one[50] with the Jumonville affair,[51] the "shots heard around the world" at Lexington and Concord ignited the second one.

General Howe left for England on May 24 when his resignation tendered last October was accepted. General Henry Clinton is now commander in chief. Before Howe left, John

---

[50] Referring to the Seven Year's War, called the French and Indian War in North America.

[51] The opening battle of the French and Indian War (May 28, 1754), when Lieutenant Colonel George Washington's forces met French forces commanded by Joseph Coulon de Villiers de Jumonville, resulting in Jumonville's death.

André and John Montresor organized a *Mischianza*[52] to honor him on May 18. It was quite a gala, costing 3,312 guineas. Fourteen of Philadelphia's loveliest young women would be escorted by Knights of the Blended Rose, in silver and pink, and Knights of the Burning Mountain, in orange and black. A joust was staged to determine which of their ladies were fairer. After the joust fought on gray chargers, the knights and their ladies adjourned to a hall for dancing. At 10:00 p.m., the windows were opened to view a massive fireworks display designed by Captain Montresor. At midnight, supper was served by twenty-four marines dressed as Nubian slaves. During supper an explosion echoed through the hall. André reassured the guests it was more of Montresor's magic to trouble the Rebels at Valley Forge. But, in fact, it was Americans blowing up a supply depot in Germantown. Undaunted, André continued with the *Mischianza* until 4:00 a.m. In addition to André, Banastre Tarleton was also a favorite of the young ladies.

May God bless you, Father

June 19, 1778
Dear Father,

We are leaving Valley Forge today. I stayed up late last night to get this letter off to you. Washington found out the Brits were leaving Philadelphia yesterday. In a war council, Generals Wayne and Lafayette, over General Charles Lee's objections, convinced Washington to aggressively pursue the British across New Jersey. He is sending Benedict Arnold to Philadelphia to act as military commandant.

On May 1, another barbaric atrocity was committed by Simcoe's troops, along with some Bucks County Loyalists. General John Lacey was at Crooked Billet, pursuing his role of preventing farmers from supplying the British, when he was attacked. His forces were routed—prisoners and wounded being

---

[52] Italian for a "medley" or "mixture."

bayoneted. Some badly wounded lying in buckwheat straw were burned alive when the straw was set alight.

On May 18, Washington sent Lafayette with two thousand troops from Valley Forge to gather intelligence on possible British plans to evacuate Philadelphia. On the nineteenth, we encamped near a Lutheran church on Barren Hill. On the twentieth, we had a frontal attack from Clinton and Grey, and with Grant attacking on our left, their forces were in excess of five thousand. Lafayette used the church's steeple as a command post to observe British positions. We were about to be encircled when we were able to escape back over the Schuylkill River at Matson's Ford using a route the British were unaware of. Our total losses were light, but unfortunately we lost six of our Oneida Indian scouts.

On May 5, von Steuben was officially named inspector general. He has done an admirable job of improving the army. The next day we had an incredible *feu de joie* to celebrate the French treaty. On May 27, Congress authorized the establishment of a Troop of Marechausee. Their role is to apprehend deserters, marauders, drunkards, rioters, and stragglers. The troop includes executioners under command of Prussian immigrant Captain Bartholomew von Heer, who, being Prussian, understands the value of strict discipline.

We now have a cavalry. You may remember that I mentioned a charge by Count Casimir Puɫaski with Washington's Life Guards at Brandywine. Soon after the battle, Congress named him a brigadier general and commander of the Corps of Continental Light Dragoons.[53] In March, the Pulaski Cavalry Legion was created. Michael Kovats, a retired hussar[54] of the Austro-Hungarian Army, was named the Legion's colonel commandant. In this role he trained the men in the tradition of Hungarian hussars. Earlier in his career he actually had trained Puɫaski. Also joining this unit was Puɫaski's friend from France, Chevalier Charles Armand Tuffin, marquis de la Rouërie, who goes by the name of Colonel Armand. Armand did a lot of the recruiting. Some of his recruits were British and Hessian deserters. Word is that Washington is not pleased with that idea.

---

[53] Mounted infantry or light cavalry units.
[54] A member of mounted light infantry.

As an aside, Kovats wrote a letter to Benjamin Franklin expressing his desire to fight for our cause. However, the letter had a disparaging remark about Emperor Joseph of Austria. Because Joseph is the brother of French Queen Marie Antoinette and because France has allied with us, Franklin was working to obtain Austria as an ally. Franklin could not recommend Kovats because of the letter. Kovats had to use other acquaintances to obtain his commission.

I am not sure when I'll next see you so I will tell you about my friend Peter Francisco. He was born in the Azores. He was kidnapped by pirates when he was four or five years old. He was abandoned on a wharf in Virginia. A local judge raised him. He is a giant—6 feet 8 inches and 260 pounds. Washington presented him with a five-foot sword after he complained that ordinary army-issue swords were too light.

Another thing I wanted to tell you personally, because up to this time I dared not put it into writing: During the encampment at Valley Forge, we were kept well informed about British activities and plans. Charles Darragh was getting numerous visits at camp from his fourteen-year-old brother who lives in Philadelphia. British officers met in the Darragh home. Lydia Darragh would listen to the discussions. She then told her husband what she had heard. Her husband then wrote what she heard in a type of shorthand on small slips of paper. Lydia would sew the notes inside the buttons of her young son's coat. When he arrived, Charles would cut off the buttons, interpret the notes, and relay the information to Washington's staff.

Your son, Moses

June 29, 1778
Dear Father,

I regret I couldn't see you on our way out of Valley Forge. We took a northerly route crossing the Delaware River at Coryell's

Ferry[55] several miles upstream from Trenton. We were in fast pursuit of General Clinton's ten thousand troops with eleven thousand of ours. We were amazed at how fast the British moved because of their long supply wagon train. On the twenty-fourth, Washington held a council of war, during which a solar eclipse occurred, at Signer John Hart's farm. Charles Lee, along with several other generals, cautioned against an attack. However, Wayne, Lafayette, Greene, Knox, and Hamilton encouraged attack. They had greater confidence in the troops due to the training they received from von Steuben in Valley Forge.

On the twenty-seventh, Washington ordered that Lafayette make an attack on the British rear column the next morning. Lee protested to Washington, stating that since he was senior to Lafayette he should lead the attack instead of Lafayette. Early yesterday morning, Washington got word from General Philemon Dickinson of the New Jersey militia that the British were moving away. At that point Washington ordered Lee to attack with five thousand troops to halt the British withdrawal. During Lee's attack, Washington would bring up the remainder of our forces.

Sadly Lee did not make a definitive plan for the attack and had not made himself familiar with the terrain. Soon he got into an intense battle with General Clinton and decided to retreat. As Washington was coming up, he ran into Lee's retreating men. Furiously, he relieved Lee of command and rallied the troops to attack. Wayne held the center as Washington sent Stirling to the left and Greene to the right. Stirling and Greene caught Clinton and Cornwallis in an enfilading fire.

Although the temperature was over 100 degrees, we pressed on until darkness. During the battle, an artilleryman's wife found a spring from which she carried water to the crew to swab the cannons and to quench their thirst. When her wounded husband was carried off, she replaced him on the crew. An enemy cannonball went between her legs, tearing away her petticoat. She's been named "Molly Pitcher." We expected to continue the battle today, but the British left last night.

Your son, Moses

---

[55] Present-day Lambertville, New Jersey.

July 5, 1778
Dear Uncle Eb,

When we left Philadelphia, the Queen's Rangers, being Americans and familiar with the route, guided the way on our 100-mile trip to Sandy Hook, New Jersey. We had only ten thousand troops, because General Clinton, learning a French fleet was on its way but not sure of its destination, had sent three thousand troops to West Florida and the West Indies before leaving Philadelphia. We had 1,500 wagons of baggage. The train was twelve miles long. Many forage depots had been set up for us. At first we made fast time, but then we encountered many obstacles. The New Jersey Rebels burned bridges, muddied water wells, and felled trees across the road.

On June 27, fearing an attack, Clinton moved the wagon train forward and formed a rear guard to protect it. At 4:00 a.m. on June 28, Clinton had von Knyphausen in charge of leading our forces toward Sandy Hook. When this move was detected, we were attacked in the rear by General Charles Lee. Clinton had no trouble routing them, sending them into a disorganized retreat. The retreating troops ran smack into General Washington, who expected to meet British troops not his own!

Washington rallied the Rebel troops. I have to admit his bravery cannot be questioned. He was dangerously riding out in front of his forces. This gallant show gave great enthusiasm to the Rebels, and the battle turned against us. The battle raged for five to six hours until sundown. No one is sure of the casualty numbers. There are reports of less than one hundred killed and less than two hundred wounded on either side. Because of the brutal heat, there were many deaths from heat stroke and fatigue. Sadly we had five hundred to six hundred deserters. Most of the deserters were from Hessian units. The talk is they wanted to go back to Philadelphia to see the girlfriends they met over the winter.

On the trip to Manhattan from Sandy Hook, I learned from a Rebel prisoner that both Alexander Hamilton and Aaron

Burr had horses shot from under them and that Washington's white mount, a gift from New Jersey's governor, collapsed of sunstroke. I imagine Philadelphia celebrated Independence Day yesterday. When I was able to, I really enjoyed visiting you at Blaze Horse this past winter.

God Save the King, Zack

❧

July 14, 1778
Dear Moses,

Thank you for your letter regarding the Battle of Monmouth. I was so relieved that you survived it well. I also got a letter from Zack. He made it to Manhattan.

A few days ago we got horrific news from the Wyoming Valley.[56] Colonel John Butler led four hundred Loyalists and five hundred Seneca Indians from Fort Niagara to attack the settlers in the valley region. As you know, this area has been disputed between Connecticut and Pennsylvania, leading to several Pennamite-Yankee Wars[57] among the settlers. Butler's force reached the area on June 30 and took over Fort Wintermoot. Meanwhile, the Connecticut militia, under Lieutenant Colonel Zebulon Butler, was gathering at Forty Fort.

On July 3, the militia, now up to four hundred men, decided to attack John Butler's forces at Fort Wintermoot. Unfortunately they walked right into an ambush. That night several prisoners were taken to a rock, now known as Bloody Rock. They were lined up around the rock where an Indian woman, Queen Esther, smashed their skulls with her tomahawk. John Butler claimed he took 227 scalps, which he turned over to the British for bounty money, and burned over 1,000 homes.

On July 8, a French fleet, under the command of Admiral Charles Henri Theodat, comte d'Estaing, arrived in Delaware

---

[56] An area of present-day Scranton and Wilkes-Barre, Pennsylvania.
[57] Pennamites were claiming the area for Pennsylvania, while the Yankees were claiming the area for Connecticut.

Bay. When the treaty with France was signed on February 6, King Louis XVI wasted no time. On February 8, Louis appointed d'Estaing to command a squadron departing for North America. The fleet finally left France on April 13 with a force of 10,600 on sixteen ships. When they cleared Gibraltar on May 20, d'Estaing ordered his captains to open their sealed orders, revealing the stunning news of France declaring war on Britain and their destination. They were hoping to find the British here but arrived too late. On the ninth, Silas Deane and Conrad Alexandre Gérard de Rayneval left the fleet and came to Philadelphia as the fleet left for New York. Today Gérard presented himself to the Continental Congress as France's ambassador, and Deane was informed Congress would investigate him in response to charges leveled against him by Arthur Lee, one of the other American commissioners in France.

While the French now recognize our independence, they were not the first nation to do so. Back on December 20, 1777, Morocco recognized our independence. On July 11, Congress resolved that the term "United States of America" be used on all bills of exchange. It is the first official use of the term. On July 1, a court-martial for General Charles Lee was appointed, with General Lord Stirling sitting as president. His charges were (1) disobedience of orders, (2) misbehavior before the enemy, and (3) disrespect to the commander in chief. I'll let you know the result.

May God bless you, Father

July 29, 1778
Dear Mr. Chaplin,

I'm writing about what started as a secret mission. In early May, I joined a group of Virginians under Lieutenant Colonel George Rogers Clark. We were told we were enlisting for service in Virginia's Kentucky County to assist the locals against Indian depredations. Kentucky was in a state of terror ever since British lieutenant governor and superintendent of indian affairs Henry Hamilton, located at Fort Detroit, received orders from Lord Germain in London through Quebec governor Frederick Haldimand to arm the Indians, use them as allies, and encourage their raids on American settlements. Hamilton is known as "Hair Buyer," because it is said he pays the Indians for American scalps brought to him.

When we got to the Falls of the Ohio[58] on May 27, we learned the real purpose of our mission. We learned we were headed to Illinois country to capture British forts located there. Going to Kentucky, populated by many Americans, was one thing, but going into Illinois, being full of Indians, British soldiers, and French habitants, our lifelong enemies, was quite another. When Clark proposed this mission to Governor Patrick Henry, he approved the plan but ordered that it must be carried out in secrecy.

On June 24, we left the Falls during a solar eclipse. As we were going down the Ohio River, William Linn, coming from Fort Pitt, caught up to us with news of the French alliance. On June 28, we left the mouth of the Tennessee River to travel overland to Kaskaskia 120 miles away. For part of the way we used a French military route, following numbers on trees painted red. So as not to signal Indians we were in the area, we were not allowed to shoot deer for meat. Fortunately there were a lot of berries to eat.

We got to Kaskaskia just before dark on July 4. The forces were split. Clark led some men to the fort, while the rest of us surrounded the town. Clark captured Lieutenant Governor Chevalier Philippe de Rocheblave in his bed. A signal was given for us to capture the town. The habitants,[59] aligned with the British, were quite frightened but did not put up a fight. Clark assured Father Pierre Gibault, a Sardinian priest, no one would be harmed with a peaceful surrender. Announcing the French alliance proved powerful. Being Independence Day, their church bell, a gift of Louis XV, was rung to celebrate.

---

[58] Present-day Louisville, Kentucky.
[59] French settlers and the inhabitants of French origin.

On July 6, Joseph Bowman, along with some Kaskaskia residents, captured St. Philip, Prairie du Rocher, and Cahokia. Father Gibault was sent to Vincennes on the fourteenth to notify the habitants there to pledge allegiance to the "Bostonnais."[60] Rocheblave is being sent as a prisoner to Williamsburg. I'm sending this letter with his escort.

Sincerely, Roelof

⁓

July 30, 1778
Dear Moses, Ben, and Teunis,

In April, a proclamation was sent to the Hessians. A soldier who deserts will receive fifty acres. A captain who brings in forty men gets eight hundred acres of woodland, four oxen, one bull, two cows, and four sows and does not have to serve in the American Army. It will be interesting to see if there are any takers.

Teunis, on May 6, Ethan Allen, who you told us of being captured at Montreal, was exchanged for British general Archibald Campbell. Campbell had been captured when he arrived in Boston on June 17, 1776, not knowing that the British had evacuated Boston in March. Allen told a hilarious story when he was being held prisoner in England. His captors had hung a portrait of George Washington in the privy. After Allen returned from a trip to the privy, his captors asked how he felt seeing a portrait of Washington in the privy. Allen replied, "The world knows nothing will make an Englishman s**t quicker than the sight of George Washington."

On May 8, General Charles Lee, captured by Banastre Tarleton in December 1776, was exchanged for British general Richard Prescott. You might remember Prescott was exchanged for General John Sullivan in September 1776. He was captured a second time in July 1777, being abducted from his headquarters, without his breeches, in Rhode Island.

---

[60] Habitants' term for Americans.

117

On July 4, a duel took place between Generals John Cadwalader and Thomas Conway. As a result of the Conway Cabal, Cadwalader considered Conway's conduct toward Washington offensive. Cadwalader fired first, hitting Conway in the mouth and exclaiming, "I've stopped the damned rascal's tongue anyhow."

Last night, Plunket Fleeson, who supplies Washington with tents and camp equipage, stopped by the Blaze Horse, telling of a letter from Ben Franklin ordering coonskin hats and whale oil candles to be sent to Paris. He also told of the harrowing trip John Adams had on his way to France when he was sent over to replace Silas Deane. Adams left Boston on a 24-gun frigate in February, taking with him his ten-year-old son, John Quincy Adams. On the way over, the ship was struck by lightning, killing a crew member. Later they captured a British ship. They finally got to Bordeaux on April 1 and to Paris on the eighth.

Ben and Teunis, there is quite a bit of discussion at the Blaze Horse regarding General Benedict Arnold in his role as Philadelphia's military commander. Folks have noticed he has acquired quite a large stable of horses and that he's selling goods left by the British not of use to American military and perhaps pocketing the proceeds.

Sincerely, Eb Chaplin

⟨∾⟩

September 1, 1778
Dear Father,

After Monmouth, Washington sent some of us to White Plains, New York. The French fleet, under Admiral Comte d'Estaing, arrived off Sandy Hook, New Jersey, on July 11. Local pilots advised d'Estaing that his ships might not clear the sandbar at Sandy Hook. Since this precluded a joint French-American attack on New York City, a few days later Washington sent Alexander Hamilton, fluent in French, to propose a joint operation against Newport, Rhode Island. The French agreed, and Washington informed General John Sullivan in Providence, Rhode Island. To keep d'Estaing informed of any British action, Washington had lookout sites set up as express posts, with each post having two saddled horses for quick departures.

On July 22, d'Estaing left for Newport and I went with Generals James Varnum and John Glover to Rhode Island. The French fleet arrived on July 29. Sullivan and d'Estaing met to establish a battle plan. Their plan never materialized, because so many New England militia units were late in arriving, and when they did arrive, there weren't enough boats to ferry them to Aquidneck Island. And then to our dismay, on August 9, British Admiral Richard Howe arrived with a fleet. On the tenth, d'Estaing gave chase, but then a furious storm hit. On the twentieth, d'Estaing's fleet reappeared with heavy damage. D'Estaing informed Sullivan that because his ships were so badly damaged by a hurricane while at sea he was sailing to Boston for repairs.

On August 29, the British attacked. I was with General Nathanael Greene, commanding the American right. Out in front, Colonel John Laurens (whose father, Henry Laurens, is president of the Continental Congress) commanded a light infantry advance guard. They were quickly thrown back by the British. Our first attack came at about 10:00 a.m. The attacks continued to and fro until late afternoon. Late on the thirtieth, Sullivan decided to withdraw all the troops from Aquidneck. He also received word from Washington that Admiral Howe was back on his way with more troops.

Despite all the heavy fighting, our losses were minimal: 30 killed and 137 wounded. Surprisingly, yesterday I ran into Ben. He told me how much he admired Benedict Arnold but also said that Teunis had some doubts about Arnold's integrity. I also talked to Lafayette, just arriving back from Boston, where he had been sent to calm things down with the French. He was mortified to have missed the battle.

Your son, Moses

∽

September 2, 1778
Dear Uncle Eb,

My stay in New York after getting back from Philadelphia was short-lived. On July 9, I went to Newport, Rhode Island, with 1,850 soldiers under General Richard Prescott, sent there by General Clinton to assist General Robert Pigot. The British got word that a French fleet was sent to America. Their fear was that the French might come to dislodge the British in Rhode Island. In December 1776, the British occupied Newport because of the warmer waters for the fleet and to quarter troops that couldn't be quartered in New York due to the great fire.

General Prescott was coming back to Rhode Island for the first time since he had been captured in July 1777. General Howe got Prescott back in an exchange for his prisoner, American General Charles Lee. On July 29, the French fleet, under Admiral d'Estaing, arrived. Before a joint American-French assault could take place, a fleet of Admiral Richard Howe arrived on August 9. Seeing the British fleet, d'Estaing reboarded the troops he had disembarked and went after Howe.

As American troops moved on to the northern part of Aquidneck Island, Pigot moved his forces down to Newport. Looking for additional help, Pigot invited Negroes to join the "King's troops" with promises of pay and provisions. Since few joined, they were impressed as manual laborers and wagon drivers. A siege went on for several weeks. On August 20, the French fleet reappeared but then left the next day.

At daybreak on August 29, we noticed that all the American tents had been struck. Pigot promptly ordered an attack—General Prescott on the right, General Francis Smith in the center, and General Friedrich Wilhelm von Lossberg on the left. I was in the battle on the left, along with the King's American Regiment and two regiments from Ansbach-Bayreuth. We made several attempts to dislodge the American right but were repeatedly repulsed. The battle went on until late in the afternoon.

Artillery fire continued all day on the thirtieth. On the thirty-first, all the Americans had left Aquidneck Island. Our losses were 38 killed and 210 wounded. General Henry Clinton arrived on September 1 with 4,300 troops. A Hessian soldier remarked, "He came too late, just as the English usually do."

God Save the King, Zack

❧

September 9, 1778
Dear Uncle Eb,

In late July, General John Sullivan put out a call, raising New England militia units to report to Newport, Rhode Island. We left Salem on August 4. As we marched to Rhode Island, we were joined by the "Boston Cadets," smartly adorned with black coats faced with red and having expensive buttons with the inscription "Inimica Tyrannis" (Enemy of Tyranny). Also with us were Signer William Whipple (New Hampshire militia general), John Hancock (Massachusetts militia general), and Paul Revere (Massachusetts artillery).

When we got there, there was a shortage of flatboats to get us over to Aquidneck Island, where Newport is located. The French had disembarked troops to help us fight the British. But because Sullivan hadn't gotten enough men over to Aquidneck and because a British fleet was spotted, the French left. From August 11 to August 14, we endured wind and bone-chilling rain. We were kept busy extending trenches, emplacing batteries, and cannonading the British positions. We had almost 10,000 men, but when the French came back and then instead of joining us sailed off to Boston, our ranks melted down by 2,300 men.

The Rhode Islanders were so desperate for men that they formed a regiment of slaves, free Negroes, and Narragansett Indians. They were placed under the command of Colonel Christopher Greene, whom I met on the Quebec Expedition. I was not with them in the battle but heard they were terrific fighters.

Early in the morning of the twenty-ninth, the British attacked. I was on our left wing under General John Glover. At one point, one of our officers remarked that we were getting reinforcements. Luckily another officer recognized that their uniforms were not blue and *buff* but blue and *yellow*—Germans. If they had gotten behind us, it would have been disastrous. The battle raged until late afternoon. We were off of Aquidneck by early morning on the thirty-first. Later that day I ran into Moses. We traded a lot of stories.

On my way back to Salem, I went through Boston. There, on September 8, I witnessed a tragedy. Because d'Estaing left Newport without assisting us, there was deep anti-French sentiment in Boston. Two French bakers left their ships in Boston Harbor, where the ships were being repaired, to acquire bread from their counterparts onshore. After heated exchanges, a riot broke out with fifty dockworkers mauling two French officers. One of them died from his injuries. It's good to be back home.

Sincerely, Ben

January 5, 1779
Dear Mr. Chaplin,

Militarily, the year 1778 did not go well for us in the South. It started badly when forays into East Florida were repelled. In December, Savannah fell to the British.

In February, the Georgia Assembly authorized an expedition by Governor John Houstoun to East Florida. Congress authorized Southern Commander of the Continental Army General Robert Howe to proceed in conjunction with Georgia's militia. The expedition got underway in April, but progress was slow due to lack of provisions and a lack of slaves to build roads. Howe and Houstoun couldn't agree on tactics. Houstoun wanted to continue on to St. Augustine, while Howe wanted to take Fort Tonyn on St. Mary's River, occupied by "Burnfoot" Brown's Loyalist East Florida Rangers. On June 28, Brown withdrew, burning the fort.

On the thirtieth, Howe sent about one hundred cavalry under General James Screven after Brown. At Alligator Bridge[61] on the Nassau River in Florida, Screven met not only Brown, but about two hundred British under command of Major Mark Prevost. After a pitched battle, Screven's men were able to escape. Regrettably on November 22, Screven, trying to assist in thwarting another advance by Prevost, was mortally wounded near Midway Church.

General Howe had conflicts with many other commanders. When his authority was questioned by Christopher Gadsden, Howe challenged him to a duel. On August 30, the duel took place. Howe fired first, grazing Gadsden's ear. Gadsden, instead of firing at Howe, intentionally shot backward over his own left shoulder and demanded Howe fire again. Howe refused, and the two made amends.

On December 23, 3,500 British troops sailing from Staten Island, under command of Lieutenant Colonel Archibald Campbell, landed on Tybee Island near Savannah. Due to knowledge that General Augustine Prevost was on his way north from St. Augustine, Florida, to join with Campbell, General Howe moved from Charleston to Savannah with 850 troops. Campbell decided not to wait for Prevost and on the twenty-ninth made his attack on Savannah. The key to the victory was that a slave, Quamino Dolly, told Campbell of a trail through a swamp that Howe thought was impenetrable. Howe's casualties were 83 killed, 11 wounded, and 453 captured. The British casualties were 7 killed and 17 wounded. We also heard that the British committed brutal acts, such as bayoneting citizens not engaged in the action.

Sincerely, Felix

January 15, 1779
Dear Father,

Except for one major tragedy, things have been quiet. The tragedy occurred in the early morning hours this past September 28. On

---

[61] Near present-day Callahan, Florida.

the twenty-second, the British sent five thousand troops up the eastern side of the Hudson River from New York City to forage. It was a massive operation with many ships to haul goods back to New York.

On the twenty-seventh, Lieutenant Colonel George Baylor, with his 100-plus dragoons referred to as Mrs. Washington's Guards, was ordered to take a position between our army and the British. That night Baylor and his men encamped in houses and barns near Old Tappan, New Jersey. During the night, British general Charles Grey approached Baylor's men with Tory guides. Grey, as he did at Paoli, attacked with bayonets, flints removed from the muskets. Grey's men killed, wounded, or took as prisoners sixty-nine men. Baylor was bayoneted repeatedly and had several sword swipes but survived and was taken prisoner.

On November 30, we started our winter encampment at Middlebrook, New Jersey. Initially we lived in tents but now have our cabins built. Unlike Valley Forge, there was plenty of timber to build the cabins. The cabin specifications call for the cabins to be sixteen feet long, fourteen feet wide, with seven-foot-high walls. While it is colder, it is nice to be able to sleep in a cabin rather than on the ground. This fall, while making camp, we had to make sure our bedroll was raised slightly above the ground. If you slept directly on the ground, you could easily have snakes trying to rest near you, seeking warmth.

Scurvy has been a problem in our encampments. The New England soldiers introduced us to spruce needle tea to fight scurvy. Their ancestors learned this from the Indians. Due to Washington's friendship with Juan de Miralles, Spain's royal commissioner to Congress, we've been getting limes from Cuba, which also combat scurvy.

The encampment is in the Watchung Mountains. From here we can keep a close watch on the British in New York City. The citizens of the area are friendly. General Washington and his wife are using the home of John Wallace as his headquarters not far from here.

So far very little snow has fallen. The temperatures are quite mild. We recently received a batch of uniforms from the French.

Some of the uniforms are blue, and others are brown. I hope we have a peaceful winter.

Your son, Moses

⚬⚬⚬

January 29, 1779
My dear son Moses,

Thank you for your letters regarding the Battle of Rhode Island and your current winter encampment. Again, I was so relieved to hear no harm came to you in the past several months. I have several news items for you.

Last July I got a letter from Roelof telling me that he was on a secret mission to capture British outposts in the Illinois country to stop the Indian depredations in Kentucky country. The mission was led by George Rogers Clark, with the support of Patrick Henry. On July 4, they captured Kaskaskia on the Mississippi River. They then captured two more outposts and were going to make an attempt on Vincennes.

You wrote about the massacre at Old Tappan in northern New Jersey. In October, we had some action in southern New Jersey, resulting in another massacre by the British. The British sent Major Patrick Ferguson down to Chestnut Neck[62], which was used as a base for privateers who were capturing British ships and their supplies. You may not be aware that these privateers were valuable in getting supplies to Valley Forge during your encampment. On the sixth, Ferguson captured some supplies and learned that General Casimir Pułaski's Legionnaires were on the way. Ferguson went on to raid the Batsto Iron Works. A few days later a deserter from Pułaski's forces told Ferguson that the Legionnaires were encamped at Little Egg Harbor. Ferguson and Loyalists attacked at daylight on the fifteenth, killing fifty men. Pułaski managed to regroup, causing Ferguson to retreat to his boats.

On August 12, General Charles Lee was found guilty of all charges at his court-martial. On December 5, over the strong

---

[62] Present-day Port Republic, New Jersey.

objections of Samuel Adams, Lee was relieved of his command. On December 24, because of all the disparaging remarks Lee made about Washington, John Laurens challenged Lee to a duel. Lee was slightly wounded. Both men were preparing for a second shot when the duel was stopped by Laurens's second, Alexander Hamilton.

As you know, Benedict Arnold is military commander of Philadelphia. I am getting more stories here at the Blaze Horse of Arnold abusing his office for his benefit. Allen McLane, of the 1st Delaware Regiment, told me he sent a letter to General Washington warning that he felt Arnold was engaged in "profiteering." When I heard this I harkened back to a letter four years ago from Ben who mentioned that Teunis felt Arnold's reputation was not the best.

May God bless you, Father

April 1, 1779
Dear Mr. Chaplin,

I am now home. After taking Kaskaskia, we had a lot more action. After Father Gibault returned from Vincennes, having sworn the habitants to American allegiance, Clark sent Captain Leonard Helm to command Fort Sackville and the habitant militia. On January 29, we received word from Francis Vigo, an Italian fur trader, that "Hair Buyer" Hamilton had retaken Fort Sackville on December 17. Clark immediately made plans to take back the fort. A batteau, the *Willing*, was built, armed with two four-pounder cannons. It set off for Vincennes on February 4 under command of John Rogers. We left, 170 strong, on the fifth for Vincennes, 160 miles away.

We had oxen pulling our supply wagons. Later on, of course, they became beef. We followed buffalo trails for most of the trip. The season was not typical. We were inundated with rain instead of getting snow. On the fourteenth, we crossed the Little Wabash and Fox Rivers with a canoe built the day before. On the eighteenth, we were close enough to hear the morning cannons at Fort Sackville. On the twenty-second, we crossed the Wabash ·River in neck-deep water. Not only did we have a difficult time crossing, but so did the horses with their packs. Our drummer boy floated across on his drum.

On the twenty-third, we crept up toward Fort Sackville. The habitants of Vincennes were notified of our presence. No one betrayed us. At 8:00 p.m., we fired our first shots at the fort. Being sharpshooters, we were able to pick off British defenders through the fort's portholes. As dawn appeared on the twenty-fourth, Hamilton saw sufficient flags unfurled for a 500-man army. Then some of our men captured a band of Indians with fresh Kentucky scalps. They proved very useful.

At 9:00 a.m., Clark asked for Hamilton's surrender. He refused and sent Captain Helm out as his negotiator. Clark told him that Helm, a prisoner of his, could not represent him. Then Clark lined up the Indians in plain view of Hamilton and proceeded to have them tomahawked, one by one. When the Ottawa chief, Macutté Mong, was tomahawked, the first blow did not kill him. He handed the tomahawk back to finish the task. Hamilton still would not surrender. Clark then announced that if he did not surrender, no quarter would be given. Having seen the fate of the Indians, Hamilton surrendered at 10:00 a.m. on the twenty-fifth. The American flag was raised, and Fort Sackville was renamed Fort Patrick Henry. The *Willing* arrived on the twenty-seventh. Luckily we didn't need her.

Sincerely, Roelof

April 30, 1779
Dear Uncle Eb,

After being in Rhode Island and getting back home to Salem, I decided to again take part in a prisoner's march. This will be my third experience after conducting prisoners from Bennington and then from Saratoga. General William Heath was put in charge of marching the prisoners, referred to as the Convention Army, taken at Saratoga from Cambridge, Massachusetts, to Charlottesville, Virginia. While almost six thousand prisoners were taken at Saratoga, we are marching just over four thousand, because there were so many escapees. We left on November 9, 1778. Just before we left, the general from Brunswick, Baron Riedesel, managed to purchase a pretty English carriage to transport Baroness Frederika Charlotte, her three children, and her two maids.

Also, before we left we heard about the raids by British Major Christopher Carleton, nephew of General Guy Carleton. Carleton came up Lake Champlain in late October from Île aux Noix on the Richelieu River. After they got to Crown Point, raids were made into New York and the Vermont Republic. On those raids many supplies were destroyed and many cattle were captured and taken back to Quebec.

When we got to Newburgh, New York, General Washington greeted General Heath and the top English and German officers. I was so hoping our route would take us through Philadelphia so that I could see you at the Blaze Horse. And since Benedict Arnold is now the military governor of Philadelphia, I was hoping to see him too. Unfortunately the route went through Lancaster, Pennsylvania. There the Pennsylvania militia was to take over as escorts. They did not show up when they were supposed to, and we were without escort for two days. At that point we lost many of the German Brunswicker prisoners. When they found out that many citizens of the area spoke German, they took the opportunity to desert.

We arrived in Charlottesville on January 17 during a raging snowstorm. The prisoners are housed very near Monticello, Thomas Jefferson's home. Jefferson has often entertained General William Phillips, along with Baron and Baroness Riedesel. After one of their dinings, Jefferson sold a pianoforte to the Riedesels, because the baroness loved it so much. I am not sure how long I'll be here, but the task keeps one busy.

Sincerely, Ben

June 24, 1779
Dear Mr. Chaplin,

Since Savannah was captured, we've had a lot of action down here, including another attempt to capture Charleston. Soon after Savannah's capture, British general Augustine Prevost sent Lieutenant Colonel Archibald Campbell to Augusta, Georgia, capturing it on January 31. While there he sent Colonel James Boyd, a Tory from South Carolina who had joined the British, to the backcountry of North and South Carolina to recruit Loyalist troops.

As word got out that Boyd had a force of 700, Colonel Andrew Pickens with 250 South Carolina militiamen, decided to go after Boyd. Pickens was joined by another one hundred Georgia militiamen. On February 14, Pickens caught up with Boyd at Kettle Creek.[63] Pickens decisively defeated the Tories. The British deaths were forty to seventy, including Colonel Boyd. While lying mortally wounded, Boyd, also from South Carolina and knowing Pickens, asked Pickens if he would deliver a broach to his wife and tell her of his death. Pickens told Boyd that he would.

When General Benjamin Lincoln arrived, replacing General Robert Howe as Southern commander, he made his headquarters at Purrysburg, South Carolina. Soon after General John Ashe arrived from North Carolina, Lincoln sent him to repair the Freeman-Miller Bridge on Brier Creek.[64] Meanwhile, the British decided to abandon Augusta. While Ashe was encamped at Brier Creek on March 3, Lieutenant Colonel Mark Prevost's forces going back to Savannah made a surprise attack on Ashe. The Patriot losses were staggering, 150 killed and 227 captured. British losses were minimal. Speaking of prisoners, we've heard that most of the 200-plus prisoners taken at Savannah who were confined on prison ships have not survived.

---

[63] Near present-day Washington, Georgia.
[64] Near present-day Sylvania, Georgia.

In late April while Lincoln headed toward Augusta, General Augustine Prevost decided to make an attack on Charleston. As the British advanced, General William Moultrie fell back to defend Charleston. On May 11, the British were engaged in battle by Pulaski's Legion, who had been sent south by General Washington. Not only was the Legion thrown back, its colonel commandant, Michael Kovats, was killed. Prevost sent surrender terms to the citizens of Charleston. Moultrie, given overall command of Charleston, rejected the terms. On the twelfth, learning that Lincoln was approaching Charleston, Prevost withdrew his forces to James and Johns Islands.

On June 16, Prevost left with most of his forces back to Savannah. He left a rear guard force of nine hundred men under Lieutenant Colonel John Maitland. On June 20, Lincoln decided to attack the British at Stono Ferry.[65] Unfortunately, Lincoln, who used mostly militia troops, was no match for the Hessians and Scottish Highlander British forces.

Sincerely, Felix

July 4, 1779
Dear Father,

To celebrate the Fourth, we had a massive *feu de joie* at noon. Ever since the British took Stony Point in May, we've been busy building the Putnam Battery on part of what was Fort Montgomery. The battery is a watch point on the Hudson River for West Point. Even though we've been working hard, a few of us took the time to catch some turtles. We made turtle soup to help celebrate the Fourth. One of the turtles was filled with eggs. We hard-boiled them to add to the soup making it even more delicious. Topping it off, a friend had pilfered a bottle of sherry from a Loyalist farmhouse, which we used to garnish the soup.

By the end of the day, the joy had turned to anxiety. Word came in regarding a cavalry skirmish at Pound Ridge, New York,

---

[65] Near present-day Hollywood, South Carolina.

about twenty-five miles east on the Connecticut border. The British learned that the Second Continental Light Dragoons, also known as Sheldon's Horse, commanded by Colonel Elisha Sheldon, were at Pound Ridge. Also living nearby was local militia Commander Major Ebenezer Lockwood, who was wanted by British general Clinton.

Clinton sent Lieutenant Colonel Banastre Tarleton and two hundred of his British Legion to Pound Ridge to drive off Sheldon's Horse and to capture Lockwood. On his way, Tarleton asked a Loyalist for directions. While he was told to go south, Tarleton headed north. When he realized his mistake, he turned south. He was spotted by a vedette[66] posted by Sheldon. Having been warned by a Patriot spy about Tarleton, Sheldon posted vedettes and kept his men armed and horses saddled. When the vedette told Sheldon of approaching horsemen, he sent Major Benjamin Tallmadge to investigate and soon learned they were British.

Tarleton charged into Sheldon's encampment at Lockwood's farm. Sheldon, with only ninety men, had to retreat. As Tarleton's men were rounding up cattle, Sheldon doubled back with some militia and drove Tarleton off. Tarleton went to burn Lockwood's house, which was being used as a hospital, but the British surgeons protested. He told them to drag the wounded outdoors, searched the house, and then torched it. On the way back he torched the Loyalist's house for having given "wrong" directions. Nice guy, that Tarleton!

Our anxiety is caused by the fact that when Tarleton searched Lockwood's home, he found Tallmadge's saddlebags. Last year Tallmadge was made chief intelligence officer by General Washington. The bags included major correspondence with Washington about intelligence activities in New York with the Culper Spy Ring set up by Tallmadge and Washington. Washington suggested the name of Culper from Culpeper County, Virginia. Tallmadge directs several secret operatives in and around New York City.

Your son, Moses

---

[66] A mounted sentry or picket.

◈

July 16, 1779
Dear Father,

Last night and early this morning we had great excitement. We captured Stony Point! In May, the British garrisoned it with about six hundred men, including Loyalists, under the command of Lieutenant Colonel Henry Johnson. Stony Point is a rocky promontory along the Hudson River and becomes an island at high tide. The British built earthen flèches[67] and wooden abatis as their defense, calling it "Little Gibraltar." We watched the work from Buckberg Mountain.

In early July, Washington got a complete layout of the fortification. Captain Allan McLane knew a local lady who wanted to visit her two Loyalist sons. McLane disguised himself and under a white flag of truce went with her to the fort. While she visited her sons, he did his scouting.

Last night we attacked. I was with General Wayne, along with 750 others, going around the south. Colonel Richard Butler, with three hundred men, led the northern flank move. Neither of our outfits had powder or ammunition—only bayonets. We attached white pieces of paper to our hats to recognize each other in the darkness. Major Hardy Murfree, with 150 men, led a frontal attack on the center to divert attention from the flanking moves. It worked, drawing a British attack in which he repulsed and captured Johnson. However, the light from their cannon flashes from their flèche #1 exposed us.

Where we were headed, abatis extended into the river, and at the end they usually placed a gunboat. We got lucky. Being unseasonably cold due to northerly winds, their ship, the *Vulture*, moved down to Haverstraw Bay and the gunboat followed it. This allowed us to go around the abatis in boot-top water instead of having to chop through it. As we were charging in, General Wayne was knocked down by a shot to the head. It turned out to be only a slight wound.

---

[67] A fieldwork consisting of two faces forming a salient angle with an open gorge.

Washington had offered rewards for the first men into the fort. That honor went to Lieutenant Colonel Francois de Fleury. Being the first in, he rushed to the flagpole, cutting down the British colors. Peter Francisco was the second man in. We learned from the British after the battle that five of our deserters had told Johnson we were about to attack. Fifteen out of our 1,300 men lost their lives. The British had twenty killed, and we took over five hundred prisoners.

Your son, Moses

❦

August 16, 1779
Dear Uncle Eb,

I am writing this letter at sea, returning from a rescue mission to Fort George at Majabigwaduce[68] in the Maine district. On May 30, General Francis McLean, with seven hundred troops, was sent from Nova Scotia by General Henry Clinton to establish fortifications in the new province of New Ireland. In 1778, Lord Germain had ordered that a province be established between the Penobscot and St. Croix Rivers to be populated by Loyalists fleeing from their American homes. McLean's first duty was to build Fort George.

When the Rebels in Massachusetts got word, they decided to send a fleet to knock out Fort George. Sailing from Boston on July 19, the fleet of twenty-two transports, seven warships, and twelve privateers went to Penobscot under command of Commodore Dudley Saltonstall. The transports carried a 1,200-man landing force under command of General Solomon Lovell. Paul Revere was in charge of the artillery.

The fleet arrived on July 25. After some shelling, the troops stormed ashore on the twenty-eighth. Lovell's forces almost succeeded in taking Fort George until British ships opened fire. Over several days Lovell pleaded with Saltonstall to take out three Royal Navy sloops. Saltonstall refused. As a result, Lovell would not attack Fort George.

---

[68] Present-day Castine, Maine.

On August 3, we set sail with ten warships for Maine from New York under command of Vice Admiral Sir George Collier. We arrived in Penobscot Bay on the thirteenth. The next day the Rebel fleet went up the Penobscot River, running their ships aground and burning them. The infantry and marines abandoned their siege on the fort, escaping into the forest. Our losses were 25 killed and 34 wounded. McLean estimates the Rebel casualties were about 150.

With the number of troops on each side, it would seem the odds were in favor of the Rebels, especially since the fort was not yet completed when the Rebels arrived. I hope this will give the law-abiding residents of New Ireland greater confidence in their safety as they settle the area.

God Save the King, Zack

August 20, 1779
Dear Zack,

Thank you for your recent letter regarding Penobscot Bay. It's Interesting the Americans made another attempt in the Maine/Nova Scotia area. Except for the raid on Charlottetown, St. John's Island, by the Marblehead Regiment on November 17, 1775, none have been successful. Over the years, raids failed at Fort Cumberland and Liverpool, Nova Scotia.

Being my nephew, while it is upsetting that you remain a King's Friend, I do pray that you survive this conflict. But having said that, I must let you know my feelings on certain aspects of this struggle. The atrocities being inflicted on American soldiers by the Hessians described by you and Moses are horrifying.

It is not bad enough that Hessians are committing cruel tactics, but the policies carried out by Simcoe's Queen's Rangers and Skinner's Greens are as disgusting. The wanton slaughter at Quinton's Bridge and Hancock's Bridge and the burning alive of wounded soldiers at Crooked Billet can't be defended.

The British prison ships in Wallabout Bay at New York are a disgrace to mankind. It's bad enough that thousands of prisoners ·are crammed below decks, but to provide only starvation portions of food (and worse yet that rats are considered a delicacy) is appalling. Last year it took a woman—Elizabeth Burgin, who would bring food to the prisoners—to assist in an escape of two hundred prisoners. The British immediately put out a bounty of £200 for her capture. Thankfully she hasn't yet been apprehended.

In reporting the Battle of the Brandywine to me, you mentioned Sandy Flash was a guide for the British on Howe's flanking move. After the battle, Sandy went on a rampage against the Patriots. He was finally seized, attempting to rob a farmer. He was sentenced to hanging. When he was hanged, the rope was too long and the hangman had to jump onto his shoulders to "finish the job."

While the British occupied Philadelphia, I was continually on tenterhooks. Many taverns were taken over by the British to use as jails. I had to be very discreet during this time, because I feared that the Blaze Horse would be appropriated as a jail and I might be a prisoner in my own enterprise.

Sincerely and may God bless you, Uncle Eb

September 11, 1779
Dear Uncle Eb,

I read your last letter with great interest and heartfelt feelings. While I know you are disappointed that I have stayed loyal to the Crown, and while I cannot condone this rebellion, I respect the fact that you are striving for a new kind of governance in America. Since you made many comments, I am responding to them.

There is no way I can condone the atrocities of the Hessian soldiers. However, I wonder how it must feel to have been rounded up by your head of state, sold to another country, stuffed on ships like herring, being at sea for several weeks bound for an unknown land, and then be expected to be the "model warrior." Unlike the American or British soldiers, they are not fighting for a cause. Interestingly, the Hessian officers do not discourage looting because they feel it prevents desertion. You may not know it, but most of the British recruits are Irish or Scots, because the English feel as if they would be fighting their fellow countrymen.

You mentioned Simcoe and Skinner. While Cortlandt Skinner is a New Jerseyian and John Graves Simcoe is a British career officer, both are zealots for the Crown. The actions you described were gruesome, but in the hot action of battle, cruel results can and do occur.

I too hear of some bad conditions on prison ships. My understanding is that if a prisoner accepts the opportunity to join the British Navy, they will be released—so far no takers. The prison ships are criticized, but where are we to keep our prisoners? We do not have excess land to incarcerate them. Some have been sent to England. I know of Elizabeth Burgin. She came on board the *Jersey*, drugged a guard's beer, grabbed his keys, and freed the prisoners.

Uncle Eb, I was very aware of your situation during the occupation. When I left Boston, I was on General Howe's ship on our journey to Halifax. I got to know him. I told him that you were my uncle and if possible to have his soldiers frequent the Blaze Horse. You might remember that my friends Johann Ewald and Lord Rawdon frequented the Blaze Horse often. Both are very influential. I don't want to pat myself on my back, but I wanted you to know that I cared.

Sincerely, Zack

September 28, 1779
Dear Moses, Ben, Roelof, Teunis, and Felix,

Thank you Moses, Ben, Roelof, and Felix for the information you sent in your letters. It kept the patrons at the Blaze Horse well informed. Teunis, I haven't heard from you since Saratoga. I was wondering if you might be involved in the Sullivan-Clinton Expedition ordered by Washington against the Loyalists and Indians in upstate Pennsylvania and the heartland of New York State.

Moses, I was happy to hear that you escaped the raid on Stony Point unscathed. Your mention of the action at Pound Ridge by the Second Continental Light Dragoons reminded me that on August 13, 1777, they, under the command of Captain Jean-Louis de Vernejoux, performed the first cavalry charge on American soil at the Battle of the Flockey. That action put a big dent in the Loyalist activity in Schoharie County, New York.

Moses, you mentioned Benjamin Tallmadge and the Culper Ring. It was interesting to learn that Culper was derived from Culpeper County, Virginia. Roelof mentioned meeting John Marshall of the Culpeper Minutemen at the Battle of Great Bridge. And then you, Moses, mentioned John Marshall won all the races at Valley Forge. I'm not sure if you are aware of this. Washington wanted an invisible ink for his espionage work with the Culper Ring. Sir James Jay, who was knighted by King George III in 1763, invented a "sympathetic stain" for this work. Those corresponding were given two bottles of liquid. Liquid from bottle #1 was used to write the message. The recipient then used the liquid from bottle #2 to recover it.

Ben, your description of the march of the Convention Army from Cambridge to Virginia was interesting. I was sorry that you couldn't visit me at the Blaze Horse. Now that Roelof is back from his western excursion, perhaps the two of you can meet up. Roelof, your description of the capturing of Kaskaskia and Vincennes was almost too hard to believe. Getting a toehold in those territories may prove valuable if we are ever to convince the British to end this war.

Felix, while it was disappointing to hear of the fall of Savannah and Augusta, it was good to hear that once again we saved Charleston. I just wanted to tell you that I recently heard from Zack. He was on an expedition to Penobscot Bay, where the Brits chased out the Patriots.

We now have Spain officially on our side. They have been helping us over the years with powder and stores of clothing. They've given our merchant and privateer ships "most favored nation" status to use the port of Havana. On April 12, Spain and France signed the Treaty of Aranjuez, which joined Spain with France against Britain in our war for independence. Interestingly, King Carlos III of Spain is the cousin of French King Louis XVI's grandfather, King Louis XV. Yesterday the Continental Congress appointed President John Jay as minister to Spain. Samuel Huntington, of Connecticut, is our new president. John Jay and Sir James Jay are brothers.

On September 22, interesting news came to the Blaze Horse that Congress would award Major Light-Horse Harry Lee with a gold medal and $15,000 to be distributed among his men for his raid on Paulus Hook.[69] While it was a daring raid, I have not heard of recompense being awarded before for a specific action. After the raid on Stony Point, Captain Allan McLane obtained precise information from a British deserter on the fort at Paulus Hook, New Jersey, which had been evacuated by General Hugh Mercer after the fall of New York City in September 1776. McLane and Lee convinced Washington that they should storm Paulus Hook.

At 3:00 a.m. on August 19, Lee, with four hundred troops, attacked the fort with steel (bayonets and swords only). They easily overwhelmed the defenders. Lee intended to burn the barracks, but when he saw they contained many sick soldiers, women, and children, he decided not to. Being fearful of British reinforcements coming from New York, he decided to leave, even without spiking the cannons. Lee lost 2 men but captured 159 and killed or wounded 30.

Ben and Teunis, Benedict Arnold has been the talk of the town. He married Peggy Shippen on April 8. In February, Joseph Reed, presiding officer of the Supreme Executive Council of Pennsylvania, presented Congress with eight charges against Arnold. One of the charges was that he appropriated public wagons of the state for private use. In April, Congress threw out four of the charges but recommended that the other four be

---

[69] In present-day Jersey City, New Jersey.

turned over to a court-martial. The court-martial was scheduled to start on June 1, but Reed asked for a delay so he could prepare ·more evidence. It will be interesting to see what happens.

Sincerely, Eb Chaplin

October 10, 1779
Dear Uncle Eb,

When I got home, I saw your letter. Your thoughts were correct—I was on the Sullivan-Clinton Expedition. After Saratoga I was so hoping my fighting days were over. After the Cherry Valley massacre last November 11, I feared I might have to get back into action because of it and other Indian and Loyalist depredations. The massacre at Cherry Valley, New York, was led by the Loyalist Butler's Rangers, Joseph Brant, and Seneca Chief Cornplanter. They slew thirty, including women and children, and took another thirty into captivity.

When General James Clinton's portion of the expedition was formed, I decided to join. Clinton was part of a force to carry out Washington's order of May 31 to do battle against the hostile tribes of the Six Nations[70] and lay waste to their territories due to the massacres at Wyoming Valley and Cherry Valley. Because of a family tradition, I'm alive to tell you the story. Almost 150 years ago, my great-grandfather came from the Netherlands and settled near Schenectady to trap beaver. He married the daughter of a Mohawk chief. All these years our family has kept familiar with the Mohawk tongue. Initially it was to communicate with family members. But as conditions changed, it was prudent to understand the language of your potential enemy.

We left Schenectady, with one thousand under Clinton to rendezvous with General John Sullivan at the confluence of the Susquehanna and Chemung Rivers. We went to the headwaters

---

[70] The hostile tribes were the Seneca, Cayuga, Onondaga, and Mohawk allied with the British. The Oneida and Tuscarora were allied with the Americans.

of the Susquehanna, Lake Otsego. Since the Susquehanna is not navigable, we built a large dam at the lake to create a huge head of water. We also were busy building 250 batteaux to haul supplies down the river. When there was enough head of water, the dam was broken, providing river navigation.

Two of us volunteered to scout ahead of the troops. The second day out, we ran into a bountiful patch of wild raspberries. As we were gorging on berries, four Indians came upon us in surprise. Each of us had a rifle and hatchet. The Indians only had tomahawks. My partner, who survived the Cherry Valley massacre, wanted to immediately shoot two of the Indians and then fight off the other two with our hatchets. I begged him not to shoot. I noticed the Indian's headdress was three feathers up. I knew they were Mohawk. I also noticed they seemed to be nervous. I started talking to them in their tongue. They wanted to know why we were here. I told them we were scouting ahead of four thousand soldiers. I told them the soldiers were only a few hours behind and if they killed us, they'd be tracked down. They believed my tall tale and decided to leave. Had I not known Mohawk, I'm convinced both of us would now be ashes in some Indian camp.

On August 22, we got to Fort Sullivan.[71] With General Sullivan there were three other brigades: General Enoch Poor, New Hampshire and Massachusetts; General William Maxwell, New Jersey; and General Edward Hand, Pennsylvania. We left Fort Sullivan on the twenty-sixth with over four thousand men traversing up the Chemung River valley. On the twenty-ninth, we were near the Indian village of Newtown.[72] Colonel Daniel Morgan in the vanguard discovered the ambush laid by the Indians behind breastworks in a horseshoe shape. Behind these fortifications were 25 British Regular troops, 250 Butler's Rangers, and over 1,000 Indians led by Joseph Brant, and Seneca Chiefs Cornplanter and Sayenqueraghta.

Sullivan ordered an artillery attack. Along with Poor's men, we made an attack. For a while we were mired in a swamp. We were able to extricate ourselves but then were met by a counterattack by Brant. But when Lieutenant Colonel Henry

[71] Present-day Athens, Pennsylvania.
[72] Present-day Elmira, New York.

Dearborn came up, the counterattack was crushed. Our forces had eleven men killed. Their losses were also minimal, but they were forced off.

We then went on to the Finger Lakes area with a scorched-earth policy. We destroyed over forty Iroquois villages. We also destroyed 160,000 bushels of corn and a vast quantity of vegetables and fruit raised by the Indians for their winter food supply. The British will have to house and feed them over the winter. Won't they appreciate that? We got back to Fort Sullivan on October 3. A New Hampshire officer said, "The nests are destroyed, but the birds are still on the wing." If this is true, we will be facing more atrocities from the Indians.

I was glad to get home in time for the harvest. I would not like to have Sarah face that task alone once again. I don't think I've told you that Sarah and I have been blessed with a son, Jellis. I'm sick of this war. It's time to say, "Bye, George!"

Sincerely, Teunis

October 16, 1779
Dear Mr. Chaplin,

On September 3, some French ships arrived at Charleston with word that Admiral Comte d'Estaing was heading to Savannah from the West Indies. On the eleventh, General Benjamin Lincoln headed to Savannah from Charleston to link up with the French. Washington, in addition to sending Pulaski's Legion south, sent General Lachlan McIntosh down from Fort Pitt with his Georgia troops. After Valley Forge, Washington had sent him there as commander of the Western Department. In September 1778, he and General Andrew Lewis made the Fort Pitt Treaty with the Delaware Indian Nation. One of the proposals was that the Delaware Nation become the fourteenth state.

I went to Savannah with Lieutenant Colonel Francis Marion, whose plantation isn't far from Moncks Corner. On the way we were joined by McIntosh's Georgia troops. I formed a friendship with Major Samuel Emory Davis.[73] By the time we got to Savannah, d'Estaing had landed his troops. On the sixteenth, he offered British general Augustine Prevost the opportunity to surrender. Prevost wanted twenty-four hours to decide. It was nothing more than a delaying tactic so that his forces could build redoubts and other fortifications. It also gave British Lieutenant Colonel John Maitland time to bring his troops in from Beaufort, South Carolina.

On October 3, the French started an almost continuous bombardment of Savannah. On the sixth, Prevost asked that women and children be allowed to leave the city. D'Estaing, fearful of another delaying tactic, refused. That had to be sorrowful news for General McIntosh, whose wife and children were in Savannah.

Lincoln and d'Estaing decided to launch an attack the ninth. The main attack was against the Spring Hill Redoubt, thinking it was manned by Loyalist militia and could be easily overrun. The opening of the attack was eerie. As the French, including several hundred free Negroes from Haiti, charged, they shouted in unison, "Vive le Roi,"[74] while the Scottish troops played their bagpipes. Being in white uniforms, the French were easily picked off by the Loyalist riflemen. Admiral d'Estaing was wounded twice.

We, under McIntosh and Marion, went in to assist. Swedish Count Colonel Curt von Stedingk managed to plant a French flag on the redoubt, and one of our men planted a South Carolina flag. The British vigorously counterattacked. Seeing this, General Pułaski's Legion attacked. Pułaski was wounded by grapeshot. Bodies were piling up everywhere. Many French were impaled on the abatis surrounding the redoubt. A four-hour truce was called to bury the dead. Our combined killed and wounded came to almost nine hundred, while theirs were about fifty. General Pułaski was taken to the American privateer *Wasp*. A few days later, he died while clutching an icon of the Black Madonna of Częstochowa.

Sincerely, Felix

---

[73] He would father Confederate States President Jefferson Davis.
[74] French for "Long live the king."

·October 30, 1779
Dear Moses, Felix, and Teunis,

Teunis, I was astounded by your experience with the Mohawk Indians encountered on the Sullivan-Clinton Expedition. The fact that you know their tongue is remarkable after all the years that have elapsed since your Mohawk great-grandmother married your Dutch great-grandfather. The fact that you were able to convince them to leave you alone is even more amazing. While the expedition laid waste to so much Indian territory, we are hearing that General Washington is disappointed that the expedition did not take Forts Niagara and Oswego and that the indiscriminate ravages caused many Tuscarora and Oneida to defect to the British cause.

Felix, your report of the huge losses at Savannah makes this battle as bloody as Bunker Hill. I was glad to hear that you survived this bloodbath. The sad part is that now we have had two disappointments with the French—first at Newport and now at Savanah. I couldn't help but chuckle about your mentioning the Fort Pitt Treaty with the Delaware Nation. It was never acted upon by Congress!

Moses, back in 1775 when you were in Cambridge, you mentioned that Dr. Benjamin Church, a member of the Sons of Liberty, was found to be a spy. He has been held as a prisoner ever since. This is now old news, but in 1778, Massachusetts passed the Banishment Act that specified that three hundred people were not to return to Massachusetts. On the list were Dr. Church and former Royal governor Thomas Hutchinson. No problem for Hutchinson, because he is in England. Dr. Church was sent on a ship to Martinique. The ship never arrived. I suspect Dr. Church has become shark food!

Zack wrote about the Penobscot Bay fiasco. As a result of that adventure, Commodore Dudley Saltonstall and Lieutenant Colonel Paul Revere were court-martialed. Saltonstall was dismissed from the navy, but Revere won acquittal. Also, in 1778, despite an impassioned defense by John Adams, "Father of the Navy," Commodore Esek Hopkins was relieved of his command by Congress for going to the Bahamas instead of going after Lord Dunmore, as ordered.

On October 2, the Continental Congress adopted blue as the official color of uniforms. Up to this time the more common colors were brown or green, or simply buckskin. Some units even wore red!

Sincerely, Eb Chaplin

November 25, 1779
Dear Moses, Ben, Teunis, Roelof, Felix, and Zack,

I want to share some interesting news from a letter received in Philadelphia from Benjamin Franklin in Paris. On November 1, 1777, John Paul Jones left for France on the *Ranger* to bring news of Burgoyne's surrender to our delegation in Paris. In April 1778, Jones took a voyage into the Irish Sea. On the twenty-second, he raided Whitehaven. It has been some time since England has been "invaded." Then he went to Kirkcudbright Bay, Scotland, trying to capture the earl of Selkirk. All he got there was the earl's silver! On the twenty-fourth, he engaged HMS *Drake* off of Carrickfergus, Ireland. He captured the *Drake,* taking her to France.

Because of his exploits, Franklin convinced the French to give Jones a new ship with forty-two guns. Jones named her *Bonhomme Richard* in honor of Franklin's *Poor Richard's Almanack*. On August 14, 1779, she left France, capturing several merchant ships as prizes. Then on September 23, she came across forty-one ships laden with timber from the Baltic for English shipbuilders. The convoy was escorted by the 44-gun HMS *Serapis* under command of Captain Richard Pearson.

The battle started as a full moon was rising. The battle raged for several hours, with *Serapis* raking *Bonhomme Richard* with deadly effect. Jones decided to grapple the *Serapis*. When Pearson asked for surrender, Jones's reply was "Sir, I have not yet begun to fight!" Pearson tried to swarm *Bonhomme Richard* but was repulsed and surrendered at around 10:00 p.m. The *Bonhomme Richard* was damaged badly and eventually sank. Jones transferred his flag to *Serapis* and took her to the Dutch United Provinces.

This created a problem for Jones. The Dutch, at this time, do not recognize the United States. To avoid becoming a "pirate," the Dutch registered Jones's flag as a Dutch flag. This is rather ironic based on their previous action at Statia.[75] On November 16, 1776, when the *Andrew Doria*, carrying a copy of the Declaration of Independence, arrived at Statia, Governor Johannes de Graaff returned a salute to her from the cannons at Fort Oranje—the first foreign salute to our flag. There is a lot of trade with Statia—our tobacco and rice traded for Dutch powder, munitions, and tea. Franklin sends his mail through Statia, feeling it is a safer route.

Sincerely, Eb Chaplin

---

[75] Common name for Sint Eustatius, a Dutch island in the Caribbean.

Chapter Five

Kings Mountain was the joyful annunciation of that turn
of the tide of success which terminated the Revolutionary
War with the seal of our independence.
—Thomas Jefferson

In 1780, the British tried a new tactic. They decided to put in an all-out effort to take the southern colonies. In their third attempt of the war, they took Charleston. After taking Charleston, the British pushed across South Carolina, scoring bloody victories at Camden and Waxhaws.

South Carolina became a brutal, bloody civil war between Loyalists and Patriots. There were numerous battles, with mixed results. A turning point for the Patriots was their winning the battle at Kings Mountain, South Carolina.

In October 1780, the French arrived in Rhode Island with seven thousand troops. General Washington met with French General Rochambeau to discuss strategy. After his meeting with Rochambeau, Washington went to West Point, New York, to confer with American General Benedict Arnold. Arnold was not there—he had joined the British.

· December 25, 1779
Dear Uncle Eb,

A few months after returning from the operation at Penobscot Bay, I was involved in a mission to destroy Rebel boats and military supplies in New Jersey. On the night of October 26, we, the Queen's Rangers along with the Bucks County, Pennsylvania, Volunteers, under the command of Colonel Simcoe, went from Staten Island via Perth Amboy, New Jersey, to do the destruction. We also had word that New Jersey governor William Livingston was at the Middlebrook encampment. Livingston wasn't there, but we found out there were Loyalists imprisoned at Somerset Courthouse. We freed the prisoners, but on our way back to Perth Amboy we made a wrong turn and were headed to New Brunswick, where we ran into an ambush set up by the Middlesex County militia. Simcoe's horse was shot from under him and was taken prisoner by Colonel Armand. We managed to get out of there, but not before being pursued once again by the militia. During this chase, Captain Peter van Voorhees, of the New Jersey Continentals, joined in and was shot off his horse and then hacked to death by swords.

Back on June 30, General Clinton issued the Philipsburg Proclamation. It extended Dunmore's Proclamation issued in December 1775 in Virginia, which granted freedom to slaves in Virginia provided they were willing to serve the Royal Forces. Clinton's new document proclaimed all slaves in the newly established United States belonging to American Patriots free, regardless of their willingness to fight for the Crown. This ought to stir up quite a "hornet's nest" for the Rebels!

General Clinton has received orders from London to start a Southern campaign. He brought troops down from Newport, Rhode Island, here to New York to join a combined military and naval expedition to Charleston. The expedition includes over twelve thousand soldiers and sailors on ninety-troop ships and fourteen warships. Later on, Lord Rawdon is to join us with another 2,500 troops. Because of Simcoe's capture, the

Queen's Rangers aren't going on this voyage. I am with the Bucks County Volunteers. General Cornwallis, "Old Grizly," is on the expedition, along with John André, Johann Ewald, Patrick Ferguson, and Banastre Tarleton.

We leave tomorrow. Hopefully this Southern campaign will be successful so that we can end this disgusting, bloody rebellion against the Crown once and for all. Before I close, I want to say that I hope you and your family had a happy Christmas. I know Moses couldn't be with you, but I hope he too had a good Christmas.

God Save the King, Zack

April 1, 1780
Dear Uncle Eb,

As I mentioned on Christmas Day, I was leaving for Charleston, South Carolina, the next day. I had no idea how frightful the voyage would be. We soon ran into vicious storms, and by January 10 we were off the coast of St. Augustine, East Florida. Many horses suffered broken legs and had to be thrown overboard. Lieutenant Colonel Banastre Tarleton lost all of his horses. On some days because of the storms, sails were lowered and the rudders tied down, leaving us at the mercy of the ocean, but fortunately no ships collided. On January 24, we were back out into the Gulf Stream. By this time, General Henry Clinton was quite unhappy with Admiral Mariot Arbuthnot's capabilities.

Finally on February 1, we caught sight of the Tybee Lighthouse off of Savannah. On the fourth, Clinton put 1,400 troops ashore under General James Patterson to mount a diversion toward Augusta, Georgia. Lieutenant Colonel Tarleton and Major Patrick Ferguson were put ashore for the purpose of obtaining horses to replace those lost at sea. There was much discussion among Clinton's staff on how and where to land at Charleston. It was eventually decided to put the ships under command of Captain George Elphinstone, who had knowledge of the inlets south of Charleston. He did a superb job of getting the troop ships up the narrow inlets and past sandbars. We started disembarking on February 11 on Edisto Island. Captain Johann Ewald's jägers were the vanguard as we made our way to Johns Island and then to James Island. We encountered a Negro who volunteered to guide us. The problem is he spoke Gullah[76] and was difficult to understand. The malaria-ridden woods and swamps we traveled through were full of wolves, snakes, and poisonous insects.

At one point Ewald saw troops from Pulaski's Legion across a creek. Ewald thought he recognized an old friend from Germany with them, waved a white flag, and conversed with them. They told us to be careful of the alligators in the creeks. Unfortunately, a few Hessians did not understand and were dragged off by the gators. Meanwhile, the British troops were collecting livestock for food and Negroes for work detail. They were attacked by Chevalier Pierre-François Vernier, who was now leading Pulaski's Legion. The jägers managed to drive them off. Today we began building works on Charleston Neck for the siege of Charleston.

God Save the King, Zack

☙

May 1, 1780
Dear Moses, Ben, Teunis, and Roelof,

A few days ago General Benedict Arnold resigned as military governor of Philadelphia. His delayed court-martial finally met in December. On January 26, the court-martial threw out two charges and found him guilty on two others: (1) improperly issuing a safe-conduct pass for the schooner *Charming Nancy* and (2) imprudent use of army wagons for his own commercial trade. The verdict imposed a reprimand to be issued by General Washington. On April 6, Washington published

---

[76] An English-based Creole that is marked by vocabulary and grammatical elements from various African languages.

this formal rebuke of Arnold's behavior: "The Commander-in-Chief would have been much happier in an occasion of bestowing commendations on an officer who had rendered such distinguished services to his country as Major General Arnold; but in the present case, a sense of duty and a regard to candor oblige him to declare that he considers his conduct [in the convicted actions] as imprudent and improper." Apparently the rebuke led to his resignation.

After the court-martial, Congress made an inquiry into Arnold's expenditures. Arnold requested £10,000 in reimbursements of his personal funds, financing the Quebec campaign. Unfortunately, he could not produce receipts. Ben, you mentioned he lost his personal papers at the Battle of Valcour Island. Congress, instead of reimbursing him, ruled that he owed them $9,000. Even though he had a lot of Tory acquaintances, his lifestyle was more extravagant than expected as military governor. We heard in the Blaze Horse he once paid £1,000 for a pipe[77] of wine.

Roelof, your mission with George Rogers Clark, and Teunis, your being on the Sullivan-Clinton Expedition, will prove very beneficial once this war ends. The French ambassador warned Congress that unless we occupied the territories west of the Appalachian Mountains, they would not support our claim to them. That is one reason, Teunis, even though you got into New York's heartland, that Washington was disappointed about not taking Fort Niagara and Fort Oswego.

The Royal Navy has been engaging in unlimited search of neutral shipping for French contraband. Neutral countries were getting fed up with this policy, including Russia. In March, Czarina Catherine II of Russia issued a Declaration of Armed Neutrality, a basic doctrine of maritime law regarding neutral rights at sea during war. Sweden and Denmark-Norway soon joined to form the League of Armed Neutrality. Many French and Dutch ships are now entering our ports under the Russian flag.

---

[77] A pipe of wine holds 126 gallons.

I just received a letter from Zack. After surviving a harrowing trip, the British are now commencing a siege of Charleston. Let's hope General Lincoln can hold them off.

Sincerely, Mr. Chaplin

May 13, 1780
Dear Mr. Chaplin,

The past few months have been quite tough. First, we lost Savannah, and yesterday we lost Charleston. The Charleston affair went on for over a month. While I was in Charleston, I sadly learned that Tarleton attacked my hometown, Moncks Corner. However, I was fortunate to escape Charleston before the surrender.

While the British were attempting to get to Charleston, we were busy building fortifications, which included hornwork, bricks made of lime and oyster shells, on which to mount cannons. In front of each of these were two ditches, the outside one being protected by abatis. After the siege started, British sappers[78] were busily opening trenches toward the city. Before the British had Charleston surrounded, General Benjamin Lincoln requested the South Carolina government to arm Negroes to help defend the city. That request was flatly refused.

On April 8, Admiral Arbuthnot managed to get his gunboats in the harbor to shell us. On the tenth, General Clinton asked for surrender. General Benjamin Lincoln told him his duty was to resist. On the thirteenth, Lincoln wanted to evacuate. General Lachlan McIntosh was in total agreement. But Lincoln eventually decided not to evacuate because he believed Congress would want the city defended. Lincoln did advise Governor John Rutledge to leave.

---

[78] Soldiers digging trenches in a zigzag pattern toward the enemy's fortification to avoid enfilading fire form the enemy. The term "sapper" comes from the French *saper*, "to dig or to trench."

On the eighteenth, 2,500 more British troops arrived with Lord Rawdon, putting more pressure on us. On the twenty-first, Lincoln offered to surrender in return for the honors of war—defenders could leave the city with colors flying, bands playing, and bayonets fixed. Clinton refused. On the twenty-fifth, Lincoln again felt the city could not be held and an attempt should be made to get the troops out. Lieutenant Governor Christopher Gadsden and the Governor's Council threatened to open the city to the enemy if Lincoln attempted escape. On May 6, the British managed to drain the canal, allowing them easier entrance to the city. Then they began to fire hot shot, which started many fires. On May 11, Gadsden came to Lincoln, asking him to surrender on the best terms he could get. Clinton's terms were unconditional surrender.

Along with Generals Lincoln, McIntosh, and William Moultrie, Signers Thomas Heyward Jr., Arthur Middleton, and Edward Rutledge were taken prisoner. Gadsden was paroled to his house in Charleston.

Sincerely, Felix

May 26, 1780
Dear Father,

Our encampment this past winter was at Jockey Hollow, near Morristown, New Jersey. As you know, this was an extremely cold winter. Conditions were much worse than at Valley Forge. When we arrived in early December, there were several inches of snow on the ground. Through the winter we had over twenty snowfalls. We again built our sixteen-by-fourteen-foot cabins, each housing twelve soldiers. Because of the problems at Valley Forge, the cabins were built according to a precise plan developed by Baron von Steuben, which improved sanitary conditions. As a result, very few soldiers died of disease. Also, trees in the area were quite plentiful. General Washington made his headquarters in the Ford Mansion in Morristown. He was joined by his wife, Martha.

Food was a terrible problem. Some soldiers resorted to plundering for food and clothing. Those caught were whipped. While the locals favor our cause, they were reluctant to sell supplies to the army because of the devaluation of paper currency. (For example, when the officers wanted to hold a dance, they had to pay $13,600 for facilities and musicians, which would have cost $300 in silver. The cost of a horse is $20,000.) As a result, officers resorted to taking food and giving certificates to those not willing to sell.

One of the more frequent meals consisted of firecake made from buckwheat, rye, and Indian corn. We would sing at midday, "What have you for dinner boys? Nothing but firecake & water sir," and would sing at night, "Gentlemen the supper is ready. What is your supper lads? Firecake & water, sir." At other times some ate bark or even cooked leather boots. Sadly, any soldier who brought a pet with him soon lost it to the cook pot.

Our encampment is located about thirty miles from New York. From here we could keep watch on the British wintered around New York. Beacons were on hills surrounding the encampment so that the New Jersey militia could warn us of any British activity or excursions. When General Clinton left New York for Charleston, General von Knyphausen was put in charge. General Washington thought von Knyphausen would be more aggressive than Clinton. As a result, Washington had General Stirling attack the British early in the morning of January 15 with 2,500 soldiers in five hundred sleds. Unfortunately, the British were warned by Loyalists. Even though the attack was not successful, it must have had an effect because we were not attacked all winter.

As I mentioned earlier, we had a lot of snow. At times it was so deep the guard could not be changed. Besides the snow, it was so, so cold. We heard that New York Harbor was completely frozen over with ice several feet deep. On March 27, Washington held a council of war to consider whether or not to send troops to Charleston, which was under attack by the British. The vote was a unanimous "no."

We did have some diversions. General Washington declared St. Patrick's Day a holiday. Some say it was in deference to the large force of Irish American soldiers in camp. On April 19, the new French ambassador Chevalier de la Luzerne and Juan de Miralles visited. Miralles is a Spanish arms dealer and royal commissioner to Congress sent by King Carlos III of Spain. He has been very helpful getting uniforms, rifles, gunpowder, flour, and other food supplies from Cuba. General von Steuben organized a massive parade and fireworks display for the foreign dignitaries. Sadly, Miralles became ill and passed away on the twenty-eighth.

On May 10, we got some exciting news. General Lafayette arrived in Boston on *L'Hermione* returning from France. Since he left in late 1778, he worked with Ben Franklin to obtain additional aid from the French. He reported that six thousand French soldiers would be sailing to America under command of General Jean-Baptiste de Rochambeau. Maybe this will help us to finally say, "Bye, George!" He also reported that this past December, his wife, Adrienne, had given birth to a son. I should also mention that in January, General Greene's wife, who accompanied him in camp, also presented him with a son.

Yesterday was a very tense day. A number of Connecticut soldiers attempted to start a mutiny because of bad conditions. Colonel Return J. Meigs, of Connecticut, and Colonel Walter Stewart, of Pennsylvania, managed to convince them that conditions were no worse for them than for any other soldier and were able to quell the mutiny.

Today had been designated as the day of execution for those charged with crimes in the camp. Three were to be executed by firing squad, and eight were to be hanged. Those to be hanged were standing under their gallows when a pardon was granted to all eleven criminals by General Washington.

I am not sure what will happen next; however, I am certain that soon the British will be up to something.

Your son, Moses

·June 1, 1780

Dear Uncle Eb,

After a rather tranquil year in Virginia guarding the Convention Army, I have been suddenly thrust back into the thick of battle—worse than Bunker Hill. Guard duty can be quite boring, but when the German prisoners found out I was a cordwainer, I was kept busy. They are paid well and needed shoes after the long march from Massachusetts. It was a good way to make some extra cash. I had another special treat: being introduced to pawpaw fruit. It has yellow-green skin and soft orange flesh with a creamy, custard-like consistency and a delicious, sweet flavor.

All this peacefulness came to an end in April when I joined the Virginia troops under Colonel Abraham Buford, former leader of the Culpeper Minutemen. Our mission was to assist in the defense of Charleston. On May 6, we got to Lenud's Ferry,[79] South Carolina, on the Santee River, no more than twenty miles from Felix's home. Across the river the dragoons of Lieutenant Colonel William Washington and Lieutenant Colonel Anthony Walton White were encamped. At about 3:00 pm., Lieutenant Colonel Banastre Tarleton and his British Legion attacked the unsuspecting dragoons. All we could do was watch the slaughter. We heard later eleven dragoons were killed and sixty-seven captured. Washington and White escaped by swimming for their lives. When news arrived that Charleston surrendered, we were ordered by General Isaac Huger to retreat to Hillsboro, North Carolina.

On our way to Hillsboro, the British learned that Governor John Rutledge, who had fled Charleston, was traveling with us. British general Cornwallis ordered Tarleton to overtake us and capture Rutledge. On the twenty-eighth, warned by an old friend Henry Rugeley, now a Tory, Rutledge left us, taking a different route. On May 29, near Waxhaws,[80] as Tarleton was pursuing

---

[79] Near present-day Jamestown, South Carolina.
[80] Near present-day Lancaster, South Carolina.

us he sent a message requesting Buford to surrender. Buford rejected by saying he would "defend to the last extremity."

We formed a line of defense as Tarleton's cavalry charged. Our orders were not to shoot until the horsemen were ten to thirty yards away. That order did not allow us time to get off a second shot before they were upon us. The dragoons were riding over men and hacking with their sabers. Buford hoisted a white flag. At this point Tarleton's horse was shot from under him, and his men went crazy. As our men were surrendering, no quarter was given by the dragoons. Wounded men and men with their hands raised in surrender were slaughtered. I never ran so fast in my life and managed to get away with about one hundred others. Our losses were 113 killed, 150 wounded, and 53 captured. Their losses were 5 killed and 12 wounded. I am happy to be alive in Hillsboro.

Sincerely, Ben

❧

June 4, 1780
Dear Uncle Eb,

It was a long siege of Charleston beginning on April 1. At first Clinton tried desperately not to bombard too heavily, because he wanted the support of the citizens. We were getting bombarded with scrap iron and broken glass. Clinton had to resort to red-hot shot, which started many homes to catch on fire in the city.

Finally, on May 11, we heard the drums beating a parlay. In the parlay negotiations, General Clinton would not allow General Benjamin Lincoln to surrender with the honors of war. On May 12, General Lincoln surrendered Charleston. We took over three thousand soldiers, along with three signers of the Declaration of Independence, and Generals Benjamin Lincoln, Lachlan McIntosh, and William Moultrie as prisoners. The soldiers were immediately confined to prison ship hulks. Slaves taken by the British from the citizens of Charleston were sent to the West Indies for sale.

As we were laying siege, Clinton had Tarleton patrol the countryside around Charleston to cut off lines of communication. On April 12, Clinton ordered Tarleton to take Moncks Corner, where General Isaac Huger was positioned with five hundred men, keeping open an avenue of communication and an escape route to the interior from Charleston. At 3:00 a.m. on the fourteenth, Tarleton attacked and completely surprised the Rebels. General Huger and Lieutenant Colonel William Washington managed to escape. Major Vernier asked for quarter but instead was sabered to death. A big prize was 184 horses, of which 82 were trained cavalry mounts. Major Ferguson was with Tarleton and was so enraged by the actions by some of Tarleton's dragoons that he wanted them lined up and shot. Lieutenant Colonel James Webster intervened and had the men sent to Charleston, where they were whipped.

On April 18, Lord Rawdon arrived with an additional 2,500 troops, which further helped our cause. General Clinton decided to return to New York. He has turned command over to General Earl Cornwallis, who is also to set up a chain of supply depots. He appointed Ferguson inspector of militia in South Carolina. His mission is to recruit Loyalist militia in the Carolinas and Georgia and to intimidate any colonists who favor American independence. I'll be leaving for New York tomorrow.

God Save the King, Zack

June 25, 1780
Dear Father,

As I mentioned in my last letter, we expected some action from the British. It came quickly on June 7. During the night of the sixth, over five thousand troops, under command of General von Knyphausen, boarded boats on Staten Island, crossing the Arthur Kill[81] to Elizabeth, New Jersey. We learned later their goal was to attack

---

[81] Arthur Kill separates Staten Island from New Jersey. It's an anglicization of the Dutch name of *Achter Kill,* meaning "Back Channel."

our encampment by coming up through Hobart Gap. General von Knyphausen had received word that our forces were much smaller than they were, that morale was low, that several mutinies had taken place, and that the locals would offer no resistance.

As the sun arose on the seventh, the British encountered a small group of New Jersey militia and quickly drove them off. At around 8:00 a.m., General Maxwell met the British at Connecticut Farms.[82] Eventually the British drove Maxwell's men toward Springfield. Late in the day General Washington and his force of over 150 Life Guards arrived. That night the British, upon hearing that numerous New Jersey militia units were assembling, decided to withdraw. Upon leaving Connecticut Farms, the British set fire to numerous houses. Tragically Hannah Caldwell, the wife of Army Chaplain Reverend James Caldwell, was shot and killed inside her home.

We moved out of our Jockey Hollow winter quarters on the twenty-second. On the twenty-third, we were once again attacked by von Knyphausen. Washington had left General Nathanael Greene in charge. Greene placed Colonel Elias Dayton and Colonel Israel Angell to defend Springfield on the left on Galloping Hill Road and placed Lee's Legion to defend Springfield on the right on Vauxhall Road. At the Galloping Hill Bridge, Angell's artillery was running low on wadding.[83] At this point Chaplain Caldwell brought up a load of Watts Hymnals from his Presbyterian church, telling them to use the paper from the hymnals for wadding and shouting, "Give 'em Watts, boys!"

Recognizing that Angell's men could be surrounded, Greene ordered them back to Springfield. Meanwhile, as Lee's men were slowly retreating, Greene sent General John Stark with four hundred reinforcements. That action, along with New Jersey militia streaming in, caused von Knyphausen to call off the attack and return to Elizabeth. As he withdrew, he burned every house in Springfield, except for four belonging to known Loyalists.

Your son, Moses

---

[82] Present-day Union Township, New Jersey.
[83] Material used in guns to seal gas behind a projectile or to separate powder from shot.

❦

June 26, 1780
Dear Uncle Eb,

On the seventeenth, I was among the troops returning to New York with General Henry Clinton from Charleston. The trip was nothing like going there last December, which lasted over a month with ferocious seas. We left on the fifth, taking just twelve days coming back.

When Clinton heard that General von Knyphausen made an assault against the Rebels on June 7, he was outraged. However, von Knyphausen convinced Clinton that an attack on the Rebels could be successful because word was out that General Washington had taken a large number of troops to resupply West Point. A battle plan was put into place for the twenty-third.

Clinton sent General Alexander Leslie with six thousand men up the Hudson River to prevent Washington from doubling back if he got word of the British attack on Jockey Hollow. General von Knyphausen, with another six thousand men, would take the route through Springfield on to Hobart Gap toward Jockey Hollow. We, the Queen's Rangers, along with the New Jersey Volunteers, also known as Skinner's Greens, were in the vanguard. We easily overwhelmed the Rebel outpost at Elizabeth.

Skinner's Greens couldn't make headway at Connecticut Farms. We made a flanking move and drove the Rebels out. We were then diverted by von Knyphausen to Vauxhall Road toward Springfield. There we encountered Major "Light-Horse Harry" Lee and his Legion. We managed to initially drive them back, but their fire from the woods gave us great difficulty. That is where I took a ball in the left bicep. While it was very painful and badly bleeding, we got help from another New Jersey Loyalist unit and managed to drive Lee's men back. As we were driving them back, General Stark appeared with four hundred reinforcements. In addition, more New Jersey militia units were flooding in. With that, von Knyphausen decided to withdraw back to Elizabeth.

We got back to Staten Island, crossing on a bridge made of boats. Our casualties, of whom I am one, were over three hundred killed, wounded, or captured. I pray that my wound will be treatable so that my arm will not have to be amputated.

God Save the King, Zack

❦

July 14, 1780
Dear Mr. Chaplin,

After the surrender of Charleston, Lieutenant Colonel John Moore, a commissioned British officer from North Carolina, went back to his area to recruit Tory forces. The news of the British victory at Waxhaws further buoyed his efforts. In June, he managed to assemble over one thousand Tories at Ramseur's Mill.[84] With that gathering of Tories, Colonel Francis Locke collected about four hundred militiamen from several North Carolina counties. At daybreak on June 20, even though highly outnumbered, Locke decided to attack. After a hot battle, many of the Tories ran off. Only a few managed to join Moore on his escape to Lord Rawdon at Camden.

Upon hearing of this I decided to go north to join Colonel Thomas Sumter, who was elected as commander in chief of South Carolina militia. He is known as "The Gamecock." Back in 1762, he traveled with three Cherokee Indian chiefs to London. He served as their interpreter at their audience with King George III. Sumter's plantation was burned to the ground by Banastre Tarleton in May.

On the night of July 11, Mary McClure arrived at Sumter's camp after a thirty-mile horse ride to tell her father, Captain John McClure, that Captain Christian Huck, with 150 British Loyalists, came to their home and that her brother, James, was tied up awaiting execution. A little later Colonel William Bratton's slave, Watt, sent by Bratton's wife, Martha, arrived, telling Bratton that Huck was at their home, where Huck

---

[84] Present-day Lincolnton, North Carolina.

threatened to cut Martha's throat with a reaping hook. With that we raced for the Tory camp. We learned Huck's men were encamped at Williamson's Plantation.[85] We got there at first light on the twelfth. Huck had no patrols out or any pickets posted. We crept up, and when the British troops called out for us to disperse, we blistered them with our rifles. Huck, along with thirty-five Tories, was killed. We also rescued prisoners from a corn crib who were slated for execution. Several of the Tories captured were hanged. One, however, was not when Martha Bratton identified him as being the man who saved her from having her throat cut by Huck. Mr. Chaplin, you may know Christian Huck, his being a Philadelphian. He may have frequented the Blaze Horse.

Just today we heard some more good news. Jane Thomas was at Ninety Six, visiting her husband, when she overheard that Major Patrick Ferguson was going to send a detachment to Cedar Springs,[86] where her son, Colonel John Thomas Jr. was encamped with the 1st Spartan Regiment. She quickly rode sixty miles to warn her son. Thomas and his men kept their campfires going while they concealed themselves in a nearby woods. The 150 Tories arriving early on the twelfth, thinking they caught the Patriots wrapped in their blankets, were met with a blaze of fire from the woods. Those who weren't killed fled.

Sincerely, Felix

❧

August 3, 1780
Dear Father,

Today General Benedict Arnold arrived at West Point to take over its command. Washington considers this an extremely important strategic fortress on the Hudson River. After Arnold's resignation as military governor of Philadelphia, Washington asked Arnold to take a field command. Word is that Washington

---

[85] Present-day McConnells, South Carolina.
[86] Near present day Spartanburg, South Carolina.

was astonished when Arnold asked for command of West Point instead. On June 29, Washington agreed to Arnold's request.

You may recall I told you that when General Lafayette returned from France, he indicated the French were going to send thousands of troops to our aid. On July 10, Admiral Chevalier de Ternay arrived with 5,500 troops at Newport, Rhode Island. The French had a code name for this undertaking: *Expédition Particulière*. The troops are under the command of General Rochambeau. Unfortunately, another 2,500 troops did not get here, because they couldn't escape the British blockade at Brest, France.

Soon thereafter the Culper Ring learned that British general Clinton was going to launch an attack on the French at Newport. When the Culper Ring sent a message to Washington's headquarters of the British plan, Washington was not in camp. Fortunately, Captain Alexander Hamilton had access to the "stain" and decoded the message. Immediately, General Lafayette was sent to warn General Rochambeau of a planned attack by the British. When Washington learned of this, he sent out "secret papers" indicating that he was planning an attack on Clinton in New York City. As expected, the "secret papers" were intercepted by the British, and the attack on the French was called off.

You may remember that I mentioned that Washington's Life Guards saved the day at Springfield. Officially they are called the Commander-in-Chief's Guard. They are an elite bunch. Each man has to be between five feet eight inches and five feet ten inches. They are decked out in splendid uniforms. Their coats are dark blue, faced with white. Waistcoat and breeches are white. They wear dark blue dragoon helmets with a white feather with a royal-blue tip and a white cockade.[87] They have a special flag. The flag is white with Lady Liberty leaning upon the Union shield, handing the commander in chief's flag (blue with thirteen six-pointed stars) to a Guard holding his horse. Above Lady Liberty and the Guard is a ribbon with the motto of "Conquer or Die." I am convinced the motto came from the

---

[87] A knot of ribbons, or other circular- or oval-shaped symbol of distinctive colors, which is usually worn on a hat.

Bedford flag, which had the motto *"Vince aut Morire,"* meaning the same in Latin.

Speaking of flags, the 1st Pennsylvania Rifles, commanded by General Edward Hand, have quite a unique and colorful standard. It is a dark green flag, with a red insert in the middle. On the red portion is a hunter with a spear directed at a tiger partially ensnared in a net. At the bottom of the standard is the motto *"Domari Nolo"* ("I refuse to be subjugated"). Hand's men are good to know. They hail from Conestoga Valley in Lancaster, Pennsylvania. Most have a good supply of cigars from Conestoga, which they call "stogies." Most of us chew tobacco, but their "stogies" are a real treat.

General Washington has two horses: Nelson and Blueskin. Nelson is a light sorrel with a white face and white legs. Nelson is his battle horse. Blueskin is a light bluish gray, almost white. Because Blueskin is skittish under fire, the general uses Blueskin for ceremonies.

I also want to tell you about drummer boys. They are very young but provide a very useful service. Their uniforms are the opposite of the fighting troops. For example, if the troops have blue uniforms with red facings, they have red uniforms with blue facings. That is to signal the enemy they are drummers, not armed men. Because of the noise in battle, they beat out different tattoos as command signals, such as attack, speed up, slow down, withdraw, cease fire, or parlay. They also carry a cat o' nine tails[88] in a bag. Since the drummers are to report infractions to officers, they will be taunted by the soldiers "to not let the cat out of the bag."

Being a city boy, I am learning from the country lads some neat things. For instance, when I have a headache or other type of pain, I've learned to chew on willow bark to obtain relief. And since we cannot get real tea, we use a plant called New Jersey tea as a substitute. Now that the goldenrods are in bloom, we use their flowers as tea—a nice change of taste.

Father, some of us have been wondering why the French and Spanish are assisting our cause. Because of having fought the

---

[88] A type of multitailed whip used as an implement to inflict severe physical punishment.

French in the French and Indian War, it is puzzling to us. We would appreciate if you could help us to understand.

Your son, Moses

⁶⟋⟍⁹

August 7, 1780
Dear Mr. Chaplin,

After defeating Huck at Williamson's Plantation, I remained with Sumter's men. Being a farrier, I am kept busy shoeing horses. Most of our men are mounted so that they can do hit-and-run tactics, easily travel long distances, and be able to retreat quickly if things turn out nasty. Because many of the battles can result in saber fights, the men need head protection. As a farrier I am very familiar with many blacksmiths and have decided to make horsemen's caps for the mounted militia.

The first step is to get a block of wood turned so that it fits on one's head. Then leather would be shaped on the "cap," greasing it with tallow and turning it before a fire until it becomes almost as hard as a sheet of iron. Then two small straps of steel are attached—one reaching from ear to ear and the other in the opposite direction. They are then lined with strong cloth padded with wool. A small brim is attached to the front and bearskin applied to the length of the cap. Then the cap is decorated with horsehair, white feathers, and deer's tails. It is heavy to wear but effectively protective.

On July 28, we headed to Waxhaws to join Major William Richardson Davie's North Carolinians. On the thirtieth, Sumter and Davie decided to attack two British outposts set up by Lord Rawdon: Rocky Mount[89] and Hanging Rock.[90] It was decided that Sumter would attack Rocky Mount, while Davie would create a diversion at Hanging Rock. I rode with Davie and eighty others. Before we got to the British encampment of five hundred men, we noticed Loyalist-mounted infantry bivouacked at a house outside

---

[89] Near present-day Great Falls, South Carolina.
[90] Near present-day Heath Springs, South Carolina.

the main encampment. Since we were dressed similarly to the Loyalists, we rode casually toward the house unchallenged past their sentries, dismounted, and opened fire. As the Loyalists fled, they ran right into dragoons sent around back by Davie. They were hacked up pretty good. So as not to impede our getaway, we took no prisoners but obtained sixty horses.

When we rejoined Sumter, we found out that his attack with six hundred men on Rocky Mount was unsuccessful. Only 150 New York Volunteers, under command of Lieutenant Colonel George Turnbull, were well fortified in three log buildings with firing loopholes surrounded by a ditch and abatis. Without artillery, Sumter could not dislodge them. The fortifications were set on fire but were extinguished by a heavy rainstorm.

With Davie knowing the layout of Hanging Rock, Sumter decided to attack on August 6. When we got there, Davie suggested we tie our horses and approach by foot. Sumter overruled him, saying we would ride in, dismount, and attack. The plan was for a three-pronged attack (left, center, and right), but in the confusion we all attacked on the left. The defenders included Banastre Tarleton's British Legion and "Burnfoot" Brown's Rangers. However, neither Tarleton nor Brown was present. Upon our attack, the Loyalists fled. Sumter's men soon were plundering, especially the rum, which led to many becoming drunk. As things were coming to an end, we were attacked by the British Legion, but without Tarleton we drove them off. The Tory losses were over two hundred, while we had twelve killed and forty wounded.

While Davie was at Waxhaws, he met a thirteen-year-old who told him that he and his mother tended to the wounded after the battle. His name is Andrew Jackson. Davie gave the boy a pistol and made him a mounted orderly or messenger for which he was well fitted, being a good rider and knowing all the roads. Davie is heading back to North Carolina. He vowed he would never again serve under Sumter, because his corps suffered much while tying their horses under heavy fire from the Tories. Sumter can inspire passion in his troops, but his leadership, I feel, is not sound.

When British general Clinton took over Charleston, he proclaimed that all colonists would be granted protection by the British upon the condition they would not fight against them. Before he left for New York he modified the proclamation that beginning on June 20 they would have to take an oath to promise to fight for the British when called upon. If not, they would be treated as enemies. That revision created quite a partisan rally, sending many men to join Sumter's forces. Even Chief New River, with his Catawba Indians, joined Sumter.

I mentioned in a previous letter that Captain Christian Huck was killed in our battle at Williamson's Plantation. When we were encamped at Waxhaws, we heard a horrific story about him. Two days after the Battle of Waxhaws, Huck was patrolling the area for resistors to the Crown. They accused a young Quaker, Samuel Wyly, of being in the militia at Charleston. Wyly produced his parole papers. Huck refused to recognize the parole and held a trial. The jury consisted of three Loyalist militiamen and three of Huck's junior officers. Wyly was sentenced to be drawn and quartered. After they finished, the different parts of his body were set up on pikes along the road as a warning to others.

Before Clinton left for New York, he also appointed Major Patrick Ferguson inspector of militia in South Carolina. As a result he has been actively recruiting Tories. On August 1, a detachment of Ferguson's men attacked Colonel Elijah Clarke's Georgia militia at Green Spring.[91] Clarke's men drove them off and inflicted major casualties, driving survivors back to Ferguson's camp. I've decided to venture over to the area where Ferguson is working to assist the partisans in their efforts. While there I can shoe horses and make horsemen's caps.

Sincerely, Felix

❧

August 15, 1780
Dear Moses, Ben, Teunis, Roelof, and Felix,

Moses and his friends were wondering why the French and Spanish were assisting us. I thought the rest of you may have

---

[91] South of present-day Spartanburg, South Carolina.

had the same question. But before I go into that, Ben, I could hardly believe the story you told about your trying to surrender at Waxhaws and that Tarleton's British Legion would give no quarter. I also got a letter from Zack telling me he got back to New York from Charleston in mid-June and just a week later he was wounded in his left bicep at the Battle of Springfield.

With the fall of Charleston and the capturing of General Benjamin Lincoln, Congress named General Horatio Gates to command the Southern Department on July 13. General Washington lobbied for Nathanael Greene to be named. However, Congress had a bad taste for Greene because of his protest to Congress in 1777 when French army officer, Philippe Charles Tronson du Coudray, was given the rank of general. The problem occurred because Congress made General Coudray senior to Generals Greene, Knox, and Sullivan. That was solved when du Coudray drowned in the Schuylkill River in September 1777! Visiting the Blaze Horse, General Charles Lee, upon hearing of Gates's assignment, warned of Gates: "Take care lest your Northern laurels turn to Southern willows."

At first blush it seems odd that France and Spain would support us. They are predominantly Roman Catholic; we are predominantly Protestant. They are monarchies; we are rebelling against a monarchy. Spain could also be wary of designs we might have on her North American colonies. However, both lost heavily in the Seven Years' War fought around the globe (called the French and Indian War in North America). In North America, France lost Canada, and Spain lost Florida. They are motivated by revenge against the British for those losses.

Initially their assistance was covert. In 1775, Spain supplied gunpowder to Charleston. Silas Deane and Benjamin Franklin worked closely with French Foreign Minister Comte Vergennes and continued to obtain military supplies. In 1776, Pierre Beaumarchais formed a French company, Roderigue, Hortalez et Compagnie, financed by one million livres each by France and Spain to conduct the covert aid. By 1777, France had supplied five million livres in aid, mostly gunpowder. Franklin's popularity in Paris, as well as our victory at Saratoga, convinced the French to formally ally with us. Eventually Spain agreed to join France.

Congress recently named former president Henry Laurens as minister to the Dutch Republic. His main task is to obtain a loan from the Dutch for $10 million. The Dutch too have been aiding us, mainly through the use of their port in Statia.

I hope this helps in answering your question why France and Spain are actively helping us.

Sincerely, Eb Chaplin

❧

August 20, 1780
Dear Mr. Chaplin,

It didn't take long after I left General Sumter before I became engaged in quite a hot battle. North Carolina Colonel Charles McDowell's scouts learned that two hundred Tories were encamped at Musgrove's Mill[92] on the Enoree River. Soon we had a force of over two hundred men under command of Colonel Isaac Shelby's "Overmountain Men" from Watauga[93] (who on July 30 had captured Thicketty Fort[94] and all ninety-four Tories without firing a shot), Colonel Elijah Clarke's militia from Georgia, and Colonel James Williams's militia from South Carolina.

We rode all night on the seventeenth to get to the Enoree using the cover of darkness and the coolness of the night for benefit of our horses. We did not even stop to let the horses drink. At the break of day on the eighteenth, we arrived. Our attempt at surprise was thwarted when we ran into an enemy patrol. We also received unsettling news from a local man who told us that the previous day, two hundred New Jersey and New York Volunteers, along with one hundred South Carolina Royalists, arrived from Ninety Six under command of Lieutenant Colonel Alexander Innes. Now we were facing five hundred men instead of two hundred.

---

[92] Near present-day Cross Anchor, South Carolina.
[93] A trans-Appalachian region of North Carolina that is now part of Tennessee.
[94] Near present-day Gaffney, South Carolina.

The commanders decided they had no choice but to attack. After our horses were sent to the rear with guards, the commanders had us form a semicircle of three hundred yards, crossing the road that led to Musgrove's ford. In a half hour we raised breast-high works composed of brush and downed logs. Shelby was in overall command. His men were on the right, with a reserve of forty men kept in the rear, Clarke was on the left, and I was with Williams in the center.

We used an "old-as-war" tactic of sending a group of troops, led by Captain Shadrach Inman of Georgia, toward the Tory encampment crossing the Enoree. They, of course, retreated while firing as they were chased back by the Tories. When the Tories were within 150 yards, they opened fire but overshot us. At seventy-five yards, Shelby gave the signal to fire. It was explosive, but the Tories would not be stopped, and they then charged with bayonets. Most of our men did not waver and, indeed, counterattacked with shrill Indian war cries. We were able to force them back. They had a heavy loss of officers, including Lieutenant Colonel Innes, who was shot off his horse. Their losses were sixty-three killed, ninety wounded, and seventy captured, almost half of their men. Four of our men were killed, including Captain Inman.

We were so euphoric after the battle that we planned to go on to attack Ninety Six. But as we were about to head out, a courier arrived with the news that General Gates was defeated at Camden. We were advised to get out of this area. As part of my flight, I am on my way back toward home to join up with Colonel Francis Marion.

Sincerely, Felix

August 21, 1780
Dear Uncle Eb,

I must be one lucky guy. I survived Bunker Hill, then Waxhaws, and on the sixteenth the Battle of Camden. A few weeks after we got to Hillsboro from the Waxhaw massacre, General Johann de Kalb arrived with Continental troops from Maryland and Delaware. I became friends with Captain Peter Jaquette of the Delaware Blues. They were a lively group, dancing around the campfire to music of fiddles while everyone else was tired out and asleep. After a few days we moved our encampment to Buffalo Ford on Deep River.[95]

Soon thereafter I was pleasantly surprised when Felix arrived with Colonel Francis Marion. De Kalb sent Marion out to scout for intelligence and supplies. Felix is very active with the South Carolina partisans. Felix, being a farrier, told me he is kept busy not only fighting but putting his profession to advantage because the partisans are primarily mounted warriors.

On July 25, General Horatio Gates arrived to take over command of the Southern Department, relieving General de Kalb. I was extremely disappointed. De Kalb was well liked, and I couldn't forget that Teunis told me at Saratoga how horribly Gates treated General Benedict Arnold. We were joined by General Richard Caswell with his North Carolina militia and by General Edward Stevens with his Virginia militia. We were also joined by Colonel Armand's Legion and seventy mounted South Carolina Volunteers. When Colonel William Washington arrived with his cavalry unit, he was sent off, with Gates telling him he didn't feel cavalry would be of use in the South. On the twenty-seventh, we hurriedly started on our way to Camden, South Carolina. We were promised there would be ample supplies of food and rum rations. On our march we passed right by Waxhaws—foreboding memory.

Soon Marion rejoined us, but Gates sent him off too. Then General Thomas Sumter convinced Gates to let him have four hundred of Gates's troops to raid a British supply convoy on its way to Camden from Ninety Six. We found out later that on the fifteenth, Sumter's men captured supplies at Carey's Fort and Wateree Ferry.

On the fifteenth, not far from Camden, alongside the Great Wagon Road,[96] we rested to eat before we were to commence a

---

[95] Near present-day Ramseur, North Carolina.
[96] A road stretching 730 miles from Philadelphia, Pennsylvania, to Augusta, Georgia.

night march at 10:00 p.m. There was very little meat. We were served a mush mixed with molasses and a gill of molasses as a substitute for the rum we didn't have. I was wise enough not to take any molasses. I was afraid of the consequences. Those who did take molasses suffered all night with the "trots."

At 2:00 a.m., Armand's Legion ran right into Tarleton's Legion, scouting ahead of General Earl Cornwallis's British forces of 2,200. After a brief skirmish, we rested on our arms until dawn. During the predawn hours, Gates was deciding what to do. Gates thought we had seven thousand men. Colonel Otho Holland Williams, on Gates's staff, reported, after getting counts from the commanders, we had three thousand. With Gates's astonishment at the number, he called a council of war. No one spoke until General Stevens advised "now to do anything but fight!" Gates deployed us Continentals under de Kalb on the right, Caswell's North Carolina militia in the center, and Stevens's Virginia militia on the left. Gates, having been a British soldier, should have known the British always deploy their strongest, most experienced troops on the right. Incredibly, Gates deployed his weakest troops against their strongest!

Cornwallis deployed Lord Rawdon's Volunteers of Ireland, backed up by Tarleton's Legion, on the left, artillery in the center, and Lieutenant Colonel James Webster on the right. During the battle, Williams was relaying messages to Gates, well in the rear. Meanwhile, we could plainly see Cornwallis in the thick of action. When Webster attacked the Virginia militia, they ran. We almost threw Rawdon's men back, but when the Virginia militia ran, Webster turned left, throwing back the North Carolina militia and our forces. General de Kalb received eleven bayonet wounds. When Tarleton circled around our rear, we had to get out of there. Fortunately, we escaped via a swamp where Tarleton's horse couldn't follow.

Colonel John Eager Howard led us to Charlotte through swamps and forests. General Gates rode off on his fine steed, making it to Hillsborough, 170 miles away, in three days! On his flight he encountered Major William Richardson Davie and then General Isaac Huger coming with troops. Davie wanted to engage Tarleton, but Gates called out that Davie should retire to

Charlotte. When Davie asked Huger if he should follow Gates's orders, Huger told him, "Do as you please, you'll never see him again." We lost 250 killed (none were of Virginia militia who ran) and 700 wounded, who were all captured. We Continentals and the North Carolina militia took the heaviest losses. We later learned the British had 68 killed and 256 wounded. We also heard that when General Cornwallis came upon General de Kalb, he had him taken to Camden on a litter to care for his wounds. He died three days later.

Tarleton was relentless in his pursuit. At Rugeley's Mills[97] he and Armand's Legion had a skirmish, but Tarleton prevailed. When I got back to Deep River, I was glad to see that my friend Peter Jaquette had also escaped. He told me that the Delaware Blues lost one-quarter of their troops. He also told me they were named for the Blue Hen gamecocks used in cockfighting.

On the Braddock campaign during the French and Indian War, Gates was wounded but carried off by another British soldier before he was scalped. Right now, because of this horribly mismanaged engagement resulting in so many deaths, I regret the Indian lost his quarry.

Sincerely, Ben

September 29, 1780
Dear Mr. Chaplin,

Getting back to join Colonel Marion was quite tricky. British Major Patrick Ferguson was roaming about northwest South Carolina and into North Carolina. Banastre Tarleton's British Legion was working north central South Carolina after the Battle of Camden. When I safely reached Marion, he told me that the British had burned his home. I also learned that on the same day I was at Musgrove's Mill, Lieutenant Colonel Banastre Tarleton, with 160 men, attacked General Thomas Sumter as his 800 men were swimming and drinking in their camp at Fishing

---

[97] Near present-day Westville, South Carolina.

Creek.[98] Sumter got away but lost 150 killed and wounded, with 300 captured.

After Camden, on August 20, Marion found out the British were holding prisoners at Great Savannah.[99] Marion attacked the camp, releasing about 150 Continental soldiers. Astonishingly, eighty-five refused to follow him, insisting they be allowed to go on to the prison ships at Charleston. Eventually all but three of those who followed him deserted.

Early on September 3, one of Marion's scouts reported that Major Micajah Ganey, with 250 Loyalists, were close by. Early on the fourth, fifty-three of us set off, putting white cockades in our hats to be able to distinguish each other in the heat of battle. Our advance guard encountered fifty of Ganey's mounted troops, killing or wounding thirty, driving off the rest. As we continued, we were met by two hundred infantries. Marion, knowing he was outnumbered, had us retreat and set up an ambush at Blue Savannah.[100] The Tories were taken completely by surprise and ran into a swamp.

British general Cornwallis put Major James Wemyss in charge of clearing up eastern South Carolina of Rebel sympathies. He has been on a rampage of burning, hanging, and slaughtering farm stock. Marion decided we should get out of the territory for a spell and hide in swamps in North Carolina near the border. Wemyss's barbarity has men joining Marion.

On September 28, after having been back in South Carolina a few days, we received news that Colonel John Coming Ball, with forty-five Loyalists, was at Red House Tavern on Black Mingo Creek.[101] We decided on a surprise night attack. However, when a sentry heard our horse's hooves as we crossed a bridge, surprise was lost. We expected Ball would fight from the tavern. But with the sentry's warning, Ball had his men in a field. As we got to within thirty yards of the Tories, they opened with a blaze of fire. Some of our men fell back from the shock but soon were moving forward again. This attack routed them, with

---

[98] Near present-day Great Falls, South Carolina.
[99] Today beneath the waters of Lake Marion in South Carolina.
[100] Near present-day Rains, South Carolina.
[101] Near present-day Rhems, South Carolina.

most escaping into a swamp. Today Marion announced that in the future, blankets will be used to cover the bridge's planks for any further bridge crossings. By the way, Colonel Ball is the brother-in-law of former Continental Congress president Henry Laurens. Since Ferguson is causing a ruckus up in North Carolina, Colonel James Williams is rounding up South Carolinians to assist the "overmountain" men. I am going up to join them.

Sincerely, Felix

❧

October 2, 1780
Dear Father, Teunis, and Ben,

Today I witnessed the hanging of the wrong man. British general Clinton's chief intelligence operative, Adjutant General John André, was hanged today as a spy. It should have been Benedict Arnold swinging from the gallows.

On September 24, General Washington—going back to his headquarters in Tappan, New York, after having met in Hartford, Connecticut, on the twentieth with French General Rochambeau—decided he'd inspect West Point to see how General Benedict Arnold was coming along there. He sent Major James McHenry ahead to let Arnold know he was coming and that he desired breakfast for his staff. When Washington got to West Point, neither Arnold nor his wife, Peggy, were there to greet him. Washington was upset by the lack of respect shown by Arnold's absence and further upset by the fort's appalling disrepair.

As Washington was preparing for dinner, with still no sight of Arnold, Alexander Hamilton handed him a packet of letters. After skimming through the letters, he sent Hamilton at full speed down the river. The letters had been retrieved from John André's boot the day before when he was apprehended by three "skinners" as André was attempting to get back to General Clinton in New York after meeting with Arnold at West

Point. The packet included a plan of the fortifications of West Point, an American engineer's analysis of how to defend the fort, and a copy of the secret minutes of General Washington's last council of war. When Hamilton returned, he did not have Arnold in custody but did have a letter from Arnold addressed to Washington composed before he escaped down the Hudson River to the British. In the letter, Arnold revealed he felt a sense of injustice that had been festering longer than his war wounds. He also requested Washington to provide safe passage of his wife, Peggy, to her family in Philadelphia.

The man the "skinners" apprehended identified himself as John Anderson, having a pass signed by Benedict Arnold. They decided to take "Anderson" to the military post at North Castle, New York. "Anderson" there convinced the commander at Tarrytown—Colonel John Jameson, a former Culpeper Minuteman—to send him back to Arnold at West Point. However, Washington's chief of intelligence, Benjamin Tallmadge, offered intelligence to Jameson that a high-ranking officer was planning to defect to the British. As a result, "Anderson" was detained, but a messenger was sent to West Point to tell Arnold they were holding a prisoner.

When Arnold learned of "Anderson's" arrest, he bade farewell to his wife, rushing to a barge where he ordered its crew to take him, under a white flag of truce, to the British ship *Vulture*, which sailed down the Hudson River to British headquarters. He told the crew that if they too defected he would obtain promotions for them in the British Army. They all refused. When they reached the *Vulture*, Arnold had the entire crew taken prisoner.

"Anderson" was taken by Tallmadge to Colonel Elisha Sheldon, whereupon André revealed his true identity and mission. Washington convened a board of senior officers to investigate the matter. The presiding officer was General Nathanael Greene, along with fourteen others, including Generals Lord Stirling, Marquis de Lafayette, Robert Howe (who also sat on Arnold's court-martial), Baron von Steuben, Henry Knox, John Glover, Edward Hand, John Stark, and James Clinton. On the twenty-ninth, the board found André guilty of being behind American lines "under a feigned name and in a disguised habit" and ordered that "Major André ought to be considered as a Spy from the enemy and that agreeable to the law and usage of nations, it is their opinion, he ought to suffer death."

When André was sentenced, he requested that, being an officer, he be executed by a firing squad. Washington refused his request but did not tell André, who would find that out as he was led to the gallows, whereupon he said, "I am reconciled to my death, but I detest the mode." André would not let his executioner, a Tory prisoner who would be paid for his work with his freedom, to place the noose around his neck. André did this himself and then tied a handkerchief over his eyes and produced a second handkerchief for tying his hands behind his back. Asked if he had any last words, André said, "Only bear witness that I died like a brave man." The wagon was suddenly pulled away as we watched in silence.

Hamilton and Lafayette so well liked André that they pleaded with Washington that he not be hanged. Our feeling is that Washington wouldn't relent because he was so highly offended at the way the British dealt with Nathan Hale. Apparently Clinton offered a prisoner exchange for André. When Washington demanded Arnold, the deal was off.

We learned from Tallmadge that soon after Arnold was put in command of West Point, Arnold approached him, asking for a list of his spies in New York. Tallmadge, working directly for Washington, would not divulge the names to Arnold.

Sincerely, Moses

❧

October 3, 1780
Dear Uncle Eb,

I am sure you remember my bringing along a very personable young man, Major John André, to the Blaze Horse. Sadly he was hanged by the Rebels yesterday, accusing him of being a spy.

André was captured while returning to New York City from West Point with important papers General Benedict Arnold was sending to General Henry Clinton. With all the humiliation Arnold received after his heroic exploits at Quebec City, Valcour Island, Danbury, and Saratoga, being investigated by Congress and then court-martialed, Arnold made a decision to "come over" to the king's side.

In late 1779, Arnold toyed with the idea of coming over. Discussions took place between André and Arnold. As you know, Arnold's wife, Peggy, was acquainted with André. He also broached the subject with Colonel Beverly Robinson of the Loyal American Regiment, who was so instrumental in taking Fort Montgomery. After he resigned as military governor of Philadelphia, the British convinced Arnold to lobby for commander of West Point. Gaining that strategic position on the Hudson River would be quite a grand prize.

Arnold and Clinton couldn't agree on a price. On August 15, Clinton made a final offer of £20,000 but no indemnification for losses, and a commission of brigadier general. Arnold accepted on the thirtieth. André was sent to West Point and met with Arnold on September 21. On the way to West Point, André had met with Robinson, who warned him about trusting himself to the honor of a man who was seeking to betray his country. André was supposed to come back via ship, but a mix-up resulted in his coming overland, resulting in his capture.

When Clinton heard that André was on trial as a spy, he was extremely disheartened to learn that André was in civilian clothes. Clinton had given specific orders that André remain in British uniform. If he had been apprehended thusly, he would merely have been a prisoner of war. When Robinson learned that André was captured, he personally appealed to Washington for his release. Robinson and Washington well knew each other in Virginia before Washington chose to abandon the Crown. Because the plot failed, Arnold's remuneration was reduced to £6,315, £500 for Peggy, and £360 pension for life. Today the Queen's Rangers were instructed to wear a black-and-white feather in their hats to honor Major André. I'm hoping Clinton succeeds in his effort to induce more generals to come over. By the way, I have fully recovered from my wound at Springfield.

God Save the King, Zack

~

October 8, 1780
Dear Mr. Chaplin,

On October 6, we got to the Cowpens, a space, owned by a Loyalist, used as a staging area by farmers getting their cattle ready for market. While at camp, word came in from a spy that Ferguson was six miles from Kings Mountain, where he planned to make his stand.

After the Battle of Musgrove's Mill, Ferguson sent a direct message to Colonel Isaac Shelby warning overmountain men to desist from rebellion or he would bring fire and sword down on them and hang their leaders. When Colonel Isaac Shelby received this threat, he, along with Colonel John Sevier, organized militia units from Watauga. As news of the threat spread, Colonel William Campbell (a brother-in-law of Patrick Henry) from the overmountain section of Virginia also formed a militia. As they crossed over the mountains from Sycamore Shoals, they encountered "shoe-tongue" depth snow.

When we got to the Cowpens, Shelby, Sevier, and Campbell were there, along with militia units from North Carolina led by Colonel Charles McDowell, Colonel Benjamin Cleveland, Colonel Joseph Winston, and Major William Chronicle. Colonel James Williams, Colonel Edward Lacey of South Carolina, and Colonel William Candler of Georgia were there too.

Kings Mountain was shaped like a foot. It ran 600 yards southwest (the heel) to northeast (the toes) and had varied widths of 60 to 120 feet. It had a spring to supply Ferguson's troops with water. The top was mostly cleared, because the locals had used it for years as a deer hunting camp. Its sides were rock strewn and heavily wooded. Ferguson moved in with about one thousand men. He especially valued the one hundred rangers of his Provincial Corps.

They were well trained and could be depended upon in heavy fighting. There were three outfits in his Provincial Corps: King's American Regiment (New York Loyalists), New Jersey Volunteers (New Jersey Loyalists), and the Queen's American Rangers (Loyalists from Connecticut, New York, and New Jersey). The rest of his force included North and South Carolina militia Loyalists. His second in command was Captain Abraham DePeyster of the King's American Regiment. He also brought to the mountain his two girlfriends, Virginia Sal and Virginia Paul.

Since this Patriot army was made up of many militia units, a leader was needed. Colonel William Campbell was selected as the leader. The commanders made a selection of nine hundred of the fittest and fastest mounted men. These horsemen, followed by eighty-five foot soldiers, left the Cowpens at 9:00 p.m. on a rainy October 6. On the way, a Loyalist courier, who had a note from Ferguson to Cornwallis requesting aid, was intercepted. When we arrived about a mile from the ridge, we halted and hitched our horses. We then proceeded on foot to encircle Ferguson's force. Before forming up, Campbell made the rounds of each corps. His message was plain: anyone not wishing to fight should immediately leave for home. No one left. He told them when the center columns were ready for attack, the signal would be an Indian-type war whoop. The center would consist of Campbell and Shelby; the right Sevier, McDowell, and Winston; and the left Williams, Chronicle, and Cleveland.

At 3:00 p.m. on October 7, we were at the base of Kings Mountain. The Loyalists fired the first shots when they spotted Shelby's approaching column. Shelby instructed his men not to fire. Then minutes later, Campbell ordered, "Shout like hell and fight like devils." The battle was on. The approach had been so fast that Ferguson's men were caught by surprise. Our approach was aided by the wetness of the ground, which muffled footsteps. We used the trees and rocks to our advantage. As the battle began, the Patriots noticed a lady on horseback riding down the mountain. Shouts went up to "let the lady pass." It was Virginia Paul. She was returning from delivering chickens to Ferguson's men. Under interrogation she told us that Ferguson could be recognized because he was wearing a red-and-white checkered shirt over his uniform.

Soon after our initial onslaught, DePeyster ordered a bayonet charge. At first, some fell back but eventually regrouped to repel it. The Loyalist forces were at a disadvantage because they were shooting downhill and thereby would often shoot over our heads. Ferguson was charging around the mountaintop, giving commands with his silver whistle. He had two horses shot from under him. At one point, DePeyster suggested surrender. Ferguson retorted that he "wouldn't yield to such a damned banditti." As Loyalists raised white flags, Ferguson slashed them out of their hands with his sword.

Knowing what Ferguson was wearing, he was simultaneously hit by eight shots from Sevier's sharpshooters. He fell from his horse, catching his spurs in the stirrup. He was carried away by four Loyalist soldiers and laid on a blanket, where he expired. Virginia Sal, who died early in the battle (her beautiful red hair probably made her an easy target), was laid beside him. Now DePeyster waved the white flag of surrender. Many of us ignored the white flags. Remembering what happened at Waxhaws where Tarleton gave no quarter, we were yelling we're giving "Tarleton's Quarter." Many of the surrendering men asking for quarter were killed. Eventually Campbell got control of the men, and the butchering of Loyalists stopped. The 65-minute battle was over. We had 28 fatalities, sadly including Colonel Williams. The wounded numbered 64. The Loyalists had 157 fatalities, 163 wounded, and 698 taken prisoner, including Virginia Paul. As I was departing to return home, some Loyalist prisoners were being put on trial. I'm not sticking around to see what transpires. More than likely they'll all be sentenced to be hanged.

Sincerely, Felix

❦

October 20, 1780
Dear Uncle Eb,

I was devastated by Moses's letter telling of the "going over" of General Benedict Arnold. As you know, I went with him on the expedition up through Maine to Quebec, and I was with him to help build a navy used at Valcour Island. I personally had great respect for him. In addition, I think of his bravery at Danbury, his impact on lifting the siege of Fort Stanwix, and his heroic leadership at Saratoga. When I read about the court-martial in Philadelphia, I didn't make much of it, thinking it was more of a political spectacle than a serious charge.

Ever since General Gates ran away from us soldiers after the Battle of Camden, we have been virtually leaderless. Fortunately, the militias are very active in fighting the British. On September 5, William Richardson Davie was named colonel commandant of all cavalry in the Western District of North Carolina. On September 8, British general Charles Cornwallis brought his troops to Waxhaws. Davie decided to take on the British Legion with a night march on the twentieth. However, when he got near the British encampment, he learned the Legion had relocated. On the morning of the twenty-first, he found them at a plantation owned by one of his men, Captain James Wahab. Major George Hanger was in charge of the Legion, because Banastre Tarleton was ill. The attack was very successful. Over twenty of the Legion were killed, and ninety-six horses were taken, which enables all of Davie's men to be mounted. Sadly as they left, Wahab's Plantation[102] was set ablaze.

On the twenty-fourth, scouts found that General Cornwallis was moving his forces to Charlotte. On the twenty-sixth, Davie had his men at the Charlotte Courthouse hidden behind a stone wall. From three hundred yards away, the bugle sounded the charge as Hanger's (Tarleton was still ill with yellow fever) Legion mounted an attack at full gallop, Tarleton style. Davie's men waited until the Legion was within sixty yards before delivering a crushing volley. The Legion formed again for another attack. With another well-directed barrage, they moved off in confusion. General Cornwallis then ordered Hanger to attack again. After receiving withering fire, they wheeled off behind houses. By now the British infantry was in earnest attack, and feeling he could hold no longer hold out, Davie ordered a retreat.

---

[102] Near present- day Van Wyck, South Carolina.

We received another bit of good news recently when we found out that militia groups from several areas slaughtered Ferguson and his Loyalists at Kings Mountain. We are all hoping that General Gates will be replaced. That would be really exulting news.

Sincerely, Ben

October 23, 1780
Dear Moses, Ben, and Uncle Eb,

Moses, when I received your letter about Benedict Arnold "going over," I exclaimed to myself I could have told you so. At Fort Ticonderoga in May 1776, I was telling Ben that Colonel John Brown told me he felt that Arnold would sacrifice his country for money, that Arnold had deserted in the French and Indian War, and that Arnold threw a fit after Colonel Hinman arrived to command Fort Ticonderoga after the raid with Ethan Allen. On the other hand, I remember Arnold coming to lift the siege of Fort Stanwix and his heroic leadership at Saratoga. By the way, we learned that soon after General Philip Schuyler resigned from the Continental Army, the British offered him a command. He indignantly refused.

I was truly saddened to learn that Major John André had been executed for spying. I met him when he became a prisoner after the surrender of Fort Saint-Jean in November 1775. Besides being so personable, he was so talented. He could draw, paint, sing, and write verse. He was a very talented mapmaker. He was fluent in French, German, and Italian.

This fall has been a nightmare in the areas north and west of our farm. Major Christopher Carleton executed a Burning of the Valleys raid out of Fort Ticonderoga. In 1778, he raided the east side of Lake Champlain. This time it was on the west side with not only his British Regulars, but with assistance from Loyalists, Hessians, Indians, and John Enys's Rangers. He captured Fort Anne, Fort George, and Fort Edward.

Meanwhile, Sir John Johnson, with his King's Royal Regiment of New York and Indians, was destroying the Schoharie Valley. The Schoharie Valley had been supplying eighty thousand bushels of wheat to Washington's army. On October 17, Johnson attacked Middle Fort.[103] Making no progress, Johnson sent forth a truce party. When Tim Murphy, who shot General Fraser at Saratoga, fired a shot over their heads, Johnson decided to withdraw.

On the nineteenth, Johnson had a battle at Stone Arabia,[104] where my friend Colonel John Brown was killed. Uncle Eb, after Fort Ticonderoga was taken in 1775, Ethan Allen sent John Brown to Philadelphia to inform the Continental Congress. Perhaps he stopped by the Blaze Horse.

Sincerely, Teunis

December 26, 1780
Dear Mr. Chaplin,

It looks like Virginia has ducked another British bullet. Soon after I arrived back from Vincennes, the first bullet hit when the British sent Admiral George Collier from New York. He arrived on May 9, 1779, at Portsmouth. After capturing Fort Nelson and its supplies of artillery, he destroyed it. Then after burning 137 vessels at Hampton Roads and torching the shipyards at Suffolk and Gosport, he returned to New York within a fortnight. His leaving left a bad taste for the Loyalists, who were hoping he'd stay to assist them.

Our second bullet hit when General Alexander Leslie arrived this last October 21 with 2,200 men. This came as a complete surprise to Governor Thomas Jefferson, who had advised Congress that it didn't seem probable that the British would come to Virginia again. What he seemed to forget is that

---

[103] Near present-day Middleburgh, New York.
[104] Near present-day Canajoharie, New York.

the British saw Virginia as a vital supplier to our forces in the Carolinas.

As a precaution, Jefferson sent the British prisoners at Charlottesville up to Maryland. He left the Brunswicker prisoners in place, because he didn't feel they'd rejoin the British. The seat of government had been moved farther inland from Williamsburg to Richmond. When the British didn't move out of Portsmouth, Jefferson warned Maryland governor Thomas Sim Lee that a British deserter reported that Leslie was planning to attack Baltimore.

To our great relief, General Cornwallis ordered Leslie to Charleston to assist in his efforts in the Carolinas. On November 15, Leslie left Portsmouth without taking hundreds of slaves who'd fled their masters in return for their promised freedom. After Leslie left, Jefferson ordered General Peter Muhlenberg to disband the 4,000-militiamen force he'd organized. Based on rumors that the British may be sending another force to Virginia, I hope that doesn't come to haunt us.

Since I've returned to Boyne Manor, it's been difficult from an economic sense. Virginia produced one hundred million pounds of tobacco. Because of the British blockades ruining the market, production is down to two million pounds. We've turned to corn, wheat, and cotton to help supply soldiers. The problem is we're being paid with state certificates that at this time are impossible from which to collect.

Here's wishing you a belated happy Christmas, Roelof

January 1, 1781
Dear Uncle Eb,

Happy New Year! I am sharing peach brandy with friends in celebration. We are not only celebrating the New Year, but more importantly that General Nathanael Greene was sent down here to lead the Southern Department. Greene arrived in Charlotte, North Carolina, on December 2. On his way down from Philadelphia, he stopped to plead with Governor Thomas Jefferson to supply provisions. Jefferson told him that Virginia was impoverished and couldn't provide aid. Baron von Steuben, who accompanied Greene from Philadelphia, stayed in Virginia to forward reinforcements and supplies. Further, on the way he had the Dan, Catawba, and Yadkin Rivers totally reconnoitered by Lieutenant Colonel Edward Carrington, Colonel Tadeusz Kościuszko, and General Edward Stevens.

I was especially happy to see General Daniel Morgan arrive on December 3. I know him well from the Quebec Expedition in 1775. Teunis spoke highly of his actions at Saratoga. Supplies were in great need. Greene managed to convince Colonel William Richardson Davie to serve as his commissary general. Davie protested that he knew nothing of money and accounts. Greene said not to worry since there was no money for which to account!

Greene sent a note to General Marion requesting that he provide intelligence regarding any troop movements of General Cornwallis from Charleston. Greene requested a meeting with General Sumter, who refused even though Governor Rutledge sent a carriage for him.

On December 4, Morgan sent Colonel William Washington with eighty dragoons to Rugeley's Mills[105] to investigate intelligence of 114 Tories encamped there. When he got there, all the Tories were in a barn and could not be dislodged with musket fire. Washington then had his men make a fake cannon out of a pine log and move it into position. Washington then asked Colonel Henry Rugeley to surrender. Upon seeing the "gun," all surrendered.

Greene decided to move the army out of Charlotte. Some went east with him to Cheraw, South Carolina, and the rest of us went west with General Morgan to Grindal Shoals.[106] While there, Morgan heard that Colonel Thomas Watts and his Loyalist Georgia militia were destroying Patriot settlements. On December 29, Washington found the Tories at Hammond's

---

[105] Near present-day Westville, South Carolina.
[106] Near present-day Jonesville, South Carolina.

Store.[107] Washington killed or wounded one hundred men, took forty prisoners, and captured fifty horses without a loss of life. We are constantly getting reinforcements: General Andrew Pickens, South Carolina; General William Lee Davidson, North Carolina; and Colonel Elijah Clarke (though because of wounds couldn't come himself), Georgia.

Hopefully this will be the year when we can finally say, "Bye, George."

Sincerely, Ben

⁓

January 8, 1781
Dear Uncle Eb,

In late December, General Clinton asked General Benedict Arnold to lead an expedition to invade Virginia. We left New York on December 20 with 1,600 men, half of whom were army and the other half navy. We were out to sea only a few days when we were hit with terrific storms. To lighten the load to prevent our sinking, the ship with cannons dumped several overboard. The horses panicked on another ship, resulting in forty of the one hundred being led overboard.

While Arnold was the lead commander, the navy was overseen by Captain Thomas Symonds. Traditionally, naval forces are allowed to keep as "prizes" any bounty captured from enemy vessels. Arnold thought this unfair and proposed that the prizes be split evenly between the army and navy.

Along with me are old friends, Captain Johann Ewald and Colonel John Graves Simcoe. After Arnold came over, he was busy recruiting deserters. I've come to know John Champe, who deserted from Lee's Legion in October. Both Clinton and Arnold hold him in high esteem. Ewald is not fond of Arnold. He told me that Clinton gave a secret order to Simcoe and Colonel Thomas Dundas that they were to take command upon Arnold's death or "incapacity." Does Clinton not trust Arnold?

---

[107] Near present-day Joanna, South Carolina.

On the thirty-first, we landed at Newport News and marched to Hampton with little resistance. Then we sailed up the James River. On January 3, we reached Hood's Point, where we expected a stout defense. We quickly dispatched the defenders to reach Westover Plantation, where Arnold established headquarters. Westover is owned by Mary Willing Byrd, a cousin of Arnold's wife, Peggy. Mary Byrd's[108] brother is Thomas Willing, one of the Pennsylvania delegates who voted against the Declaration of Independence. While there we satiated our appetites by butchering many cattle. The neighboring plantation, Berkeley, owned by Signer Benjamin Harrison, was put to the torch.

On the fifth, we raided Richmond, Virginia's new capital. Again we met little resistance. We were hoping to capture Thomas Jefferson, but he managed to run away. We did enjoy the fine wine and Antigua rum that we found in Jefferson's house. Arnold wrote a letter to Jefferson, saying that if he could move the city's tobacco stores and military arms to his ships, he would leave Richmond unharmed. Jefferson answered on the sixth with a livid refusal. Richmond was then set ablaze, a weapons foundry blown up, and many slaves taken. Today we are back at Westover.

God Save the King, Zack

January 15, 1781
Dear Moses, Ben, Teunis, Roelof, and Felix,

Teunis, you asked if I remembered John Brown and John André. I sure do. Brown was sent to Congress by Ethan Allen to report the taking of Fort Ticonderoga in 1775. While in Philadelphia, he took meals at the Blaze Horse. I knew John André well. He planned the *Mischianza* in honor of General Howe. Felix, you asked if I knew Christian Huck. During the British occupation of Philadelphia, he often came to the Blaze Horse to spout his Loyalist feelings. After the British evacuated, his property was

---

[108] A descendant of hers was Richard E. Byrd, who was the first to fly over the South Pole in 1929.

confiscated. Felix, you also mentioned the barbarity of Major James Wemyss. When he was in the Blaze Horse he told me he'd been slightly wounded at the Battle of Brandywine.

Felix, I was delighted to hear your report on Kings Mountain. Not since Saratoga have we heard such inspirational news. When Thomas Jefferson heard it, he made the following statement: "Kings Mountain was the joyful annunciation of that turn of the tide of success which terminated the Revolutionary War with the seal of our independence." I hope he is correct with such a strong testimonial.

As I previously wrote, former president Henry Laurens was sent to the Dutch Republic to enlist further aid. He had in his possession a proposed treaty. His ship was captured off Newfoundland by the British. Even though he threw all his papers overboard, the British retrieved the proposed treaty. As a result, Great Britain declared war on the Dutch Republic and imprisoned Laurens in the Tower of London.

After the fall of Charleston, we had some Loyalist activity in Sussex County on the Delmarva Peninsula. Loyalists down there are known as "refugees." The "refugees" cause havoc on those supplying Patriots and don't hesitate to supply the British. They were active in supporting Lord Dunmore before he was chased out of Virginia in 1776. Sensing a possible British victory when Charleston fell, they started the Black Camp Rebellion. Delaware militia General John Dagworthy was sent in to put it down. It will probably be the only action he'll see. He wanted to be a general in the Continental Army. But because he disputed the authority of Washington in the French and Indian War, his request was declined by Washington.

Costs of this war are getting way out of control. The current rate for a horse is $20,000. A pound of pork costs £8. It takes 22,000 pounds of pork, 40,000 pounds of flour, 1,800 gallons of peas, and 1,800 pounds of butter to feed 110 soldiers per year.

In November, two generals captured at Saratoga, Baron Friedrich Riedesel and William Phillips, were exchanged for General William Thompson, captured at Trois-Rivières, and General Benjamin Lincoln, captured at Charleston.

Sincerely, Eb Chaplin

Chapter Six

We fight, get beat, rise, and fight again.
—Nathanael Greene

In an effort to regain control of the south, the Continental Congress sent Nathanael Greene to take command. The effort gained an enormous victory at the Cowpens. After that, General Greene employed a strategy of avoiding direct conflict unless attacked. This approach, along with the continued partisan efforts, resulted in the British expending precious resources chasing Greene to the point that British general Cornwallis abandoned the Carolinas and headed to Yorktown, Virginia.

In May 1781, Washington and Rochambeau met to determine strategy regarding an attack on New York City. In August, Rochambeau informed Washington that a French fleet under command of Admiral de Grasse left the Caribbean en route to the Chesapeake Bay area. Washington decided to march the American and French Armies to Virginia. Before Washington and Rochambeau got to Virginia, Admiral de Grasse defeated a British naval force.

January 18, 1781

Dear Uncle Eb,

What a difference a general makes! Yesterday we had a magnificent victory due to the superlative strategy and inspiration provided by General Daniel Morgan. Our force of a little over 1,000 defeated Lieutenant Colonel Banastre Tarleton's force of almost 1,100 by inflicting 110 deaths and capturing 712 prisoners, of which over 200 were wounded. Our losses were 12 killed and 60 wounded.

On the sixteenth, we arrived at a location called the Cowpens. It was an area five hundred yards long by five hundred yards wide, an open meadow, sparsely wooded and free of undergrowth kept clear by thousands of grazing cattle gathered every spring before being driven to Camden or Charleston for slaughter. The Green River Road ran through it. To its rear was the Broad River. The field had a slight rise followed by two swales, which we used to our advantage. Having the Broad River in the rear would make it hard for the militia troops to run from the British like they did at Camden.

Knowing Tarleton was not far off when we got here, Morgan called his staff together to lay out his plans. At Camden, General Gates called a council to ask, "What is best to be done?" With Morgan—no advice asked for—he told them how this battle was to be fought. Morgan knew that because so many of our men were militia, they would be fearful of a bayonet attack by the British.

Here is what he laid out. At the top of the rise he would place three hundred from the militia units from South Carolina, Georgia, and North Carolina under command of General Andrew Pickens. To support Pickens's right, one hundred riflemen from Augusta County, Virginia, were placed. Sixty selected Georgia, and sixty selected North Carolina sharpshooters were placed on either side of the road 150 yards ahead of the militia. Behind the militia 150 yards, in the first swale, were placed 280 Maryland and Delaware Continentals, along with 200 Virginia militiamen, who were former Continentals under command of Lieutenant Colonel John Eager Howard. Peter Jaquette and I were in this deployment. Behind us was Colonel William Washington with eighty of his Light Dragoons, along with forty-five other mounted men slightly hidden in another swale lined with trees to help conceal them. The militia's horses were picketed well behind Washington's men.

Morgan personally toured the camp that night, talking to each group, giving out specific instructions. He told the first line of sharpshooters that after firing two rounds they were to run back to the line of militia. They were specifically to aim at officers and sergeants. He told the militia that after firing three rounds they were to run back past our line of Continentals. The Continentals were told the plan that the militia was to run after three shots so that we didn't think the militia had panicked. Knowing this, we knew to hold our ground. As the militia retreated, Washington's task was to protect them if they were attacked by cavalry. As Morgan made his rounds, he showed the many scars on his back from the five hundred whiplashes he received from the British during the French and Indian War. He told us that tomorrow we would give "Bloody Ban" his whipping.

Two hours before daybreak, a scout reported Tarleton was five miles away. Just before 7:00 a.m., the attack started. As the sharpshooters and militia ran, the British charged ferociously, thinking the battle would soon be over. They were totally surprised when they ran into us, but soon we were up against the vaunted Fraser's Highlanders. Howard gave a command to the Virginians to cover our right flank. In the confusion, they thought it was a command to retreat, and we all started to follow them. Morgan came dashing up and ordered us to about-face and deliver a volley into the faces of the astonished Highlanders. Then we heard Howard shout, "Charge, bayonets."

As the British were fleeing, Tarleton tried to regroup his men, but to no avail. Washington, who had driven off British dragoons trying to reach the retreating militia, then decided to go after Tarleton. There was quite a fight. Washington broke his saber at the hilt in fighting a British officer but was saved when his Negro body servant shot his attacker with his pistol. Then Washington managed to deflect a saber slash from Tarleton with the hilt of his broken sword. Before riding off, Tarleton pulled his pistol but missed Washington with the shot.

We found out after the battle that the cannons being used against us were captured from us at Camden, which we had captured from the British at Saratoga. We also found that many of the "British" prisoners were Americans captured at Camden. They chose to serve with the British rather than go to the prison ships in Charleston Harbor. They told us they were put in the front portion of the attack. Many merely dove to the ground, hoping they would be recaptured.

I can't believe that this overwhelming victory took only a little over an hour to accomplish. Morgan's plan worked almost to perfection. We will be moving out shortly. When Cornwallis hears of this, he'll be on his way.

Sincerely, Ben

⟡

January 25, 1781
Dear Mr. Chaplin,

When I got back from Kings Mountain, I again sought out Colonel Francis Marion. When I met Marion, he was riding a beautiful sorrel gelding, named Ball, which was captured at Black Mingo Creek. It had belonged to Colonel John Coming Ball.

On October 24, Marion learned that Loyalist Lieutenant Colonel Samuel Tynes and eighty Tories were near Tearcoat Swamp.[109] As we approached during the night of the twenty-fifth, we could see their campfires. We attacked shortly after midnight. Those who could, fled into the swamp, including Tynes. We took twenty-three prisoners and many horses. Many of the prisoners decided to join our forces.

---

[109] Near present-day Gable, South Carolina.

A few days later, Tynes was captured. This news infuriated Cornwallis, who sent Tarleton to deal with us. On November 7, Tarleton encamped at the plantation of General Richard Richardson. Richardson had been taken prisoner at Charleston, imprisoned at St. Augustine, and then due to being ill paroled to his plantation, where he died in September. We saw the campfires and proceeded toward them. Mary Richardson, the general's widow, sent her son to warn us that the campfires were Tarleton's, with four hundred troops and two grasshopper cannons.[110] Being badly outnumbered, we galloped away. We had a cat-and-mouse game for several days before Tarleton decided to go back to chasing "The Gamecock," explaining that even the devil could not catch the "Swamp Fox."

We heard that Sumter had two successes in November. On the ninth, at Fish Dam Ford,[111] he thwarted an attack by that barbarian, Major James Wemyss. Wemyss was wounded and captured. Regrettably, Sumter paroled him. Then on the twentieth, Sumter was attacked by Tarleton at Blackstock's Farm.[112] On the way to Blackstock's, Tarleton stopped at the Dillard residence, forcing Mary Dillard to provide a meal. While preparing the meal, she overheard Tarleton's plan. Later she slipped away and rode off to warn Sumter. Sumter was wounded in the attack but was able to repel the attack and inflict heavy losses.

On New Year's Day, Marion received the news that Governor John Rutledge promoted him to general. Yesterday we, along with Lee's Legion, attempted to capture Georgetown. However, not having cannons, we could not dislodge the Loyalists. We've also gotten word that many of the Camden Battle prisoners took service in Jamaica to strengthen British garrisons versus the Spanish. I guess that's preferential to rotting away on a British prison ship.

Sincerely, Felix

---

[110] Grasshopper cannons were made of bronze instead of iron. They could be moved by men much like a handcart. When fired, the recoil made the gun jump backward, hence *grasshopper.*
[111] Near present-day Blackstock, South Carolina.
[112] Near present-day Union, South Carolina.

❧

February 18, 1781
Dear Uncle Eb,

After the Cowpens, General Daniel Morgan had us head northwest toward North Carolina to escape British general Charles Cornwallis. Since we heard that Cornwallis had been reinforced by troops under command of Generals Alexander Leslie and Charles O'Hara and a Hessian regiment that had been sent by General Clinton in New York to Charleston in December, we had to make fast time. Because of the incessant rain and the number of prisoners we had, it was a tough go.

We learned that on January 27, General Cornwallis ordered his baggage train burned, destroying tents, clothing, and the soldiers' rum ration so the British could travel faster. He retained only enough wagons for medical supplies, salt, and ammunition. On January 31, we managed to ford the Yadkin River, even though it was very high. General Nathanael Greene directed General William Lee Davidson, with eight hundred troops, to guard several fords on the Yadkin. We were sent on our way to Guilford Courthouse. General Greene sent Lieutenant Colonel Edward Carrington to gather boats on the Virginia side and get them to the North Carolina side of the Dan River to be used when we got there.

At dawn on February 1, General Cornwallis led the charge across the Yadkin at Cowan's Ford.[113] Because the Yadkin was extremely high, many of their soldiers drowned. Early in the crossing attempt, General Davidson was killed. After the skirmish, many of the soldiers and civilians moved toward Tarrant's Tavern,[114] where they, due to the cold weather, were busy drinking rum. Even though he was badly outnumbered, Lieutenant Colonel Banastre Tarleton attacked at around 2:00 p.m., killing ten.

On February 10, due to being quite ill, General Morgan left us. He was replaced by Colonel Otho Holland Williams. Greene's idea was to retreat at a fast pace to wear out Cornwallis. Williams was to stay between us and Cornwallis to mask our

---

[113] Today beneath the waters of Lake Norman in North Carolina.
[114] Near present-day Mooresville, North Carolina.

destination. When we got to the Dan River on Valentine's Day, there were many boats awaiting us, including many flat-bottomed boats built by Colonel Tadeusz Kościuszko during his reconnoitering efforts. When Cornwallis got there, all of our forces had crossed into Virginia. Not being able to cross without boats, he decided to head to Hillsborough, where he issued a proclamation for loyal subjects to join his forces.

I enjoyed your letter regarding events elsewhere. You mentioned inflationary costs. We have it here too. It cost me a hundred continental dollars for a half pint of whiskey. We've been told that tomorrow we head back to North Carolina.

Sincerely, Ben

February 21, 1781
Dear Father,

Militarily, there's been little action this winter. On January 22, Lieutenant Colonel William Hull attacked the headquarters of the Tory lieutenant colonel James De Lancey at Morrisania.[115] Hull burned the barracks, a pontoon bridge over the Harlem River, and a great amount of forage. He captured fifty-two prisoners, along with some horses and cattle.

Our main excitement was provided by two mutinies. On January 1, the Pennsylvania Line encamped at Jockey Hollow mutinied. General Anthony Wayne attempted to quell the mutiny but because he was somewhat sympathetic to their grievances did not take drastic action. While the winter hasn't been harsh, the rations are meager, the clothing is wretched, and the pay often is not disbursed. The Pennsylvania troops began a march to Philadelphia to lodge complaints against Congress and the Pennsylvania state government. On the sixth, agents sent by British general Clinton offered the men their back pay from British coffers if they gave up their Rebel cause. Clinton misjudged the reason for the mutiny. These men were indeed Patriots who just wanted to be treated

---

[115] Located in what is now the Bronx, New York.

fairly. In fact, the British agents were hanged with horse collars. Pennsylvania president Joseph Reed and council member and former General James Potter met with the troops at Princeton on January 7. Even though negotiations ended the mutiny, less than half the troops returned to Jockey Hollow.

On January 20, the New Jersey Line encamped at Pompton, New Jersey, mutinied. When General Washington got word on the twenty-first at New Windsor, New York, he sent General Robert Howe with New England troops to quell it. Howe surrounded the mutineers on the twenty-sixth. On the twenty-seventh, Washington arrived by sleigh. The leaders of the mutiny were identified, whereupon two of them were executed by a firing squad of their fellow mutineers.

When Washington learned that new British general Benedict Arnold was sent to Virginia by General Clinton, he decided to send General Lafayette down there to combat him and attempt a capture. If Lafayette captures Arnold, he has orders to hang him. I will be going along with Lafayette. We will be leaving shortly and hope to see you at the Blaze Horse.

Back in October, many of us were mystified by a strange occurrence. One of Lieutenant Colonel Henry Lee's most trusted sergeant majors deserted to the British. When some of Lee's men failed to recapture him, Lee didn't seem to care. Today Lafayette told me what transpired. The sergeant major John Champe had been handpicked by Lee upon Washington's request to find a man to go into New York to capture Arnold and bring him back alive to Washington. We have no idea what happened, because Arnold has not been captured.

Your son, Moses

༄

March 14, 1781
Dear Uncle Eb,

Soon after we crossed the Dan River back to North Carolina, we learned that General Cornwallis was heading out of Hillsborough because it was barren of supplies and lacking in Tory support. General Greene again sent Colonel Otho Holland Williams as a screen between us and the British, with Lee's Legion and General Andrew Pickens's militia as his "eyes." Meanwhile, Cornwallis sent Tarleton's British Legion to protect the Loyalist militia assemblies. Lee had difficulty getting information from the locals on British positions, because they spoke only German.

We were steadily obtaining reinforcements. Generals John Butler and Thomas Eaton brought in one thousand North Carolinians; Generals Edward Stevens and Robert Lawson brought in several hundred Virginians; and General Friedrich von Steuben sent down four hundred troops from Maryland. Disappointingly, Colonel William Campbell promised one thousand Virginia overmountain men but showed up with less than one hundred.

On February 25, Lee and Pickens were told by some women that Tarleton's men were gathering between the Haw and Deep Rivers. Trying to find Tarleton, two Tory mounted men looking for Tarleton came upon Lieutenant Colonel Lee, thinking he was Tarleton because both units had green jackets, and Lee's men had affixed red plumes to their caps. Lee asked the Tories that he be escorted to their leader. Lee's men were escorted past the British mounted men by the Tories to their leader, Colonel John Pyle. As Lee tried to introduce himself to Pyle, some of Pickens's men hidden in the woods opened fire. Lee's men then started hacking away with their sabers. Pyle shouted that they were attacking their own, still not aware of the dupe. Many of Pyle's men yelled, *"Ich ergebe mich,"* but no one understood the German term for "I surrender." Many of Lee's men were shouting, "Buford's Play," or "Tarleton's Quarter." It was over in a few minutes, with 250 of Pyle's men killed or wounded.[116]

On March 6, Cornwallis got very close to Williams, and the race was on. Williams managed to beat Cornwallis to the ford at Weitzel's Mill[117] on Reedy Ford Creek. Pickens's South Carolina and Georgia militia managed to cover the crossing from Tarleton's attack. After everyone was safely

[116] This encounter took place near present-day Graham, North Carolina.
[117] Near present-day Gibsonville, North Carolina.

across, Pickens's militia units so resented the fact that they had to expose themselves to protect the Continentals that they insisted on going back home. Pickens expressed his apologies and mortification to Greene. Greene reluctantly agreed to their departure but asked Pickens to continue where possible to raid British posts.

Tonight we are at Guilford Courthouse with over 4,400 troops. Cornwallis is twelve miles away along the Great Salisbury Wagon Road. I expect that soon we will be in combat.

Sincerely, Ben

⁓

March 28, 1781
Dear Uncle Eb,

I'm finally getting a chance to write about the Battle at Guilford Courthouse that took place on the Ides of March. After the battle, we retreated to Troublesome Creek and dug breastworks in case the British came to attack. We soon learned that Cornwallis was encamped at Guilford Courthouse for several days. When he left, we followed him. Today, Greene decided to call off the chase. Cornwallis is on his way to Wilmington, North Carolina, which fell to the British on February 1.

Before dawn on March 15, scouts brought word that Cornwallis was on the move. We could hear the gunfire from skirmishes between Lee and Tarleton. Even though outnumbered two to one, Cornwallis, having trained soldiers versus our heavy makeup of militia, did not hesitate to attack, appearing at about 1:30 p.m.

General Greene's battle plan was essentially the same as Morgan's at the Cowpens but altered slightly due to different terrain. The first line was composed of 1,000 North Carolina militiamen behind a rail fence, flanked on the left by Lee's Legion, along with riflemen, and flanked on the right by Washington's Dragoons, also with riflemen. The second line, three hundred yards behind, consisted of 1,200 Virginia militiamen. Twenty paces behind them, General Stevens posted riflemen with orders to shoot anyone who ran. He was not going to let what happened ·at Camden happen again. Peter Jaquette and I were on the third line, five hundred yards back, with the Maryland Continentals on the left, under command of Colonel Otho Holland Williams. General Isaac Huger commanded the Virginia Continentals on the right.

The first line fired a galling and destructive fire on the British attack. But when the British burnished bayonets, they ran behind the second line. The second line of Virginia militiamen stood their ground until they were overrun. As we were attacked, we wounded General O'Hara of the Guards, who then turned command over to Colonel James Stuart, who soon became engaged in a sword fight with Captain John Smith of Maryland. Smith eluded Stuart's thrust and managed to kill Stuart.

As we were embroiled with O'Hara's Guards, Washington's Dragoons charged in. When Cornwallis saw this, he ordered his cannons to fire grapeshot at the melee, which included his own troops. While it broke up the fight, he killed as many of his soldiers as he did ours.

Soon General Greene ordered a retreat. While the British "won" the battle, they lost 25 percent of their men, with 93 killed and 413 wounded. We had 79 deaths, along with 184 wounded. We also had almost 900 militiamen decide to leave us to go home.

Sincerely, Ben

April 1, 1781
Dear Moses, Ben, Teunis, Roelof, Felix, and Zack,

On March 1, the Articles of Confederation were finally ratified. All but Maryland had ratified the Articles by 1779. Maryland resisted because of land ownership in the west. The charters of Virginia, the Carolinas, Georgia, Connecticut, and

Massachusetts stretched their western border to the Mississippi River. Maryland's charter did not have that provision and felt the western lands should belong to the United States. When Thomas Jefferson persuaded Virginia to cede its claims, Maryland ratified.

The British declaration of war on the Dutch Republic has already had an impact. On February 3, the British took Statia. This is a big loss to us. Much powder, other military supplies, and mail from Europe came through Statia.

Recently, Christopher Gadsden was a surprise visitor in the Blaze Horse. I knew him when he was a delegate from South Carolina in the Continental Congress. When Gadsden was captured at Charleston, he was granted parole by General Clinton. After Clinton left, General Cornwallis had him arrested and sent him to St. Augustine, East Florida. He was offered parole there, but Gadsden refused, claiming that the British had already violated one parole and would not give his word to a false system. As a result, he spent the next forty-two weeks in solitary confinement in a prison room at the old Spanish fortress of Castillo de San Marcos. When he was released, he was sent to Philadelphia. Hearing of the victory at the Cowpens, he went back to South Carolina to offer his services there again.

When the British sent Benedict Arnold to Virginia, Washington sent Marquis de Lafayette there too. In February, on their way to Virginia, Moses brought Lafayette to the Blaze Horse. Lafayette told us that after the Battle of Rhode Island he spoke to Washington about leading a force to capture Canada. Washington told him he'd be more valuable going back to France and requesting more aid from King Louis XVI. When he got to France, he was put under house arrest for eight days for having come to America without permission. He was soon released and spent time hunting with the king. While there he and Adrienne had a son, whom he named George Washington Lafayette. His trip back to France resulted in Rochambeau being sent here. Lafayette told a funny story: When he and General Nathanael Greene went to d'Estaing's ship to plead with the French not to leave Rhode Island, Greene said that even if negotiations fail, they'd at least get a good French meal! But then on the boat ride to the ship, Greene got seasick!

Ben, you asked if I knew John Pyle. The Pyles lived in Kennett Square and would stop by the Blaze Horse when in Philadelphia. Zack wrote me that he went to Virginia with Arnold.

Sincerely, Eb Chaplin

April 30, 1781
Dear Father,

Since I was curious, I asked Lafayette why he would be involved in our fight for independence. He told me that he joined the Freemasons in Paris. At the lodge meetings he would hear speeches calling for the liberty and sovereignty of the people. When he heard of our cause, he felt he had to become an advocate for the rights of man. He named many Americans involved in masonry, including George Washington, Benjamin Franklin, John Hancock, Sam Adams, Paul Revere, John Paul Jones, Peter Muhlenberg, John Stark, James Monroe, and Hugh Mercer.

We got to Head of Elk, Maryland, on March 3, but there were not enough boats to take us down Chesapeake Bay. We continued our march to Annapolis, but Lafayette, knowing that the French were sending 1,100 troops to Virginia, left alone and arrived at Yorktown on the fourteenth. When he learned that Admiral Destouches returned to Rhode Island, he came back to Annapolis. We started back north on April 3. However, on the twelfth, Lafayette received word to continue back to Virginia. We crossed the Potomac River on the twenty-first, arriving in Alexandria. A few days later we arrived at Fredericksburg, Virginia. We were also told that Washington sent General Anthony Wayne with the Pennsylvania militia to Virginia. We have not yet seen any trace of Wayne.

We got to Richmond on April 29. That evening as Lafayette was having dinner with General Thomas Nelson Jr., he was told that British generals Benedict Arnold and William Phillips were walking along the James River not far from where Lafayette and Nelson were dining. An officer told Lafayette he had some crack riflemen who could take them both out. Lafayette declined the request, stating that they would be defeated on the field of battle.

We were surprised by his decision. Our understanding was that Lafayette was told to hang Arnold if he was captured. And he could have settled an old score, because General Phillips manned the British artillery at the Battle of Minden,[118] which killed Lafayette's father. Perhaps he thought back to his first battle at Brandywine, where British Major Patrick Ferguson opted not to shoot at General Washington.

Your son, Moses

༺༻

May 11, 1781
Dear Uncle Eb,

After General Greene decided to call off the chase with Cornwallis, his strategy was to cut off the British supply depots. He sent Colonel Lee and General Marion to threaten communication between Camden and Charleston. He sent General Sumter to do the same between Camden and Ninety Six and sent General Pickens with a like task between Ninety Six and Augusta, Georgia.

We went directly to Camden, encamping on Hobkirk's Hill on April 20. Greene felt Colonel Francis Lord Rawdon's defenses were too strong to attack. Not learning this until after the battle, we had a deserter that informed Rawdon we had no artillery and were low on supplies. Rawdon decided to attack on April 25, completely to our surprise. Initially, Rawdon attacked with a very narrow approach. When Greene spread us out to try to envelope him, Rawdon threw in the Volunteers of Ireland, and we were repulsed. Colonel Washington's cavalry was to make a

---

[118] The Battle of Minden was fought in the Seven Year's War in 1759, located in present-day northeast Germany.

flanking move, but his route took him into Rawdon's hospital area, and they got bogged down trying to take prisoners, thereby ·never making it to action. Greene was so upset by troops fleeing instead of standing strong that he directed a court-martial to convene for over twenty deserters. All were found guilty, but only five were executed. We had about 130 casualties, while the British had about 250 casualties.

After the battle, we moved about, including a stay at Rugeley's Mills. While there I met Andrew Jackson, a fourteen-year-old boy, returning to his home at Waxhaws. When he refused to clean a Tory officer's boots, he was struck in the head with a sword and taken prisoner. He was in prison in Camden while our battle was raging. After the battle, he and others were exchanged for British prisoners. During the battle, Captain John Smith, who killed British Colonel James Stuart in a sword fight at Guilford Courthouse, was taken prisoner. Rawdon was going to have him executed. However, under a flag of truce, Greene managed to get Smith released.

Yesterday Rawdon evacuated Camden. Meanwhile, General Pickens forwarded to Greene a note that he intercepted sent from Rawdon to Lieutenant Colonel John Harris Cruger instructing Cruger to abandon Ninety Six and take his troops to Augusta. Because of that, we are now on our way to Ninety Six. We also learned that Lee and Marion captured Fort Watson. One by one, we are taking the British supply depots.

Sincerely, Ben

May 13, 1781
Dear Mr. Chaplin,

Over the past month we've been busy taking out two British supply posts: Fort Watson[119] and Fort Motte. These posts were set up by the British to help supply Camden and Ninety Six from Charleston. In February, General "Gamecock" Sumter

---

[119] Near present-day Summerton, South Carolina.

attacked Fort Watson. He was unsuccessful and suffered fifty-six casualties.

On April 14, riding with General Francis Marion, we met up with Lieutenant Colonel Henry "Light-Horse Harry" Lee, recently reinforced with North Carolina and Maryland Continentals. On the fifteenth, we got to Fort Watson. We were hoping to get them to surrender by cutting off access to water from Scott Lake. Their commander, Lieutenant James McKay, had his men dig a well. Without artillery, laying a siege was not working. We were also quite fearful of British or Loyalist reinforcements arriving.

On the eighteenth, Major Hezekiah Maham suggested that we build a tower. For five days we labored, and on the night of the twenty-second it was erected. At dawn on the twenty-third, we started firing from the tower. This action allowed others to remove the abatis surrounding the fort. With this turn of events, Lieutenant McKay raised the white flag. We captured all 114 men and then destroyed the fort.

We then decided to take Fort Motte, arriving on May 7. By the tenth, we completed a 400-foot trench toward the fort. Lieutenant Donald McPherson was asked to surrender. He refused. We got word that Lord Rawdon's forces were not far away. Desperate measures were called for. The fort was erected around the house of Mrs. Rebecca Motte. Lee asked permission to set her house on fire to drive the British out. Not only did Mrs. Motte give permission, but she had in her possession a bow and several arrows brought from the East Indies and especially prepared to carry combustible material. The arrows ignited the house. With his men running from the burning house, McPherson surrendered on the twelfth. We took 183 prisoners.

Since most of her house was saved, that night Mrs. Motte invited both the Patriot and British officers to a meal. During the meal, Marion received word that Lee's men ordered three Loyalists to be hanged. When Marion heard it, he reminded Lee that he, Marion, was in charge. He cut down the one prisoner who was not yet dead and told Lee's men that he would personally kill the next man who harmed a prisoner.

There is virtually no money to pay us South Carolina militiamen. General Sumter has put into effect "Sumter's Bounty," whereby state militia would be paid in slaves confiscated from Loyalists' estates. While General Andrew Pickens also uses the practice, General Marion refuses to implement it.

Sincerely, Felix

❧

May 29, 1781
Dear Uncle Eb,

Today General Arnold leaves for New York. We are not sure if it is by his request or if he is being recalled for other reasons. My friend Johann Ewald absolutely despises him. After taking Richmond, Ewald discovered that American General von Steuben had some troops at Hood's Point. Instead of giving Ewald command, Arnold gave command to Major Beverly Robinson Jr., the son of New York Loyalist Colonel Beverly Robinson, who assisted in Arnold's defection; he led them into an ambush. Ewald learned that Clinton's staff was upset when they found out that much of the tobacco captured at Richmond was not destroyed but kept by Arnold as spoils. Naval Captain Symonds and Arnold have had many quarrels on the subject of splitting bounty. There's also talk that Arnold wants to attack Philadelphia. His initial direction here was to establish a base at Portsmouth and to recruit Loyalists to join our forces. The devastating of properties and the freeing of slaves have not been ideal recruitment tools. Defenses at Portsmouth are meager. On the other hand, Arnold's forces have all but destroyed Virginia's navy.

Arnold always carries two pistols so that in the event he is captured he can escape the hangman's noose. A prisoner told Arnold that if he was captured, his left leg would be cut off, buried with full military honors, and the rest of him would be hanged.

In late March, General William Phillips arrived with additional troops and replaced Arnold as commanding general.

He immediately decided that Portsmouth was inadequate and needed additional work. He decided to move inland. On April 18, we easily took Williamsburg, which was lightly defended by militia Colonel James Innes. However, when we got to Petersburg on April 25, General von Steuben put up a gallant fight before finally fleeing. As we were on our way back to Portsmouth, Phillips ordered that no private property be damaged. We think it was a result of his being treated so well by Thomas Jefferson when he was a prisoner of war at Charlottesville.

On May 9, we reached Portsmouth, with Phillips being very ill. There Phillips got a message from General Cornwallis that he and Lieutenant Colonel Tarleton were on their way from the Carolinas and that we should return to Petersburg. He made his headquarters at Bollingbrook Plantation. On May 13, Phillips died while Bollingbrook was being shelled by newly arrived American General Marquis de Lafayette. Ewald was devastated by Phillips's death but was happy to learn Cornwallis would now be in charge instead of Arnold. Many troops are convinced Arnold had Phillips poisoned.

God Save the King, Zack

❧

June 13, 1781
Dear Mr. Chaplin,

As you probably know by now, the rumor of the British coming to Virginia proved to be true with the arrival of Benedict Arnold. Since the senior Continental Army officer in Virginia was General Friedrich von Steuben, Jefferson allowed him to head military actions against Arnold. Steuben had few troops of his own. His main objective had been to supply and send troops to General Greene in the Carolinas. Steuben became totally disgusted with Jefferson. Steuben asked that slaves be ordered to construct fortification, he asked that militia terms be extended, and he asked that horses be impressed. Even though the British were stealing horses at will, Jefferson refused all of Steuben's requests.

George Rogers Clark was in Richmond attempting to get permission for a raid on Fort Detroit. Clark was asked by Jefferson to assist the militia against the British. Clark agreed and laid an ambush at Hood's Point. The militia had no idea who Clark was and ran when fire was returned. Clark decided he'd had enough. To make matters worse, when the British burned Richmond, Clark lost his vouchers to the flames for his military actions in the amount of $15,000.

Knowing militia troops were needed, the Virginia legislature tried to enact a draft. This was met by riots in the western counties where the citizens were as concerned with Indians as they were with the British. The eastern shore counties refused the draft, as they were totally hemmed in by the British.

There were two failed attempts by the French to assist. In mid-February, a small fleet under Captain le Gardeur de Tilly decided his ships had too much draft to go upriver to attack Arnold's fleet. In March, Admiral Chevalier Destouches left Newport, Rhode Island, for the Chesapeake with 1,200 troops, but British Admiral Mariot Arbuthnot got there first from New York. On March 16, they battled off the Capes, with the French doing considerable damage. However, Destouches left feeling he was outgunned.

On the night of June 3, Jack Jouett, forty miles away from Charlottesville, observed Tarleton's British Legion. Fearing they were on the way to capture legislators who were meeting in Charlottesville, he rode off to warn them. Jefferson left five minutes before Tarleton got to Monticello. Jefferson escaped to another home of his, Poplar Forest. Monticello was unscathed by the British. Was that due to Jefferson's kind treatment of British general William Phillips when he was a prisoner of war at Charlottesville, or was it because of King George's birthday? When Jefferson heard of Phillips's death, he described him as "the proudest man of the proudest nation." On the other hand, Jefferson offered five thousand guineas for the capture of Arnold. His term up, Jefferson was replaced by Thomas Nelson as governor.

Sincerely, Roelof

June 15, 1781
Dear Moses, Ben, Teunis, Roelof, Felix, and Zack,

Back in 1778, Loyalists from the Philadelphia area and mercenary Waldeckers were sent to Pensacola, West Florida, under command of British general John Campbell. Word was recently received of a major battle at Pensacola, where the British not only had significant losses, but with the capitulation of Pensacola they agreed to turn control of West Florida over to the Spanish.

During 1779 and 1780, the Spanish took British fortifications at Manchac, Baton Rouge, Natchez, and Mobile. At Manchac and Baton Rouge, the Spanish were assisted by French militia from Attakapas Parish. In October 1780, Spanish Field Marshal Bernardo de Galvez set out from Havana to attack Pensacola. Unfortunately the fleet was badly damaged when hit by a hurricane. Undaunted, de Galvez set out once again on February 13, 1781, arriving at Pensacola on March 9. When Campbell got to Pensacola, he built additional fortifications: Fort George, Prince of Wales Redoubt, Queen's Redoubt, and Fort Barrancas Colorada. With these strong fortifications, unsuccessful initial attacks convinced de Galvez he had to lay a siege. Trenches were dug, and bunkers and redoubts were built.

The British forces, numbering about three thousand, were made up of British Regulars, Waldeckers, Pennsylvania and Maryland Loyalists, and Indians. With later reinforcements, the Spanish force reached almost eight thousand. Trench warfare went on for several days. Then on May 5 and 6, another hurricane hit. On May 8, an American Tory deserter fired a cannon shot that hit the powder magazine in the Queen's Redoubt. On the ninth, the Spanish charged the fortifications, causing Campbell to wave the white flag of surrender. Over 1,100 prisoners were taken to Havana to exchange for Spanish prisoners being held on British prison ships.

There was an interesting development out west in February. Two Milwaukee chiefs, El Heturno and Naquiguen, went to

St. Louis to convince the Spanish to attack British Fort St. Joseph[120] in the western district of Connecticut. A force of Spanish volunteers and Indians took the fort by surprise. But disturbingly, the Spanish raised their flag to claim the area. While the Spanish are our allies against Britain, there is no issue with their taking West Florida from the British, because it was territory they lost after the French and Indian War; however, we cannot tolerate their claiming our territory.

I'll close with this. Here is what Charles Fox said to the British Parliament when news reached London of Cornwallis's "victory" at Guilford Courthouse: "Another such victory would ruin the British army." Is it time to say, "Bye, George"?

Sincerely, Eb Chaplin

June 19, 1781
Dear Uncle Eb,

We got to Ninety Six on May 21. When we got here, General Greene ruled out a direct assault because of a formidable defense of a Star Fort with 550 Loyalists under the command of Colonel John Harris Cruger. In addition, we did not have heavy artillery. Greene felt only a siege could bring down Ninety Six.

Greene sent General Andrew Pickens to Augusta, Georgia, to keep British reinforcements from Ninety Six. Greene had previously sent Lieutenant Colonel "Light-Horse Harry" Lee to capture other outposts. On the twenty-first, Lee and Colonel Elijah Clarke destroyed Fort Galphin.[121] Lee and Clarke then moved toward Fort Grierson at Augusta. On the twenty-third, they encircled it. Its commander, Colonel Grierson, and his eighty men attempted to flee to nearby Fort Cornwallis under command of Colonel Thomas "Burnfoot" Brown. All were captured, given no quarter, and slaughtered. The Patriots were exacting revenge for the treatment Brown was known to hand out.

---

120 Near present-day Niles, Michigan.
121 Near present-day Jackson, South Carolina.

Lee and Clarke then went on to Fort Cornwallis to join Pickens. The fort was too strong for a direct assault. Lee suggested building a "Maham tower," as done at Fort Watson. On June 1, the tower was completed, which allowed cannon fire into Fort Cornwallis. On June 4, Brown was asked to surrender. He asked for one more day because it was King George III's birthday. The next day Brown surrendered specifically to Continental forces to avoid Grierson's fate if he had fallen into the hands of the Patriot militia.

During this time we were busy digging a system of parallel trenches under the direction of Colonel Tadeusz Kościuszko. The first parallel was finished on June 1, the second on June 3, and the third on June 10. The defenders tried to dig a well, but not being successful, slaves brought in water from the town. Greene learned on the eleventh that Lord Rawdon was marching from Charleston. On the thirteenth, a thirty-foot tower was built so we could shoot down into the fort. The cannon fire was not powerful enough to breach the walls of the fort, and the defenders were shooting heated cannonballs at the tower.

Yesterday, fearing Rawdon's arrival, Greene ordered an assault of fifty men on the fort. Some had axes to cut away the sharpened stakes extending from the fort's walls, while others had hooks to pull down sandbags positioned on top of the fort wall to add height, which hampered our ability to shoot at the defenders. These men were repulsed, with over half giving their lives. The wounded are being tended to before we leave tomorrow.

Sincerely, Ben

❦

July 19, 1781
Dear Mr. Chaplin,

General Marion and Lieutenant Colonel Lee's Legion were under the command of General Sumter when Sumter decided to attack the British, who were near my home at Moncks Corner. On the fourteenth, British Lieutenant Colonel John Coates withdrew to Biggin Church. At 3:00 a.m. on the seventeenth, Coates burned the church and decided to go down the Cooper River to Quinby Bridge. Coates loosened the planks of the bridge, which he would remove when his baggage train caught up. However, Lee captured the baggage train before it got to the bridge. Several of our troops attacked but, because of the dislodged planks, could not follow up.

After crossing the bridge, Coates took a defensive position in the many buildings of Shubrick's Plantation.[122] After we, Marion's forces, and Lee forded the river, they decided the British position was too strong to attack. At about 3:00 p.m., Sumter finally arrived and insisted upon attacking. Then we learned he failed to bring artillery along. Sumter positioned us to attack across open fields, while he had his men stay behind the protection of the plantation's slave buildings. We were able to drive the British back, but when they counterattacked Sumter's men with bayonets, we had to go to their assistance. As darkness fell, Sumter ordered a retreat to continue the battle the next day.

There was no battle the next day. We had captured one hundred prisoners and three hundred horses. Then we found out that a captured paymaster's chest containing 720 guineas[123] was distributed to Sumter's men only. With this news and the disgust with Sumter's strategy, most of Marion's men, including me, left. Lieutenant Colonel Lee took his forces to rejoin General Greene. Both Marion and Lee told Sumter they would never again fight with him.

Governor John Rutledge put an end to "Sumter's Bounty." I also need to tell you about some other practices Sumter had. One punishment was "spicketing"—a Tory was suspended over a sharp pin, with his bare foot tenuously perched on the point, slowly driving the pin through the foot. Many times slaves offered services, thinking they were offering their services to

---

[122] About seventeen miles southeast of Moncks Corner, South Carolina.

[123] A guinea equaled twenty-one shillings (or one pound, one shilling). A pound equaled twenty shillings. A shilling equaled twelve pence. A continental dollar equaled seven shillings, sixpence (or two and two-third dollars equaled a pound).

Tories. They would be whipped and half hanged before they were distributed as "bounty."

Sincerely, Felix

◦❥◦

August 5, 1781
Dear Uncle Eb,

Earlier this month, General Cornwallis moved the army from Portsmouth to Yorktown, Virginia. He felt the deeper water near Yorktown would be better suited for British battleships. Also, across from Yorktown is Gloucester Point, which will enable our command of the York River. I am on Gloucester Point with the forces of Banastre Tarleton's Legion, John Graves Simcoe's Queen's Rangers, and Johann Ewald's Hessian jägers.

We aren't getting as much support from the Loyalists as expected. Admiral Collier arrived in 1779 and departed, and then General Leslie arrived in 1780 and departed. Their fear once again surfaced in June when General Clinton ordered Cornwallis to send over two thousand troops to New York, where he expected an attack by Washington and his French allies. Again, Loyalists expected Cornwallis to abandon them and return to North Carolina. On July 21, Clinton rescinded the order.

After we left Petersburg, we learned that John Champe, who deserted to us in New York in October 1780, deserted back to the Rebels. Simcoe had an embarrassing situation. Two of his men were found to have ravished a nine-year-old girl. When Cornwallis learned of it, he ordered the two soldiers to be hanged.

While Cornwallis sent Tarleton off to capture Jefferson at Monticello, we headed for Jefferson's Elk Hill plantation. It was totally wasted. His corn and tobacco crops were destroyed. Stocks of cattle, sheep, and hogs were taken to feed our army. Any horses capable of service were taken and the throats slit of young horses that couldn't be of use to us. All the barns and fences were burned.

212

In July, after being at Williamsburg for some time, Cornwallis decided to cross the James River at Jamestown Ferry and continue to Portsmouth. Meanwhile, we'd been skirmishing with Lafayette's troops but could not subdue them. Knowing that Lafayette might chase us to the James River, Cornwallis set up a trap. He sent "deserters" out with the message we had crossed the James River. He left some jägers near Green Spring Plantation[124] as a rear guard to entice the advancing enemy. He arranged troops in marshlands on either side of the causeway to the James River. Lafayette sent General Wayne straight toward us. When they reached an "abandoned" cannon, we struck. Even though outnumbered three to one, Wayne ordered a bayonet charge, and Lafayette came in on the flank. Eventually the Rebels retreated. Tarleton wanted to chase them, but Cornwallis wanted to finish the job of getting across the James River.

God Save the King, Zack

August 13, 1781
Dear Father,

One of Washington's orders to Lafayette was to secure an open line of communication between Virginia and Philadelphia. As a result, we've had numerous skirmishes with the British troops, but because they outman us, we have made sure not to get drawn into any major battles.

On June 10, General Anthony Wayne finally arrived with his troops. We are now at almost equal strength with the British. We learned why Wayne took so long to get here. Wayne had to deal with two mutinies on his way down from Philadelphia. When the Pennsylvania line mutinied in January, Wayne tried to work with the soldiers' grievances—not this time. He held courts-martial, resulting in a dozen mutineers paying with their lives.

When Cornwallis came up from North Carolina, he was inundated with runaway slaves. Soon the slaves found out that

---

[124] Located five miles west of Williamsburg, Virginia.

they would be sent to ships, either to be sent to the West Indies or impressed into the British Navy. As a result, many came to our side to serve as teamsters. Lafayette convinced William Armistead to allow his slave, James,[125] to join the Continental Army. Lafayette put him to work as a spy. Posing as a runaway slave, he worked for British general Benedict Arnold, and when Arnold left, Cornwallis took him on as a servant. He has been invaluable. Lafayette feeds James false information regarding our side, which James conveys to Cornwallis.

We noticed that Cornwallis left Williamsburg on July 4. We're guessing that he was going to Portsmouth, so he'd have to cross the James River. On July 6, near Green Spring Plantation, Lafayette ordered Wayne to attack with five hundred men. We were steadily driving the British back when we got reinforcements of six hundred more men. As we reached an abandoned cannon, we were suddenly struck from both sides by about three thousand troops. We were stunned, but Wayne, instead of initially retreating, ordered a bayonet charge. This action temporarily stalled the British attack and allowed Lafayette, who from his vantage point realized a British trap was sprung, to bring in a covering force to help manage a retreat. Cornwallis, himself, led a countercharge but, because of receding daylight, decided not to pursue so that he could get his troops across the James River. We are at West Point wondering if Cornwallis will remain in Yorktown, where he moved to a fortnight ago.

Your son, Moses

⸎

August 17, 1781
Dear Uncle Eb,

I am with General James Clinton's troops from New York, and he has joined with the allied forces under General Washington

---

[125] After the war, James returned to William Armistead to continue his life as a slave. In 1787, Lafayette assisted in obtaining James's freedom. In gratitude he became James Armistead Lafayette.

and French General Rochambeau. Back in May, the two generals met in Wethersfield, Connecticut, to prepare for an attack on New York City. At that time Rochambeau informed Washington that Admiral de Grasse had left France for the Caribbean with orders to coordinate his naval activities with the allied forces. The French Army came from Newport, Rhode Island, to link up with Washington's forces near White Plains, New York, on July 6. As the French troops moved across Connecticut from Rhode Island, Duc de Lauzun's Legion acted as a screen for those troops.

On August 14, Rochambeau received word that de Grasse would not bring his fleet to New York. He told Rochambeau that his fleet would be in the Chesapeake area in early September. This news changed the allied plans. Instead of an attack on General Henry Clinton in New York, we will march to Virginia to attack General Cornwallis at Yorktown. Meanwhile, many "secret" messages about an attack on New York sent by Washington over the most dangerous routes were, as planned, intercepted by the British. A French bakery was built. Phony encampments were built along the New Jersey shore. Boats were built to use to cross over to Staten Island. All a ruse.

Before I left home, the British were again raiding in the Lake Champlain area. This time Lieutenant Colonel Barry St. Leger led the raids. He got into trouble for shooting a Vermont militia sergeant and had to apologize. Unknown to St. Leger, Quebec governor-general Frederick Haldimand was negotiating with Ethan Allen for Vermont to become a new British province.

When I got here I heard that after Arnold went over, Washington wanted to capture British general Clinton by sending Americans to New York wearing captured British uniforms. Talking about uniforms, we were impressed by the resplendent uniforms of the French—much different from my buckskin and linsey-woolsey[126] getup.

Due to the high demand for ropes, sails, clothing, and paper, the market price for hemp is quite high. As a result I've turned to growing hemp. Being away, Sarah will be stuck with the

---

[126] A coarse fabric woven from linen warp, or sometimes cotton, and coarse wool filling.

harvest once again. We've been told we start our trek to Virginia tomorrow. I hope I can see you at the Blaze Horse as we pass through Philadelphia.

Sincerely, Teunis

⟨∿⟩

September 6, 1781
Dear Moses, Ben, Teunis, Roelof, and Felix,

Moses, Ben, Roelof, and Felix, I had the great pleasure of seeing Teunis at the Blaze Horse yesterday. He is marching with the allied army of Washington and the French under command of Rochambeau to Yorktown, Virginia. They left the area of White Plains, New York, on August 18. Originally the allied army was hoping to take New York City from the British, but when French Admiral de Grasse set sail for Chesapeake Bay, the decision was made to switch tactics.

Over the past few days, both armies marched through the streets of Philadelphia. The uniforms of the French were magnificent. It was just about four years ago that we last saw such an exhibition. However, the colorful British and Hessian uniforms gave us great trepidation. Yesterday the feeling was different. Most of the French uniforms are white with different-colored facings on their coats, depending on their regiment. The hussars wear a distinctively different cap from their American or British counterparts.

Ben, a few days ago John Pyle came to the Blaze Horse. He told me of the massacre his men suffered from Lee's Legion. Not only were they hacked by Lee's men, but they also were speared by Catawba Indians. He saved himself by diving into a pool and breathing through a reed to avoid drowning. He lost several fingers in the fight. A bit later he became an adjutant[127] in Cornwallis's headquarters. When he asked for a promotion to general, it was refused. Sometime later he left and came back up to Kennett Square. When he learned Washington would be

---

[127] A military officer who acts as an administrative assistant to a senior officer.

216

here, he requested a meeting, declaring he thought he'd been on the wrong side. He then informed Washington of Cornwallis's battle plans, which he had memorized. Felix, Pyle told me he'd been taken prisoner at Moore's Creek but later escaped.

Teunis, I can't say I was surprised by your report about Ethan Allen. In September 1778, he asked that the Continental Congress recognize the Vermont Republic. That was turned down because Vermont was claiming land east of the Connecticut River, which rightfully belonged to New Hampshire, and most of Congress felt that Vermont was part of New York. By the way, in regard to your decision to raise hemp, the Declaration of Independence was written on paper manufactured from hemp.

Ben, Congress awarded a gold medal to Daniel Morgan, silver medals to John Eager Howard and William Washington, and a sword to Andrew Pickens for their efforts at the Cowpens.

Sincerely, Eb Chaplin

September 9, 1781
Dear Uncle Eb,

We lost at Guilford Courthouse, but Cornwallis left for North Carolina. We lost at Hobkirk's Hill, but Rawdon left for Charleston. We couldn't win the siege at Ninety Six, but Cruger left for Charleston. Yesterday we lost at Eutaw Springs,[128] but Lieutenant Colonel Alexander Stewart left for Charleston. Except for Charleston, the British have basically evacuated South Carolina. Are we close to saying, "Bye, George"?

When General Greene got word that Washington was trying to encircle Cornwallis in Virginia, Greene wanted to make sure no British troops from South Carolina got to Virginia to assist Cornwallis. The decision was made to attack the British encampment of two thousand at Eutaw Springs. In July, due to illness, Lord Rawdon left and was replaced by Lieutenant Colonel Alexander Stewart.

---

[128] Near present-day Eutawville, South Carolina.

Because General Marion, the "Swamp Fox," is so familiar with the area, he was invaluable to Greene's strategy of how to attack with our force of 2,200. Greene used the tactic he used at Guilford Courthouse, whereby the militia would be in front and we Continentals were behind them. We completely surprised the British as they were having breakfast.

Marion's men initially performed brilliantly but were driven back by a bayonet charge. We then came in and took over the encampment. Unfortunately, because of hunger, many of our men were more interested in plundering food and rum than continuing to chase off the British. The British right flank under Major John Marjoribanks was their stronghold. Also riflemen of the New York Volunteers were able to keep up a strong fire from inside a large brick house. Greene sent Colonel William Washington to clear out Marjoribanks. Unfortunately, his horse was shot from under him and he was wounded. A British soldier was about to finish Washington off with his sword, but Marjoribanks gallantly turned the sword aside. Washington was captured.

Marjoribanks, seeing the disorder of our troops, rallied his troops, and we were driven from the field. Our losses were heavy: 139 killed and 375 wounded. While the British had fewer killed or wounded, over 400 were captured. While we lost, General Greene made this statement relative to his campaign: "We fight, get beat, rise, and fight again."

It was good to see Felix again after last seeing him a year ago. I told him about the young boy I met, Andy Jackson. Felix had heard of him from Major Davie. We also traded stories about General Sumter.

Sincerely, Ben

September 21, 1781
Dear Father,

On August 30, the French fleet of Admiral Comte de Grasse arrived in the Chesapeake. He had left Brest, France, in March, arriving in Martinique in early April. He had with him six million livres. In July, 3,300 troops were boarded in Saint-Domingue.[129] His next stop was Havana. Being grateful for shipments of American wheat, the Spanish provided five million livres. The Spanish also provided de Grasse with pilots. The French suspected the British, under Admiral Samuel Hood, knew that de Grasse was headed to America. As a result, de Grasse opted not to take the direct route past Bermuda but to take a route between Florida and the Bahamas, for which he needed the Spanish pilots. This maneuver eluded Hood. Hood got to the Chesapeake first, but seeing no French, he went on to New York.

On September 2, Marquis de Saint-Simon's troops were unloaded at Jamestown. That night General Anthony Wayne, on his way to meet General Lafayette, was mistakenly shot in the thigh by a French sentry thinking Wayne was British. Some ships were left there to blockade the James River, and others blockaded the York River. On the fifth, the British fleet of Admiral Thomas Graves was spotted off the Virginia Capes. The French left the Chesapeake to do battle. During the battle, the British had 5 ships damaged, 1 ship scuttled, and 336 casualties. The French had 2 ships damaged and suffered 220 casualties. The battle broke off that night, but the fleets maneuvered for several days. On the twelfth, de Grasse returned to Chesapeake Bay, and two days later the British fleet left for New York.

At this point, there are over 10,000 American troops. The French force totals about 8,600. On the other hand, we estimate the British have about 5,000 men, most in Yorktown and some at Gloucester Point. Washington, suspecting that Gloucester Point may be used by General Cornwallis as either a route to launch an attack north toward Philadelphia or to merely escape, has sent French General de Choisy to Gloucester Point to hem in the British.

Today Washington and Rochambeau met with de Grasse. It took some convincing, but de Grasse promised to stay until the end of October.

Your son, Moses

---

[129] Present-day Haiti.

∽

September 23, 1781
Dear Uncle Eb,

When we got to Gloucester Point, we were quickly put to work building defenses. We built four redoubts and three batteries.[130] We are hemmed in by General George Weedon's Virginia militia and Duc de Lauzon's Legion, both under command of French General Claude Gabriel de Choisy.

We also were taken across the York River to assist in building defensive earthworks around Yorktown. Along the earthworks, somewhat left of center and protruding outward, we built a battery named the Hornwork. Battery firing could cover three sides. Along this inner fortification were eight redoubts and ten batteries. Outside of the inner fortification, we built three more large redoubts. The Fusilier's Redoubt was on our far right, eight hundred yards west of the inner line on a cliff above the York River. Southeast of the inner fortification, about 350 yards away, Redoubt 10 was built. It too was on a cliff above the York River. Redoubt 9 was built seven hundred feet away farther inland.

On August 25, Admiral Samuel Hood arrived with his fleet from the West Indies. He was expecting to find a French fleet here. Seeing nothing, he sailed to New York. On August 30, we were astounded to find a 24-ship French fleet in Chesapeake Bay. On September 5, Admiral Thomas Graves, along with Hood, arrived from New York with nineteen ships. The French immediately left the Chesapeake to do battle. We weren't sure what happened but knew the result when the French fleet reappeared on September 12 and set up a blockade of Chesapeake Bay. On the fourteenth, Graves decided to return to New York.

On the sixteenth, General Cornwallis received word that General Clinton was sending Admiral Robert Digby from New York with four thousand troops. During the night of the seventeenth, fire ships were sent toward the French ships, blocking the mouth of the York River. Unfortunately, the fire

---

[130] A battery is a grouping of artillery pieces for tactical purposes.

ships were set ablaze too soon, which enabled the French to cut their cables and sail away.

Knowing Allied American-French troops are on the way and a French fleet is sitting offshore, Cornwallis has decided to do more work to strengthen Yorktown's fortifications. We have about 5,000 troops and over 1,500 slaves to work on the defenses. We've torn down most of the houses in Yorktown to obtain more timber and to clear a field of fire for our artillery. I am quite worried that if we do not get reinforcements soon from Clinton, we could be in big trouble.

God Save the King, Zack

September25, 1781
Dear Uncle Eb,

It was so great to see you. Shortly after leaving Philadelphia, we were joined in Delaware by Colonel Moses Hazen's Canadian Regiment. They had come down the Delaware River and then up the Christiana River to join us. When they arrived, I ran into Clement Gosselin, whom I hadn't seen since we met on the way to Quebec City in 1775. He is French but speaks English. It is good to know him, because he easily gets information from the French. Hazen's men have played an important role as interpreters.

He told me about a French-speaking Loyalist spy, Miss Jenny, who was infiltrating the French troops. On one of her trips back to New York, she was stopped by a French guard. Both the French and Washington's men interrogated her, but she insisted she was just looking for her French-Canadian father. Finally, she was released, but not until her head was shaved. I guess British general Clinton believed all the false information on troop movements she reported. By the way, when we left, General Washington kept General William Heath with four thousand troops in the vicinity of New York City.

Clement also told me what Rochambeau's aide-de-camp, Baron Ludwig von Closen, said when they first met the American troops, "It was really painful to see these brave men, almost naked with only some trousers and little linen jackets, most of them without stockings, but would you believe it? Very cheerful and healthy in appearance." He also remarked that the Negro Rhode Island Regiment was the most neatly dressed.

We also were joined by a group of Oneida and Tuscarora Indians, under the leadership of Colonel Louis Cook, whose real name is Atayataghronghta ("He Unhangs Himself from the Group"). His mother was a Saint-François Abenaki Indian, and his father was a Negro. He fought against the English during the French and Indian War. He joined our cause and was commissioned an officer by Congress. He has a silver pipe with GW etched into it.

As we crossed Cooch's Bridge in Delaware, it was one of the few places where the entire allied army was on the same road. Many times we were marching on different roads parallel to one another. When we got to Head of Elk, Maryland, there weren't enough boats to take us down Chesapeake Bay. We then marched to Annapolis, while others went to Baltimore. Admiral de Grasse sent boats up to get us to Virginia. Today we are in Williamsburg. We were joined by 3,300 French troops (Regiments d'Agenois, du Gatinois, and de Touraine) from the West Indies under command of General Claude-Anne-Montbleru, marquis de Saint-Simon, who were disembarked by Admiral de Grasse on September 2. The word is that we will start a siege of Yorktown on the twenty-eighth.

Sincerely, Teunis

⌒⌒

September 26, 1781
Dear Mr. Chaplin,

I am with the militia of General Thomas Nelson Jr. right outside Yorktown. Troops came from all over. Lafayette has been here since April. In early September, Admiral de Grasse dropped off soldiers he brought from the West Indies. A few days ago the ·allied army of Washington and Rochambeau arrived. We also are expecting heavy siege guns and more French troops to come in with Admiral Barras from Newport.

After Cornwallis and Tarleton arrived, Loyalists became more confident and started causing trouble. In southwest Virginia, Colonel Charles Lynch, who is also a judge, decided to hold informal courts handing out "lynching" sentences to Loyalists, which resulted in whippings, property seizure, coerced pledges of allegiance, and conscription into the military.

In April, British general Phillips ordered Captain Thomas Graves up the Potomac to prevent Lafayette's arrival. However, since Lafayette had not arrived, he took to plundering and destroying plantations on both sides of the Potomac. Graves docked in the Potomac where Mount Vernon is located. Graves requested provisions from Lund Washington, who has been overseeing Mount Vernon. When Lund refused, Graves told him Mount Vernon would be burned. Lund had a discussion with Graves and subsequently agreed to supplying provisions if Graves returned seventeen slaves who had run away. Lund sent the provisions, but no slaves were returned. When General Washington heard about it, he was furious with Lund.

Because Tarleton was causing havoc across Virginia, the militia wanted a spy to keep eyes on him. A soldier who had walked back to his home after the Battle at Guilford Courthouse, Peter Francisco, volunteered. He had been quite heroic in that battle, and he helped move a cannon so it wouldn't be captured at the Battle of Camden. Peter is a huge man and very strong. He was at Ward's Tavern[131] in July when nine of Tarleton's men arrived. One of the dragoons told Peter to give him the silver buckles on Peter's shoes. Peter told him he'd have to take them himself. When the dragoon bent over to take the buckles, Peter grabbed his sword, killing him. Peter chased the other dragoons off and captured eight horses.

Earlier this year, Henry "Hair Buyer" Harrison was exchanged. We captured him at Vincennes in February 1779.

---

[131] Near present-day Jetersville, Virginia.

Since that time he was kept in a tiny, almost lightless cell in leg irons. The British tried desperately to have him exchanged as a prisoner of war. Governor Thomas Jefferson refused. His rationale was that "Hair Buyer" was being held as a war criminal. Based on the atrocities he committed, I can surely agree with that.

Sincerely, Roelof

Chapter Seven

The play, sir, is over.
—Marquis de Lafayette

In September 1781, the Allied American and French forces reached Yorktown, Virginia, to begin a siege of the British positions. Having the French was an advantage, because they were experienced in siege warfare. Continual bombarding and daring raids convinced British general Cornwallis to surrender on October 19, 1781.

While the surrender at Yorktown for all practical purposes ended the war, it was not over. In 1782, bloody battles took place in Kentucky and Ohio. Partisan activity continued in South Carolina. Loyalists committed a brutal massacre in New Jersey.

The British evacuated Savannah and Charleston in 1782. In March 1783, another attempt was made to remove Washington as commander in chief. Washington deftly turned aside the mutiny attempt.

On September 3, 1783, the Treaty of Paris was signed. In December 1783, the British evacuated New York City. Washington made a historic decision about his role as commander in chief.

◥◞

September 30, 1781
Dear Father,

We arrived outside of Yorktown yesterday. Even though
Washington is quite familiar with the area, having participated
in cockfighting before the war, he had sent General Louis
Duportail to work with General Lafayette to determine the best
locale to start a siege of Yorktown. The French are arrayed to
our left in front of the British right. We are on the right in front
of the British left. Our line is divided into three divisions, left
to right: General Friedrich von Steuben, General Marquis de
Lafayette, and General Benjamin Lincoln.

I learned some very interesting news about the Battle of
the Capes between de Grasse and Graves. In July, the Culper
Spy Ring provided Allan McLane with the British Royal Navy's
signal book. Washington immediately sent McLane to the West
Indies, where McLane presented the signal book to Admiral de
Grasse. Since de Grasse won the battle, it must have been helpful.

The Battle of the Capes was also very useful, because it
allowed Admiral Jacques-Melchoir de Barras to get his eight
ships here bearing heavy artillery and siege guns. British
Admiral Graves had intelligence that Barras was leaving
Newport, Rhode Island, and his goal was to stop Barras. Barras
took a circuitous route, avoiding the British, and while the
naval battle ensued, Barras managed to slip in. In midsummer,
Barras had received orders from France to lead an expedition
against Newfoundland. When the allied movement formed,
Rochambeau convinced Barras to ignore those orders so that
he could bring armaments to Virginia.

I told Lafayette that I met General Rochambeau's aide-de-
camp, Axel von Fersen. He is about my age. Since the French
Deux-Ponts Regiment is made up of Germans, I assumed he
too was German. Lafayette told me that he was a Swedish
count. Then Lafayette shocked me when he told me that it was
rumored that von Fersen was a lover of the French queen, Marie
Antoinette. Because the rumors around Versailles made things

uncomfortable for von Fersen, he was only too glad to come to America with Rochambeau.

I had the pleasure of Lafayette introducing me to Billy Lee, General Washington's valet. Billy is a mixed-race slave. Washington purchased him for £61, 15 shillings in 1768. To keep them together, Washington, at the same time, purchased Billy's brother, Frank, for £50. Billy is always at Washington's side. He accompanied Washington on surveying trips before the war. A superb rider, he served as Washington's huntsman on fox hunts. He was at Washington's side at Princeton when the general led the attack on the British. He went with Washington to Cambridge in 1775 and hadn't been back to see his family until now.

Your son, Moses

October 7, 1781
Dear Mr. Chaplin,

I am very familiar with the area around Yorktown. Before the war it was a popular place to hold cockfights. Because Cornwallis got here almost two months before we did, he made an attempt to spoil all the water in the vicinity. One of our main tasks has been to locate sources of potable water. While doing that task, we've been busy running down pigs to feast on roasted pork.

On September 28, General Nelson, who is also governor of Virginia, made a request of British general Cornwallis to allow the citizens of Yorktown to leave before hostilities started. Cornwallis granted the request. We are not sure how many took the opportunity, but we do know that some citizens did not leave.

We have been very busy making gabions, fascines, and saucissons[132] to be used in the construction of siege trenches.

---

[132] Saucissons are large fascines. The word is derived from a type of French sausage.

We do this work in ravines, out of range of British artillery and out of sight of British eyes.

On October 1, General Duportail plotted the lines for the trenches known as the first parallel. On the fifth, being engaged as sappers, we followed the engineers to trace lines for the parallel with strips of pine wood laid end to end. During the evening of October 6, before we started digging, General Washington rode up, dismounted, grabbed a pickax, and with his hands broke the first ground for the siege.

The trenches are ten feet wide and four feet high. We dug like badgers all night, and by dawn the first parallel over half a mile was complete. True to European tradition, on the seventh, a trench opening ceremony was held. French and American troops marched to their respective trenches, with drums beating and banners unfurled. When in the trench, banners were planted in full sight of the British.

The British then started a deluge of cannon fire, which stopped when they witnessed a jaw-dropping sight. Lieutenant Colonel Alexander Hamilton commanded the 2nd Battalion of Hazen's Brigade to mount the epaulement[133] and execute the manual of arms from von Steuben's Regulations for the Order and Discipline of the Troops of the United States—an impressive display, yes, but too dangerous.

Sincerely, Roelof

October 9, 1781
Dear Uncle Eb,

We got to Yorktown on September 29. It didn't take long for the action to start. The French noted a lack of activity in the outer British redoubts. When they investigated, they were surprised to see that the British had abandoned them. The French not only took them but fortified them to use against the British.

---

[133] A barricade of earth used as a cover from flanking fire.

On September 30, the French made an attack on the Fusilier's Redoubt. It is star shaped and heavily protected by abatis. The French drove off the British pickets, but that action drew grapeshot and musket fire from the redoubt. The French retreated but then attacked a second time, getting into the ditch around the redoubt. Again they retreated but tried a third attack. By this time the British ships in the York River opened up, and the French were finally beaten back.

On October 1, the army's workhorses finally arrived. With the arrival of the horses, they were put to work hauling artillery from the James River that Admiral Barras brought from Rhode Island. As we were doing this work, we encountered many slaves infected with smallpox that Cornwallis had turned out of Yorktown. Many were found dead, and we had to avoid those who hadn't died. We were ordered to air our bedding daily.

I got separated from my Canadian friend Clement Gosselin, because Hazen's men were positioned with General Lafayette in the center. Our outfit under General James Clinton is positioned with General Lincoln on the far right.

Work started on digging trenches on October 6. The trench is called a parallel. We had rain before we started digging the trenches. It also rained most of the night. While it was uncomfortable in the wetness, we had easier digging than expected.

Our general Knox and French Colonel Commandant Francois Marie d'Aboville marked where the batteries should be placed. The French, more experienced with siege warfare, managed to complete their portion of the parallel and battery positions before we did. At 3:00 p.m. today, d'Aboville touched off the French cannonade on the British. As we got into the action, the noise was indescribable.

Sincerely, Teunis

October 11, 1781
Dear Uncle Eb,

In my last letter, I mentioned the deafening noise as some of the allied artillery pieces were put into action. When all the batteries were completed yesterday, the bombardment totally dwarfed that on the ninth. Even though Knox and d'Aboville had basically selected their artillery positions, they asked for an attack on the British lines. It was a ruse to get the British, firing at the attack, to better reveal the location of their guns so that the allied guns could be more advantageously placed.

I had mentioned that the French opened the cannonade. At 5:00 p.m. on the ninth, General Washington arrived at Battery 13A, the farthest battery on the right, located along the York River facing British Redoubt 10. Washington touched the fuse. The cannon roared, sending a ball into Yorktown, striking house to house.

On the tenth, all the batteries were completed. The French concentrated their fire on Fusilier's Redoubt. It is a strong fortification. If the French expect to get into Yorktown, it will have to be neutralized. The American bombardment concentrated on the Hornwork, where we were able to set up a pretty good cross fire.

As the cannonade continued, the British guns started to go silent. We are not sure if it was because their weapons were too damaged to fire or if their gunners' positions had become too hazardous to maintain. We could see that their fortifications were being heavily damaged. The American gunners used a smart tactic to improve their results. Before each shot, gunners made a mark with chalk on the platforms along the wheels. If the shot had been well directed, the carriage would be placed exactly in that same place again.

At 8:00 p.m. last night, the French started tossing hot shot at the British ships. This is a dangerous procedure, because a hot shot is put down the barrel, which contains powder. To prevent an explosion, the powder is covered with a wad followed by a cushion of water-soaked hay. Then the cannon shot is placed into the muzzle, and immediately the fuse is ignited. The French wanted to clear out the ships, which were effective in covering Fusilier's Redoubt. One ship hauled anchor, but another was hit and when attempting to flee collided with others spreading quite a conflagration.

Sincerely, Teunis

~~~

October 12, 1781
Dear Mr. Chaplin,

With all the shelling going on, the ditches around the redoubts along the trench were suffering damage. To strengthen the redoubts, we were busy making wooden palisades to fortify the ditches. The palisades are twelve feet long, with one end pointed. During the night on the tenth, we started to dig the trench for the second parallel. These trenches are three feet deep and three feet wide at the top but only two feet wide at the bottom. These trenches will only handle soldiers, while the trenches of the first parallel were broad enough to handle carriages. By the morning of the eleventh, the second parallel was completed. It ends about three hundred yards from British Redoubt 9. There is a strong epaulement at the ending of the trench.

At noon on the tenth, we were surprised to see a white flag elevated above the enemy works. Two British soldiers escorted former Virginia Secretary of State Thomas Nelson, General Nelson's uncle, to the American lines. Earlier in the day, Washington, at the behest of Nelson's sons, sent a white flag to General Cornwallis, asking for the old gentleman's release. Cornwallis had been using Nelson's home as his headquarters. Surprisingly, surely aware Nelson could provide intelligence, Cornwallis honored Washington's request.

Nelson told Washington that the French and American artillery was taking a heavy toll. Many Yorktown citizens had taken refuge in caves beneath the cliffs along the York River. Many British soldiers also were taking refuge there. Nelson advised that the forces on Gloucester Point were very effectively hemmed in by the allied troops led by French General de Choisy.

Because of a lack of forage, Tarleton had more than one thousand horses destroyed. He also told us that on the first artillery shot by the Americans, the ball hit a house where British officers were dining, killing Commissary General Perkins. The biggest news, however, was that Major Charles Cochrane had eluded the French fleet to bring a message from General Henry Clinton in New York to Cornwallis. Cochrane reported that Clinton was in the process of sending Admiral Robert Digby with four thousand troops on thirty ships.

Another item of interest happened on the tenth. General Nelson was in a battery commanded by General Lafayette. Lafayette asked Nelson where to direct his cannons. Nelson pointed to his own house, explaining that since Secretary Nelson's house was now in ruins, his house was most certainly being used as headquarters by Cornwallis. To top it off, Nelson offered five guineas to the gunner who was the first to hit his house.

Sincerely, Roelof

October 16, 1781
Dear Father,

Two days ago, the fourteenth, there was a lot of anticipation among the troops. All day the cannonade was directed at the Fusilier's Redoubt and Redoubts 9 and 10. A lot of hot shot was directed at the abatis surrounding those redoubts. Due to the abatis being apple wood, not pine, the abatis would not ignite. Late in the day, we learned that Redoubts 9 and 10 were going to be attacked. I am sure that because of the intelligence that the British were sending four thousand troops, the command decided that we had to hasten a termination to the siege.

The attack on Redoubt 10 was undertaken by the Americans. General Lafayette wanted Lieutenant Colonel John-Joseph de Gimat to command the attack. Instead, Washington selected

Lieutenant Colonel Alexander Hamilton to command. Light infantry troops from Massachusetts, Connecticut, Rhode Island, New Hampshire, and New York, numbering four hundred, were selected for the attack. Gimat and Major Nicholas Fish led the attack. Lieutenant Colonel John Laurens was directed to sweep around the rear of the redoubt to cut off enemy troops trying to escape.

In darkness the attack commenced, in silence, with muskets empty. This was a bayonet and spontoon[134] charge. Surprisingly the men got through the abatis easier than expected. The British and Hessian defenders were completely surprised and were shooting over the attackers. In ten minutes the redoubt was quickly overwhelmed and captured. Considering all the action, the casualties were quite light on both sides.

The storming of Redoubt 9 fell to the French. General Baron de Viomenil was in command. They too had four hundred men consisting of chasseurs and grenadiers from the Gatinois Regiment and the Deux-Ponts Regiment. Rochambeau specifically selected Deux-Ponts because of their fighting reputation. Gatinois was led by Lieutenant Colonel Baron de l'Estrade. Deux-Ponts was led by Graf Wilhelm von Forbach of Zweibrücken (*Vicomte Guillaume de Deux-Ponts* in French). The French had a much tougher time getting into the redoubt. They had to hack through abatis with axes. It took a half hour to capture. Due to the Gatinois wearing white uniforms, some of the Deux-Ponts were killed by mistake, because the Deux-Ponts were wearing blue uniforms similar to the Hessians in the redoubt.

After the redoubt action, the second parallel was extended to get closer to the lines of the British left. On the fifteenth, both redoubts were armed with our artillery. This morning, at about 4:00 a.m., we were completely taken by surprise when the British, under Lieutenant Colonel Robert Abercromby, led an attack on a French battery. He did manage to spike several cannons but was eventually driven off. Washington rewarded

---

[134] A shafted weapon, six to seven feet in length, having a pointed blade with a crossbar at its base.

the Deux-Ponts with an artillery piece for their gallant efforts at Redoubt 9.

Your son, Moses

❧

October 19, 1781
Dear Father,

At 10:00 a.m. October 17, the fourth anniversary of the surrender at Saratoga, amidst a tremendous allied cannonade, a drummer appeared above the British ramparts beating a chamade.[135] Soon an officer appeared waving a white handkerchief. All shelling stopped. An American officer sent the drummer back, blindfolded the British officer, and conducted him to General Lafayette, who in turn conducted him to General Washington's headquarters.

The note from Cornwallis proposed a cessation of hostilities for twenty-four hours and that two officers appointed from each side meet at the Moore residence to settle terms for surrender. The British officer returned to his lines, and the allied bombardment resumed. With another white flag, the officer returned for Washington's response. Washington sent him back with the message that Cornwallis needed to send back a written proposal within two hours. Again artillery recommenced.

At 4:30 p.m., Cornwallis sent his proposal of terms: the garrisons of Yorktown and Gloucester Point shall be prisoners of war with the customary *honours*; the British soldiers shall be sent back to Britain, and German soldiers shall be sent back to Germany under engagement not to serve against France, America, or their Allies until released or exchanged; and all arms and stores shall be delivered to the American forces. What? Did Cornwallis forget the dishonorable surrender required of General Lincoln at Charleston? Did Cornwallis not remember

---

[135] A chamade is a certain beat of a drum, or sound of a trumpet, which signaled to the enemy a proposition to be made to their commander.

that American prisoners of war were dying daily aboard British prison ships?

Washington responded that hostilities would be suspended for the night and if his terms were agreed to, the commissioners would meet to formulate the official terms of surrender. Washington's terms were that the same honors would be granted as were granted at Charleston, soldiers would be allowed to keep personal items, officers would be allowed to keep their sidearms, and everything else would be turned over to the Allies. Cornwallis had 120 minutes to agree before hostilities again commenced. Cornwallis responded favorably and agreed to impose further cessation of his artillery at 5:00 a.m. the next morning.

The morning of the eighteenth had a very strange feeling. There was virtually no noise, and soldiers were peering across from each other. Just the day before, they were trying to kill each other or were trying to escape from being killed by the other side. The commissioners were named. Washington named his aide-de-camp, Lieutenant Colonel John Laurens, whose father was being held as a prisoner in the Tower of London. Rochambeau named Vicomte Louis-Marie de Noailles, the bother of Lafayette's wife, Adrienne. Cornwallis named Lieutenant Colonel Thomas Dundas and Major Alexander Ross, who is a close personal friend of Cornwallis.

There was an interesting development on the eighteenth. General Lincoln approached the American trenches to relieve General von Steuben. Citing European precedent, von Steuben claimed that since his troops were in the trenches when negotiations for the surrender began, they had the right to continue on duty until capitulation. When Lincoln protested, Washington sustained von Steuben. The Regiments Bourbonnais and Deux-Ponts continued on duty in the French trenches. Not used to siege warfare, we Americans aren't familiar with these European traditions of trench opening ceremonies and the protocol of the honor to holding a trench during capitulation proceedings.

On the eighteenth, the commissioners met at the Moore residence, located about a mile southeast of Redoubts 9 and 10.

Ross and Dundas wanted to be accorded the terms rendered to Burgoyne at Saratoga. Laurens and de Noailles stood firm and stated the British would get the same terms they rendered Lincoln at Charleston. The surrender would be without honors—the garrison would march out with colors cased and drums beating a British or German march. The truce was extended to 9:00 a.m. on October 19.

There was controversy regarding the Loyalists. Cornwallis requested immunity for Loyalists serving with his army. Washington, who more than likely would like to have seen the Loyalists hanged, refused that request. He pointed out that the jurisdiction for the treatment of Loyalists rested with the United States government. However, Washington agreed that the sloop HMS *Bonetta* would be at Cornwallis's disposal to carry dispatches and private property. The *Bonetta* was designated a cartel ship, meaning it could proceed on its humanitarian voyage to New York but then had to be turned over to the French.

The surrender at Gloucester Point had a slight difference. Because the garrison there was contained but not under siege, Tarleton's cavalry would be allowed to ride forth with swords drawn, but the infantry would surrender with cased colors.

Washington informed Cornwallis that he expected the Articles of Capitulation to be signed by 11:00 a.m. on the nineteenth and the garrison to march out at 2:00 p.m. At noon, the Union Jack was lowered. The British signers of the articles were General Charles Lord Cornwallis and Naval Captain Thomas Symonds. The Allied signers were General George Washington for the United States, and Le Comte de Rochambeau and Le Comte de Barras (signing for Comte de Grasse) for the French.

Today, at 3:00 p.m., an hour later than specified, the British garrison marched out. As they marched out, the French were on their right and we were on their left. We were astonished to see that the march out was led by British general Charles O'Hara, second in command to Cornwallis. Was Cornwallis ill or too embarrassed to show? General O'Hara rode up to General Rochambeau to present his sword of surrender. Was O'Hara intending to slight Washington, or was he merely trying to avoid him? Rochambeau pointed to Washington, across from him, directing O'Hara in that direction. O'Hara then presented his sword of surrender to Washington. Washington refused to accept it. He pointed to General Benjamin Lincoln, his second in command. Lincoln symbolically held it a moment before returning it to O'Hara.

The garrison marched out to a tune we did not recognize. Some thought it was titled "The World Turned Upside Down." If that is what they played, it certainly was appropriate. As the British were to deliver their colors, a problem developed. They resented having to hand them over to noncommissioned officers. Lieutenant Colonel Alexander Hamilton solved the issue. He had a commissioned officer receive the colors to hand over to sergeants. As the British marched out, they refused to look at the Americans. All had their heads turned right, looking at the French. When General Lafayette saw this, he ordered his band to strike up "Yankee Doodle." All heads turned left! Now they were looking at us! I am sending this letter with Tench Tilghman, whom Washington is sending to Philadelphia with the news of Yorktown's surrender.

Your son, Moses

October 29, 1781
Dear Uncle Eb,

As I write this, I am totally devastated. I am on HMS *Bonetta* going back to New York. With the surrenders at Yorktown and Gloucester Point, I have to admit that the Rebels will win their revolution against the Crown. Most disappointingly, we were told several times that General Clinton was sending help. They came too late! The first word was back on September 16. Then on September 29, we received word that troops were sent to arrive on October 5. Finally, on October 10, Major Cochrane slipped by the French to tell us four thousand troops were on the way. I don't know why Clinton gave Cornwallis these hopes of relief when he didn't leave New York until October 19, the day of the surrender. Clinton's ships appeared on the twenty-fourth, and now we are sailing back to New York with the fleet.

On October 3, our forces were foraging when they were engaged by Lauzon's Legion. Soon Tarleton's Legion came to engage Lauzon, and the Battle of the Hook was on. There was some hand-to-hand combat, but Tarleton retired when Lieutenant Colonel John Mercer's Virginia militia joined the battle.

During the intense allied bombardment, we witnessed cannonballs skipping across the York River, hitting our shores. General Cornwallis had many women and children brought across to us from Yorktown. After Cornwallis observed the allies' second parallel having been completed on the twelfth, he ordered Lieutenant Colonel Thomas Dundas to bring reinforcements to Yorktown from Gloucester Point. That same day, Major Cochrane, who brought the news of Clinton's sending reinforcements, was decapitated by a cannon shot while standing next to Cornwallis. Realizing dealings were getting dire, Cornwallis, on the night of the sixteenth, attempted to evacuate Yorktown to Gloucester Point. After the first boats got across, a violent storm hit, blowing boats downstream, putting an end to the attempt.

On the seventeenth, Cornwallis decided to surrender. I was very worried about what the terms would be regarding Loyalists. Cornwallis requested immunity for Loyalists who fought with his army. Washington would not agree, because the treatment of Loyalists was the jurisdiction of the government, not his to agree to in terms of surrender. However, he gave us a way to escape Virginia by placing the *Bonetta* at Cornwallis's disposal to carry messages to Clinton but then turn the *Bonetta* over to the French after it arrives at New York. As a result, Cornwallis loaded a lot of us Loyalists on the *Bonetta*. Many slaves are also on board, including Deborah, who was one of Washington's slaves.

God Save the King, Zack

November 5, 1781
Dear Uncle Eb,

Yesterday Admiral de Grasse left with his fleet. On October 21, General Washington was rebuffed by de Grasse as he tried to convince him to attack Charleston, teaming up with General Nathanael Greene to drive the British out. Also today General Anthony Wayne is being sent down to the Carolinas. I am on my way north with Hazen's Canadians, taking Hessian and Ansbacher prisoners to Lancaster, Pennsylvania. Hopefully I can see you at the Blaze Horse on my way back home.

I can't believe I had the fortune to witness a second major capitulation of the British. I can't help remember how polite we were to the British at the surrender in Saratoga, while witnessing the crude conduct of the British here. Instead of handing over their weapons, they tried to destroy them. While the German troops marched out respectfully and in perfect step, the British were sullen or drunk. At the surrender, Captain John Parke (Jacky) Custis, Washington's stepson, watched from a carriage, very sick with fever. Today he died.

After the ceremony, Baker General Christopher Ludwig baked six thousand pounds of bread for the British soldiers. As did Gates for Burgoyne's officers, General Washington invited the British officers to dine with the Allied officers. There was one exception—American officers balked at inviting Banastre Tarleton. While dining, Cornwallis stated he had no funds to pay his soldiers. Rochambeau advanced Cornwallis £150,000 in silver for that purpose.

General Nelson, seeing many slaves boarding the *Bonetta*, protested. However, the French reminded him the *Bonetta* was a cartel ship so no inspection would be allowed. In addition to local slaves escaping, many Loyalists were on the *Bonetta*.

I learned the Allies fired 15,437 artillery rounds during the siege. That amounts to 1,700 rounds per day, or 71 rounds per hour. More than one a minute! Our casualties were a little over 100; the French about 250; and the British over 500, along with over 7,000 prisoners.

A few days after the surrender, Banastre Tarleton was riding his horse in Yorktown. A citizen brandishing a wooden stick demanded he get off. Tarleton meekly gave up the horse. I guess he remembered the great line General Lafayette uttered at the surrender: "The play, sir, is over." Perhaps we can now really say, "Bye, George."

Sincerely, Teunis

❧

November 6, 1781
Dear Moses, Teunis, Roelof, Felix, and Ben,

On October 24, Philadelphia was treated to the joyous pealing of the Liberty Bell when the news of the Yorktown surrender was delivered by Tench Tilghman to the president of Congress, Thomas McKean. Moses, later that day, he delivered your last letter to the Blaze Horse. Fireworks were planned but had to be delayed for two days due to rain. In the Blaze Horse, shouts of "Bye, George" were celebrated.

On November 3, the captured enemy standards arrived. Seeing the standards really made all believers. They were placed before Congress and French Ambassador Anne-César de La Luzerne. Most of us were impressed by the intricacy and colors of the Hesse-Kassel and Ansbach-Bayreuth standards.

Moses, Roelof, and Teunis, thank you for your letters describing all the events during the Yorktown Siege. I also want to let you know that Ben and Felix have been sending news from their actions in the Carolinas. Ben has been with General Greene in many battles. While the British were victors, they managed to wear out Cornwallis, eventually sending him to Yorktown. Felix has been with Francis Marion most of the time. From what he writes, Marion is most impressive.

I do have some painful news. In early September, British general Henry Clinton attempted a diversion to draw Washington away from New York. The ruses set up by Washington evidently worked quite well, because by that time Washington and Rochambeau were well on their way to Yorktown. As the diversion, Clinton sent General Benedict Arnold to Connecticut.

At sunrise on September 6, Arnold arrived on the Thames River. Upon seeing Arnold's fleet, Fort Griswold fired two cannon rounds as a signal that an enemy was approaching. Arnold, being familiar with the signal, immediately had one of his guns fire a third round, changing the signal to a victorious friend arriving. Arnold's men landed at New London and set some fires. One of the storehouses lit contained gunpowder, and when it ignited most of the town was in flames. Arnold sent British Colonel Edmund Eyre and the New Jersey Loyalist Skinner's Greens, with 800 men, to attack Fort Griswold, defended by about 150 men under command of Lieutenant Colonel William Ledyard. After a gallant fight, Ledyard surrendered his sword to a British officer, who took it and plunged it into Ledyard. The word is that Clinton was not impressed with Arnold because he lost 25 percent of his men.

Sincerely, Eb Chaplin

January 1, 1782
Dear Uncle Eb,

As this New Year arrives, I am very troubled regarding my future. Since Yorktown, I feel it is quite evident that unless Britain makes some drastic changes in its military strategy, Britain has lost its American colonies. As a result, I am trying to plot a course of action. I am sure that I will have to leave America. New York City is full of Loyalists from many parts of the country. The way Loyalists and their properties are treated, we feel it would be unsafe to try to remain in America.

I've been thinking about how the greatest military nation in the world could be defeated by what I consider rebellious tyrants. First, King George appointed Lord Germain as his secretary of state for America to lead the war effort. This is a man who was convicted by a court-martial of malfeasance in the face of the enemy at the Battle of Minden in 1759. Second, there was a continual change of commanders in chief. Thomas Gage was replaced by William Howe, who was replaced by Henry Clinton, who is now replaced by Sir Guy Carleton. Third, there was constant dissension between generals (Clinton versus Howe, Cornwallis versus Clinton) and uncooperativeness at times between the army and the navy. Fourth, in seven years only two expeditionary forces were sent—to New York in 1776 and to Canada in 1777. Included in both were German mercenaries who were fighting only for the money or loot they received. Fifth, the American soldier had total dedication. My friend Johann Ewald told me that he was impressed when he found books on captured prisoners, such *as Instructions of the King of Prussia to his Generals* or Thielke's *Field Engineers*. Sixth, supply lines for food and armaments had to reach all the way to Canada, Jamaica, Ireland, and England.

Some of my friends are considering going to England. I don't think I'd fit into their culture. After all, I am an American. Many are considering Nova Scotia or other parts of Canada. Since working as a ropewalker, I don't think there is a great opportunity for that profession there. I don't want to go to East Florida or the Bahamas, because I think they will be returned to Spain after the war. Because of my feelings against slavery, I don't think Jamaica would be a fit. Perhaps my best option would be Bermuda. Bermuda was enticed by your Congress but stayed Loyal.

God Save the King, Zack

❧

February 22, 1782
Dear Moses, Teunis, Roelof, Felix, and Ben,

Today we are really busy in the Blaze Horse getting ready for a big group of people to celebrate General Washington's birthday. After Jacky Custis was buried, he and Martha came to Philadelphia. While the army was sent to the Hudson Highlands in New York, Washington is making his headquarters at the house that was confiscated from Loyalist John Penn, former governor of Pennsylvania. Washington is advising and entreating Congress to maintain and fully support the Continental Army. Funding to pay the soldiers has been a constant problem. Since the victory at Yorktown, there are some in Congress who don't feel an urgent need to support the army, thinking it will soon disband with expected peace talks.

General Rochambeau and his French troops are encamped in Virginia at Williamsburg, Hampton, Halfway House, Gloucester, Jamestown, and Yorktown. Speaking of funding, Robert Morris, our new superintendent of finance, managed to arrange a loan from Rochambeau when he came through Philadelphia on the way to Virginia last September. Morris has been tireless in his attempts to fund the war effort. He told me his frustration is that the Articles of Confederation have the power to maintain a wartime army but have no power to levy taxes to support it. At this point, Congress has asked for $6 million from the states to fund the army but has collected only $125,000.

Morris himself has financed a lot of the war effort from his own pocket. Another man involved in financing the war is Haym Salomon. He is a Polish-born Jewish immigrant who became a financial broker in New York City. In 1776, the British arrested him as a Patriot spy. He was pardoned and used as an interpreter with their Hessian troops. When the British discovered he was helping American prisoners escape and encouraging Hessians to desert, he was sentenced to death. He escaped and came to Philadelphia, where he continues his financing work.

Moses, it was so good to see you on your way north to your winter encampment. Let's hope the winter isn't being too hard on you. Teunis, I was so happy to see you at the Blaze Horse on your way back to your home. Ben, I received a letter from Zack expressing his concern about where he might live after a peace treaty. Since you were so close to him growing up, I am sending his letter to you. Perhaps you can give him some advice.

Sincerely, Eb Chaplin

❧

July 12, 1782
Dear Uncle Eb,

After the Battle of Eutaw Springs, we camped at Round O[136] to keep an eye on the British left flank. General Marion was keeping an eye on the British right flank along the Cooper River. Last December 1, General Greene drove the British out of Fort Dorchester,[137] capturing two artillery pieces. You might remember my mentioning that British Major John Marjoribanks saved William Washington's life at Eutaw Springs. We later learned that Marjoribanks died on October 22, 1781, from wounds suffered in the battle.

After Yorktown, Washington sent Generals Anthony Wayne and Mordecai Gist to assist Greene in wrapping up the Southern campaign. Greene sent Wayne to Georgia on January 12. I joined his small force. Because we had such a small force, Greene advised Wayne not to attack Savannah but to keep the British there contained and to drive out Tories and Indians who were allied with the British. Wayne devised a trick he used on the Indians. While our uniforms were blue, they were lined on the inside in red. Because we wore our uniforms inside out, the Indians thought we were British troops and would welcome us in, resulting in quite a few captures. Wayne also advised the Indians that because the British held only Savannah, the British would no longer be able to support them.

Another tactic Wayne used was to encourage Tories to defect to the Patriot cause as "reclaimed Citizens." Wayne had proclamations sent into Savannah written in English and German, promising deserters, on condition that they serve with him until the enemy surrendered or left Georgia, a full pardon, two hundred acres of land, a cow, and two breeding swine. This action produced immediate results, with many Hessians accepting the offer.

---

[136] Near present-day Walterboro, South Carolina.
[137] Near present-day Summerville, South Carolina.

On the night of June 23, "Burnfoot" Brown had Creek Chief Emistisiguo attack us. We beat them back with a bayonet charge, killing Emistisiguo. Finally, yesterday, British Colonel Alured Clarke surrendered. The British troops shipped out to Charleston. Tory civilian refugees, including "Burnfoot" Brown and his King's Rangers, numbering 2,500, along with 4,000 slaves, were sent to St. Augustine. We later learned that back in May the new British commander in chief, Sir Guy Carleton, had sent word to Savannah it would be evacuated as soon as Carleton could provide ships.

Sincerely, Ben

August 5, 1782
Dear Moses, Teunis, Roelof, Felix, and Ben,

John Paul Jones's *Serapis* is no more. In 1780, the French commissioned the *Serapis* a privateer. A year ago it was off the coast of Madagascar when a sailor accidentally dropped a lantern into a tub of brandy. The flames eventually reached a powder magazine, with the resulting explosion destroying the ship.

Between year-end and February, the following exchanges took place. British general George Cornwallis was exchanged for Henry Laurens, who had been held in the Tower of London. British general Charles O'Hara was exchanged for General Landis McIntosh, captured at Charleston. British general John Burgoyne was exchanged for General William Moultrie, also captured at Charleston.

The marquis de Lafayette returned to France, arriving there on January 22, where he saw his new daughter, Marie Antoinette Virginie. When received at Versailles, he was promoted to maréchal de camp. On April 19, 1782, the Dutch Republic recognized our independence.

Early this year, Colonel Matthias Ogden of New Jersey suggested to Washington that King George's son, Crown Prince

William Henry, and Admiral Robert Digby be captured. The Crown prince arrived in New York City on September 26, 1781, and became a friend of Digby. The thought was that, if captured, the Crown prince could be exchanged for the American prisoners rotting on British prison ships. Washington approved the plan until he was notified by his spies in New York City that General Clinton had doubled his sentries. Washington called off the plan.

On August 2, Washington received a letter from Admiral Digby and Sir Guy Carleton that Great Britain had commenced negotiations in Paris for ending the war. The American negotiators are Benjamin Franklin, John Adams, John Jay, and Henry Laurens. The British negotiators are David Hartley and Richard Oswald. Oswald was a former partner of Henry Laurens in the slave trade.

Ben, your friend Peter Jaquette stopped by the Blaze Horse. Since Peter is from Delaware, Allan McLane's name came up. I mentioned McLane's prophecy on Benedict Arnold, his exploits at Stony Point and Paulus Hook, and his getting the British Naval signal book to the French. I was shocked when he characterized McLane as "more to plunder and make money, than to destroy the common enemy."

Sincerely, Eb Chaplin

September 1, 1782
Dear Mr. Chaplin,

I've heard that negotiations started back in April with the British for a peace treaty. One would think that at Yorktown we meant that it would be "Bye, George." Unfortunately, the British continue to stir up trouble in the Ohio and Kentucky country. I have distressing news to report from Ohio and Kentucky, as well as a heroic act by a lady in Kentucky.

The Moravian Church set up missions to convert Lenape Indians to Christianity in Ohio in 1772. In September 1781, the British forced the Christian Indians and Moravian missionaries from Gnadenhutten, taking two of the missionaries to Fort

Detroit, accusing them of treason for providing military intelligence to the American garrison at Fort Pitt. They were eventually acquitted of the charge. In February of this year, about one hundred Indians returned to Gnadenhutten for food. In March, a militia force from Pennsylvania arrived to accuse the Indians of making raids on settlements in Pennsylvania. The Lenape denied the charges, but the militia took a vote to kill them all. When they were told, the Lenape requested time to prepare for death by praying and singing hymns through the night. Two Lenape boys managed to escape to tell the story. We have so few Indian allies. This horrible tragedy is not going to help matters.

Earlier this year a proposal was made to General Washington that an expedition be organized to capture and destroy Fort Detroit, from which the British were organizing the Indian raids on settlers in the west. While Washington agreed, he indicated there were no funds to accommodate it. Reluctantly, Washington's friend Colonel William Crawford came out of retirement to lead the expedition. With almost five hundred Pennsylvania Volunteers, the expedition left for Detroit on May 25 to destroy it and to destroy Wyandot and Delaware Indian encampments near Sandusky in the Ohio country.

On June 4, the expedition reached Sandusky Plains and got into a battle with the Delawares and Wyandots. After intense fighting, Crawford's men gained possession of a grove known as Battle Island. The next day it became obvious that the British had known about the expedition because Captain William Caldwell, with his British Rangers and Shawnee Indians, arrived. When the reinforcements arrived, Simon Girty called for a surrender, which was refused.

That night Crawford and Dr. John Knight got separated from the main force. On June 6, the forces were attacked at Olentangy and eventually were able to drive off the Indians, enabling a retreat. On the seventh, Crawford and Knight were captured by Delaware Indians. Knight was found alive in July by hunters in Pennsylvania.

Late on August 15, the settlers in fortified Bryan's Station[138] in the Kentucky country became aware they were surrounded by

---

[138] Located near present-day Lexington, Kentucky.

a hostile force of Indians. To withstand a siege, the fortification would need water. The next morning, Jemimah Johnson suggested that all the women of the fort go to a nearby spring to fill water buckets. Her thought was that, because this would be normal activity, the Indians would not suspect that the settlers knew they were there. Eventually the Wyandots and British/Canadian Rangers, under command of Captain William Caldwell and Simon Girty, attacked with burning arrows. One of the burning arrows struck the crib of Jemimah's son.[139] With the water fetched, that fire and others were extinguished. Eventually two men slipped out to obtain help.

Militia arriving from Lexington and Boone's Station fought their way into Bryan's Station, causing Caldwell and Girty to abandon the siege the morning of the seventeenth. On the eighteenth, several militia units pursued the Indians. One of the units was under command of Lieutenant Colonel Daniel Boone. On the morning of the nineteenth, the troops reached the Licking River, near a spring and salt lick known as the Lower Blue Licks[140], where they caught sight of a few Indians. Boone became suspicious because of the obvious trail the Indians left. He felt the Indians were trying to lead them into an ambush. The other leaders prevailed and crossed the river. After crossing and going up a hill, they were attacked by Caldwell's forces that had been hiding in ravines. Boone and his men retreated. During the retreat, Boone's son Israel was killed. The militia lost sixty men. Caldwell may not have had any men killed.

I just wonder when the British will stop this slaughter coming out of Fort Detroit. Let me know if you hear anything about Colonel Crawford's fate.

Sincerely, Roelof

---

[139] The baby was Richard Mentor Johnson. He is reputed to have killed Tecumseh during the War of 1812. He became the ninth vice president of the United States, serving under Martin Van Buren. He is the only vice president to be elected by the Senate because he did not have enough electoral votes to win outright.
[140] Near present-day Mount Olivet, Kentucky.

December 15, 1782
Dear Mr. Chaplin,

After Eutaw Springs, the Tories had one last hurrah on September 13, 1781, up in North Carolina at Lindley's Mill.[141] On the twelfth, Colonel David Fanning's North Carolina Loyalist militia captured North Carolina governor Thomas Burke. The next day, General John Butler pursued Fanning and had quite a bloody battle for four hours at Lindley's. Eventually Butler was flanked and had to retreat. Dr. John Pyle attended to wounded on both sides. Over the next year, Fanning tried to obtain a pardon from Butler. Fanning would break the agreements as fast as he got them. Finally, this past September, he went to St. Augustine.

With the surrender at Yorktown, General Washington sent Generals Mordecai Gist and Anthony Wayne down. Wayne was to clean up Georgia, and Gist was to assist Generals Marion and Greene in keeping the British holed up in Charleston. In March, British general Alexander Leslie requested a truce with Greene so that the British could obtain food for his garrison and the city's inhabitants. Greene refused. On August 27, Greene sent General Gist out to Combahee Ferry[142] to stop the British from plundering plantations. As the British started to move downriver, Gist sent Lieutenant Colonel John Laurens after them. The British set up an ambush, resulting in the death of Laurens.

When Cornwallis left the Carolinas, the British had almost no mounted troops at their disposal. Earlier this year we encountered a mounted unit they formed of former slaves, called the Black Dragoons. Patrolling outside the Charleston lines, the Black Dragoons have committed horrible depredations, including the murder of Hessian deserters they locate. Colonel Tadeusz Kościuszko became obsessed with defeating them.

[141] Near present-day Snow Camp, North Carolina.
[142] Near present-day Green Pond, South Carolina.

They kept eluding him, except for one minor skirmish in early November.

The last military deaths down here occurred on November 14 on James Island. Kościuszko, heavily outnumbered, attacked and routed three hundred British Regulars escorting a wood party. Of the seven deaths, five were Patriots.

Since the British troops evacuated from Savannah were sent to Charleston, General Greene ordered General Wayne to Charleston. British general Leslie agreed he would not destroy Charleston when he left if his troops were allowed to leave safely. Yesterday the British evacuated Charleston and, along with his troops, took 3,800 Loyalists and 5,000 slaves. Can we now say, "Bye, George"?

Sincerely, Felix

❧

January 1, 1783
Dear Uncle Eb and Zack,

Happy New Year! Zack, Uncle Eb sent me your letter regarding your concerns about where you might live after this war ends. I am sorry for not responding earlier, but I was heavily involved with General Anthony Wayne in Georgia, driving out the British and "Burnfoot" Brown's ruthless Loyalists.

Zack, as you know, I was disappointed when you decided to be a King's Friend instead of supporting the quest for independence. I so much remember when your family visited us in Salem as we were growing up. I think your idea of relocating to Bermuda is wise, and I feel I can help you. When I joined the Salem Minutemen, William Browne was our colonel. It turned out he was a Tory and was replaced. In 1776, he sailed off to London. In 1781, the British appointed him governor of Bermuda. If you go to Bermuda, let Browne know that you are my cousin.

Zack, you mentioned ideas on why the Patriots defeated the largest army in the world. Your mention of long supply lines was proved here in the Carolina campaign, with Cornwallis facing that very issue. I also would mention that your European troops expected normal supplies, while Americans could live with depravity.

Uncle Eb, after Savannah was evacuated, General Wayne was sent to Charleston to keep the British contained there. While there, I once again met Felix. Zack, I shared your letter with Felix. He pointed out the issue of how Patriots were treated by Loyalist provincial troops, especially Tarleton's Legion, which worked against the British cause by raising Patriot fervor. We both witnessed Tarleton's conduct in the Carolinas but later heard about an incident in Virginia when Tarleton sabered a young boy standing alongside the road just to make sure the boy wouldn't communicate to others that Tarleton was in the area. We both feel that Tarleton should not be returned to England but be tried as a war criminal.

Felix also told me about John Laurens being killed. Sadly, soon after his father is released from the Tower of London, he learns the sorrowful news of his son having been killed by the British.

Uncle Eb, on my way back to Salem I will stop by the Blaze Horse to visit you. One of my greatest disappointments of this struggle is that we did not capture Canada. I am of the opinion that sometime in the future we will be fighting Britain again.

Sincerely, Ben

January 15, 1783
Dear Roelof,

Your reports of what I would call British terrorist tactics aren't confined solely to the west. We recently had an incident close to home on the New Jersey shore. Last October 25, a Cape May privateer, Andrew Steelman, intercepted a British cutter that ran aground along the northern coast of Long Beach Island with a cargo of tea. After removing the cargo, the exhausted crew bedded down on the beach next to their spoils of war. During the night, John Bacon and his band of Loyalist Pine Robbers knifed to death twenty of the crew. On December 27, the New Jersey militia ran into Bacon's men at Cedar Bridge. The militia had him cornered when they were attacked by local Pine Barren Loyalists, allowing Bacon to get away.

You were asking about Colonel Crawford's fate. After Dr. Knight, who managed to escape, made it back to civilization, he related the gruesome story. When he and Crawford were captured, in retaliation for Gnadenhutten, the Indians had resolved to kill any American captives. Crawford's face was painted black, a sign he was to be executed. He was stripped naked, beaten, and tied to a pole a few yards from a large fire. Then he was poked with burning pieces of wood from the fire, and hot coals were thrown at him, which he was forced to walk on. He begged Simon Girty, who was present, to shoot him. Girty was unwilling or afraid to intervene. After about two hours of torture, he fell down unconscious. He was scalped, and a woman poured hot coals over his head, which revived him. He began to walk about insensibly as the torture continued. After he finally died, his body was burned.

Let me fill you in on Simon Girty. He was born in western Pennsylvania. During the French and Indian War, when he was fourteen, he was captured by the French and Seneca Indians. He was adopted by the Senecas and came to prefer their culture. At first he sided with us, but after being accused of treason for supposedly planning the seizure of Fort Pitt, he has served with the British as both an interpreter and leader of Indian raids.

As you mentioned, negotiations started in April of last year on a peace treaty with Britain. Just a few days ago, word was received that on November 30 preliminary articles for a treaty were signed. Hopefully that means "Bye, George!" Additionally, let's hope this stops the terrorist tactics by the British.

Sincerely, Cousin Ebenezer

March 16, 1783
Dear Father, Teunis, Roelof, Felix, and Ben,

Yesterday General Washington, arriving from Newburgh, defused a conspiracy at our encampment in New Windsor, New York. Because so many soldiers and officers are discontented with their treatment by Congress, Washington encouraged General Henry Knox to send a letter of grievances to Congress. It read in part, "We have borne all that men can bear—our property is expended—our private resources are at an end, and our friends are wearied out and disgusted with our incessant applications." The letter was delivered to Congress by General Alexander McDougall, a former delegate to Congress from New York.

Apparently the letter caused quite a flurry with Congress. General Horatio Gates was sent to Newburgh to be Washington's second in command. After he got here, a letter was distributed among the officers, which could lead to the conclusion that two thing were under way: a mutiny against Washington and a coup d'état against Congress. The letter was written by Major John Armstrong, Gates's aide-de-camp. The letter also notified the officers of a meeting to be held on March 10.

Washington, after seeing the disturbing letter, put out an order canceling the illicit meeting. In the meantime, Washington received a letter from Alexander Hamilton, now a delegate to Congress, suggesting Washington would likely need to use his great prestige to "keep a complaining and suffering army within the bounds of moderation." He also received a letter from his friend Virginia Delegate Joseph Jones, warning him of "dangerous combinations" and "sinister practices" in the army. Washington issued an order that a meeting for officers would occur on March 15. The Ides of March—coincidental or cleverly calculated? Washington implied in the order that he would not attend.

Yesterday, the fifteenth, the officers met with General Gates, who, acting as presiding officer in Washington's absence, opened the meeting. After several minutes, a small door offstage opened with Washington striding in. Washington then addressed the hostile crowd. After finishing, he felt his points had not been received well. He then reached into his pocket to retrieve Jones's letter, identified as coming from a member of Congress. He paused for some time instead of reading the letter. Many in the crowd wondered what was wrong. Eventually Washington reached into his pocket for a pair of new reading glasses. Then he went on to speak: "Gentlemen, you will permit me to put on my spectacles, for I have not only grown gray but almost blind in the service of my country." When he finished reading, he deliberately folded the letter, removed his glasses, and quickly exited. At this point, with many in tears, General Knox offered resolutions in appreciation of their commander in chief and their loyalty to Congress. The conspiracy collapsed. Support for Gates disintegrated.

Sincerely, Moses

❧

April 5, 1783
Dear Moses, Teunis, Roelof, Felix, and Ben,

As I mentioned earlier, a provisional treaty was signed by the American and British commissioners last November 30. I've learned more about it. Benjamin Franklin drew up eight points: (1) complete independence for the United States from Great Britain; (2) settle boundaries for the colonies; (3) move Canadian border north to its position prior to the Quebec Act of 1774; (4) freedom for Americans to catch fish and whales in the waters off Newfoundland; (5) Britain to pay reparations for burning American towns; (6) Parliament to confess its error for waging the war; (7) each country to extend trading privileges to the other; and (8) Britain to cede all of Canada to America. Franklin felt the first four points were essential. John Adams warned that if Britain did not permit America to fish off the coasts of Newfoundland and Nova Scotia, and to dry their fish on those shores, America would wage another war to seize that territory. John Jay insisted that Spain was to have no territory in America east of the Mississippi River.

For almost a year and a half, John Adams's fifteen-year-old son, John Quincy, has been serving as private secretary to Francis Dana in Saint Petersburg, Russia. Dana was sent as our minister to Russia in 1780. Even though Czarina Catherine II of Russia issued the Declaration of Armed Neutrality in 1780, she refuses to recognize Dana.

After General Horatio Gates's defeat at Camden, Congress passed a resolution for a board of inquiry, the prelude to a court-martial, to look into his conduct. Gates vehemently opposed the inquiry. Late last year Congress repealed the call for an inquiry, and to add insult to injury, especially after his role in the Conway Cabal, Gates was sent to Washington's encampment at Newburgh, New York, to be Washington's second in command. As we heard from Moses, sending Gates to Newburgh was a bad decision.

In November 1781, Pennsylvania petitioned Congress to settle the dispute in the Wyoming Valley as to whether it belonged to Pennsylvania or Connecticut. Five commissioners were appointed by Congress to settle the issue. After meeting from November 12 to December 30, 1782, the commissioners decided Connecticut had no right to the lands in controversy. However, Connecticut was allowed to keep its claims west of Pennsylvania.

Yesterday word was received that Tory John Bacon, mastermind of the Long Beach Island Massacre, was captured by a militia posse near Tuckerton, New Jersey. When he tried to escape, he was shot by militia Captain John Stewart.

Sincerely, Eb Chaplin

April 15, 1783
Dear Moses, Teunis, Roelof, Felix, and Ben,

Today Congress ratified a provisional treaty of peace with Great Britain. I cannot express enough elation with the words of Article

1: "His Brittanic Majesty acknowledges the said United States, viz., New Hampshire, Massachusetts Bay, Rhode Island and Providence Plantations, Connecticut, New York, New Jersey, Pennsylvania, Delaware, Maryland, Virginia, North Carolina, South Carolina and Georgia, to be free sovereign and Independent States; that he treats with them as such, and for himself his Heirs & Successors, relinquishes all claims to the Government, Propriety, and Territorial Rights of the same and every Part thereof."

Article 2 defines the boundaries of the United States with British North America. Basically the northern border is latitude 45 degrees for New York and then through the middle of the Great Lakes (except Lake Michigan) all the way to the Lake of the Woods. The Mississippi River is the western boundary. The southern boundary is basically latitude 31 degrees.

Article 3 gives the United States the right to take fish of every kind on the Grand Bank and on all the other banks of Newfoundland, and in the Gulf of Saint Lawrence. Article 8 provides that navigation of the Mississippi River shall forever remain free and open to the subjects of Great Britain and the citizens of the United States. The other articles deal with payment of debts, Loyalist reparations, and freeing of prisoners by both sides.

Everyone feels that our commissioners did a fantastic piece of work to gain such a favorable peace treaty. Franklin tried hard to obtain Canada. He reasoned that ceding Canada would remove all occasions for future quarrel. The British didn't buy it. On the other hand, the British want strong language for Loyalist reparations. Franklin was adamantly against any compensation for Loyalists but yielded to the weak language in the treaty to get agreement. Jay was disappointed that Spain regained possession of East Florida and West Florida.

It is very fortunate that back in February 1781, Franklin rejected French Foreign Minister Count de Vergennes's scheme of having Russia and Austria-Hungary act as mediators to settle the war. That proposal offered a truce whereby the British would claim the territory its armies controlled—all of Georgia and South Carolina, the area of northern New York where Indians were spreading terror, and New York City.

Sincerely, Eb Chaplin

April 19, 1783
Dear Father, Teunis, Roelof, Felix, and Ben,

Today is the eighth anniversary of the first shots at Lexington and Concord. At noon today General Washington announced to all of the troops the cessation of hostilities with Britain. We all got an extra ration of liquor to join the general in a toast wishing "perpetual peace, independence, and happiness to the United States of America."

Sir Guy Carleton told Washington that he got word in early April that Britain had declared a cessation of hostilities on February 4. On April 14, Washington allowed, at the request of Carleton, a messenger to pass through our lines to carry word to British general Haldimand in Quebec announcing the cease-fire. To speed communications, Washington sent an Indian runner directly to the British officer commanding at Fort Niagara, telling him of the cease-fire and urging him to keep Indians off the warpath.

While Washington knew of the cease-fire from the British, he waited until he was informed directly by Congress. Again he held the information from us for a few days to make the announcement on the Lexington/Concord anniversary.

I am so glad this war is over. I've been in it almost from the beginning. I've been in many a battle, and I've been so lucky not to have been wounded or killed. I've had to endure many a cold and wet night without proper shelter or clothing. But when I consider what the prisoners have had to undergo, I feel even luckier. It is sickening to hear that more soldiers died on prison ships than in battle. While I recognize that the British had no land area on which to hold prisoners, they didn't have to confine the prisoners so brutally. It is shameful that rats were considered a delicacy. There is also word the British fed the prisoners poisoned bread. All 2,800 prisoners captured after the Battle of Fort Washington are no longer alive.

While we were dedicated in our resolve to win this War of Independence, we have to be thankful for the French assistance. I was especially impressed by how Generals Washington and Rochambeau worked so well together.

When the next white flag goes through the British lines, I am going to send a note to Zack, wishing him well and hopefully finding out what his plans are.

Sincerely, Moses

May 10, 1783
Dear Mr. Chaplin,

Ever since the British evacuated Charleston, things are slowly getting back to normal. It may have been a War of Independence, but here in South Carolina and Georgia it was a vicious civil war—neighbor versus neighbor, father versus son, brother versus brother—and it didn't matter if man or woman. The carnage carried out by the Tories—burning Patriot homes and farms, wantonly destroying crops, or senselessly taking or butchering farm animals—created ill feelings that may take decades to fade.

I'll give you an example of an incident that occurred in Wilkes County, Georgia. Six Tories came to the house of Nancy Morgan, demanding that she tell them where she was hiding Patriots they were chasing. She told them there were none around. They killed her last turkey, ordered her to cook it for them, and insisted on something to drink. She provided the Tories corn liquor, and as she cooked the turkey she noticed the Tories had stacked their weapons together in a corner. One by one she began passing the weapons through a crack in the wall to her daughter outside. A Tory, seeing this, lunged toward the remaining weapons. Nancy grabbed a weapon and shot him. A second Tory then made a try for the weapons, and he too was shot. She held off the rest. Meanwhile, her daughter had blown on a conch shell to signal neighbors that Tories were present. When they and her husband arrived, they wanted to shoot the remaining four Tories. Nancy said that would be too good and had them hanged one by one.

Here's the latest disgusting incident. Juan Manuel de Cagigal, Spanish governor of the Bahamas, received dispatches to end hostilities by April 9, because the preliminary peace treaty had the Bahamas being returned to the British. More than likely Loyalist Colonel Andrew Deveaux had the same intelligence but regardless attacked the Spanish, who surrendered on April 14.

On March 10, Captain John Barry, with the *Alliance* carrying 72,000 Spanish silver dollars, became engaged with a British ship in the Straits of Florida.[143] Barry managed to win the battle to get the much-needed money to Newport, Rhode Island.

I know soon we can indeed say, "Bye, George," but even though this conflict is ended, I am concerned about the Indians. While the British were here they took care of the Indians' needs. Now the British are gone. Will this augur new hostilities?

Sincerely, Felix

June 21, 1783
Dear Moses, Teunis, Roelof, Felix, and Ben,

Philadelphia is no longer the capital. In fact, the turmoil here is almost frightening. On June 17, the four hundred soldiers of the Continental Army stationed here sent a message to Congress demanding payment for their services, threatening action if their demands weren't addressed. Congress ignored the request, and fortunately the soldiers did not take action on their threat.

On the nineteenth, Congress received word that eighty soldiers from Lancaster were on their way to join the soldiers in Philadelphia. The next morning, almost five hundred soldiers mobbed the Pennsylvania State House,[144] not allowing the delegates to leave. Bravely, Alexander Hamilton, a delegate

---

[143] Off the coast of present-day Cape Canaveral, Florida.
[144] Now known as Independence Hall.

from New York, addressed the soldiers, asking them to allow Congress to meet to address their concerns.

The night of the twentieth, a committee headed by Hamilton sent a note to the Pennsylvania Supreme Executive Council to protect Congress from the mutineers. This morning Pennsylvania president John Dickinson refused the request. The official response was that the council was unsure that the local militia would protect Congress from their fellow soldiers. We think there are two other reasons: (1) Dickinson, having been an officer in the militia, was sympathetic to the soldier's grievances, and (2) the council refused to allow Pennsylvania, a sovereign state, to be subjugated by the demands of a few members of Congress.

Congress decided to pack up and get out of Philadelphia. Continental Congress president Elias Boudinot, who is from New Jersey, suggested that Congress move to Nassau Hall in Princeton, New Jersey. Even though the conspiracy at Newburgh was diffused, Congress needs to take these grievances seriously. At least we can't blame General Gates for this incident!

In May, British Colonel Alured Clarke was here to manage the evacuation of British and Hessian prisoners. When Clarke stopped at the Blaze Horse, he commented on how healthy the prisoners appeared. Too bad the same isn't the case for American prisoners on those ships. I was quite impressed by Clarke. He told me that he recently learned his next post would be as the governor of Jamaica.

Sincerely, Eb Chaplin

July 31, 1783
Dear Uncle Eb,

Earlier this month I got word from General James Clinton that General Washington was taking a trip up from Newburgh to visit the battlefields at Saratoga and to visit Fort Ticonderoga. I decided to join the entourage, which included General Philip

Schuyler, and Lieutenant Colonel Alexander Hamilton, whose wife, Elizabeth, is General Schuyler's daughter. It was nostalgic to be back at Freeman's Farm, Bemis Heights, and the place of surrender in Saratoga. Being back at Fort Ticonderoga brought back memories of its surrender to Ethan Allen. It also brought back sad thoughts about the loss of General Richard Montgomery at Quebec. Now that the war is basically over, Montgomery was the most senior officer killed in the conflict. Interestingly, Montgomery, from his time in the British Army during the French and Indian War, was a close friend of Henry "Hair Buyer" Hamilton.

It's been almost two years since I saw you at the Blaze Horse after dropping the German prisoners from Yorktown off at Lancaster. While going back home with Hazen's Canadians, I learned that his men were often ostracized by American troops and were not allowed to partake of Catholic sacraments. That is so pitiful. They fought with us the entire war and now cannot go back to their own homes for fear of being taken prisoner by the British if they cross into Canada. My friend Clement Gosselin told me that Hazen absolutely loathed Benedict Arnold.

I was glad to get your letter that peace negotiations are moving along. Let's hope we can truly say, "Bye, George!" The proposal about the border with Canada is really important. The proposal of Britain ceding all of Canada I don't feel will happen. Without getting it straight about the borders, there will be more bloodshed, war or no war. So much trouble started when Britain pushed the Quebec Act down our throats. That effort stopped a lot of migration to the west and led to the Indians killing so many settlers. I was involved in too many battles with the Indians during this war to ever want to go through it again.

I am of the view that the British will not get out of the western forts of Oswego, Niagara, Detroit, and Mackinac. The British in Canada will incite the Indians to attack Americans from those forts. Oswego and Niagara are too close to my home for comfort.

Sincerely, Teunis

❧

August 20, 1783
Dear Mr. Chaplin,

As this War of Independence is all but over, I've been thinking about how we managed to win against the greatest military and naval power of the world. Of many thoughts, three different types of incidents come to mind. One is the memory of the clownish little French Irish drummer boy trooping all the way with us to Vincennes, who sang comical songs to encourage the soldiers to push him on his drum across flooded rivers—a brave little boy suffering with troops fighting for freedom.

Another is an incident of bravery at Fort Henry[145] on September 11, 1782, when the fort with 20 Patriots was besieged by 260 Indians and 60 British troops. Soon the defenders were running low on gunpowder. Betty Zane, sixteen years old, offered to run to another building sixty yards away to bring in a keg of powder stored there. As she ran out, the Indians did not shoot because she was a "squaw." The powder keg was too heavy for her, so she poured some gunpowder in her apron and ran back to the fort. This time she was shot at. One shot tore her dress. The extra gunpowder enabled the Patriots to endure the siege.

And then there is the incident of making a challenging choice based on one's conviction. In January 1776, Peter Muhlenberg, a Shenandoah Valley preacher, based the sermon to his congregation on the third chapter of Ecclesiastes, which starts with "To everything there is a season ..."; after reading the eighth verse, "a time of war, and a time of peace," he declared, "And this is the time of war," as he removed his clerical robe to reveal his colonel's uniform.

From a tactical and strategical viewpoint we had two other advantages. From our experience in the French and Indian War, we knew how to raise troops from all areas of the colonies. To augment their forces, the British had to rely on recruiting Loyalists or convincing the neutral populace to becoming

---

[145] Located in present-day Wheeling, West Virginia.

Loyalists. Their policies drove many a potential recruit to the Patriot cause.

We may be joyous in being able to say, "Bye, George," but I have two major concerns. Peace treaty or not, the British will stay in Fort Detroit, sending Indians throughout the territory between it and Fort Pitt to terrorize any American inhabitants. While the British were in Virginia, they offered freedom to runaway slaves. Boyne Manor lost fifteen slaves that ran off to the British. Who knows where they are now? Two of our slaves, Nero and Trajan, returned to Boyne Manor, telling me the British would put them to work on ships or they would be sent to the West Indies. More than likely they would have been sold to a sugar plantation owner in Barbados or Jamaica, with a British officer reaping a handsome dollar amount. Two of my slaves came back, but will slave insurrection become a future fear?

Sincerely, Roelof

December 4, 1783
Dear Father, Teunis, Roelof, Felix, and Ben,

At noon on November 25, General Washington—officers at his side, eight abreast including Major Benjamin Tallmadge— entered New York City even as some of the British were still boarding vessels. Washington wanted to get into the city quickly to ensure that the British would not burn it as they left. Tallmadge, who has directed the effective espionage network around New York City from 1778, wanted to get there quickly to protect his spies, who had posed as Loyalists, from attack by Patriots who lived there during the British occupation.

One of the first to be visited was James Rivington, publisher of the *Royal Gazette*, a Loyalist pro-British newspaper. While Washington met behind closed doors with Rivington, some of the officers indicated that they heard the clink of two bags of gold being dropped on a table. We later learned that it was

Rivington who had provided Allan McLane with the British Royal Navy's signal book.

General Washington presented three men with the Badge of Military Merit. The badge is purple and in the shape of a heart. Sergeant William Brown of the 5th Connecticut Regiment received his for his courage in the attack on Redoubt 10 at Yorktown. Sergeant Elijah Churchill of the Second Continental Light Dragoons received his for gallantry in action in the attack led by Tallmadge on the Loyalist outpost, Fort St. George,[146] on November 23, 1780. Sergeant David Bissell of the 2nd Connecticut Regiment received his for his spy work in New York City. He went to the city posing as a deserter. To be more effective Bissell served with Benedict Arnold for thirteen months.

Today at noon, General Washington met with his officers at Fraunces Tavern. After a light lunch, he raised a glass of wine with a toast: "With a heart full of love and gratitude, I now take leave of you. I most devoutly wish that your latter days may be as prosperous and happy as your former ones have been glorious and honorable." One by one, the officers silently came forward to embrace him. He's on his way back to Mount Vernon.

Finally with finality, we can say, "Bye, George." By the way, my attempt to get word to Zack was successful. He is taking Ben's suggestion in going to Bermuda.

Sincerely, Moses

❧

December 25, 1783
Dear Teunis, Roelof, Felix, and Ben,

On September 3, the Treaty of Paris, guaranteeing our independence, was signed. Signing for the United States were Benjamin Franklin, John Adams, and John Jay. David Hartley signed for Great Britain. At the signing, Franklin wore the same suit he wore when he was in the privy council's cockpit in January 1774. While Congress instructed the delegates to

---

[146] Located in present-day Mastic Beach, New York.

include France in the negotiations, Adams and Jay took it upon themselves to exclude France and make the treaty with Britain directly. Franklin had the dirty work of conveying the news to French Foreign Minister Vergennes. Congress hopes to ratify the treaty next month.

In September, the French Army passed through Philadelphia from Virginia on its way to Boston for embarkation to the West Indies. We had a party at the Blaze Horse to honor the French. Along with Rochambeau, we entertained Generals Choisy, Duportail, Lauzon, Vioménil, and Counts von Fersen and von Forbach.

We invited General Washington, on his way back to Mount Vernon, to the Blaze Horse for an ox roast I had planned for Moses's return home. Washington told some interesting stories about events I had been unaware of. He told us that after the Battle of Brandywine, Ephrata Cloister was being utilized as a hospital. The cloister was famous for publishing books. Knowing the cloister would have a large supply of paper for publishing, he raided the supply of paper to use as shot wadding. Those unfortunate pacifists not only lost their paper supply but had to burn down the buildings used as hospitals due to being disease ridden.

Washington also told us that he did not trust the Quakers, who were also pacifists. Before Trenton, he seized grain from the Quaker gristmills to make sure they would not provide it to the British. Before Brandywine, he had all the Quaker gristmills disabled, again to make sure that flour would not get to the British. I reminded him that even though the Quakers, and the Moravians in the Lehigh Valley, were pacifists, they did provide hospitals and nursing to the troops.

Washington told us he was on his way to the State House in Annapolis, Maryland, where the Continental Congress was now convening, and he sent a message ahead to let them know he was going to resign his commission as commander in chief and wanted to know the protocol. Thomas Jefferson, who was in charge of protocol, informed Washington to enter the Maryland State House precisely at noon on December 23. Washington, as a gesture of thanks, invited Moses and me to attend the ceremony.

As Moses and I journeyed to Annapolis, we discussed how it was possible that we won our independence. I think it gets down to a few things. Our troops were fighting for the divine cause of liberty. Their troops, far from home, were fighting for a pay day and loot. While we lost more battles than we won, the Fabian tactics led to our overall victory. In addition, the partisan passion and effort in the South was extremely effective. The British use of Indians in New York, the west, and Georgia turned many a neutral observer into a Patriot. And, of course, the French assistance was vital.

At noon on the twenty-third, Washington entered the Maryland State House. He was introduced by Secretary Charles Thomson. Thomson, who is from Philadelphia, is the only person who has been present for every minute of Congress. After Washington made a short speech, he drew from a pocket his commission as commander in chief and handed it to President Thomas Mifflin, the only member of Congress who was also present at Washington's commissioning in 1775. Mifflin lauded his services and his distinguished merits as a gentleman. As Washington left the room, Moses and I, along with many others, shed some tears.

As we returned to Philadelphia, it occurred to us what a significant act his resignation was. He could have decided to take it upon himself to use his commission as a justification to become head of state of the new nation. He decided to return to civilian life and let Congress do its work. He chose the route taken by Cincinnatus rather than the route taken by Julius Caesar.

During the British occupation of Philadelphia in the winter of 1777/78, Zack's Hessian friend, Johann Ewald, asked if he could set up a Christmas tree in the Blaze Horse. This was a German tradition we did not observe. I was so impressed by the occasion that I've put up a Christmas tree ever since. Today Moses and I cut an evergreen and are now decorating it with ribbons, pieces of fruit, and candles. We wish each of you a happy Christmas and a hearty "Bye, George."

Sincerely, Eb Chaplin

Chapter Eight

The American war is over but this is far from being the
case with the American Revolution. On the contrary,
nothing but the first act of this great drama is closed.
—Dr. Benjamin Rush

While the Treaty of Paris was signed in September 1783, it had to be
ratified by both sides before the war officially concluded. The ratification
process faced difficulties that were eventually surmounted. While the
War of Independence was a triumphant victory, there were concerns
about what the new country faced.

❦

January 22, 1784
Dear Moses, Teunis, Roelof, Felix, and Ben,

We finally received word that Congress ratified the Treaty of Paris. Weather, so severe beyond all memory—bitter cold, ice storms, and blizzards—caused quite a delay. Since December 13, Congress has attempted to obtain a quorum. The Articles of Confederation require nine states to approve the treaty. Further, each state had to have two delegates present to vote. As of January 12, there were only seven states who had delegates to vote: Massachusetts, Rhode Island, Delaware, Pennsylvania, Maryland, Virginia, and North Carolina. New Hampshire and South Carolina each had one delegate present. There were no delegates from Connecticut, New York, New Jersey, or Georgia.

Some delegates suggested that the treaty be ratified by the seven states present. Thomas Jefferson opposed that action, angering many delegates. The treaty stipulated both nations were to exchange ratifications in Paris by March 3, 1784. Finally on January 3, Jefferson relented and proposed a letter be sent to Benjamin Franklin in Paris asking for an extension. Meanwhile, President Mifflin was sending riders out to bring delegates in. On the thirteenth, Roger Sherman and James Wadsworth from Connecticut arrived, along with John Beatty from New Jersey. South Carolina Delegate Richard Beresford was extremely ill while boarding here at the Blaze Horse. Despite his illness, he ventured out into the appalling weather, arriving on the fourteenth. Congress now had its nine votes and ratified the treaty.

The treaty was embossed with the Great Seal of the United States and signed by President Thomas Mifflin and Secretary Charles Thomson. Thomson quickly prepared two diplomatic pouches to be sent to London and Paris. Colonels David S. Franks and Josiah Harmar were sent to New York to gain voyage to their ports in Europe.

The treaty was also sent to all the states, along with a Proclamation of Peace penned by Thomas Jefferson. The proclamation included language that Congress "promised to observe all its articles as far as should be in our powers" and "the good citizens of these United States are to carry into effect every clause and sentence of the treaty."

Sincerely, Eb Chaplin

July 4, 1784
Dear Moses, Ben, Teunis, Roelof, Felix, and Zack,

Because we recently got news the war was formally over, the Fourth of July celebration at the Blaze Horse is extremely boisterous. It's over, but it wasn't easy. Because of an ice barrier between Long Island and Staten Island, the couriers, Franks and Harmar, sent to New York couldn't get out to sea until February 21. Franks took a London-bound ship. Harmar took *Le Courier de L'Amerique,* a French packet, arriving March 25, after a rough 33-day voyage, in L'Orient, the French naval base in Brittany. From there he rode to Paris, delivering the ratification documents to Franklin in Paris on March 29.

The British, because Europe was experiencing a winter unlike anyone could remember, readily accepted the explanation that inclement weather was the cause in the delay of the ratified treaty. Upon hearing of America's ratification, George III signed Britain's ratification on April 9. The treaties were exchanged in Paris on May 12. Franklin sent the British ratified treaty to Secretary Thomson, along with a statement: "The great and hazardous enterprise we have engaged in, is, God Be praised, happily completed." He also sent word that his belief about the abnormally cold winter in America and Europe was due to gases from the eruptions of Iceland's Laki volcano.

Britain too must be relieved the war is over. Besides trying to hold her American colonies, she was engaged in a world war—battling the French, Spanish, and Dutch in the West Indies, and battling the French and Dutch in India. In fact, her last battle of the war with the French occurred at Cuddalore, India, in June 1783.

Signer Dr. Benjamin Rush recently stated, "The American war is over but this is far from being the case with the American Revolution. On the contrary, nothing but the first act of this great drama is closed." This is so true because I have my own concerns: The federal government under the Articles of Confederation cannot raise funds on its own. The treaty allows passage on the Mississippi River, but with West Florida now in Spanish hands, there is no access. And British troops have left the east coast cities but still occupy western forts—Niagara, Detroit, and Mackinac. Challenges going forward, but I am confident we can overcome them.

Sincerely, Eb Chaplin

Epilogue

There have been thousands of books written on the War of Independence, also known as the Revolutionary War or American Revolution. Many cover the entire war; many are about a specific battle (e.g., Battle of the Brandywine); many are about epic events (e.g., Paul Revere's ride); many are about significant figures (e.g., George Rogers Clark). My book, *Bye, George,* tries to capture the essence of all of the above, along with interesting anecdotes, in an attempt to inspire an interest in this memorable event of American history to those not before interested in history.

Each of the letter writers in *Bye, George* is an ancestor of mine. Ebenezer Chaplin (Uncle Eb) was on an alarm list of Minutemen in 1776. Moses Chaplin and Ebenezer (Ben) Thompson served in Rand's Company of Moore's Regiment of New Hampshire Volunteers. They were discharged one day after the surrender at Saratoga. In *Bye, George,* Zaccheus (Zack) Witt is portrayed as a Loyalist. In real life he served in Lewis's Company of Moore's Regiment of New Hampshire Volunteers. Teunis Swart and Roelof Staley served in the 3rd Regiment, Tryon County, New York, Militia. Felix Porter served in the 14th Regiment, Albany County, New York, Militia.

Being a member of the Peter Jaquette Chapter, Delaware Society of the Sons of the American Revolution, I included Peter in *Bye, George.*

I would like to offer special thanks to these people who contributed to my writing *Bye, George.* It began with Beth Rorke, former education director at Brandywine Battlefield, when she took me on as a tour guide. Current education director at Brandywine Battlefield Andrew Outten has guided me many times as I was writing *Bye, George.* Fellow tour guide Verne Weidman has joined me on many site tours and has been a source of inspiration. There are two tour guides, one at Guilford Courthouse and one at Stony Point, who gave me outstanding one-on-one tours, from whom I sadly neglected to get their names.

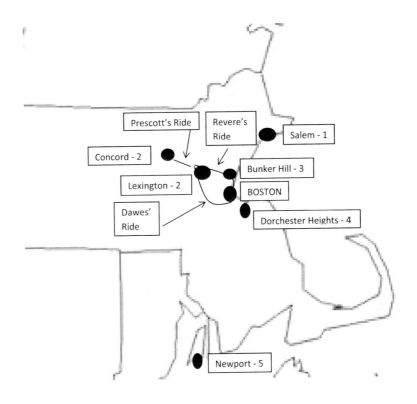

DIRECTORY

1	Salem Bridge Alarm	February 26, 1775
2	British Attack on Lexington and Concord	April 19, 1775
3	Battle of Bunker Hill	June 17, 1775
4	Washington's ruse at Dorchester Heights leads to evacuation of British from Boston March 17 by Howe	March 5, 1776
5	Battle of Rhode Island	August 29, 1778

APPENDIX 1 - MAP 1.2 - FORT TICONDEROGA AND QUEBEC CAMPAIGN

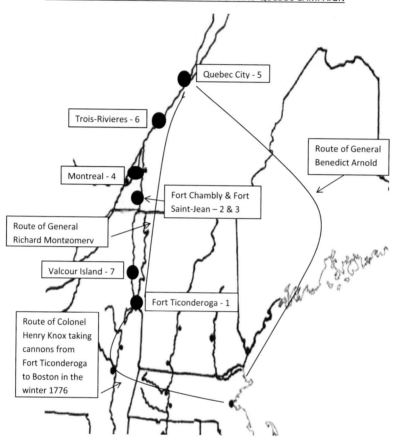

DIRECTORY								
1	Capture of Fort Ticonderoga	5/10/75	4	Montreal	11/13/75	7	Valcour Island	10/11/76
2	Fort Chambly	10/18/75	5	Quebec City	12/31/75			
3	Fort Saint-Jean	11/2/75	6	Trois-Rivieres	6/8/76			

APPENDIX 1 - MAP 1.3 - ACTIVITIES IN VIRGINIA

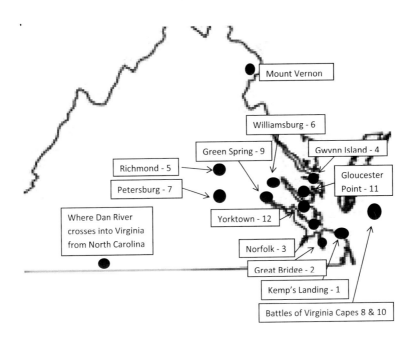

DIRECTORY					
1	Kemp's Landing	11/15/75	7	Petersburg	4/25/81
2	Great Bridge	12/9/75	8	Virginia Capes – First	3/16/81
3	Destruction of Norfolk	1/1/76	9	Green Spring	7/6/81
4	Gwynn Island	7/8/76	10	Virginia Capes – Second	9/5/81
5	Richmond	1/5/81	11	Battle of the Hook	10/3/81
6	Williamsburg	4/18/81	12	Siege of Yorktown	9/28/81 to 10/19/81

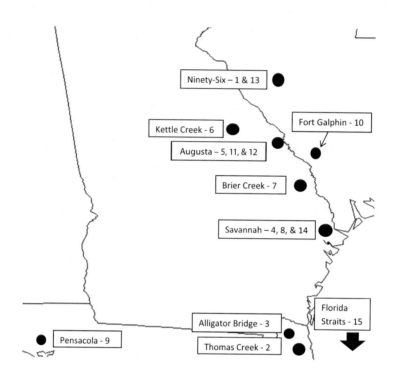

DIRECTORY								
1	Snow Campaign	11/19-12/22/75	6	Kettle Creek	2/14/79	11	Fort Grierson	5/23/81
2	Thomas Creek	5/17/77	7	Brier Creek	3/3/79	12	Fort Cornwallis	6/5/81
3	Alligator Bridge	6/30/78	8	Savannah	10/9/79	13	Ninety-Six	6/18/81
4	Capture of Savannah	12/29/78	9	Pensacola	5/9/81	14	Evacuation of Savannah	7/11/82
5	Capture of Augusta	1/31/79	10	Fort Galphin	5/21/81	15	Florida Straits	3/10/83

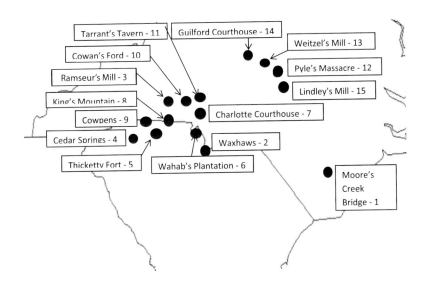

DIRECTORY								
1	Moore's Creek Bridge	2/27/76	6	Wahab's Plantation	9/21/80	11	Tarrant's Tavern	2/1/81
2	Waxhaws	5/29/80	7	Charlotte Courthouse	9/26/80	12	Pyle's Massacre	2/25/81
3	Ramseur's Mill	6/20/80	8	King's Mountain	10/7/80	13	Weitzel's Mill	3/6/81
4	Cedar Spring	7/12/80	9	Cowpens	1/17/81	14	Guilford Courthouse	3/15/81
5	Thicketty Fort	7/26/80	10	Cowan's Ford	2/1/81	15	Lindley's Mill	9/13/81

APPENDIX 1 - MAP 1.6 - ACTIVITIES IN SOUTHERN SOUTH CAROLINA

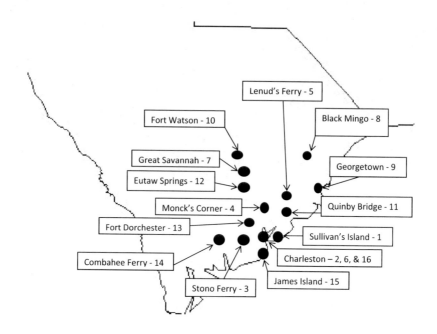

DIRECTORY								
1	Sullivan's Island	6/18/76	7	Great Savannah	9/4/80	13	Fort Dorchester	12/1/81
2	Charleston	5/11/79	8	Black Mingo	9/29/80	14	Combahee Ferry	8/25/82
3	Stono Ferry	6/2079	9	Georgetown	1/24/81	15	James Island	11/14/82
4	Monck's Corner	4/14/80	10	Fort Watson	4/23/81	16	Charleston Evacuated	12/14/82
5	Lenud's Ferry	5/6/80	11	Quinby Bridge	7/17/81			
6	Surrender of Charleston	5/12/80	12	Eutaw Springs	9/8/81			

278

APPENDIX 1 - MAP 1.7 - LOWER NEW YORK & CONNECTICUT

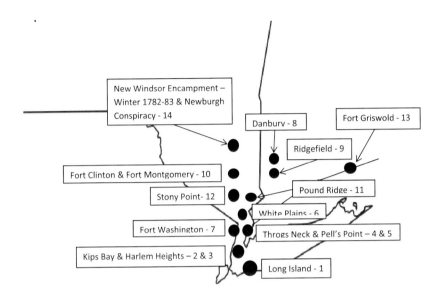

DIRECTORY								
1	Long Island	8/27/76	6	White Plains	10/28/76	11	Pound Ridge	7/2/79
2	Kips Bay	9/15/76	7	Fort Washington	11/16/76	12	Stony Point	7/16/79
3	Harlem Heights	9/16/76	8	Danbury	4/25/77	13	Fort Griswold	9/6/81
4	Throgs Neck	10/12/16	9	Ridgefield	4/27/77	14	Newburgh Conspiracy	11/15/83
5	Pell's Point	10/18/76	10	Fort Clinton & Fort Montgomery	10/6/77			

279

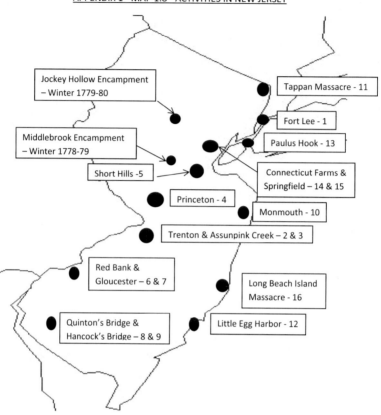

Jockey Hollow Encampment
– Winter 1779-80

Tappan Massacre - 11

Fort Lee - 1

Middlebrook Encampment
– Winter 1778-79

Paulus Hook - 13

Short Hills -5

Connecticut Farms &
Springfield – 14 & 15

Princeton - 4

Monmouth - 10

Trenton & Assunpink Creek – 2 & 3

Red Bank &
Gloucester – 6 & 7

Long Beach Island
Massacre - 16

Quinton's Bridge &
Hancock's Bridge – 8 & 9

Little Egg Harbor - 12

DIRECTORY								
1	Fort Lee	11/20/76	7	Gloucester	11/25/77	13	Paulus Hook	8/19/79
2	Trenton	12/26/76	8	Quinton's Bridge	3/18/78	14	Connecticut Farms	6/7/80
3	Assunpink Creek	1/2/77	9	Hancock's Bridge	3/21/78	15	Springfield	6/23/80
4	Princeton	1/3/77	10	Monmouth	6/28/78	16	Long Beach Island Massacre	10/25/82
5	Short Hills	6/26/17	11	Tappan Massacre	9/27/78			
6	Red Bank	10/22/77	12	Little Egg Harbor	10/15/78			

APPENDIX 1 - MAP 1.9 - ACTIVITIES IN UPPER NEW YORK

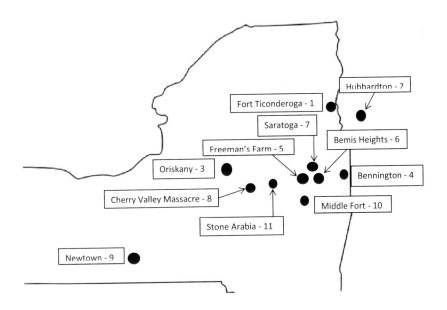

DIRECTORY					
1	Fort Ticonderoga Surrender	7/5/77	7	British Surrender at Saratoga	10/17/77
2	Hubbardton	7/7/77	8	Cherry Valley Massacre	11/11/78
3	Oriskany	8/6/77	9	Newtown	8/29/79
4	Bennington	8/16/77	10	Middle Fort	10/17/80
5	Freeman's Farm	9/19/77	11	Stone Arabia	10/19/80
6	Bemis Heights	10/7/77			

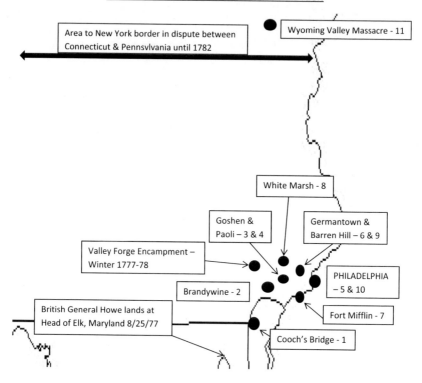

DIRECTORY					
1	Cooch's Bridge	9/3/77	7	Fort Mifflin	11/16/77
2	Brandywine	9/11/77	8	White Marsh	12/7/77
3	Goshen (Battle of Clouds)	9/16/77	9	Barren Hill	5/20/78
4	Paoli Massacre	9/20/77	10	Philadelphia Evacuated	6/18/78
5	Philadelphia Occupied	9/26/77	11	Wyoming Valley	7/3/78
6	Germantown	10/4/77		Massacre	

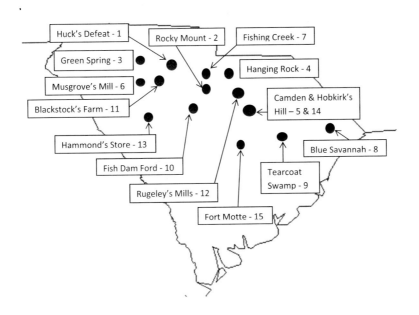

DIRECTORY								
1	Huck's Defeat	7/12/80	6	Musgrove's Mill	8/18/80	11	Blackstock's Farm	11/20/80
2	Rocky Mount	7/30/80	7	Fishing Creek	8/18/80	12	Rugeley's Mills	12/4/80
3	Green Spring	8/1/80	8	Blue Savannah	9/4/80	13	Hammond's Store	12/29/80
4	Hanging Rock	8/6/80	9	Tearcoat Swamp	10/25/80	14	Hobkirk's Hill	4/25/81
5	Camden	8/16/80	10	Fish Dam Ford	11/9/80	15	Fort Motte	5/12/81

283

APPENDIX 1 - MAP 1.12 - ACTIVITIES IN THE WEST

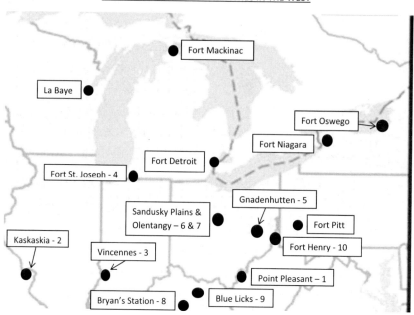

DIRECTORY					
1	Point Pleasant	10/10/74	6	Sandusky Plains	6/4/82
2	Kaskaskia	7/4/78	7	Olentangy	6/6/82
3	Vincennes	2/25/79	8	Bryan's Station	8/16/82
4	Fort St. Joseph	2/12/81	9	Blue Licks	8/19/82
5	Gnadenhutten Massacre	3/8/82	10	Fort Henry	9/11/82

Appendix 2: Guide to Participants

Name	Role	Afterward
Abercromby, Sir Robert	British lieutenant colonel	Commander in Chief, India.
Acland, John Dyke	British major	Grateful for the treatment received when recuperating as a prisoner of war, upon returning to England he challenged Lieutenant Lloyd to a duel when the latter spoke poorly of Americans at a dinner party. Although he survived the duel, he caught a cold during it, from which he died.
Adams, John	Member Continental Congress; signer; second cousin of Sam Adams	Second US president; father of sixth US president, John Quincy Adams; died July 4, 1826, at ninety, fifty years after signing.

Adams, Sam	Member Continental Congress; signer; second cousin of John Adams	Massachusetts governor.
Agnew, James	British general	Killed at Germantown October 4, 1777.
Alexander, William	(See Lord Stirling)	
Allen, Ethan	Colonel commandant of Green Mountain Boys	Negotiated with British for Vermont becoming a British province.
André, John	British adjutant general	Hanged as British spy October 2, 1780. Later buried in Westminster Abbey.
Angell, Israel	American colonel	Died May 4, 1832, in Rhode Island.
Arbuthnot, Mariot	British admiral	Named admiral of the Blue in 1793; died in London in 1794.
Armand, Charles	American colonel from France	Active in the Breton Association against the French Revolution.
Armstrong, John (Sr.)	American general	Armstrong County, Pennsylvania, named for him.
Armstrong, John (Jr.)	American major; aide-de-camp to Gates	As secretary of war during War of 1812 elected not to defend Washington, DC, which allowed the British to burn it.

Arnold, Benedict	American general	The earl of Balcarres when introduced by King George III to Arnold, exclaimed "What, the traitor Arnold?" Arnold challenged the Earl to a duel. Arnold fired, and the earl walked away. Arnold asked why he didn't fire. The earl replied, "I leave you to the executioner." Arnold died a broken man in 1810 in London.
Baker, John	American colonel	Baker County, Georgia, named for him.
Ball, John Coming	South Carolina Loyalist militia colonel	Eventually left the service of the British.
Barras, Jacques-Melchoir Saint-Laurent, Comte de	French admiral	Promoted to lieutenant general of the French Naval Armies.
Barry, John	American naval captain	First commissioned officer of Continental Navy. Known as the "Father of the American Navy." Given rank of commodore by President Washington in 1797.
Baylor, George	American colonel	Never recovered from wounds at Tappan Massacre; died in Barbados March 1, 1784.

Baum, Friedrich	Brunswick lieutenant colonel	Killed at Bennington August 16, 1777.
Beaumarchais, Pierre	French playwright, musician, diplomat, publisher, arms dealer, and revolutionary	Returned to Paris in 1796 after living in exile in Germany; died in Paris in 1799.
Brant, Joseph (Thayendanegea)	Mohawk military leader	Initiated formation of Western Confederacy of Indians.
Bratton, William	American colonel	Served in South Carolina Senate.
Breymann, Heinrich	Brunswick colonel	Killed at Bemis Heights October 7, 1777.
Brown, John	American colonel	Killed at Stone Arabia, New York, in 1780.
Brown, Thomas (Burnfoot)	Loyalist colonel of King's Carolina Rangers	Died on St. Vincent Island August 3, 1825.
Browne, Montfort	Governor of Bahamas	Exchanged for Lord Stirling.
Browne, William	Salem, Massachusetts, militia colonel	Governor of Bermuda.
Buford, Abraham	American colonel	Settled in Kentucky, where he helped found that state's horse racing industry.
Burgoyne, John	British general	Member British House of Commons.
Burr, Aaron	American lieutenant colonel	Third US vice president; in duel July 11, 1804, shot Alexander Hamilton, who died the next day.

Butler, John	American general	Member North Carolina Senate.
Butler, John	British colonel	Political leader in Upper Canada (now part of Ontario).
Butler, Richard	American colonel	Killed by Miami Indians at Battle of the Wabash in 1791.
Butler, Zebulon	American colonel	Commissioner of Luzerne County, Pennsylvania.
Cadwalader, John	American general	Member Maryland State Assembly; shot Thomas Conway in mouth during duel July 1778.
Caldwell, William	Captain of Rangers in British Indian Department	Superintendent of Indians in the Western District of Canada.
Campbell, Archibald	British general	Governor of Jamaica; governor of Madras.
Campbell, John	British general	Replaced Sir Guy Carleton as commander in chief, North America, in 1783.
Campbell, Mungo	British lieutenant colonel	Killed at Fort Montgomery.
Campbell, William	American colonel	Member Virginia House of Delegates.
Candler, William	American colonel	Served in Georgia Legislature; descendant Asa Griggs Candler, founder of Coca-Cola.
Carleton, Christopher	British major	Died June 14, 1787, in Quebec City.

Carleton, Guy	British general	Governor of Canada; member British House of Lords.
Carrington, Edward	American lieutenant colonel	Served as the foreman of the jury that acquitted Aaron Burr of treason in 1807.
Caswell, Richard	Member Continental Congress; American general	North Carolina governor.
Champe, John	American sergeant major	Sergeant at arms for Continental Congress in 1783.
Choisy, Claude Gabriel, Marquis de	French general	General in French Revolution sent to Avignon to hold inquiry of the Massacre of La Glacière.
Chronicle, William	American major	Killed at Kings Mountain.
Church, Dr. Benjamin	First surgeon general of US Army	Disappeared sailing for Martinique in 1778 when banished from Massachusetts.
Clark, George Rogers	American lieutenant colonel	In 1793, he accepted from Citizen Genet a commission as "Major-general in the armies of France, and commander-in-chief of the French Revolutionary Legion in the Mississippi Valley."
Clarke, Alured	British colonel	Commander in chief, India; promoted to field marshal July 22, 1830, by King William IV.

Clarke, Elijah	American colonel	Tried to form Trans-Oconee Republic in 1794.
Cleveland, Benjamin	American colonel	Commissioner in the Pendleton District of South Carolina.
Clinton, George	American general	Fourth US vice president.
Clinton, Henry	British general	Governor of Gibraltar.
Clinton, James	American general	Member of New York Convention adopting US Constitution.
Closen, Baron Ludwig von	French colonel from Bavaria	Fought with Napoleon, retiring after Napoleon's defeat.
Colburn, Reuben	Shipbuilder	Never paid for batteaux and supplies for Arnold expedition.
Collier, George	British admiral	Member of British Parliament.
Colombe, Chevalier de la	Lafayette's aide-de-camp	Went to live in New York after release from imprisonment with Lafayette.
Conway, Thomas	American general	Survived shot in mouth in duel with John Cadwalader July 1778; governor of French colonies in India.
Cornstalk (Hokoleskwa)	Shawnee Indian chief	Killed in 1777 by American militiamen.
Cornwallis, Charles Lord	British general	Governor-general of India.
Crawford, William	American colonel	Tortured to death by Indians in June 1782.

Cruger, John Harris	Loyalist colonel of DeLancey's Brigade	Went to London in 1783, dying there in 1807.
Cushing, Thomas	Member Continental Congress	Lieutenant governor, Massachusetts.
Dana, Francis	Minister to Russia	Chief justice of Massachusetts Supreme Court.
Davidson, William Lee	American general	Killed at Battle of Cowan's Ford.
Davie, William Richardson	American colonel	Deputy to the Constitutional Convention of 1787 but left before he could sign the document.
Dayton, Elias	American colonel	Served in New Jersey Assembly.
Deane, Silas	US commissioner in France	Died mysteriously awaiting return to United States from England September 23, 1789, to collect war debts owed him.
Dearborn, Henry	American colonel	Fifth US secretary of war.
De Lancey, James	Loyalist lieutenant colonel	Moved to Nova Scotia after war, serving on governing council.
Delaplace, William	British captain	Died on sixtieth birthday, 1790, in Great Britain.
DePeyster, Abraham	Loyalist captain of King's American Regiment	First treasurer of New Brunswick province in Canada.

D'Aboville, Francois Marie	French colonel commandant, chief of artillery	First inspector general of artillery under Napoleon.
D'Estaing, Jean Baptiste Charles Henri Hector, Comte	French admiral	After testifying in favor of Marie Antoinette, sent to guillotine April 28, 1794, writing, "After my head falls off, send it to the British, they will pay a good deal for it!"
Destouches, Charles René Dominique Sochet, Chevalier	French admiral	Died in poverty in 1794 as a result of supporting the Royalists in the French Revolution.
Dickinson, John	Member Continental Congress	Signer of US Constitution.
Dickinson, Philemon	American general	Member US Senate; John's brother.
Digby, Robert	British admiral	In 1783, evacuated 1,500 Loyalists from New York to Nova Scotia; Digby, Nova Scotia, named for him.
Donop, Karl Emil von	Hesse-Kassel colonel	Killed at Red Bank October 25, 1777.
Duane, James	Member Continental Congress	Member of New York Convention, adopting US Constitution.
Du Boysson des Aix, Chevalier	De Kalb's aide-de-camp	Brigadier general, North Carolina militia.
Dundas, Thomas	British colonel	Governor of Guadeloupe.

Dunmore, Lord (John Murray)	British Royal governor of Virginia	British governor of the West Indies in Nassau.
Duportail, Louis Lebègue dePresle	American general from France (chief engineer)	Fled to United States from France during French Revolution; died at sea in 1802, returning to France.
Eaton, Thomas	American general	One of largest slaveholders in North Caronia in 1790.
Elbert, Samuel	American colonel	Georgia governor.
Elphinstone, George	British naval captain	Admiral in numerous sea battles off Europe, Africa, and India; supervised Napoleon's final exile to Saint Helena.
Enos, Roger	American general	Member of the Vermont Board of War from 1781 to 1792.
Ewald, Johann	Hesse-Kassel captain	General for Kingdom of Denmark-Norway.
Ewing, James	American general	Vice president of Pennsylvania.
Eyre, Edmund	British colonel	Died in Ireland in 1791.
Fanning, David	North Carolina Loyalist militia colonel	Convicted of rape in New Brunswick in 1801, pardoned but ordered to leave, settling in Digby, Nova Scotia, dying there in 1825.
Ferguson, Patrick	British major	Killed at Kings Mountain October 7, 1780.

Fermoy, Matthias de	American general from French West Indies	Resigned 1778; returned to West Indies.
Fish, Nicholas	American major	Served seven years as president of Society of the Cincinnati.
Fersen, Count Hans Axel von	Aide-de-camp to Rochambeau	Murdered by a mob in Stockholm, Sweden, on June 20, 1810, on suspicion that he was connected in the death of the Swedish Crown prince Carl August.
Fleury, Francois de	American lieutenant colonel from France	Held French commands in India.
Forbach, Wilhelm von	Graf (count) of Zweibrücken	General in Bavarian Army.
Forman, David	American general	Died September 12, 1797, in Bahamas after being captured by British privateer.
Francisco, Peter (Pedro)	American soldier born in Azores	Virginia State Senate sergeant at arms.
Franklin, Benjamin	Signer; obtained Treaty of Alliance as commissioner to France	Negotiated Treaty of Paris; deputy (signer) to Constitutional Convention.
Fraser, Simon	British general	Killed at Bemis Heights October 7, 1777.
Gadsden, Christopher	Delegate First Continental Congress	British prisoner of war released in 1781; designer of Gadsden Flag: "Don't Tread on Me."
Gage, Thomas	British general	Recalled to England September 1775.

Galloway, Joseph	Delegate First Continental Congress	Loyalist moving to England in 1778.
Galvez, Bernardo de	Spanish field marshal	Viceroy of Spain; died at age forty in 1786 with rumor that he was poisoned by his enemies. Galveston, Texas named for him.
Ganey, Micajah	South Carolina Loyalist militia major	Agreed to lay down arms to avoid confiscation of his property by the South Carolina Legislature.
Gansevoort, Peter	American colonel	Presided over court-martial of General James Wilkinson in 1811.
Gates, Horatio	American general	Served in New York Legislature.
George III	King of Great Britain	Reign: October 25, 1760, through January 29, 1820.
Germain, Lord George (Viscount Sackville)	British secretary of state for America	Member British House of Lords.
Gimat, Jean-Joseph Sourbader de	American major from France	Governor of Saint Lucia.
Girty, Simon	Liaison/interpreter between British and Indians	Blind when died 1818 in Canada.
Gist, Mordecai	American general	Retired to South Carolina plantation.

Glover, John	American general	Served in the Massachusetts State Legislature; his eldest son, Captain John Glover, was captured in 1778 by the British and was lost at sea while being transported to prison in England.
Grasse, Francis Joseph Paul, Marquis de Grasse Tilly, Comte de	French admiral	In April 1782, he was defeated and taken prisoner by Admiral Rodney at the Battle of the Saintes. He was taken to London and while there briefly took part in the negotiations that laid the foundations for the Peace of Paris (1783).
Grant, James	British general	Governor of Stirling Castle.
Graves, Samuel	British admiral	Died in England 1787.
Graves, Thomas	British admiral	Baron Graves: Londonderry, Ireland.
Graves, Thomas	British naval captain	Became an admiral in 1812.
Greene, Christopher	American colonel	Killed by New York Loyalists May 13, 1781.
Greene, Nathanael	American general	Died at his Georgia estate, "Mulberry Grove," June 19, 1786, of sunstroke.
Grey, Charles (No Flint)	British general	Governor of Guernsey.

Haldimand, Frederick	Governor of Quebec	Died June 5, 1791, in Switzerland.
Hall, David	American colonel	Delaware governor.
Hall, Lyman	Member Continental Congress; signer	Georgia governor; founder University of Georgia.
Hamilton, Alexander	Aide-de-camp to General Washington	First US secretary of treasury; died July 12, 1804, after being shot by Aaron Burr in a duel.
Hamilton, Henry "Hair Buyer"	Quebec lieutenant governor at Fort Detroit	Governor of Bermuda and Dominica.
Hamilton, James	British general	Died in Scotland July 27, 1803.
Hamond, Andrew Snape	British naval captain	Lieutenant governor, Nova Scotia.
Hancock, John	Member Continental Congress; signer	Member of Massachusetts Convention, adopting US Constitution.
Hand, Edward	American general	Resumed practice of medicine.
Hanger, George (Lord Coleraine)	British major	Became a companion of the prince regent (later King George IV).
Han Yerry (Tewahangarahken)	Oneida war chief	Died in 1794.
Harcourt, William	British colonel	Bore the Union standard at coronation of George IV July 19, 1821.

Harrison, Benjamin	Member Continental Congress; signer	Opposed adoption of US Constitution; father of ninth US president, William Henry Harrison; great-grandfather of twenty-third US president, Benjamin Harrison.
Hazelwood, John	American commodore	Died March 1, 1800, in Philadelphia.
Hazen, Moses	American colonel	Died in 1803 at Troy, New York.
Heath, William	American general	Member of Massachusetts Convention, adopting US Constitution.
Heister, Leopold Philip von	Hesse-Kassel general	Recalled to Germany after Battle of Trenton, dying in 1777.
Henry, Patrick	Member Continental Congress	Opposed adoption of US Constitution.
Herkimer, Nicholas	American general	Died after wounds suffered on August 16, 1777, at Oriska.
Hewes, Joseph	Member Continental Congress; signer	Appointed as the new secretary of the Naval Affairs Committee in 1776, which laid the foundation of the American Navy.
Hinman, Benjamin	American colonel	Member of Connecticut Convention, adopting US Constitution.

Hood, Samuel	British admiral	Commander in chief, Mediterranean fleet; Oregon's Mount Hood named for him.
Hooper, William	Member Continental Congress; signer	Property burned by British.
Hopkins, Esek	American commodore	Served in Rhode Island General Assembly.
Howard, John Eager	American colonel	Federalist Party candidate for vice president in 1816.
Howe, Richard	British admiral; brother of William Howe	Commander of Channel Fleet against French in 1793.
Howe, Robert	American general	Served on John André's court-martial board.
Howe, William	British general; brother of Richard Howe	Involved against French 1793–95.
Huger, Isaac	American general	First federal marshal for South Carolina.
Hull, William	American lieutenant colonel	General who surrendered Fort Detroit to the British in the War of 1812.
Hutchinson, Thomas	Lieutenant governor and governor of the Province of Massachusetts Bay	Died in England 1780.
Innes, James	American colonel	First attorney general of Virginia; declined offer from Washington to be first US attorney general.

Irvine, James	American general	Held prisoner by British for four years; served as trustee for University of Pennsylvania and Dickinson College.
Jackson, Andrew	American soldier	Seventh US president.
Jameson, John	American colonel	Court clerk of Culpeper County, Virginia.
Jay, John	Negotiator, Treaty of Paris	First US chief justice.
Jaquette, Peter	American major	Returned to farming after the war; died September 13, 1834, at age eighty.
Jefferson, Thomas	Author of Declaration of Independence; signer	Third US president; died July 4, 1826, at age eighty-three, fifty years after signing.
Johnson, Henry	British lieutenant colonel	Became a baronet in 1818.
Johnson, Sir John	British Loyalist general	Served in Lower Canada Legislative Council.
Jones, John Paul	American naval captain	Rear Admiral Imperial Russian Navy.
Jones, Joseph	Member Continental Congress	Voted against ratification of US Constitution.
Kalb, Baron Johann de	American general from France	Died from wounds August 19, 1880, at Battle of Camden.
Knox, Henry	American general	First US secretary of war.

Knyphausen, Wilhelm von	Hesse-Kassel general	Military governor of Kassel.
Kościuszko, Tadeusz	American colonel from Poland	Fought with Polish resistance against Russia.
Kovats de Fabriczy, Michael	American colonel commandant from Hungary	Died May 16, 1779, at Charleston.
Lacey, Edward	American colonel	County judge of Livingston County, Kentucky.
Lacey, John	American general	Developed Ferrago Forge in Forked River, New Jersey.
Lafayette, Marie-Joseph Paul Yves Roche Gilbert du Motier, Marquis de	American general from France	Participant in French Revolution; imprisoned by Austrians; visited America in 1824–25.
Langlade, Charles	Captain in British Indian Department	Considered "Father of Wisconsin."
Laurens, Henry	President of the Continental Congress November 1, 1777, to December 9, 1778	Held a prisoner in Tower of London from October 5, 1780, to December 31, 1781; member of South Carolina Convention, adopting US Constitution.
Laurens, John	American lieutenant colonel; aide-de-camp to Washington	Killed at Battle of Combahee River August 27, 1782.
Lauzun, Armand Louis de Gontaut-Biron, Duc de	French general	Both he and his wife were guillotined by the Revolutionary Tribunal.

Lawson, Robert	American general	Member of Virginia Convention, adopting US Constitution, but voted against ratification.
Ledyard, William	American lieutenant colonel	Died September 6, 1781, when he was stabbed with his sword that he was surrendering.
Lee, Arthur	US commissioner in France; brother of Richard Henry Lee	Delegate to Continental Congress in 1782 from Virginia.
Lee, Charles	American general	Wounded by John Laurens in a duel December 24, 1779.
Lee, Henry (Light-Horse Harry)	American lieutenant colonel	Helped suppress Whiskey Rebellion; Virginia governor; delivered this tribute at Washington's funeral: "First in war, first in peace and first in the hearts of his countrymen … second to none in the humble and endearing scenes of private life."
Lee, Richard Henry	Member Continental Congress; signer; brother of Arthur Lee	President pro tempore of Senate during second US Congress.
Leslie, Alexander	British general	Died 1794 in Scotland.

Lewis, Andrew	Colonel Virginia militia; American general	Member Virginia House of Burgesses.
Lincoln, Benjamin	American general	Helped in putting down Shay's Rebellion.
Lindsay, Alexander (sixth earl of Balcarres)	British major	Governor of Jersey; governor of Jamaica.
Livingston, Philip	Member Continental Congress; signer	Died suddenly while attending Congress in 1778.
Locke, Francis	American colonel	South Carolina state attorney.
Long, Pierse	American colonel	Member of New Hampshire Convention, adopting US Constitution.
Lossberg, Friedrich Wilhelm von	Hesse-Kassel general	Became commander of Hessian troops in New York in 1782.
Lovell, Solomon	American general	Died September 9, 1801, in Weymouth, Massachusetts.
Ludington, Henry	American colonel	Aide-de-camp to Washington.
Luzerne, Anne-César, Chevalier de La	Second French ambassador to United States	Died in 1791 serving as French ambassador to Great Britain; Luzerne County, Pennsylvania, named for him.
Lynch, Thomas	Member Continental Congress; signer	Disappeared sailing for Sint Eustatius in 1779.
MacDonald, Donald	British general	Died in London in 1784.

Magaw, Robert	American colonel	Served in Pennsylvania House of Representatives.
Maham, Hezekiah	American lieutenant colonel	Prisoner of British in 1782 paroled to his home; died 1789.
Maitland, John	British lieutenant colonel	Died October 25, 1779, of fever after Battle of Savannah.
Marion, Francis (Swamp Fox)	American general	South Carolina state senator.
Marjoribanks, John	British major	Died October 22, 1781, from wounds suffered at Eutaw Springs.
Mawhood, Charles	British lieutenant colonel	Died August 29, 1780, during siege of Gibraltar.
Maxwell, William (Scotch Willie)	American general	Served in New Jersey Legislature.
McClure, John	American captain	Killed at Hanging Rock August 6, 1780.
McDougall, Alexander	American general	First president, Bank of New York.
McDowell, Charles	American general	Served in North Carolina Senate.
McHenry, James	American major	Third US secretary of war; Fort McHenry of "Star Spangled Banner" fame named for him.
McIntosh, Lachlan	American general	Died in Savannah February 20, 1806.
McLane, Allan	American captain	Collector of the Port of Wilmington.
McLean, Francis	British general	Died May 4, 1781, in Halifax, Nova Scotia.

Mercer, Hugh	American general	Died January 12, 1777, from wounds suffered at Battle of Princeton. Ancestor of World War II General George Patton.
Middleton, Henry	Member Continental Congress	Opposed to independence and left Congress.
Meigs, Return Jonathan	American colonel	US agent to Cherokee Nation.
Mifflin, Thomas	American general	Signer of US Constitution.
Monroe, James	American major	Fifth US president; supported founding of Liberia; died July 4, 1831.
Montgomery, Richard	American general	Killed at Quebec City December 31, 1775.
Montresor, John	British captain	Died June 29, 1799, in Maidstone Prison for not being able to support his expenditures during the war.
Moore, James	American general	Died April 15, 1777, of illness.
Moore, John	British lieutenant colonel	Arrested by General Cornwallis after defeat at Ramseur's Mill.
Morgan, Daniel	American general	Helped suppress Whiskey Rebellion; member US House.

Morris, Robert	Superintendent of finance; signer	Spent several years in debtors' prison, until Congress passed a bankruptcy act to release him.
Moultrie, William	American general	South Carolina governor; Fort Sullivan renamed Fort Moultrie in his honor.
Muhlenberg, Peter	American general	Member US House.
Murfree, Hardy	American major	Lived in Tennessee; Murfreesboro, Tennessee, named for him.
Musgrave, Thomas	British colonel	Colonel of Hindoostan Regiment.
Nash, Francis	American general	Killed at Germantown October 4, 1777.
Nelson, Thomas, Jr.	American general; signer	Died January 4, 1789, at age fifty.
Nicholas, Samuel	First American marine officer	Died 1790 in Philadelphia yellow fever epidemic.
Noailles, Vicomte Louis-Marie de	French lieutenant colonel	During the French Revolution emigrated to United States and became a partner in Bingham's Bank in Philadelphia; joined Rochambeau against English in 1804, dying of a bullet wound in Havana.
Ogden, Matthias	American colonel	Brought news of Treaty of Paris from Europe.

O'Hara, Charles	British general	Governor of Gibraltar; had distinction to have surrendered to both Washington and Napoleon.
Paine, Robert Treat	Member Continental Congress; signer	Prosecutor in Shay's Rebellion.
Paine, Thomas	American political activist, philosopher, and revolutionary	Went to France in 1790, becoming involved in the French Revolution; sentenced to the guillotine by Robespierre but escaped execution because jailer did not see chalk mark on the door of his cell when he was to be collected for execution; died June 8, 1809, in New York City.
Parker, Peter	British commodore	Succeeded Richard Howe as admiral of the fleet in 1799.
Päusch, Georg	Hesse-Hanau captain	Kept highly acclaimed journal of Hesse-Hanau troops during Revolutionary War.
Pearson, Richard	British naval captain	Knighted after sinking *Bonhomme Richard*.
Percy, Hugh	British general	Resigned 1777 due to his animosity toward General William Howe.
Phillips, William	British general	Died of disease in Virginia May 13, 1781.

Pickens, Andrew	American general	Member US House; uncle of John C. Calhoun, seventh US vice president.
Pickering, Timothy	American general	Second US postmaster general; second US secretary of war; fourth US secretary of state.
Pigot, Robert	British general	Warden of the Mint.
Pitcairn, John	British major	Killed at Bunker Hill; son Robert discovered Pitcairn Island in 1767.
Plessis, Thomas-Antoine du	American lieutenant colonel from France	Murdered in Haiti by mutinous troops March 3, 1791.
Pollock, Oliver	American financier	Sent to debtors' prison in Havana but paroled by Bernardo de Gálvez when he became viceroy of Mexico; died 1823 in Mississippi.
Poor, Enoch	American general	Said to have been killed in a duel with a subordinate officer September 8, 1780.
Potter, James	American general	Potter County, Pennsylvania, named for him.
Prescott, Richard	British general	Known for his harsh and cruel treatment of American prisoners; died in 1788.
Prescott, William	American colonel	Served on Massachusetts court.

Prevost, Augustine	British general	Resigned in 1779, returning to England; died in 1786.
Prevost, Mark	British major	Died 1781 in Jamaica from wounds in an uprising.
Pułaski, Casimir	American general from Poland; father of American Cavalry	Died October 10, 1779, from wounds suffered at Savannah.
Putnam, Israel	American general	Suffered paralyzing stroke December 1779.
Putnam, Rufus	American general; nephew of Israel Putnam	Active in the Ohio region of the Northwest Territory.
Pyle, John	British colonel (American commissioned as British officer by the royal governor of North Carolina)	When refused a promotion by Cornwallis, delivered British plans to Washington. King George III offered £5,000 for his capture. Returned to practice medicine in North Carolina.
Rall, Johann	Hesse-Kassel colonel	Died at Battle of Trenton December 26, 1776.
Randolph, Peyton	President, First and Second Continental Congress	Died in Philadelphia October 22, 1775.
Rawdon, Francis Lord	British colonel	Governor-general of India.
Revere, Paul	Lieutenant colonel, Massachusetts militia	Prominent in casting business.

Rayneval, Conrad Alexandre Gerard de	Signed Treaty of Alliance for France; first French ambassador to United States	Councilor of state in France.
Riedesel, Baron Friedrich	Brunswick general	Commandant, city of Braunschweig (Brunswick).
Robinson, Beverly	Colonel, Loyal American Regiment	Moved to England at end of war.
Rochambeau, Jean-Baptiste Donatien de Vimeur, Comte de	French general	Arrested during the Reign of Terror in 1793–94, narrowly escaping the guillotine. He was subsequently pensioned by Napoleon.
Rocheblave, Philippe de	Quebec lieutenant governor at Fort Kaskaskia	Served in Assembly of Lower Canada (Quebec).
Rodney, Caesar	Member Continental Congress; signer	President of Delaware.
Rogers, Robert	Colonel, Queen's American Rangers	Imprisoned by Americans after capture by privateer; went to England in 1783.
Ross, Alexander	British major	Became a general in 1802.
Rouërie, Charles Armand Tuffin, Marquis de la	(Known as Colonel Armand; see Charles Armand)	
Rush, Dr. Benjamin Rush	Member Continental Congress; signer	Died April 19, 1813, in Philadelphia as most celebrated physician in America.

Rutledge, Edward (Ned)	Member Continental Congress; signer (youngest)	British prisoner of war released in 1781.
Rutledge, John	Member Continental Congress	Deputy (signer) to Constitutional Convention.
Salomon, Haym	Businessman and financial broker	The thirteen stars above the eagle on the Great Seal of the United States are arranged in rows of 1-4-3-4-1, forming a six-pointed star in his honor. Due to the failure of governments and private lenders to repay the debt incurred by the war, he was left penniless at his death in 1785.
Saltonstall, Dudley	American commodore	Engaged in privateering ventures.
Schuyler, Philip	American general	Member US Senate.
St. Clair, Arthur	American general	Governor of the Northwest Territory.
St. Leger, Barrimore (Barry)	British (brevet) general	Involved in negotiations to bring Vermont to British side.
Sevier, John	American colonel	Governor of proposed state of Franklin; first governor of Tennessee.
Shelby, Isaac	American colonel	First governor of Kentucky.

Sheldon, Elisha	American colonel	Founded Sheldon, Vermont.
Sherman, Roger	Member Continental Congress; signer	Only signer of Continental Association, Declaration of Independence, Articles of Confederation, and US Constitution.
Simcoe, John Graves	British colonel	First lieutenant governor of Upper Canada (now part of Ontario).
Skinner, Cortlandt	British Loyalist general	Died 1799 in Bristol, England.
Smallwood, William	American general	Maryland governor.
Smith, Francis	British colonel	Promoted to major general 1779.
Smith, Samuel	American lieutenant colonel	Commanded defense of Baltimore during War of 1812.
Stark, John	American general	Died May 8, 1822, in Derryfield, New Hampshire at age ninety-three.
Stedingk, Count Curt	French colonel from Sweden	Swedish commander in chief of Finland.
Stephen, Adam	American general	Member of Virginia Convention, adopting US Constitution.
Steuben, Friedrich Wilhelm von	American inspector general from Prussia	Died in Rome, New York, November 29, 1794.
Stevens, Edward	American general	Member of Virginia State Senate.

Stewart, Walter	American colonel	Later a brevet brigadier general; died of yellow fever June 16, 1796.
Stirling, Lord	Title claimed by General William Alexander	Died January 15, 1783, in Albany, New York.
Sullivan, John	American general	Member of New Hampshire Convention, adopting US Constitution.
Sumter, Thomas (Gamecock)	American general	Member US House; member US Senate; last surviving general of the War of Independence, dying at age ninety-seven in 1832.
Symonds, Thomas	British naval captain	Being senior naval officer, signed Articles of Capitulation at Yorktown along with Cornwallis.
Tallmadge, Benjamin	American major	Married Mary Floyd, daughter of Signer William Floyd.
Tarleton, Banastre	British lieutenant colonel	Member of Parliament, actively supporting slave trade.
Ternay, Charles-Henri-Louis d'Arsac, Chevalier de	French admiral	Died in Newport, Rhode Island, December 15, 1780.
Thayer, Simeon	American major	Drowned in a stream October 14, 1800, after being thrown from his horse.

Thomas, John	American general	Died of smallpox June 2, 1776.
Thomas, John, Jr.	American colonel	South Carolina state treasurer.
Thompson, William	American general	Exchanged for General Riedesel.
Thomson, William (Danger)	American colonel	Pioneer in producing cotton for export.
Tilghman, Tench	American lieutenant colonel; aide-de-camp to Washington	Formed a business relationship with Robert Morris in Baltimore until his death April 18, 1786.
Trumbull, Jonathon	Governor of Connecticut	US paymaster general in 1778.
Tryon, William	Royal governor of New York	Returned to England; died in 1788.
Turnbull, George	Loyalist lieutenant colonel of New York Volunteers	Died in New York in 1810.
Varnum, James	American general	Supreme Court justice, Northwest Territory.
Vaughan, John	British general	Commander in chief, Leeward Islands.
Vergennes, Charles Gravier, Count de	French foreign minister	Died February 13, 1787, before he could attend the Assembly of Notables that he suggested to be called by King Louis XVI.
Vernejoux, Jean-Louis de	American captain from France	Returned to France after Saratoga.
Vernier, Chevalier Pierre-François	Cavalry major from France	Killed at Moncks Corner April 14, 1780.

Vioménil, Antoine Charles du Houx, Baron de	French general	At the attack on the Tuileries Palace, August 10, 1792, he was so severely wounded in defending King Louis XVI that he died a few weeks later.
Ward, Artemas	American general	Member US House.
Warner, Seth	American colonel	Opposed Vermont's attempt to join Canada.
Warren, Dr. Joseph	American general	Killed at Bunker Hill.
Washington, George	American commander in chief	First US president.
Washington, William	American colonel	Served in South Carolina State Legislature.
Watts, Thomas	Colonel of Georgia Loyalist militia	After the war, settled in South Carolina but later moved to England.
Wayne, Anthony	American general	Commander, Legion of the United States.
Webster, James	British lieutenant colonel	Died from wounds two weeks after the Battle of Guilford Courthouse.
Weedon, George	American general	Resumed managing his tavern.
Wemyss, James	British major	After emigrating to America, died on December 16, 1833, at Huntington, Long island.
White, Anthony Walton	American colonel	Helped suppress Whiskey Rebellion.

Wilkinson, James	American (brevet) general	General in War of 1812.
Willett, Marinus	American colonel	Mayor of New York City.
Williams, James	American colonel	Killed at Kings Mountain.
Williams, Otho Holland	American general	First commissioner of the Port of Baltimore.
Winston, Joseph	American colonel	Member US House.
Woedtke, Frederick William	American general from Prussia	Died of exposure at Lake George July 31, 1776.
Woodford, William	American general	Captured at Charleston; died on British prison ship in New York Harbor November 13, 1780.
Wooster, David	American general	Died from wounds encountered at Battle of Ridgefield.
Wright, James	Royal governor of Georgia	Regained Savannah in 1778; retired to England in 1782.
Wurmb, Ludwig von	Hesse-Kassel colonel	Division general of Westphalia.

Appendix 3: Pronunciation Guide

Name	Pronunciation	Role
Abatis	ah-bah-tee	A defensive obstacle formed by felled trees with sharpened branches facing the enemy.
Barras, Jacques-Melchoir Saint-Laurent, Comte de	bar-ras	French admiral.
Batteau (singular), batteaux (plural)	ba-toh, ba-tohz	Flat-bottomed boats used to haul cargo, men, or artillery.
Beaumarchaise, Pierre	bow-mar-shay	French covert supplier of arms.
Bonhomme Richard	bon-om ree-shar	John Paul Jones's ship.
Bostonnnais	bos-tonay	Habitants' term for Americans.
Boudinot, Elias	boo-din-ot	President Continental Congress, November 4, 1782, to November 2, 1783.
Chasseur	shah-sur	Member of French light cavalry units.
Chaudière	shaw-dee-air	River in Quebec.
Chevalier	shah-valley-yea	Rank in French nobility.

Chevaux-de-frise	shuh-voh duh freeze	A defensive obstacle with projecting spikes for military use in closing a passage.
Choisy, Claude Gabriel, Marquis de	choy-zay	French general.
Colombe, Louis Saint Ange Morel, Chevalier de la	koh-lum	Aide-de-camp to Lafayette.
Colonel	ker-nel	Title of an officer.
Coup d'état	coo day-tah	Attempt to overthrow the government by force.
Częstochowa	chenss-toh-hoh-va	City in Poland that is home to the nation's most important religious relic: the Black Madonna.
D'Aboville, Francois Marie	dab-oh-vee	Chief of French artillery.
D'Estaing, Charles Henri Theodat, Comte	des-tang	French admiral.
Destouches, Charles René Dominique Sochet, Chevalier	day-toosh	French admiral.
Du Buysson des Aix, Charles-Francois, Chevalier	do boy-zon de-say	Aide-de-camp to de Kalb; later North Carolina militia general.
Duportail, Louis Lebègue dePresle	do-pour-tie	Chief engineer of Continental Army from France.
Epaulement	eh-pol-man	A barricade of earth used as a cover from flanking fire.

Ewald, Johann	eh-vault	Hesse-Kassel captain.
Fascine	fah-seen	A rough bundle of brushwood or other material used for strengthening an earthen structure, or making a path across uneven or wet terrain.
Fermoy, Matthias Alexis Roche de	fer-moy	General in Continental Army from France.
Feu de joie	foo duh zhwa	A salute of musketry fired successively by each man in turn along a line and back.
Flèche	flesh	A fieldwork consisting of two faces forming a salient angle with an open gorge.
Gabion	gah-bee-uh	A cylinder of wickerwork filled with earth, used as a military defense.
Gerry, Elbridge	gary	Signer of Declaration of Independence.
Gimat, Jean-Joseph Sourbader de	zhe-mah	Lieutenant colonel in Continental Army from France.
Gloucester Point	glaw-ster	Peninsula between York River and Chesapeake Bay across from Yorktown, Virginia.
Gnadenhutten	ji-nay-dun-huh-tenn	Moravian mission.
Gorget	gore-zhay	Piece of plate armor hanging from the neck.

Grasse, Francis Joseph Paul, Marquis de Grasse Tilly, Comte de	grass	French admiral.
Guilford Courthouse	gill-ford	Battle on March 15, 1781.
Habitants	hobby-tawn	French settlers and the inhabitants of French origin.
Huger, Isaac	oo-zhay	American general.
Hussar	heh-zar	Units modeled on the Hungarian light infantry.
Île-aux-Noix	eel-oh-nowah	Island on the Richelieu River in Quebec, close to Lake Champlain.
Jäger	yea-gah	Member of elite Hessian infantry units.
Jumonville, Joseph Coulon de Villiers de	zhou-mohn-vee	French-Canadian officer in French and Indian War.
Kościuszko, Tadeusz	kos-chew-sko	Engineer in Continental Army from Poland.
Lafayette, Marie-Joseph Paul Yves Roch Gilbert du Motier, Marquis de	la-fy-ette	General in Continental Army from France.
Lancaster	lank-iss-ter	City 60 miles west of Philadelphia utilized as prisoner of war camp for captured British and German soldiers.
Langlade, Charles	lung-glahd	Led Great Lakes Indians as an ally of the British commanders.

Lauzun, Armand Louis de Gontaut-Biron, Duc de	lah-zohn	French general.
La Victoire	la vee-twah	Ship bringing Lafayette to America in 1777.
Lenud's Ferry	lenoes	Battle on May 6, 1780.
L'Hermione	lair-me-own	Ship bringing Lafayette back to America in 1780 with news of French troops being sent.
Livres	leave-rah	French currency during War of Independence.
Macutté Mong	ma-cootay	Ottawa Indian chief.
Maréchal de camp	mare-eh-shal de com	French military rank, third in command after general and lieutenant general.
Marechausee	mare-show-say	Original military police.
Marjoribanks, John	marsh-banks	British major.
Marquis	mar-key	Nobleman title.
Newfoundland	new-fen-land	Large island off east coast of Canada governed separately by the United Kingdom as a colony and dominion before confederating with Canada in 1949.
Noailles, Vicomte Louis-Marie de	no-ay	French lieutenant colonel.
Päusch, Georg	poysh	Hesse-Hanau captain.
Pigot, Robert	pig-ette	British general.
Plessis, Thomas-Antoine de Mauduit du	ple-cease	Lieutenant colonel in Continental Army from France.

Pułaski, Casimir	pu-waski	Father of American Cavalry from Poland.
Quebec	keb-bec	English province in Canada with a majority French population.
Redoubt	reh-daut	A small enclosed defensive work.
Regiment Bourbonnais	boar-bon-nay	French regiment.
Regiment Royal Deux-Ponts	do pont	Zweibrücken Germans fighting with the French.
Regiments d'Agenois, du Gatinois, and de Touraine	dazhen-ewa, do gaten-ewa, deh too-rain	French regiments from the West Indies.
Richelieu	ree-sha-lou	River flowing from Lake Champlain to the St. Lawrence River.
Riedesel, Friedrich Adolf	ree-day-zel	Brunswicker general.
Rochambeau, Jean-Baptiste Donatien de Vimeur, Comte de	row-sham-bow	French general.
Rocheblave, Philippe de	roash-blav	Quebec lieutenant governor at Fort Kaskaskia.
Rouërie, Charles Armand Tuffin, Marquis de la	roo-ehry	Cavalry officer from Breton, France, known as Colonel Armand.
Saint-Domingue	sohn doe-meng	Present-day Haiti.
Saint-Jean, Fort	sohn zhawn	Fort in Canada on the Richelieu River, which flows from Lake Champlain to the St. Lawrence River.

Saint-Simon, Claude-Anne-Montbleru, Marquis de	sohn see-moan	French general.
Saucisson	so-see-sohn	A large fascine; word is derived from a type of French sausage.
Schuyler, Philip	sky-ler	American general.
Schuylkill River	skoo-kill	River running past Valley Forge and through Philadelphia to the Delaware River.
Statia	stay-sha	Common name for Sint Eustatius, a Dutch island in the Caribbean.
Stephen, Adam	steven	American general.
St. Clair, Arthur	sin-clare	American general.
St. Leger, Barrimore (Barry)	sill-edjer	British (brevet) general.
Ternay, Charles-Henri-Louis d'Arsac, Chevalier de	ter-nay	French admiral.
Tilghman, Tench	till-man	American lieutenant colonel; aide-de-camp to Washington.
Townshend Act	towns-end	A 1767 act of Parliament to raise revenue by taxing imports.
Trois-Rivières	twa riv-eh-air	City in Canada.
Trous-de-loup	trood-l-oo	Shallow holes with sharpened stakes to impale feet of attackers.
Vergennes, Charles Gravier, Comte de	ver-zhenz	French foreign minister.
Vernejoux, Jean-Marie de	vair-ne-zhou	Cavalry captain from France.

Vernier, Chevalier Pierre-François	vern-yea	Cavalry major from France.
Vioménil, Antoine Charles du Houx, Baron de	ve-o-may-nee	French general.
von Fersen, Count Hans Axel	fun faya-sen	Aide-de-camp to Rochambeau.
von Knyphausen, Wilhelm	fun kah-nype-houzen	Hessian general.
von Steuben, Friedrich Wilhelm August Heinrich Ferdinand	fun shtoy-ben	General in Continental Army from Prussia.
Wemyss, James	weems	British major.
Zweibrücken	tsvy-brew-ken	A German duchy (meaning two bridges) providing troops to the French.

Appendix 4: Battle Timeline

Name of Battle	Location	Letter(s)
Point Pleasant	West Virginia	October 27, 1774
Salem Bridge Alarm	Massachusetts	February 27, 1775
Lexington and Concord	Massachusetts	April 20, 1775 June 20, 1775
Capture of Fort Ticonderoga	New York	May 14, 1775
Bunker Hill	Massachusetts	June 18, 1775 June 20, 1775
Noddle's Island	Massachusetts	June 20, 1775
Quebec City	Quebec	January 2, 1776 January 3, 1776
Fort Chambly	Quebec	January 3, 1776
Fort Saint-Jean	Quebec	January 3, 1776
Montreal	Quebec	January 3, 1776
Kemp's Landing	Virginia	January 5, 1776
Great Bridge	Virginia	January 5, 1776
Burning of Norfolk	Virginia	January 5, 1776
Snow Campaign	South Carolina	March 5, 1776
Moore's Creek Bridge	North Carolina	March 5, 1776
Dorchester Heights (Boston Evacuation)	Massachusetts	March 17, 1776
Trois-Rivières	Quebec	June 20, 1776
Sullivan's Island	South Carolina	June 29, 1776

New Providence	Bahamas	August 2, 1776
Gwynn's Island	Virginia	August 10, 1776
Long Island	New York	August 31, 1776 September 1, 1776
Kips Bay	New York	September 23, 1776 November 14, 1776
Valcour Island	New York	October 22, 1776
Harlem Heights	New York	November 14, 1776
White Plains	New York	November 14, 1776 November 18, 1776
Throgs Neck	New York	November 18, 1776
Pell's Point	New York	November 18, 1776
Fort Washington	New York	November 18, 1776
Fort Lee	New Jersey	December 15, 1776
Trenton	New Jersey	December 27, 1776
Assunpink Creek	New Jersey	January 5, 1777
Princeton	New Jersey	January 5, 1777
Danbury	Connecticut	April 30, 1777
Ridgefield	Connecticut	April 30, 1777
Thomas Creek	Florida	June 15, 1777
Surrender of Fort Ticonderoga	New York	July 9, 1777
Hubbardton	Vermont	July 9, 1777
Short Hills	New Jersey	August 5, 1777
Bennington	New York	August 16, 1777
Oriskany	New York	August 30, 1777
Lifting of Fort Stanwix Siege	New York	August 30, 1777
Cooch's Bridge	Delaware	September 9, 1777
Brandywine	Pennsylvania	September 12, 1777 September 17, 1777
Goshen (Battle of the Clouds)	Pennsylvania	September 17, 1777 September 22, 1777

Freeman's Farm (Saratoga)	New York	September 20, 1777
Valley Forge	Pennsylvania	September 21, 1777 September 22, 1777
Paoli Massacre (Action Near White Horse Tavern)	Pennsylvania	September 21, 1777 September 22, 1777
Germantown	Pennsylvania	October 4, 1777 October 5, 1777
Bemis Heights (Saratoga)	New York	October 9, 1777
Fort Clinton and Fort Montgomery	New York	October 17, 1777
Surrender at Saratoga	New York	October 17, 1777 October 18, 1777
Red Bank	New Jersey	November 1, 1777
Fort Mifflin	Pennsylvania	November 22, 1777
Gloucester	New Jersey	December 20, 1777
Whitemarsh	Pennsylvania	December 20, 1777
Spread Eagle Tavern	Pennsylvania	March 23, 1778
Quinton's Bridge	New Jersey	March 23, 1778
Hancock's Bridge	New Jersey	March 23, 1778
Crooked Billet	Pennsylvania	June 19, 1778
Barren Hill	Pennsylvania	June 19, 1778
Monmouth	New Jersey	June 29, 1778 July 5, 1778
Wyoming Valley Massacre	Pennsylvania	July 14, 1778
Kaskaskia	Illinois	July 29, 1778
Rhode Island	Rhode Island	September 1, 1778 September 2, 1778 September 9, 1778
Alligator Bridge	Florida	January 5, 1779
Capture of Savannah	Georgia	January 5, 1779
Tappan	New Jersey	January 15, 1779
Little Egg Harbor	New Jersey	January 29, 1779
Vincennes	Indiana	April 1, 1779

Carleton Raids	New York & Vermont	April 30, 1779
Capture of Augusta	Georgia	June 24, 1779
Kettle Creek	Georgia	June 24, 1779
Brier Creek	Georgia	June 24, 1779
Charleston	South Carolina	June 24, 1779
Pound Ridge	New York	July 4, 1779
Stony Point	New York	July 16, 1779
Penobscot Bay	Maine	August 16, 1779
Paulus Hook	New Jersey	September 28, 1779
Cherry Valley Massacre	New York	October 10, 1779
Newtown	New York	October 10, 1779
Savannah	Georgia	October 16, 1779
Raids by John Paul Jones	England, Scotland	November 25, 1779
Sea Battles of John Paul Jones	Irish Sea, North Sea	November 25, 1779
Siege and Surrender of Charleston	South Carolina	May 13, 1780 June 4, 1780
Lenud's Ferry	South Carolina	June 1, 1780
Waxhaws	South Carolina	June 1, 1780
Moncks Corner	South Carolina	June 4, 1780
Connecticut Farms	New Jersey	June 25, 1780
Ramseur's Mill	North Carolina	June 14, 1780
Williamson's Plantation (Huck's Defeat)	South Carolina	June 14, 1780
Cedar Springs	South Carolina	June 14, 1780
Springfield	New Jersey	June 25, 1780 June 26, 1780
Rocky Mount	South Carolina	August 7, 1780
Hanging Rock	South Carolina	August 7, 1780
Green Spring	South Carolina	August 7, 1780
Thicketty Fort	South Carolina	August 20, 1780
Musgrove's Mill	South Carolina	August 20, 1780

Camden	South Carolina	August 21, 1780
Fishing Creek	South Carolina	September 29, 1780
Great Savannah	South Carolina	September 29, 1780
Blue Savannah	South Carolina	September 29, 1780
Black Mingo	South Carolina	September 29, 1780
Kings Mountain	South Carolina	October 8, 1780
Wahab's Plantation	South Carolina	October 20, 1780
Charlotte Courthouse	North Carolina	October 20, 1780
Carleton's Burning of the Valleys	New York	October 23, 1780
Middle Fort	New York	October 23, 1780
Stone Arabia	New York	October 23, 1780
Fort Nelson	Virginia	December 26, 1780
Rugeley's Mills	South Carolina	January 1, 1781
Hammond's Store	South Carolina	January 1, 1781
Cowpens	South Carolina	January 1, 1781
Raid on Richmond	Virginia	January 8, 1781
Tearcoat Swamp	South Carolina	January 25, 1781
Fish Dam Ford	South Carolina	January 25, 1781
Blackstock's Farm	South Carolina	January 25, 1781
Georgetown	South Carolina	January 25, 1781
Cowan's Ford	North Carolina	February 18, 1781
Tarrant's Tavern	North Carolina	February 18, 1781
Morrisania	New York	February 21, 1781
Pyle's Massacre	North Carolina	March 14, 1781
Weitzel's Mill	North Carolina	March 14, 1781
Guilford Courthouse	North Carolina	March 28, 1781
Hobkirk's Hill (Second Camden)	South Carolina	May 11, 1781
Fort Watson	South Carolina	May 13. 1781
Fort Motte	South Carolina	May 13. 1781
Williamsburg	Virginia	May 29, 1781
Petersburg	Virginia	May 29, 1781

First Battle of the Virginia Capes	Offshore Virginia	June 13, 1781
Pensacola	Florida	June 15, 1781
Fort St. Joseph	Michigan	June 15, 1781
Fort Galphin	South Carolina	June 19, 1781
Fort Grierson	Georgia	June 19, 1781
Fort Cornwallis	Georgia	June 19, 1781
Siege of Ninety-Six	South Carolina	June 19, 1781
Quinby Bridge and Shubrick's Plantation	South Carolina	July 19, 1781
Green Spring	Virginia	August 5, 1781 August 18, 1781
Eutaw Springs	South Carolina	September 9, 1781
Second Battle of the Virginia Capes	Offshore Virginia	September 21, 1781 September 23, 1781
Siege of Yorktown	Virginia	September 30, 1781 October 7, 9, 11, 12, 16, 19, 29, 1781 November 4, 1781
The Hook	Virginia	October 29, 1781
Fort Griswold	Connecticut	November 16, 1781
Fort Dorchester	South Carolina	July 12, 1782
Gnadenhutton Massacre	Ohio	September 1, 1782
Sandusky Plains and Olentangy	Ohio	September 1, 1782
Bryan's Station	Kentucky	September 1, 1782
Blue Licks	Kentucky	September 1, 1782
Lindley's Mill	North Carolina	December 15, 1782
Combahee Ferry	South Carolina	December 15, 1782
James Island	South Carolina	December 15, 1782
Long Beach Island Massacre	New Jersey	January 15, 1783
Florida Straits Naval Battle	Offshore Florida	March 10, 1783
Fort Henry	West Virginia	August 20, 1783

Appendix 5: Noteworthy Events

Event	Letter(s)
Boston Port Act	August 1, 1774
Sugar Act	August 1, 1774
Stamp Act	August 1, 1774 August 16, 1774
Townshend Act	August 1, 1774
Tea Act	August 1, 1774
Massachusetts Bay Regulating Act	August 1, 1774
Philadelphia Tea Party	August 1, 1774
Benjamin Franklin in cockpit	August 1, 1774
First Continental Congress Called	August 1, 1774
Quartering Act	August 15, 1774
Quebec Act	August 15, 1774 August 21, 1774
Boston Massacre	August 15, 1774 August 16, 1774
Boston Tea Party	August 16, 1774
Sons of Liberty	August 16, 1774 July 31, 1775 October 4, 1775 July 13, 1776
Charleston Tea Party	August 20, 1774
Watauga Republic	August 20, 1774
Suffolk Resolves	October 27, 1774

Creation of Continental Association	October 27, 1774
Yorktown Tea Party	March 30, 1775
Patrick Henry's "Give me liberty, or give me death" speech	March 30, 1775
Rides of Paul Revere, William Dawes, and Samuel Prescott	April 20, 1775
Second Continental Congress Convenes	June 25, 1775
George Washington named commander in chief	June 25, 1775
Congress authorizes foray into Quebec	June 25, 1775
Olive Branch Petition	July 31, 1775
Morgan exhibits scars from five hundred whiplashes	October 4, 1775 January 18, 1781
King George proclaims colonies in state of open rebellion	October 4, 1775
Dunmore's Emancipation Proclamation	January 5, 1776
Cannons from Fort Ticonderoga hauled to Boston	March 17, 1776
Common Sense	April 1, 1776
King George procures German mercenaries	April 1, 1776
Congress sends commissioners to Canada	June 30, 1776
Resolution for independence introduced in Congress	June 30, 1776
Declaration of Independence adopted by Congress	July 8, 1776
Liberty Bell rung	July 8, 1776
Thomas Hickey hanged for treason	July 13, 1776
Use of $ to denote dollars	August 2, 1776
Signing of Declaration of Independence	August 2, 1776
Billopp House Peace Conference	September 14, 1776
William Franklin arrested	September 14, 1776
Nathan Hale hanged for spying by British	September 23, 1776
First attempted submarine attack	November 14, 1776
The American Crises	December 27, 1776

Benjamin Franklin sent to France as American commissioner	January 18, 1777
Signatures on Declaration of Independence published	January 18, 1777
Ride of Sybil Ludington	April 30, 1777
Jane McCrea killed and scalped	August 16, 1777
Betsy Ross flag	September 12, 1777
Liberty Bell removed from Philadelphia	September 26, 1777
British occupy Philadelphia	September 26, 1777
Saratoga surrender	October 17, 1777 October 18, 1777
Articles of Confederation	November 22, 1777 January 21, 1778 April 1, 1781
Valley Forge encampment	December 20, 1777
Conway Cabal	January 21, 1778
British evacuate Philadelphia	June 18, 1778
Treaty of Alliance with France	June 18, 1778
Mischianza	June 18, 1778
Queen Esther smashes skulls of Patriots	July 14, 1778
French fleet arrives	July 14, 1778
Morocco first to recognize US independence	July 14, 1778
John Adams sent to France as an American commissioner	July 30, 1778
Middlebrook encampment	January 15, 1779
March of Convention Army	April 30, 1779
Culper Spy Ring	July 4, 1779 September 28, 1779 August 3, 1780
Elizabeth Burgin on prison ships	August 20, 1779 September 11, 1779 September 28, 1779
Spain joins France to assist United States	September 2, 1779

First salute to American flag by Dutch at Statia	November 25, 1779
Philipsburg Proclamation	December 25, 1779
Arnold's court-martial	May 1, 1780
League of Armed Neutrality	May 1, 1780
Jockey Hollow encampment	May 26, 1780
Rides of Mary McClure and Watt	July 14,1780
Ride of Jane Thomas	July 14,1780
French General Rochambeau arrives	August 3, 1780
General Washington's horses	August 3, 1780
Arnold "goes over" to British	October 2, 1780 October 3, 1780
John André hanged for spying by Americans	October 2, 1780
Ride of Mary Dillard	January 25, 1781
Cornwallis fires grapeshot at own troops	March 28, 1781
Rebecca Motte gives permission to have her house fired	May 13,1781
Sumter's Bounty	May 13,1781
Ride of Jack Jouett	June 13, 1781
Francisco's Fight	September 26, 1781
Washington breaks first ground for Yorktown trenches	October 7, 1781
Washington fires first American artillery shot at Yorktown	October 11, 1781
Redoubts 9 and 10 taken at Yorktown	October 16, 1781
Yorktown surrender	October 19, 1781
Lafayette declares, "The play, sir, is over."	November 4, 1781
British evacuate Savannah	July 12, 1782
Peace negotiators named	August 5, 1782
British evacuate Charleston	December 15, 1782
Preliminary articles for treaty with Britain signed	January 15, 1783
Newburgh Conspiracy	March 16, 1783

American peace provisions presented	April 5, 1783
Nancy Morgan Hart kills six Tories	May 10, 1783
Pennsylvania Mutiny	June 21, 1783
Betty Zane retrieves powder for Fort Henry	August 20, 1783
British evacuate New York City	December 4, 1783
Washington's farewell to officers	December 4, 1783
Treaty of Paris signed	December 25, 1783
Washington resigns as commander in chief	December 25, 1783
Treaty of Paris ratified by United States	January 22, 1784
Treaty of Paris ratified by King George III	July 4, 1784

Appendix 6: What Happened to the Signers?

Name	Colony	Age	Afterward
John Hancock	Massachusetts, president of Congress	39	"There, I guess King George will be able to read that!" Member of Massachusetts Convention, adopting US Constitution.
Josiah Bartlett	New Hampshire	46	First member to vote in favor. Member of New Hampshire Convention, adopting US Constitution.
Matthew Thornton	New Hampshire	62	Not present at vote. Physician and ferry operator.
William Whipple	New Hampshire	46	Brigadier general; New Hampshire associate justice.
John Adams	Massachusetts	40	Served on Committee of Five; second US president; died July 4, 1826, at age ninety, fifty years after signing.
Samuel Adams	Massachusetts	53	Massachusetts governor.

Elbridge Gerry	Massachusetts	31	Fifth US vice president.
Robert Treat Paine	Massachusetts	45	Prosecuted the treason trials following Shay's Rebellion.
William Ellery	Rhode Island	49	Rhode Island Supreme Court justice.
Stephen Hopkins	Rhode Island	69	"My hand trembles, but my heart does not." Member Rhode Island General Assembly.
Samuel Huntington	Connecticut	45	Connecticut governor.
Roger Sherman	Connecticut	55	Served on Committee of Five; only signer of Continental Association, Declaration of Independence, Articles of Confederation, and US Constitution.
William Williams	Connecticut	45	Not present at vote; pastor, merchant, and county judge.
Oliver Wolcott	Connecticut	49	Connecticut governor.
William Floyd	New York	41	Abstained on vote for independence; member US House.
Francis Lewis	New York	63	Abstained on vote for independence; property burned by British, and wife taken prisoner; daughter married British naval officer moving to England.
Philip Livingston	New York	60	Served on Committee of Five; abstained on vote for independence; died in 1778 while serving in Congress.

Lewis Morris	New York	50	Abstained on vote for independence. "Damn the consequences. Give me the pen." Property burned by British.
Abraham Clark	New Jersey	50	Two sons captured, tortured, and beaten by British. Refused to recant signing of Declaration of Independence to free them.
John Hart	New Jersey	65	Property destroyed by Hessians; hid in forests and slept in caves to avoid capture.
Francis Hopkinson	New Jersey	38	US District Court justice in Pennsylvania.
Richard Stockton	New Jersey	45	Captured by Loyalists, imprisoned by British.
John Witherspoon	New Jersey	53	Appointed congressional chaplain by John Hancock; served as member of New Jersey Convention, adopting US Constitution.
George Clymer	Pennsylvania	37	Not present at vote; business ventures during war increased his wealth.
Benjamin Franklin	Pennsylvania	70	Served on Committee of Five; negotiated Treaty of Paris; deputy (signer) to Constitutional Convention.
Robert Morris	Pennsylvania	42	Abstained on vote for independence; financier of the revolution.

John Morton	Pennsylvania	55	Finnish descent; first signer to die, April 1, 1777.
George Ross	Pennsylvania	46	Not present at vote; judge of Pennsylvania Admiralty Court.
Benjamin Rush	Pennsylvania	30	Not present at vote; physician; founder Dickinson College.
James Smith	Pennsylvania	56	Not present at vote; law practice.
George Taylor	Pennsylvania	60	Not present at vote; supplier of cannon shot to Continental Army.
James Wilson	Pennsylvania	33	US Supreme Court justice.
Thomas McKean	Delaware	42	Pennsylvania governor.
George Read	Delaware	42	Voted against independence; chief justice Delaware Supreme Court.
Caesar Rodney	Delaware	47	President of Delaware.
Charles Carroll of Carrollton	Maryland	38	Not present at vote; US senator; died in 1832 at age ninety-five; last surviving signer.
Samuel Chase	Maryland	35	US Supreme Court justice.
William Paca	Maryland	35	Maryland governor.
Thomas Stone	Maryland	33	Promoted Maryland's approval of the Articles of Confederation, which was last state to approve.
Carter Braxton	Virginia	39	Lost much of wealth during war; his wife was a daughter of a prominent Loyalist.

Benjamin Harrison	Virginia	50	Mr. Harrison said smilingly to Mr. Gerry, "When the hanging scene comes to be exhibited I shall have the advantage over you on account of my size. All will be over with me in a moment, but you will be kicking in the air half an hour after I am gone." Property destroyed by Benedict Arnold; Virginia governor.
Thomas Jefferson	Virginia	33	Served on Committee of Five; third US president; died July 4, 1826, at age eighty-three, fifty years after signing.
Francis Lightfoot Lee	Virginia	41	Farmer.
Richard Henry Lee	Virginia	44	Proposed resolution for independence June 7, 1776; not present at vote; president pro tempore of Senate during second US Congress.
Thomas Nelson Jr.	Virginia	37	Cornwallis used his house in Yorktown, which was destroyed during battle.
George Wythe	Virginia	50	Murdered by family member in 1806 because he willed part of his property to his slaves.
Joseph Hewes	North Carolina	46	Instrumental in forming American Navy.

William Hooper	North Carolina	34	Not present at vote; property burned by British.
John Penn	North Carolina	35	Served on Board of War until 1780.
Thomas Heyward Jr.	South Carolina	29	British prisoner of war released in 1781.
Thomas Lynch Jr.	South Carolina	26	Lost at sea 1779 sailing to Sint Eustatius.
Arthur Middleton	South Carolina	34	British prisoner of war released in 1781.
Edward Rutledge	South Carolina	26	Youngest signer (110 days younger than Lynch); British prisoner of war released in 1781.
Button Gwinnett	Georgia	41	Died in a duel in May 1777 with Lachlan McIntosh.
Lyman Hall	Georgia	52	Georgia governor; founder University of Georgia.
George Walton	Georgia	27	Georgia governor; US senator.

Edwards Brothers Malloy
Thorofare, NJ USA
April 8, 2016